CAMPFIRE

JIMMY PATTERSON BOOKS
FOR YOUNG ADULT READERS

JAMES PATTERSON PRESENTS

Stalking Jack the Ripper by Kerri Maniscalco
Hunting Prince Dracula by Kerri Maniscalco
Escaping from Houdini by Kerri Maniscalco
Gunslinger Girl by Lyndsay Ely
Twelve Steps to Normal by Farrah Penn

THE MAXIMUM RIDE SERIES BY JAMES PATTERSON

The Angel Experiment
School's Out—Forever
Saving the World and Other Extreme Sports
The Final Warning
MAX
FANG
ANGEL
Nevermore
Maximum Ride Forever

THE CONFESSIONS SERIES BY JAMES PATTERSON

Confessions of a Murder Suspect
Confessions: The Private School Murders
Confessions: The Paris Mysteries
Confessions: The Murder of an Angel

For exclusives, trailers, and other information, visit jimmypatterson.org.

CAMPFIRE

SHAWN SARLES

FOREWORD BY JAMES PATTERSON

JIMMY PATTERSON BOOKS
LITTLE, BROWN AND COMPANY
NEW YORK BOSTON LONDON

Copyright © 2018 by Shawn Sarles
Foreword copyright © 2018 by James Patterson

Hachette Book Group supports the right to free expression and the value of copyright. The purpose of copyright is to encourage writers and artists to produce the creative works that enrich our culture.

The scanning, uploading, and distribution of this book without permission is a theft of the author's intellectual property. If you would like permission to use material from the book (other than for review purposes), please contact permissions@hbgusa.com. Thank you for your support of the author's rights.

JIMMY Patterson Books / Little, Brown and Company
Hachette Book Group
1290 Avenue of the Americas, New York, NY 10104
jimmypatterson.org

First Edition: July 2018

JIMMY Patterson Books is an imprint of Little, Brown and Company, a division of Hachette Book Group, Inc. The Little, Brown name and logo are trademarks of Hachette Book Group, Inc. The JIMMY Patterson Books ® name and logo are trademarks of JBP Business, LLC.

The publisher is not responsible for websites (or their content) that are not owned by the publisher.

The Hachette Speakers Bureau provides a wide range of authors for speaking events. To find out more, go to hachettespeakersbureau.com or call (866) 376-6591.

Names: Sarles, Shawn, author.
Title: Campfire / Shawn Sarles; foreword by James Patterson.
Description: First edition. | New York; Boston: Little, Brown and Company, 2018. | "JIMMY Patterson Books." | Summary: Sixteen-year-old Maddie's camping trip with family and friends in a remote mountain location turns deadly as stories told around the campfire begin coming true.
Identifiers: LCCN 2017055823 | ISBN 978-0-316-51506-1 (hc)
Subjects: | CYAC: Camping—Fiction. | Murder—Fiction. | Brothers and sisters—Fiction. | Single-parent families—Fiction. | Best friends—Fiction. | Friendship—Fiction. | Storytelling—Fiction. | Horror stories.
Classification: LCC PZ77.1.S26446 Cam 2018 | DDC [Fic]—dc23
LC record available at https://lccn.loc.gov/2017055823

10 9 8 7 6 5 4 3 2 1

LSC-C

Printed in the United States of America

To Vera Pitney
English Teacher Extraordinaire,
Who Made Me Believe I Really Could Write

FOREWORD

As a storyteller, telling scary stories around the fire was always my favorite part of a camping trip: listening to the fire crackle, holding a flashlight up to my face, whispering ghost stories and urban legends…and making everyone too terrified to crawl into their dark tents.

Campfire by Shawn Sarles took me right back to those hair-raising moments. The idea that scary stories can come to life—that the stuff of nightmares might be real—is so terrifying, I guarantee it'll give you goose bumps.

—*James Patterson*

CAMPFIRE

PROLOGUE

MADDIE DAVENPORT SAT ALONE IN THE front seat of the idling car. She fiddled with the radio, switching from pop to country to oldies before stabbing the dial and silencing it. Her restless fingers flew to her head and snagged a strand of her long, blond hair. She twirled it into a thick curl and held it there, eyeing the effect in the rearview mirror. *So pretty.* If only she had natural curls like her mother.

A frustrated sigh escaped her lips and she let the curl drop. She glanced out the front windshield and in the darkness could just make out the sign hanging in front of her mom's small office: DAVENPORT & TOWSON REALTY. Her mom had said she'd only be a minute, but that had been ten minutes ago. And did Maddie really expect anything less? She'd been late all eleven years of her life—for dance classes, track meets, birthday parties, and even school. Why would today be any different? Why would today be the day her mom decided to put her daughter ahead of her job?

Maddie pursed her lips and glanced toward the office. It was a look of pure attitude, one her mother would have withered under.

Usually she could deal with this—the lateness, the waiting around, her constant placement as first runner-up in her mom's poor attempt to balance work and family. But not today. Not after the day she'd had at school. Not after Chelsea Park had stood up during lunch and called her Saint Maddie in front of the whole cafeteria.

It had spread like pink eye, and by last period everyone had started crossing themselves in front of her. Had started bowing their heads and offering mock prayers to her.

Saint Maddie. The Patron Saint of crybabies. Of teacher's pets. Of prudes. The list had grown as the day had gone on.

Maddie looked at herself in the rearview mirror again. The insult burned deep within her. She tried to smile but couldn't keep it up. She grimaced and dropped her head, burying it in her hands. Two years of braces wasted. She'd never have anything to be happy about again. And all because she hadn't kissed Tommy Meyers during that stupid game of spin the bottle.

Why hadn't she just gone with it? The thought crossed her mind for about the hundredth time.

His Funyuns breath, for starters.

She could barely stand sitting six feet away from him. The thought of locking lips—she had almost gagged when the bottle had come to a stop, its neck pointing right at her.

And that's how she'd escaped. She'd leaped to her feet, her hand pressed to her mouth as she hurried out of the basement, out of Chelsea's house, and made her way home early.

It wasn't the smoothest of exits, but it had worked. She'd escaped. Still, Maddie had known that there'd be hell to pay Monday morning, but she hadn't cared—until, of course, she had.

Saint Maddie.

It wasn't even that bad. At least, it could have been so much worse. But it wasn't the name that got under Maddie's skin. It was the way Chelsea said it. The way her lips curled up into a sly smirk. That twinkle of mischief and malice that winked from the mean girl's narrowed eyes.

Maddie twisted in her seat and crossed her arms. She needed a plan. Something to combat the good-girl lies. A way to dirty up her image.

But what? She sighed.

Why did Chelsea have to be such a bitch?

A satisfied smirk lifted Maddie's lips.

Bitch.

She thought it again and again. See. She could be bad. But she'd need more than a few curse words to undo Chelsea's handiwork.

She flipped down the visor and looked in the mirror. She imagined herself with a nose ring. Or maybe an eyebrow piercing. That'd be edgy. But you had to have your parents' permission, which her mom would never go for. Could she pass for eighteen? Maddie sucked in her cheeks and pursed her lips.

Not a chance in hell.

Maybe makeup.

Maddie reached into the back and pulled her mom's purse onto her lap. She dug through it, picking out a tube of lipstick. She ran it across her lips, then smacked them like she'd seen her mom do.

It was bold. But would it be enough?

No. Chelsea already wore lip gloss and blush to school. Maddie couldn't copy her. That'd be worse than being the good girl.

Defeated, Maddie tossed the lipstick back into her mom's purse. They'd call her Saint Maddie for the rest of her life.

She opened the glove compartment and looked for a pack of gum. But instead of gum, Maddie's eyes fell on something else. Something that just might do the trick. She reached in and took hold of the pack, giving it a shake. Its contents rattled softly inside. She opened it. Eight cigarettes looked back at her. She unsheathed one of the thin tubes and held it gingerly, like a sleeping cobra she'd been dared to kiss.

This could work.

Without thinking, Maddie pressed the cigarette lighter down into the dashboard and waited, shooting nervous glances up at the office. She'd seen her mom smoke hundreds of these, but always on the sly. She knew her mom would be furious if she found her eleven-year-old daughter with a cigarette in her mouth.

The lighter popped with a dull thwack. It was now or never.

Maddie's hands shook as she held the cigarette to her lips and pressed the hot lighter to its tip. A soft sizzle snaked through the air. The first tinges of burning tobacco tickled Maddie's nose. She couldn't wait to see Chelsea's face. Chelsea would have to eat all those good-girl lies.

The warm smoke seeped from the cigarette. It filled her mouth with a tangy, ashy flavor. Maddie inhaled slowly and felt it stream down her throat. She could feel her chest swelling as the smoke pooled in her lungs, as it sparked inside her. It actually wasn't that bad.

Maddie took a deeper breath. More smoke poured in. Too much smoke. It caught in the back of her throat. It scratched at her insides. Her lungs rebelled. They seized up and shriveled, sending the smoke right back the way it'd come.

A grizzled cough tore through Maddie, involuntary and gruesome.

She coughed again. She couldn't stop. She coughed and coughed and coughed. Her throat grew raw. She gasped for air, but that only made it worse. With the next cough a bit of bile leaped up into the back of her throat. She swallowed it down and prayed for it to be over.

This had been a terrible idea.

Still coughing, Maddie opened the car door and jumped out. She flicked the cigarette to the ground and stomped on it, doing a little dance as she waved her arms around and tried to air out her shirt.

She hopped back in the car and rummaged through her mom's purse again, pulling out a little perfume bottle. She sprayed it around the inside of the car and on her clothes. She even put a few spritzes in her hair.

She sniffed.

Yes, she could smell the perfume, but underneath its overpowering fruitiness, the smoke lingered. And it smelled awful. She opened the glove compartment and tossed the cigarette pack back in as she rooted around for the gum. But it wasn't there. She checked her breath and started to panic. What had she been thinking? On top of being Saint Maddie at school, she was going to be grounded-for-life at home.

She looked up at her mom's office and saw a flicker of light. She said a silent prayer and kissed her freedom good-bye.

And then a violent explosion blew the office windows out into the night.

Maddie's head banged hard against the seat. Her vision went white and then black as she felt the world crashing down around her.

ONE

"EARTH TO MADDIE," A VOICE CRACKED.

Maddie jerked, the reins snapping in her limp hands. Underneath her, the horse picked up its head and snorted but kept trotting smoothly along the path.

She'd been daydreaming again. Or rather, she'd had a daymare. The same one that always haunted her. She took a deep breath and filled her lungs with fresh mountain air. She tried to shake off the bad feeling.

"Hellooo." The voice broke into her thoughts again.

This time Maddie swung her eyes around to meet those of the girl riding beside her. Maddie barely managed to stifle a laugh as her best friend, Chelsea Park, jostled uncomfortably in her saddle, almost falling off.

"When you invited me on this camping trip," Chelsea said in a strained voice, her teeth gritted the entire time, "I thought it'd be like a hiking-through-the-woods kind of thing."

"Are you really telling me you'd rather be walking up this mountain right now?"

"Well, no." Chelsea stiffened as her horse stepped around a rock in the path. "But my chances of breaking my neck are a lot smaller when I'm on my own two feet."

"Nothing's going to happen," Maddie promised, "as long as you keep those feet in your stirrups."

A panicked look crossed Chelsea's face and she jammed her feet into the stirrups as far as they'd go. Maddie couldn't keep her giggles back this time. It felt good to laugh, especially at her best friend, who rarely lost her cool.

"It's not funny." Chelsea tried, and failed, to keep a straight face as she jostled around atop her horse.

"You look like you're constipated." Maddie giggled some more.

"I do not."

Chelsea shot up in her saddle, her back ramrod straight.

"You kinda do." And Maddie mimicked her best friend's face, gritting her teeth and pursing her lips tight like she'd just taken a bite out of a lemon.

"Stop that." Chelsea swatted at Maddie, completely forgetting she was on top of a horse. She wobbled in her saddle again, but this time Maddie reached out and grabbed her.

"Relax," Maddie said. "The horse can feel when you're uncomfortable."

Chelsea's fingernails dug into Maddie's arm as she pushed herself back up on her horse. She took a deep breath, like she was about to meditate or something, and then slowly let go of Maddie. The horse continued walking along underneath her, and she didn't falter this time.

"I think I've got it," Chelsea whispered, afraid to upset the fine balance she'd found with her horse. A few strides later and she seemed marginally more comfortable in her saddle.

"Who are you trying to impress anyways?" Maddie asked.

"I thought that was obvious," Chelsea eyed Maddie conspiratorially. "But the real question is who *you* should be worried about impressing."

Maddie's cheeks flushed pink as she shook her head and looked down at the ground.

"Don't act like you haven't noticed our hot mountain guide," Chelsea pressed on.

A nervous snort erupted from Maddie's lips, and she almost fell off her horse. She flipped her eyes up to the front of their group and got a good look at the guide with his blond hair and tan skin. His bright blue eyes.

"He's kinda hot, isn't he?" Maddie confessed.

"Scorchin'," Chelsea replied.

Maddie had to roll her eyes at that one.

"Well, he's all yours."

"Oh, no," Chelsea shooed the words right back at Maddie. "He's not my type at all. You're gonna have to take this one."

Maddie hesitated. She didn't usually go after the guy. That was Chelsea's area of expertise. Maddie had never even had a boyfriend, though she'd had her first kiss. And it hadn't been at a party or with

Tommy Meyers and his Funyuns breath, though she couldn't say that it had been much better.

But this could be fun. It wasn't like she'd ever see their guide after this week. It could be nice to look and maybe even flirt a little. She was sixteen, after all, and entitled to a little crush here and there.

What had he said his name was? Maddie tried to remember, but when he'd introduced himself she'd been too busy gawking at his perfect, one-cheeked dimple.

Carl or maybe Calvin. Maddie tried to recall it.

"Caleb." Maddie said it out loud, snapping her fingers in delight as she remembered. A nervous excitement bubbled up in her stomach. Her face flushed again, warming her all over.

"This little camping trip just got a lot more exciting," Chelsea trilled, her eyes cutting mischievously to Maddie. "So here's what we're going to do—"

As Maddie listened to Chelsea unfurl her master plan, an uneasiness crept in and replaced her excitement. What had she just agreed to? Sure, Maddie had talked to boys. But what did she really know about flirting with them? Only that she wasn't very good at it.

All of a sudden her slender legs itched in their stirrups. They longed to pound against the dirt trail, to get away from Chelsea's sly gaze, the glimmers of her mean-girl past shining through. Maddie could run up this path in a flash. And the altitude training would be great for her. Her cross-country coach wanted her up to speed by July.

But why was Maddie thinking about training right now? This was supposed to be a vacation. Was Maddie really so afraid of talking to a boy?

"How about I just go up and talk to him?" Maddie offered, inter-rupting Chelsea's elaborate plans of late-night encounters beside the campfire.

"I guess that could work, too." Chelsea seemed a little deflated.

"I'll just go now then," Maddie said, effortlessly urging her horse forward.

"I'll be right behind—" Chelsea cut off as she tried, and failed, to mimic Maddie's easy moves. She lost her balance again and nearly slipped off her horse. "On second thought, I'll stay back here. I'm gonna need a detailed report, though. I'm talking every syllable and hair flip. Don't you dare forget a single thing."

"I won't." Maddie laughed at Chelsea's super-serious approach to all things boy. "Try not to break your neck while I'm gone."

And Maddie pulled in front of her best friend.

Up ahead she saw her father sidling his horse toward another with a woman riding it. Maddie's breath caught in her lungs. Her face flushed red with a painful heat. She squeezed her eyes shut and then opened them again. Her vision blurred in the bright morning light and then focused on the woman.

For a second, she'd seen her mother. But, of course, that couldn't be. How could her mind still trick her like that? She hadn't seen her mother in five years.

Maddie blinked the tears out of her eyes. It was only Mrs. Towson—Kris, Maddie corrected herself. Even out here in the wild, stripped of her usual pantsuit and three-inch heels, the woman looked all business with her short hair dyed blond, like some kind of wannabe politician.

Had her mother taken herself so seriously? Maddie couldn't remember. But Mrs. Towson—Kris—had taken over the real-estate business after her mom had died, and the woman had gone full-on power broker. It wasn't a bad look. It just could be a bit off-putting at times.

As Maddie's horse caught up to them, she could just make out their conversation.

"Enjoying the great outdoors, Kris?" Maddie's dad asked, his tone light.

"More like worrying about the paperwork piling up on my desk."

"You're supposed to relax on vacation. Unplug and unwind."

Kris shot Maddie's dad an annoyed look.

"Well, since we're miles away from civilization, the nearest cell tower, and any Wi-Fi hotspot, you can consider me good and unplugged."

Maddie heard her dad chuckle at that, though she knew Kris was deadly serious. The woman had a Blu-Tooth hooked into one ear at all times, always carrying on conversations with herself. Maddie got ready to urge her horse forward again but stopped as she saw her father lean in close and speak in a hushed voice.

"So—uh—do you think you'll have time to talk later?"

Maddie had no idea what that could be about and nudged her horse a little closer to try to listen.

"It's important, Kris," Maddie's father pressed.

"Fine," Kris relented. "But this better not be why you dragged us up this mountain."

"The trip's for the kids." Her dad looked more relaxed now, his breezy self again. "Charlie and Dylan are going off to college in the fall. This could be the last time we're all together."

Kris rolled her eyes and pulled her horse away. Maddie's father didn't seem to mind, though, as he smiled to himself and rode on.

That was weird, Maddie had to admit. But it was probably something stupid like coordinating graduation gifts for her older brother and Kris's daughter, Dylan. Maddie's dad had the annoying habit of making a big deal out of a small thing.

Maddie pulled on her reins and made her way toward her father. She sneaked a look back over her shoulder and saw Chelsea watching her, excitedly nodding her head toward the front where Caleb was riding.

Well, maybe she'd ask her dad about it later. Right now she had a date with a hot guide named Caleb. She dug in her heels and her horse picked up speed.

But just at that moment a roar ripped through the woods, followed by the crack of a gunshot. Tree branches shook as birds leaped from their roosts. The ground seemed to give way underneath Maddie. She jolted in her saddle and hung on for dear life as her horse rocketed up on its hind legs.

TWO

THE HORSE'S FRONT HOOVES PAWED THE air. Its whinnies cut shrilly through the afternoon, louder than the original beast's roar. The horse stomped and kicked and threw its head back and forth. It was like riding a jackhammer hell-bent on tattooing its name into the mountain.

Maddie couldn't think. Her teeth clacked in her mouth. Thankfully, her tongue rolled up on its own, otherwise she would have bitten it clean off. The force of the stomps hammered up her legs and rattled down her arms. The bucking threw her feet from the stirrups and jerked the reins from her hands. Her strong runner's quads strained as they squeezed the horse's back, as she clung on through sheer will.

Barely.

A picture of her body lying broken on the trail flashed through her mind. She panicked, grabbing blindly at the air, the horse's back, the saddle...anything that might save her.

Mercifully, her fingers found the horse's mane. They twisted into the fine hairs and crooked into knots, giving the horse a vicious French braid. Maddie stopped sliding, but she'd only pissed off the horse more as it continued to buck and neigh, no signs of tiring in sight.

"Hey, there," a voice rolled under the commotion. Maddie had forgotten there were other people around.

"Hey. I'm talking to you."

The voice was sterner this time. It demanded to be heard.

"Everything's gonna be all right."

Maddie tried her hardest to focus on the calm, soothing words. But she couldn't bring herself to open her eyes. She was scared. Petrified. And her fingers were slipping. If she was going to die, she'd rather go without having to witness the final, grim descent.

Fear was what made death so bad, the fear of knowing that it was all about to end. She liked to believe that her mother had burned up all in one instant. In one flash. One explosion so intense she couldn't have felt it. Gone before she had the time to think about all she was leaving behind—about her husband, who was hopeless without her, who could barely work the oven to heat up fish sticks; about her son, who still needed her to remind him that socks had to be changed *every* day and that sleeping past noon on Saturday was a terrible waste of a weekend; and about her daughter, who she'd never watch grow up, never see go on her first date or hear about her first kiss, never help her through those lowest of low moments in life when a girl needed her mother's shoulder to cry on more than anything else.

Who would Maddie miss most?

Her brother. And Chelsea. The two best things in her life. Her anchors and protectors. She would never have made it this far without them.

Maybe it wouldn't be so bad, though. At least when she was gone she wouldn't feel the pain or fear anymore. It'd be theirs then. Maddie felt her fingers loosening, letting go of their knots. She slid backward.

"Come on now," the voice persisted. "Just look here. You can trust me."

Even as her heart pounded in her ears, Maddie focused on the voice, pulling herself back up an inch, then another. Now she knew why she hadn't recognized it at first. It was Caleb speaking. She eased one eye open and spotted him, hair golden in the light, standing under her horse's pawing hooves. Her other eye snapped open. He was too close. The horse was going to kick him right in the face, knock the teeth out of his beautiful smile.

"You can trust me," Caleb reiterated, and with a jolt, Maddie realized his words hadn't been for her at all, but for the horse.

"I'm not going to hurt you. No one is. Whoa, now."

And it was like he'd spoken the magic words. The horse snorted loudly as it came down onto its front hooves and looked into Caleb's bluer-than-blue eyes. Maddie couldn't help staring, too, transfixed by the guide's piercing gaze.

The horse paused there on the ground, eyeing Caleb, marveling over him. Or maybe deciding whether to maul him next. But that few seconds was all the time Caleb needed; his hand shot up and grabbed the reins.

The horse nickered and tossed its head, but Caleb refused to let go. The earth grew steady under Maddie. She couldn't believe it. He had saved her.

THREE

"TH-THANKS." MADDIE'S VOICE SOUNDED FUNNY IN her own ears, like hearing it through a long and narrow tunnel. Maybe one with a bright light at the end of it. She looked down at her hands and could barely focus. Even though the horse had stopped moving, her whole body quivered still.

"It's all right," Caleb said in the same soothing voice. "I've got her. You can dismount if you want."

Maddie nodded slowly, hearing but not quite understanding. She looked at her hands again. They were lost in a snarl of horsehair. She concentrated on them. She bent her index finger, and it surprised her when it moved. Carefully, she untwined the rest of her fingers from the horse's mane, her knuckles coming unhinged one at a time.

"Here."

Maddie turned. It took her a beat to realize that it was her brother's hand outstretched to meet hers.

Charlie.

She grabbed for it and felt relief at the familiar rough skin of his palm, the calluses from hours spent on the baseball diamond. She leaned on him and slid off her horse. Her legs hit solid ground and faltered, threatened to buckle, but Charlie was there again, lifting her up, handling her weight easily as he slipped his arm around her waist.

"You all right?"

"Yeah," Maddie's voice wavered. "I'm fine...thanks to Caleb." She met the guide's eyes and her cheeks flared. She dropped her gaze to the ground.

"Oh, my gosh. Are you okay?" Chelsea pushed through and flung herself at Maddie, wrapping her in a crushing hug. The girl's makeup had bled around her eyes, giving her a ghoulish look. But she didn't seem to care as she held on tight to her best friend.

"I was so scared," Chelsea babbled on. "It was like slow motion— the roar—and then the gunshot—and then your horse—I don't know what I'd do if I lost you."

Actual tears dotted Chelsea's cheeks as she buried her head in Maddie's shoulder.

"I'm—I'm fine. See? Still in one piece."

Maddie held her arms out, proving it to herself as well as to Chelsea. Then she gently shrugged her best friend away. She had to wipe her own eyes now. She sniffled and looked up, trying to keep more tears from leaking out.

"I'm so glad you're okay. You wouldn't be a very good best friend if you were a pancake."

A laugh gurgled out of Maddie's mouth and a smile sneaked across her lips. She shook her shoulders back and started to feel like herself again. Until she noticed everyone looking at her.

All those eyes. All of them staring at her with the same expression, the same wide-eyed, poor-little-girl look that had dogged her for the last five years. Chelsea was the only one who'd never looked at her with those pitying eyes. Maddie's cheeks burned with embarrassment. They all thought her helpless.

And wasn't she? Hadn't she been? She tilted her head forward and let her hair swing down to hide her face.

"I think we could all use a little break," Caleb said. "Take ten. Grab some water and stretch your legs. I'll help you tie up your horses. We've still got a ways to go."

The group broke up slowly, everyone still on edge after Maddie's brush with death.

"Promise not to go endangering your life again," Chelsea said, holding up her pinkie.

"I promise." Maddie slowly lifted her head and hooked her pinkie with Chelsea's.

"Good. I'm gonna hold you to that. Now, I think I better go check on my horse before it gets too far away."

Maddie nodded and watched her best friend go, thankful that she'd invited Chelsea along on the trip.

"You sure you're feeling better?" It was Charlie's turn to check on her.

"Yes. I really am." Maddie didn't like all the attention. She was fine. Couldn't they all see that? "Now stop worrying about me and go help Dylan. Your girlfriend looks like she could use a big, strong man to haul her pack down for her."

Maddie shooed her brother away, sticking out her tongue so he'd know she was all right.

She *was* all right, wasn't she? She looked down at her hands and watched them tremble. She clenched them hastily as someone walked up to her.

"I just wanted to apologize again for that—um—freak-out," Caleb said. "I know it must have been really scary."

Caleb looked embarrassed, and Maddie hated it. She didn't want him to feel bad. Not after he'd saved her. Accidents happened.

She wanted to say all this, but her voice had abandoned her. She could only nod and hope she got her point across.

"I don't know how you stayed on for so long."

"Instinct, I guess." Maddie swallowed and could somehow form words again.

"You've got good ones, then." Caleb beamed at her. "Do you want to take my horse the rest of the way? She's sweet as can be."

"I guess…" Maddie hesitated to accept. "I mean—that's nice of you to offer."

Then she remembered Chelsea's dare. This was her chance to get closer to Caleb. She could do this. She just had to be bold. She cleared her throat and met Caleb's eyes, her best attempt at a flirtatious smile curling her lips.

"But only if I can ride alongside you."

"I'd be honored."

Caleb flashed his brilliant white teeth at her and Maddie felt her stomach flip-flop. Her knees wobbled and a giddy tremor tickled up her spine. It was such a relief—this feeling—the exact opposite of fear. Why hadn't Chelsea ever told her that flirting felt this good?

A few hours later, Maddie felt like herself again. Riding next to Caleb, she'd completely forgotten that her first horse had almost thrown her to the ground and stomped on her head. She felt light and happy. But also like such a schoolgirl. She was sixteen. Way too old to have a puppy crush. But she couldn't help it. Every time Caleb spoke, her heart skipped, her cheeks flushed, her breath came in short gasps.

She glanced back and saw Chelsea still struggling on her horse. She felt guilty for leaving her behind, but this was Maddie's chance. How often did a girl get the opportunity to flirt with an older guy? Especially one this attractive. She knew Chelsea would understand.

"You know," Caleb said, glancing at Maddie out of the corner of his eye. "I think we need a new name for you."

"A new name?"

"Yeah. A nickname. Something legendary. I mean, that was some feat, the way you held on to that horse."

"It was only luck," Maddie mumbled. "You did all the real work."

"Don't sell yourself short." Caleb set those blue eyes on Maddie and she almost melted. "You held on to that horse all by yourself. That took strength. And guts."

Caleb winked at her, and Maddie blushed from head to toe.

"Now about that name," Caleb thought out loud. "How about— how about Mustang Maddie?"

Maddie had to use every bit of willpower she possessed to keep from leaping out of her saddle.

Mustang Maddie.

She loved it, even if she didn't quite understand it.

But she couldn't let Caleb know that. She had to play it cool, erase that smile bubbling behind her eyes. It was what Chelsea would have whispered in her ear if she could. So, with her best straight face, she turned to the mountain guide.

"What kind of nickname is that?"

Had she sounded convincing? Not over-eager?

"It's something my kid sister and I used to do," Caleb explained. Then he seemed to lose his train of thought. "Actually, you kind of remind me of her."

Warning bells sounded in Maddie's ears. *Kid* sister? She had to get this flirting back on track.

"So I'm like a superhero or something?"

"Kind of."

Caleb laughed, and Maddie gave herself an inner high-five.

"It's more old-timey, though," Caleb went on. "More like a tall tale. Like—"

Caleb took both hands off his reins and waved them in front of Maddie to illustrate his point. He lowered his voice and spoke in a deep drawl, loading each word with action like an announcer at a rodeo.

"Introducing Mustang Maddie, the finest horsebreaker in all the West. She'll ride the wildest colts to the ends of the plains and back to tame 'em."

Maddie couldn't hold back anymore. Her giggle bubbled out of her.

"So like Pecos Bill."

"Exactly."

"I like it. I like it a lot."

But before Maddie could go on, the horses came to a halt. Next to her, Caleb turned and lifted his voice to speak to the rest of the group.

"Take a look, everyone."

They had stopped at the edge of a ridge. Down below them a valley opened up. It was just as breathtaking as Caleb had promised. The ground popped with bright green grass and a lake shone brilliant blue, reflecting the larger-than-life sky in a picture crisper than any HD television.

"We'll be camping down there. Welcome to your new home. At least for the next week."

FOUR

TENTS WERE HARD. ESPECIALLY WHEN THEY didn't come with instructions. Maddie stared down at the limp, olive-green canvas and winced. What dingy corner of the attic had her dad dug this out of? And how long had it been there? The thing looked more like a dead frog waiting to be dissected than a tent. Discolored splotches spotted its back. They could have been old mud stains or black mold. Maddie kicked at it, half-expecting it to jump to life and bite her. There was no way she was going to touch this thing.

Even though she and Chelsea were sharing the tent, Maddie's dad was supposed to help her—that is, put the whole thing together—but he'd disappeared the moment they'd thrown their packs down. And Chelsea had absolutely no clue how to put the tent together. Maddie looked around, hoping that maybe she could get Caleb to help.

"You need a hand?"

"More like two or three," Maddie said, a bit disappointed to see her brother.

"You're my hero," Chelsea jumped in, laying it on thick. Charlie didn't rise to her bait, though, and instead bent over and set to work on the tent.

Over his head, Chelsea shot a furtive look at Maddie, who could only shrug back. She knew why Chelsea had passed on the opportunity to flirt with Caleb. Her crush on Charlie was no secret between the best friends. But it had taken on a new wrinkle in the last few months, ever since Charlie and Dylan had surprised everyone and started dating. Chelsea insisted that that coupledom wouldn't last long and so had kept right up with her obvious attempts at flirtation. Charlie never bit, though, and today didn't look like it'd buck the trend.

"Do you need any help?" Chelsea made one last attempt with Charlie, but he only shook his head. Chelsea rolled her eyes at Maddie—boys—and walked off, but Maddie knew better than to take that as surrender. It was more of a rallying of the troops. She'd lick her wounds now and then come back with the big guns later.

"She gone?" Charlie spoke once Chelsea moved out of earshot.

"Yes, silly. She doesn't bite, you know."

"Oh—I think that girl could bite and then some."

"You might like it, if you ever gave it a shot," Maddie teased.

"That's exactly what I'm afraid of."

Charlie wasn't teasing, though, and it shocked Maddie to hear.

"Things okay with you and Dylan?"

She felt awkward asking it. She and Charlie were close. Very close.

He'd looked after her ever since their mom died. But they almost never talked about relationships. Maddie wasn't even sure if Charlie and Dylan were having sex or not.

"Yeah. They're fine."

"Fine?"

"I can't believe Dad still has this old thing." Charlie quickly changed the subject. "I don't think anyone's used it in years. Mom was always the camper. . . ."

Charlie let his thought trail off.

"I remember this one time," Maddie reminisced, "Mom decided that she needed to bond with me or something. So we pitched this old thing out in the backyard and had a girls' night under the stars."

Maddie got quiet as she remembered. They'd camped out the summer before the fire, when she'd been only ten. Her mom had pointed out all the constellations. And they'd made s'mores in the kitchen and brought them outside to eat, pretending they'd had a real campfire. They'd talked all night, about Maddie's favorite subjects in school and what color she wanted to paint her room. Even the boy she liked.

"I miss her, too," Charlie said. He waited another beat and then asked, "Can you grab that corner over there?"

Maddie scurried around the tent and pressed it flat to the ground as Charlie carefully drove a stake into the dirt. They rotated around the rest of the tent, repeating this at each corner. They didn't speak as they worked, each lost in his or her own thoughts.

"You know, I'm really going to miss you," Maddie spoke up, the sad look still on her face. "Who am I going to watch the games with on Sundays?"

It had been their tradition ever since their mom had died. The two would plop down on the sofa every Sunday during the baseball season and watch the San Francisco Giants play.

"I'll just be down the road," Charlie tried to cheer his sister up.

"It won't be the same."

Maddie realized in that moment just how much she was going to miss Charlie when he went away to college. Miss him and his complete obsession with baseball. Maddie never got tired of hearing him yammer on about the sport and all his favorite players. She still didn't know how he managed to keep all their names and stats straight in his head. And he had to have like an entire encyclopedia set's worth of baseball cards stowed in binders under his bed, all kept in meticulous, pristine shape. What would happen to those when Charlie left? He wouldn't take them with him, would he?

But Maddie loved her brother's devotion. Loved how he'd shared it with her. She couldn't think of a better way to spend a Sunday than watching the game with him, laughing as he added his own colorful commentary.

"You'll survive," Charlie said, looking Maddie right in the eyes, his brown hair tucked behind his ears, his beat-up old Giants cap snugly on his head.

That stupid baseball cap. It looked an inch from death, sun-bleached, stained with sweat and dirt. But Charlie still wore it everywhere. He'd gotten it years ago when their dad had surprised them—and their mother—with a trip to San Francisco and lower deck seats at AT&T Park. Charlie hadn't caught any foul balls that day, but their mom had bought him the cap as a souvenir, and he'd worn it every day for the rest of that summer. It'd driven Mom crazy. She'd only managed to get him to take it off in the house by threatening to stuff it down the garbage disposal. And even then he hadn't let her wash it. He couldn't let her tamper with the luck he'd built up in it, made of the hours of sweat and dirt that Charlie had poured into it as he'd trained his ass off to get good enough to make the high school team.

"I know I will," Maddie said. "But that doesn't mean I can't still be mad at you."

And she reached up and tugged the brim of her brother's cap down over his eyes, laughing as she did it, letting Charlie know that she'd be all right without him. He hadn't worn that hat for two years after their mom had died. But Maddie was glad he'd come around. She couldn't imagine him without it. He needed a little luck in his life.

Charlie pushed the cap back up his head and smiled at his sister before standing up and drumming his fingers against the taut tent canvas.

"Looks like we're all done."

"I can help with yours," Maddie offered. "If you want."

"No worries. Bryan's got it."

Charlie pointed over his shoulder and Maddie saw their cousin bent over, struggling to erect a much newer-looking tent. It wouldn't have been that hard, but Uncle Ed stood over him, barking orders, his square face made all the more severe by the crew cut he'd worn for the last twenty-five years, ever since he'd joined the army right out of high school.

"Not like that. That pole goes over there. And you laid that flap down backward. That joint there is all wrong. I don't know why this is so hard for you. Your cousin already has his up."

Bryan looked exasperated, but toiled away at the tent in silence.

"And quit slouching," their uncle snapped. "You're my son, for God's sake. Shoulders back. Chin up. Have some respect for yourself. It's not too late to cancel Stanford. The military is always looking for new recruits."

Bryan stiffened at the threat but continued working. Unfortunately for him, he didn't have the same broad build as his father. He took after his South Korean mother. Dark hair and pale skin. High, prominent cheekbones. Maddie had gotten tired of telling people that, yes, they were related, and no, he wasn't adopted. He stopped working on the tent for a second to push his round spectacles back up his nose and Maddie shot him a sympathetic look.

Bryan put his head back down and set to work, his glasses winking brightly at Maddie as they caught the light. She got up and started over toward him to help, but he waved her off. She'd only make it worse with his dad. Maddie knew this about her uncle, knew how stubborn and pigheaded he could be. And how much he bullied his son. He was always hard on Bryan, and she didn't understand why. What had happened to Uncle Ed to make him that way? How could he have come from the same family as her sweet mother? Another question to add to the list of things Maddie could never ask.

With her tent pitched and her brother off helping Dylan put up hers, Maddie headed across camp to find Chelsea. She couldn't wait any longer to gush over Caleb. And she needed help devising a plan to get close to him again. As nice as their ride had been, Maddie didn't want to have to go through another near-death experience to get him one on one.

As she walked, she spotted Aunt Julie going through their supplies, the coolers of food and drinks that had been waiting for them—
along with the half of their group who hadn't wanted to ride up the
mountain on horseback. They might have to build their own tents, but
the campsite came fully stocked. Food. A first-aid kit. An emergency
radio. All of it waiting for them in a small supply shed so they wouldn't
have to lug it up the mountain themselves.

Maddie watched her aunt as she rummaged through the coolers,
her head bent low, her straight, shoulder-length hair falling across her
face. Her aunt was so pretty. So petite. And kind. The polar opposite of
her uncle's disciplined rigidity.

How had they ever fallen in love? And then managed to stay
together this long? Maddie shook the question out of her head. Another
mystery she'd never know the answer to. She watched Julie a little longer, saw her pull out hot dog buns and a can of baked beans. She hoped
there were ingredients for s'mores in there, too. Then she kept going,
finding Chelsea pretty quickly.

"Always gotta look your best," Maddie couldn't help but needle her
best friend, "even in the wild."

Chelsea closed her compact with a snap and glowered at Maddie.

"Why didn't you tell me I looked like shit?"

"You always look beautiful to me."

"I can tell when you're lying." Chelsea used a tissue to dab at her
cheeks, then swept a curve of gloss over her lips. She threw the compact and makeup back in her pack and gave her hair a quick tousle.
"I'm surprised your brother didn't run in fear from me."

"Eh—he's seen you look worse."

Chelsea balled up her tissue and threw it at Maddie.

"God...he has, hasn't he."

"Facial Friday probably wasn't our best idea."

"Definitely not when you have a hot older brother."

Maddie's face curled up like the school cafeteria had served her a glass of spoiled milk.

"What? It's the truth. Ask any girl at school."

"You know he shaves his back, right?"

"You shut your mouth," Chelsea gasped. "Don't you dare start making up lies about him. That isn't true, is it?"

"Guess you'll have to wait and see." Maddie's eyes glinted mischievously and both girls started to snicker.

"Hey, is there something wrong with your dad?" Chelsea pointed over Maddie's shoulder. Maddie turned just in time to see her father ambling out from behind one of the tents, wincing as he rubbed his right shoulder. Had he had that talk with Kris already? If so, it didn't look like it'd gone well.

"I don't know," Maddie replied. She paused as her dad's gaze met hers. An easy smile slid over his lips, and he lifted his left hand to wave.

"There you are." Her dad's voice sounded bright, but Maddie could see the discomfort still there behind his eyes.

"Is everything okay, Dad?"

"Nothing wrong with me."

The response came out too quick. Maddie narrowed her eyes. She wasn't buying his act and she wanted him to know.

"Ah, my shoulder." Her dad broke quickly under pressure. He

always did. "Just an old skiing injury. You know, I haven't been sleeping so well the past couple of weeks. Might be time for a new mattress."

"Sure." Maddie still didn't believe him. But why would he lie to her? She opened her mouth to press more, but he beat her to it.

"I was actually looking for you all. We need some water for camp. Caleb said there was a stream just there through the woods. Could you fill up some of the thermoses for us?"

"It'd be our pleasure, Mitch." Maddie cringed as Chelsea used her father's first name. Even though he'd told her to call him that, she still hadn't gotten used to her best friend sounding so casual with her dad.

"Thanks." Her dad seemed truly relieved. "Oh, and why don't you take Abigail with you. It'll give you girls some alone time. I know you must be going crazy with all us adults around."

Chelsea had her mouth half-open, and Maddie could see the snappy retort loaded on the tip of her best friend's tongue. She quickly jabbed her elbow into Chelsea's side, and Chelsea bit down in surprise, cutting the words off at the head.

"Will do, Dad," Maddie said with all the cheer she could muster, and her dad went on his way, lifting his hand to rub his shoulder again, but then thinking better of it halfway there.

"What was that for?" Chelsea turned on her friend.

"You were about to say something mean."

"Well—" Chelsea searched for an excuse, "—yeah. So?"

"*So?* The trees have ears. And you have to spend a week out here in the middle of nowhere with these people. At least wait until the end of it to piss somebody off. I don't want to wake up with spiders in our sleeping bags."

"Or frogs in our water bottles?"

"Ew. Why'd you have to put that image in my head?"

"Just trying to cover all the bases." Chelsea grinned wickedly. "But I'll behave. For now."

"Good. Now let's go pick up the monster—"

Chelsea shot Maddie a look.

"I mean, Kris's lovely daughter, Abigail."

"Now who's being a bitch?" Chelsea couldn't keep a straight face.

"I said *you* had to behave."

The girls sniggered as they made their way to the large fire pit in the middle of camp. Caleb had dropped the canteens there, along with a big water cooler, and conveniently enough, Abigail was plopped down on a log right beside it, staring at her phone, clearly frustrated.

"But honestly, how does your dad not know that you and Abigail can't stand each other?"

Maddie could only shrug as they came up on Kris's youngest daughter. Dads could be blind about the most obvious things. Their families had known each other for years—longer than Maddie could even remember—and she and Abigail had never gotten along.

"I guess we better get this over with."

Maddie tightened her backpack straps and forged ahead. Chelsea followed right behind her.

FIVE

IT DIDN'T TAKE THE GIRLS LONG to find the path to the stream. It was wide and well marked, right where Maddie's dad had pointed. The water cooler, though, slowed them down. The canteens were no trouble, each just about twice the size of a normal water bottle, with straps that they could loop over their shoulders. Abigail had two of these around her neck and another one around her left wrist. She kept her right hand free for her phone as she cast around for any kind of cell signal. That left Maddie and Chelsea with the much harder task of lugging the large water cooler through the woods.

The cooler wasn't heavy—not when empty, at least—but the size and shape of it made it bulky and cumbersome, even for two people. Maddie and Chelsea kept having to stop and readjust their grips as the plastic slipped in their sweaty palms. Maddie felt like a baller Boy Scout, though, carrying three canteens on her own as the large cooler swayed between her and Chelsea. And it gave them an excuse to fall far enough behind Abigail that they could pretty much ignore her—and talk about Caleb.

"So, what's he smell like?" Chelsea jumped right in, unapologetic. "And don't you give me that look. You know exactly what I mean."

Maddie stopped herself mid-denial and gave Chelsea's question a real think. What *had* he smelled like? She tried to remember. She breathed in and could sense the memory tickling her nose.

"He smelled—" Maddie cast around for the right word. "He smelled like—like summer rain." She didn't know where it'd come from, but as soon as she said it, she knew it was true. "You know, that smell of damp earth and pollen and sun and..." Maddie trailed off, embarrassed.

"See," and Chelsea wasn't teasing this time, "it's not such a bad question, is it?"

Maddie shook her head and smiled.

"So what did you talk about?"

And the two girls launched into a blow-by-blow, Chelsea hanging on every one of Maddie's words, prodding her for more details here and whooping with delight there. They got so wound up in their conversation that they didn't even notice Abigail glowering at them, her foot tapping with impatience.

"We're here," she said in a snooty voice. It looked like cell phone withdrawal had already set in. "Let's fill these up and go."

The girls let the cooler fall and it *thunked* hollowly against the ground. A second later and Chelsea had popped a squat right on top of it.

"Hellooo. Let's get moving." Abigail shook her canteens at the girl.

"Cool it," Chelsea shot back. "It's not like we're in a hurry. Enjoy the mountain scenery."

Abigail stomped her foot. And when Chelsea ignored her, she huffed and let her canteens clatter to the ground.

"Fine, you can fill these up, too."

With that, Abigail turned and walked off into the woods, leaving Chelsea and Maddie behind, gawking after her.

"Where the hell is she going?" Chelsea spoke first.

"Maybe she has to tinkle."

Maddie smiled at her joke. But then her worry returned.

"Do you think she'll be all right by herself?"

Chelsea turned and gave Maddie a deadpan look.

"What's the worst that could happen? She squats in the wrong place and ends up with a nasty rash?"

"That, or—" Maddie scratched her brain for something good. "She gets eaten by a bear."

Both girls broke out into laughter at the same exact moment. Their cheer bubbled out of them, floating up to join the leaves. As their laughter ran its course, the forest grew still and they sat quietly, taking in all the nature brimming around them.

They were in the great outdoors. The wilderness. America's backyard. A far cry from their cushy suburban lives. But it was gorgeous here. Maddie marveled at how oblivious she'd been so far this trip. She hadn't noticed the towering trees all around her, throwing their cool shade for as far as she could see.

The stream, now right in front of her, was much larger than she'd imagined. Streams gurgled. But here, the water churned, a river rushing downhill toward the valley's center. It was beautifully blue, white where little rapids formed, shedding their foam caps. It wasn't a wide river. Maddie could see across to the other side. And maybe that was why Caleb had called it a stream.

They sat there together for maybe ten minutes, neither girl speaking. Maddie's eyes scanned the forest across the river. At first she didn't see much, but then her eyes adjusted, her ears tuned in to the forest's frequency, and she saw everything.

Two birds flapped onto a nearby branch. On the ground, a squirrel foraged in the fallen leaves before finding a nut and scurrying out of sight. There was so much life right here in front of her eyes if only she stopped for a moment to take it all in.

Maddie froze as a doe and two fawns cantered into sight. She didn't even dare motion for Chelsea to look. They were beautiful, their coats a soft brown speckled with delicate white flecks like they'd been dusted in powdered sugar. They picked their way to the water and carefully bent to drink.

They looked so innocent. Maddie's palms itched to reach out and touch them. Slowly, she edged forward, even though she knew she couldn't reach them from across the stream. Her arm raised a centimeter at a time and her hand opened up in invitation.

She was so close to them now, her shoes squishing in the mud of the river bank. She could make out their tracks, count their slender legs, see the nutmeg color of their twinkling eyes, so full of life and wonder. If only she had a sugar cube to offer them.

Somewhere in the forest a twig snapped. In the still air it might as well have been a gunshot. The deer tensed, perking up their ears, lifting their heads, spotting Maddie's unusual presence.

They spooked and leaped back into the forest. Maddie watched them go, disappointed but also thrilled to have seen them at all, a reminder that the world still had good things to offer, even if it could be a shitty place some of the time.

As the deer disappeared from sight, Maddie spun around to tell Chelsea about it, but her eyes caught on something—something not right. She swung her gaze back and squinted into the shadows, trying to pick it out again. But she came up empty.

She could have sworn she'd seen something there in the woods, though. A shadow maybe. Or a figure. Someone or something watching them. Her eyes strained to see more, to develop X-ray vision on the spot.

"Did you see something just now?" Maddie asked.

"See what?"

"I thought there was someone over there." Maddie pointed and Chelsea followed her finger.

"I wasn't paying attention." Chelsea didn't seem bothered by it at all. "Maybe it was Abigail trying to scare us?"

"Maybe." Maddie humored Chelsea, but she knew it wasn't Abigail. She'd been forced to have play dates with the girl since she was little. She knew her face almost better than her own.

"I'm sure it was nothing. Your eyes playing tricks on you or something."

"Yeah. Probably."

Maddie thought Chelsea was right, but she couldn't shake the bad feeling. She continued staring at the spot out in the woods, expecting a shadow to peel off and reveal itself any second now.

"How about we fill these up," Chelsea suggested, changing subjects.

Maddie nodded, taking one last hard look into the forest before turning and helping Chelsea drag the big water cooler to the river.

"Should we send out a search party?" Maddie asked five minutes later. She wiped her hands dry on her shorts and gave the pile of canteens a dubious eye.

"Abigail's a big girl," Chelsea said. She bent over the large cooler and lifted it, but then plunked it right back down on the ground. "But maybe we should make sure she hasn't fallen in a hole."

Maddie nodded, but before the girls could split up, a commotion of snapping twigs broke out behind them and Abigail stumbled through the underbrush toward them.

"What were you doing out there?" Chelsea asked, annoyed. "You didn't even help with the canteens."

Abigail breezed past, ignoring Chelsea completely. Maddie turned to defend her best friend, but a pungent odor slapped her across the face. She sniffed again, recognizing the funky smell trailing Abigail.

"Were you smoking pot?"

"Maybe." Abigail spun around and grinned, her eyes narrowing to a dazed squint. "Why do you care?"

"I don't," Maddie replied indifferently. "But your mom probably will."

"Please," Abigail shrugged. "She's oblivious. And I'll be good and aired out by the time we get back."

"Well, you better not forget these."

Chelsea chucked four of the canteens into Abigail's arms. To her merit, the girl hung on to them all. Maddie and Chelsea split the remaining canteens and then bent as one and hefted the big water cooler between them. It weighed a ton, and trickles of water ran down its sides, making the girls' hands even slicker than before. The walk back was going to take a lot longer.

"This way," Chelsea snapped, and Abigail fell in line behind them, walking slowly, her gaze floating left and right and up and down as she slid further into her high, the reverse of earlier in the day.

They walked for a while without anyone speaking, Abigail lost in her own world as Maddie and Chelsea labored with the full water cooler. Maddie's arm grew sore, but she didn't want to stop. Not in front of Abigail. She gritted her teeth and carried on, but she could see Chelsea's face out of the corner of her eye, the way she huffed, her red-cheeked look of strain. Chelsea might have had the bigger bark, but Maddie had the muscles.

After another minute Maddie took pity on her best friend and let her half of the cooler drop. Chelsea happily let go of her side as well, and the girls bent over, taking deep breaths. Maddie wiped her forehead with her shirt and unstoppered one of the canteens to take a long drink before offering it to Chelsea.

"I wish Caleb was here to carry this," Maddie said as Chelsea took the canteen and gulped down a mouthful of water. She swallowed and wiped her lips.

"You and me both."

Maddie opened her mouth, but Abigail's voice cut her off. She'd caught up to them.

"Are you two talking about Caleb again?" Abigail cocked a discerning eyebrow Maddie's way. Her initial high seemed to have burned off, leaving behind an even meaner Abigail. "Don't you think he's a bit out of your league? I mean, not that you're completely inexperienced—but older guys like Caleb expect a bit more than holding hands."

"And how exactly would you know?" Chelsea came to Maddie's defense. "Blowing through the entire baseball team hardly makes you an expert."

Abigail flushed a deep red. She opened her mouth and shut it again, pressing her lips together in a fine line of fury. She stared down Chelsea, but the girl didn't even flutter an eyelash. And then Abigail was gone, storming past Maddie and Chelsea without another word.

"Is that true?" Maddie's relief showed all over her face. That was her best friend, shutting down anyone and everyone who came for them.

"Well, maybe it wasn't the *entire* baseball team...."

SIX

THE FIRE CRACKLED AND POPPED IN the center of camp. It shot sparks into the night as a gooey marshmallow slipped from a stick and kamikazied into the flames. A caramel aroma filled the air, smoky and sweet.

"Shit! What—what did you say happened?" The curse came from Mark Towson—Kris's husband—though Maddie couldn't tell if he was yelling at his suicidal marshmallow or her dad's story.

"It was really scary," Maddie's dad went on, able to talk about that morning's events calmly now that Maddie had gotten through them unhurt. Mark didn't seem so blasé about it, though. He frowned into the fire, watching as the white confection turned brown and then black. He hadn't ridden up with them. He'd missed the morning's excitement—the roar, the gunshot, and Maddie's bucking horse.

"And the horse went berserk? Just like that?" Mark looked worried now. His knuckles glowed white around the stick that had held a marshmallow only a second before. "And there was a bear...."

Maddie heard the man gulp.

"Well, we didn't actually *see* a bear," Charlie jumped in to clarify.

"But that's what it sounded like," Dylan added.

This didn't help Dylan's father one bit. His head swiveled to one side. And then to the other, like a cheap bobble-head doll they handed out at baseball games. Maddie felt sorry for Abigail and Dylan. They had to have the most embarrassing dad on the planet. As if his overwhelming anxiety wasn't bad enough, he also had on the most ridiculous camping vest. It surprised Maddie that he hadn't already pulled a can of bear mace from one of its numerous pockets.

"These mountains aren't safe," Mark's voice rose an unflattering octave. "I told you, Kris. But you didn't believe my research. There are bears and mountain lions. Hundreds of attacks every year."

Kris only sighed, placing her fingers against her forehead as she let her husband wind himself up.

Mark's search for an impending attack turned more frantic. His head whipped around, but he couldn't see anything past their campfire's circle of light. Instead, he dropped his marshmallow stick and rushed over to his tent, reaching in and pulling out his overstuffed pack, filled with triple rations and a mini-pharmacy's worth of ointments and pill bottles. His hand grazed a long, cylindrical package and he seemed suddenly calmer. Maddie couldn't tell what it was. It was wrapped in harmless brown paper and looked kind of like a bat. But why would he have brought that with him? He wasn't planning on hitting fly balls with Charlie, was he?

"Everyone can relax," Caleb spoke up, and Mark's fingers darted back from the package like a kid with his hand caught in the cookie jar. "There's nothing to worry about."

"But there was a bear," Mark sputtered, rushing back to the campfire.

"That roar came from miles away," Caleb reassured them all.

"And the gunshot?"

"It probably was a firecracker. Kids like to set them off this time of year—getting antsy for the Fourth of July. Trust me. You have nothing to worry about. You'd know if something was about to attack you."

"But—but—"

"Honey, trust the guide. If he says it's safe, it's safe." Kris's stern voice ended the debate. Mark looked around, searching for someone to share in his hysteria, but came up empty.

"Have another marshmallow," Julie said as she came forward and handed Mark the stick he'd dropped. She skewered a new marshmallow on the end of it and pushed it out over the fire to toast. She reached up, as if to pat him on the head and say "good boy," but her hand found his shoulder instead, more of a "there, there."

Maddie lay back against a log and watched it all as she munched on her own s'more, smiling to herself. That was just like Aunt Julie. Always the mom. She took another bite and couldn't help but remember the ones she and her mom had made over their gas stove so many years ago. No s'more could ever compete with those, but these came pretty close—the smooth, rich chocolate coating her tongue; the marshmallow a light, gooey pillow of sweetness; and the graham cracker a salty crunch to give the s'more teeth. She took another bite and savored it, casting her eye around the rest of the fire, seeing how everyone was getting along.

Ever since Maddie could remember, their three families—the Davenports, the Towsons, and the Witters (her mother's family)—had gotten together for playdates, birthdays, Sunday brunches, game nights, Super Bowl parties . . . just about everything imaginable. Now that she was older, however, it seemed kind of strange to Maddie just how intertwined and dependent they'd become. They couldn't even go on vacation alone—case in point, this camping trip. Though this was more of a special last hurrah before Bryan, Dylan, and Charlie went off to college in the fall. But there was Hawaii and Disney and that cruise to the Bahamas. The weekends skiing and the cross-country road trip two years ago.

According to her dad, it went all the way back to college. Kris, Julie, and Maddie's mom—Linda—had all met there and been nearly inseparable. In an attempt to get some alone time with Linda, Maddie's dad had brought his roommate to dinner one night and asked Maddie's mom to invite her brother. Neither had had the faintest idea that things would go so well that they'd be dinnering with the other two couples for the next twenty-plus years. Even after Maddie's mother had died, the families had only gotten closer, their shared tragedy knitting them even tighter together.

There'd been some tension as of late, though. At least, Maddie had sensed it. Just the slightest twist of the screw. Maddie could see the pressure building, the cracks beginning to show around pasted-on smiles. Pretty soon, with their eldest children gone to college, they might be seeing a lot less of one another.

And maybe that was for the best. Maddie certainly didn't want to spend every weekend with Abigail.

Maddie watched as Mark finished roasting his marshmallow. Julie swooped in again, this time with chocolate and two graham crackers, which she used to pin and remove the smoking treat from Mark's stick. She handed it to him, and he thanked her with big googly eyes. He took a bite of the s'more and its insides squished out, the marshmallow sliding down and splatting right on his shirt.

From the other side of the fire, Maddie's uncle Ed pointed and laughed. Mark's face glowed red in the firelight. He looked at Julie, who looked at her husband, who was still laughing and pointing. Mark threw his stick down and slumped back to take a seat on one of the logs.

Yeah, some time apart could do them all a lot of good.

"So, should we get this party started?" Maddie's dad had appeared from the shadows beyond the campfire. He walked over to one of the coolers and pulled out a bottle of beer. He cracked it open with an effortless twist.

"Now that's what I'm talking about," Ed shouted. He abandoned his half-eaten s'more and joined Maddie's dad, pulling a can of beer out of the cooler for himself. He popped it open and took a long gulp, downing it in one go. He crunched the can in his fist like some amped-up frat boy and let out an almighty burp that curdled Maddie's ears. He grabbed another beer for himself and then began passing them out to everyone.

"Anyone think they can chug a beer faster than me?"

Kris rolled her eyes as she took a beer from him.

"You do realize you're not twenty-one anymore and the kids aren't even old enough to drink yet."

"Screw age limits. We're in the middle of nowhere. The kids can have a beer if they want. At least my kid can."

Ed tossed a beer to Bryan, who fumbled the slick can and then dropped it in the grass. He scrambled to retrieve it, but his dad had already rolled his eyes and moved on.

"I bet Charlie wants one, too. That OK, Mitch?"

Maddie's dad nodded and Ed fired off another can, which her brother caught easily.

"That's my champ."

Bryan could only glower as he listened to his father praise the son he'd rather have had. He took a feeble sip of his beer and then wandered off into the night. Ed didn't even notice him leave. He was too busy passing out drinks to everyone who wanted one.

"Well, then." Ed had finished the rounds and his second beer. He took a third and popped it open. "I think a cheers is in order."

He held his beer high and everyone joined him, Maddie and Chelsea raising their cans of soda. They were the only two not drinking, even though her dad had said it was okay. She'd be damned if she got drunk for the first time in front of him, though. There were some things dads just shouldn't see.

"To our distinguished graduates," Ed nodded in Dylan and Charlie's direction, completely unaware of his son's absence. "You're going to learn a lot in college, then realize it doesn't mean shit. So don't forget to party hard. That's about the only thing college is any good for."

It was an odd toast, but very much her uncle. Maddie clinked her soda can with Chelsea's and the girls drank along with everyone else.

"Now, let's have some fun."

"I already told you, no drinking games." Kris sounded extra annoyed with Ed, her tone terse. Ed shot her a frown, but before he could complain, Charlie jumped in with an idea.

"What about we tell some campfire stories?" He'd drunk about half his beer already and Maddie could tell it was bubbling behind his eyes, loosening him up.

"You know," Caleb spoke for the first time since dinner and everyone turned to listen, "it's bad luck to tell scary stories under a full moon."

Everyone's gaze followed his finger as it pointed up into the sky, their eyes growing big as they spotted the perfectly plump moon sitting full in the cloudless sky above them.

"They say that stories told under a full moon come true," Caleb warned.

"Bullshit," Ed spat out. "Sounds like an old superstition to me."

"Don't say I didn't warn you." A gleam sparked in Caleb's so-blue eyes and a chill ran up Maddie's spine. The mood felt suddenly dangerous. But also alive.

"Can I go first?" a voice squeaked. Maddie turned and was surprised to see Aunt Julie raising her hand. She'd opted for a wine cooler instead of beer, and her cheeks had already started to turn a rosy shade of pink.

No one argued, so Julie moved closer to the fire, her voice dropping to a low, conspiratorial murmur as she began her tale.

"Have you ever heard the one about the dancing bear?"

BEWARE WHEN THE FAIR COMES TO TOWN

Old Man Weber's field had sprung to life overnight, though not with crops. It hadn't seen a harvest since the city had foreclosed on the farmer's property more than a decade ago. Instead, the land bloomed with bright red-and-yellow tents. Rows of them had popped up, housing games of skill and chance—all rigged—while others held mouthwatering treats like fried Snicker bars, popcorn, and funnel cakes wafting their enticing aromas through the crowd. And above it all, a Ferris wheel had blossomed, unfurling its colorful swinging cars like petals on a brilliant sunflower.

The County Fair had come to town.

Jennifer stood outside by herself, waiting in line to buy her ticket. Her phone buzzed and she snatched at it, then a second later flared with embarrassment. She thrust the phone back into her pocket and shook her head. It was only her mother, reminding her to stay safe.

Not Max.

He wasn't calling. He was never going to call. He'd dumped her two weeks ago. Why couldn't she accept it?

But she couldn't think about that. The night was supposed to be fun, a distraction from her ex and all his bullshit. She shuffled forward and passed a worn ten-dollar bill to the ticket seller.

"Excuse me." A voice startled Jennifer out of her own thoughts. "Have you seen my friend?"

It took Jennifer a moment to realize the girl was talking to her.

"Sorry?"

"Have you seen her?" the girl asked shyly.

She held out a flyer with a black-and-white photograph printed on it. The girl in the picture looked about Jennifer's age, unruly brown hair flying all over the place, a mouth that took up half her face opened so wide that Jennifer could see a filling peeking out from one of her molars. She had her hand up, as if trying to stop the photographer from taking her pic-ture, and on that wrist Jennifer could just make out a tattoo—an infinity sign.

"Her name's Rachel. No one's seen her for over a week."

Jennifer felt bad for the girl.

"We're best friends," she sputtered. "And I don't—I don't—"

The girl broke into tears. Jennifer didn't know what to do, so she took the flyer.

"I haven't seen her. But I'll keep an eye out."

This seemed to calm the girl. She sniffled, sucking the snot back up into her nose, and wiped her eyes. She said thanks and moved on, another flyer ready to hand out. Jennifer looked back down at the face of the laughing girl—Rachel. She'd never seen her. But maybe she would.

She folded up the paper and slid it into her back pocket. Then she grabbed her string of red tickets and walked through the fair's gates. She had an ex-boyfriend to forget about.

As Jennifer picked her way through the fairgrounds, she tried everything. She lost at the ring-toss and could have been drunk for how badly she did at the shooting gallery. But she did manage a solid hit at the dunk tank. Visualizing Max plummeting into the chilly water had helped her focus. She rode the bumper cars and even made it through the haunted house without screaming too much. But she avoided the Ferris wheel. It was too depressing to ride that one single. And she definitely wasn't going up there with a stranger. If the wheel stopped at the top, who knew where he'd try to put his hands.

Nibbling on a deep-fried Oreo, Jennifer took stock of her ticket situation. She had just enough for one last attraction. Maybe another go at the shooting gallery. She couldn't do worse. She turned to walk back and find the booth, but right then, a tinkling caught her attention. She stopped and listened for it again.

There. Like a wind chime. Delicate and sweet, dancing above the rowdiness of the crowd. Jennifer paused and listened to it ring. She closed her eyes and felt calmer. A smile sneaked its way onto her face. It might have been the first time she'd been happy in weeks.

Slowly, Jennifer opened her eyes, and that's when she spotted him. She'd know that shaggy brown hair anywhere. Her heart leaped into her throat. She hadn't run into him at all in the past weeks. But maybe...if she talked to him, things could be good again.

He hadn't noticed her yet, so she took a step toward him. But then she saw Kara. She saw the two of them laughing. Holding hands. Out on a date?

Jennifer's heart took a suicidal leap into her stomach. She had to get away. She couldn't let Max see her alone and miserable while he held hands with another girl. She panicked and rushed into the nearest tent.

She couldn't breathe. Or rather, all she could do was breathe. In and out and in and out, too fast for any air to actually get to her lungs. She had to slow down.

And then she heard it—that tinkle. Louder now. Closer.

Her eyes popped up and she saw a man standing in the center of the tent, holding a miniature bell in one hand. His other hand was stuffed into the pocket of a flamboyant red jacket, its seams etched with brilliant gold embroidery. He wore a huge black top hat, which perfectly matched his knee-high leather boots.

The man rang the bell twice more, and a hush fell over the tent. Only then did Jennifer realize she wasn't the only one watching, wasn't the only one spellbound by this odd man in his ringmaster get-up. She shuffled forward a bit and joined the back of the audience.

An eerie silence filled the tent, anticipation and dread colliding in the air as everyone waited and wondered what would happen next. Then another bell jingled in answer. And kept jingling.

From the shadows behind the ringmaster, a burly figure twice the ringmaster's size and five times as hairy ambled forward. It took Jennifer a moment to realize it wasn't a man the ringmaster had summoned, but a wooly behemoth of a bear.

Dressed in a light pink vest and matching tutu, the bear jingled as it lumbered into full view. Jennifer looked closer and saw that it wasn't glitter shining from the tutu's fabric, but actual bells, dozens of them sewn into the hemline. The bear walked into the center of the tent and stood up on two paws, watching the ringmaster.

"Allow me to introduce you to Bambi."

The man gave his bell a quick shake, and the bear let out a magnificent roar, teeth bared to the heavens, spittle flying from its snout. The audience sucked in its breath as one and pulled back.

"Oh, now, now. Don't you all worry." The ringmaster's voice carried over the crowd's gasp. "Bambi really likes people. In fact, she's quite harmless."

The man gave his bell two shakes and the bear snapped its jaws shut and plopped down on the ground, a puppy dog lapping at its master's feet.

"See…" The ringmaster waited for the applause to go down before he continued. "As long as you know how to talk to her—"

He rang the bell again, this time a new pattern of short and long tolls, like he was speaking in Morse code, and the bear jumped back on its feet to give the man a high five.

"She'll do anything you ask."

The crowd broke into a round of applause, and the man beamed out at them all. Then he sent the bear dancing across the little stage in the center of the tent. He had Bambi prance and play dead and stand on one leg. He had her jump over hurdles and through hoops, turn not-so-dainty pirouettes. And for the grand finale, he had her take a treat from between his own teeth.

"Ladies and gentlemen," the ringmaster shouted, snapping his top hat from his head and dipping into a deep bow, "I give you Bambi."

The small crowd broke out into applause again as the bear mimicked its master. Another bow and the two walked off stage. The audience began to spill out into the night.

The show had only taken twenty minutes, but in that short time, the fair had emptied out considerably. Most of the attractions had closed up, and the few fairgoers Jennifer saw were heading toward the exit. She was ready to go home, too.

As Jennifer walked through the rows of shuttered tents, she couldn't help thinking about Max. And Kara. She paused and pulled out her phone, but stopped herself from looking down at it, from writing him an angry message. A pathetic text that would only embarrass her come morning. Instead, she squeezed her phone tight, thinking. Even if Max had called, she didn't want to speak to him. She could do so much better than him. In fact, she *never* wanted to speak to him again.

The smile from earlier in the night sneaked back across her face. She moved to put her phone away, but her fingers slipped. She looked down and saw a folded piece of paper there in her hand. It took her a second to remember the flyer. She unfolded it and looked at the missing girl again.

What was her name? She was young and happy. So pretty. She looked cool with that infinity-sign tattoo, like someone Jennifer would have liked to know. She folded the paper back up and hoped that the girl's friend would find her, that the girl had simply run off and holed up in some hotel room with a guy.

She took a step forward, but before she could take a second, she felt an arm twist roughly around her waist. A hand crammed a rag against her mouth and nose as a bitter chemical seeped in through her nostrils. It coated her tongue. Made her dizzy.

She wanted to scream. She wanted to thrash. She wanted to bite and scratch and cry and vomit.

But she couldn't do any of that.

Terror overwhelmed her as the world faded before her eyes and she collapsed.

Jennifer groaned and turned over. She didn't remember drinking the night before, but how else could she explain this feeling, like the world's worst hangover had taken her and wrung her within an inch of her life? Her head pounded. Her ears rang with an unending, dull drone. Her mouth was bone dry, and her tongue tasted like she'd swallowed a Molotov cocktail.

She opened her eyes slowly. Or at least, she thought she'd opened them. But she could only see a pitch-black nothingness. She waved her hands in front of her face to be sure. Was this what dying felt like?

She rolled over and her body hit a wall. She rolled the other way and hit another wall. Her hands flew out to both sides, and she felt rough wood beneath her fingertips, less than three feet apart. She sat up in a panic but only got a quarter of the way before her head smashed into a ceiling.

She panicked. Her fingers clawed at the lid. She kicked at the box. She tried to scream but could only croak, her throat still too dry to make a real sound. Tears rolled down her cheeks. She couldn't breathe. The walls pressed in all around her. Her prison got smaller, and she realized with heart-shattering certainty that it wasn't just a box, but her coffin.

Minutes passed and Jennifer grew tired. She lost hope. She lay there on her back and tried to slow her breathing. She had to conserve whatever oxygen she had left. If she was buried alive, maybe someone would find her still. She closed her eyes and tried to calm down.

Slowly, the night's events seeped into her mind. The fair. The bumper cars. The haunted house and the dancing bear. Seeing Max with Kara. The fingers pressing into her mouth, gagging her. All of it happening in a flash.

Her phone.

She groped for her pockets. If she could get to her phone, maybe she could call for help. But no. She must have dropped it. Or whoever had attacked her had taken it.

A yelp escaped her lips, sad and forlorn, as depressing as a dying puppy.

"Ah," a man's voice shocked her out of her stupor. "Finally given up, have we?"

"Wh—who's there?" Jennifer's voice wavered. "What do you want with me?"

The man didn't reply. Jennifer strained to hear. She tried to push aside the incessant droning still burrowing into her ears and she managed to hear something beneath it. Something wet and squelching, almost like the man was sucking the last tendrils of meat from a chicken bone.

Suddenly, the lid of her coffin flew open and Jennifer felt a rough hand reach in. Fingers snagged her by the hair and yanked her out, sending her tumbling across the room. She fell to the ground in a heap and heard a clanging behind her. The click of a padlock. She turned in a frenzy, pulling her hair out of her face just in time to see a man putting a key into his vest pocket, a barred cage door separating them.

At first, she didn't recognize him. He'd lost all of his magnificence from earlier in the night. His hair lay flat and greasy on his head, patchy in spots. Without his black boots and top hat, he looked half as tall. But he still wore his vest, bright and festooned with gold. And he had that same hand stuffed into his pocket, a familiar pose of confidence and ease.

"What do you want with me?" Jennifer asked the question again.

"It's not what *I* want," the ringmaster smiled cruelly. His hand dipped into his pocket and pulled out that damn bell. He rang it.

The sound pierced Jennifer's eardrums. It cut through her like a knife. It no longer sounded like a soothing wind chime, but like glass shattering, dreams dashed, a life snuffed out. She whipped her head around just in time to see the huge bear twist its snout around to face her.

The creature held Jennifer's gaze, unfazed as it continued gnawing on something. Blood spotted the fur around its mouth. Its teeth gnashed and Jennifer heard a bone snap. She looked closer and saw a finger, a manicured nail, the split ends of severed bones.

Jennifer's face blanched. Her stomach heaved and she vomited up the remnants of her fried Oreo.

It was a human arm. The bear was chewing on it like a drumstick, tearing flesh off at the forearm. Jennifer didn't want to watch, but she couldn't turn away. Her eyes slid down to the hand and that's when she saw it—the figure-eight symbol from before.

Rachel.

The name came back to her with a seismic bolt of thunder. It shook her out of her daze. She turned and scrambled across the floor to where the man stood, the door of the cage still between them.

"Please!" Jennifer shook the cage door as she screamed. "You can't do this!"

"Quiet now." The ringmaster looked sympathetically down at her. "You'll only make it worse."

"But—but—" Jennifer grappled for the right words, but none came.

"Shh." The man reached through the bars and placed a gloved finger against her lips. If she had been thinking straight, she would have bitten it off.

"Bambi likes to play with her dinner before eating it."

The man pulled his hand back and gave his bell four quick shakes. Jennifer swiveled her head around and watched in terror as the bear dropped its human drumstick and turned its attention on her.

Only a handful of steps separated them, trapped in the same floor-to-ceiling cage. The bear rose onto its hind legs, a towering mass of fur and muscle, of sharp teeth and flashing claws. Jennifer wished she could go back to her coffin, anything to get away. The bear would tear her apart in a heartbeat. Just like it had Rachel.

Bambi took a step forward and its costume jangled to life. It still had on the tutu and vest from the performance earlier in the night, the ones festooned with glittering bells. It took another step and the bells clanged out a sort of rhythm this time.

"Oh, God. Please. Please. You don't have to do this."

Jennifer didn't know who exactly she was pleading with, but it was the ringmaster who answered.

"I'm afraid it's out of God's hands."

"But why? Why?" Jennifer took her eyes off the bear to stare up at her kidnapper.

"Why?" The man crouched down and leaned in close so that only the cage's bars separated his face from Jennifer's. He could have licked her cheek if he'd wanted. "Because Bambi has to eat."

Jennifer's pupils widened and then narrowed again. That didn't make any sense.

"Bambi and I have been together for over a decade," the man elaborated. "She's my best friend. My only family. And family doesn't run out on each other."

The man paused here, considering his next words carefully. Slowly, he shifted positions and took his hand out of his vest pocket. Only then did Jennifer realize he'd kept it hidden away the whole time, even during the show that night. And now she understood why.

"You see, a few years ago Bambi got a little taste of human flesh." The man held up the hand he'd just taken from his vest pocket and showed Jennifer his whittled-down stump of an arm.

"She didn't mean it. We were playing, and she only got a few of my fingers. But after that, she didn't eat for days. At first, I thought it was because she felt guilty. I tried to show her I was okay, that I loved her still. But she wouldn't eat.

"I was desperate, then. My Bambi was weak. She could barely walk. I couldn't sleep, I was so worried. That's when I got an idea. It seemed crazy, I know, but I was willing to try anything to save my baby.

"It took three chops with a meat cleaver, right here below the wrist." The man pointed it out to Jennifer, and she realized just how crazy he was. Her stomach rebelled against her again, but only green bile came up. "It hurt like hell. But Bambi ate after. And has eaten ever since…as long as I provide her the right diet."

A sound like a tambourine clanged only a foot away from Jennifer, and she turned from the man to see the bear looming over her now.

"Looks like Bambi's ready for dinner."

"No!" Jennifer shrieked. Without a thought, her hands shot through the bars of the cage and grabbed the ringmaster's vest. She clawed at his buttons, his pockets, anything to get at him, to stay alive for a second more. But he only chuckled and pushed her away with ease. She fell to the floor again.

"You can't fight it. There's nowhere to hide, little girl."

But Jennifer didn't listen. Instead, she uncoiled her legs and leaped to her feet. While she'd wrestled with the man, she'd managed to grab the key from his vest pocket. Now, she fumbled with the lock. She had surprise on her side, but a hungry bear at her back.

Somehow, despite her shaking hands, she managed to get the key in the lock and twisted it open just as the bear lunged forward.

The weight of Jennifer and Bambi simultaneously crashing against the cage door popped it open like a mousetrap. The door snapped the ringmaster in the chest and he flew backward. Jennifer didn't waste a glance in his direction as she picked herself up off the floor and made for the door. She heard him laughing, though. And it unnerved her.

"I don't know where you think you're going."

Jennifer tried to ignore him. She grabbed the door handle and pulled hard. It slid open with a stubborn screech.

A cry leaped from her mouth and flew away on the wind as it whipped into the room and blew her hair back. Below her the ground whooshed by, at fifty or sixty miles an hour.

The drone she'd been hearing ever since waking up wasn't only in her head.

No. It was a train, hurtling her to God knew where.

The world raced past in a blur. If she jumped, she was dead. But if she stayed, she was also dead. She didn't know what to do.

"I'm afraid you're out of options."

Jennifer turned and saw the man leering at her. He'd picked himself up off the ground and had his bell out. He rang a command, but Bambi didn't react. Instead, the bear looked around the room uncertainly. Its snout twitched. Its tongue tasted the air. It was disoriented. It'd probably never been let out of its cage like this. In that moment, Jennifer saw her one chance at survival. She rushed forward, surprising the man. Her hand flew to his good one and she snapped up the bell. Before he could react, she'd run back into the cage and locked it behind her.

"You think those bars will save you?" the man snorted.

"No. I'm hoping this will." And Jennifer rang the bell as hard and as fast as she could. Its sound bounced off the walls of the train car, ricocheting and getting louder. She kept it up and began ringing harder when she saw Bambi start to freak out.

The bear roared to life. It swatted at the cage door. It tried to get in and claw Jennifer to ribbons, but she danced out of its reach and rang the bell even faster. The bear tried to cover its ears, but the ringing still got through.

"What are you doing?" the man cried out. "You're hurting her! Stop it!"

But Jennifer kept up the ringing, and when Bambi couldn't get to her, it turned on its master.

With one heavy swat, the man crashed to the floor. He tried getting up, but the bear hit him again and sent his body skittering close to the train car's open door. Jennifer kept up her ringing and the bear continued its attack. It hovered over the man and then dug its claws into his chest. He didn't scream, though. The bear hit him again and he coughed up blood, which Bambi happily licked off his face. Tears spilled from his eyes and a strangled cry escaped his throat. He looked up at Bambi with a glimmer in his eyes.

Was it sadness? Or love? Jennifer couldn't tell. He held the bear's gaze for a moment, and then its jaws came down and crushed his throat. He didn't move after that.

Jennifer watched as the bear plopped down on top of its master and began eating. She didn't even realize she'd stopped ringing the bell. Bambi started in on the man's stump of an arm, then the train shuddered as it rounded a bend.

The bear lost its balance. It teetered on the lip of the open door. And then the train shook again and Bambi toppled over, taking the man with her as she tumbled out of the car.

Jennifer gasped. She opened the cage and rushed out, just in time to see the bear land. It rolled on the ground, the man's lifeless body spinning around it like a towel in the dryer. It came to a quick stop and lay there, unmoving as the train chugged away. Just as she was about to travel out of sight, Jennifer saw the bear lift its head. She saw it take stock of its surroundings, and then it grabbed the man in its teeth and dragged him into the forest.

SEVEN

"JENNIFER SURVIVED THAT NIGHT," JULIE SAID as the fire flickered and sent eerie shadows dancing across her face. "But she wasn't the only survivor."

Maddie leaned in to get a better look at her. She didn't want to miss a single word.

"Bambi survived, too." Julie paused and glanced around the circle. "A few days later a park ranger came across the ravaged remains of a man. His fingers were gone, and both legs had been gnawed through.

"Only, it wasn't the ringmaster's body. And it wasn't just any woods." She paused again. Maddie had to give it to her aunt—she knew how to tell a damn creepy story. "No. They found the body right here in these mountains. Seems that Bambi never did get over the taste of human flesh. And still hasn't."

A roar suddenly filled the night and Maddie jumped, almost falling off her log. She turned her head and saw her uncle Ed laughing his head off, his finger pointed toward Mark, who had fallen on the ground and spilled his beer all over his shirt in the process.

"Wow, Julie," Ed belched, his laughter finally cutting off. "I didn't know you had that in you."

Julie rolled her eyes, then raised her wine cooler to her lips to take a sip.

"Full of surprises, isn't she?" Mark had recovered himself and looked genuinely proud of her.

"Remember whose wife you're talking about," Ed growled.

"Why don't you two grow up," Julie huffed. She tilted her head back and finished off her wine cooler. "When I get back, you better be ready to behave."

And with that warning, Julie stomped her way out of the campfire's circle of light.

"Wow, I didn't know your aunt was such a badass," Chelsea whispered to Maddie.

"She usually isn't." Maddie didn't know what had come over Aunt Julie, but she liked it. And wanted to see more of it in the future. "Another s'more?"

"Duh," Chelsea deadpanned. "I'll never say no to toasted sugar."

The girls got up and walked over to rummage through the bag of treats but found only an empty marshmallow bag.

"That sucks." Maddie frowned.

"Here. I grabbed another bag."

The girls jumped as Julie appeared behind them. She handed them a fresh bag of marshmallows and then popped open her second wine cooler.

"Thanks." Maddie could have hugged her aunt. "And great story. How'd you come up with that?"

"Oh, you know. . . ."

Julie's smile faded. Maddie followed her gaze and saw her uncle and Mark talking again. It didn't look pretty. Uncle Ed had a problem with his temper when sober, more so when he had a few beers swishing around in his gut.

"These days, the news can be scarier than Stephen King," Maddie's aunt finished half-heartedly, clearly distracted. "Excuse me, girls."

And with that, Julie made her way around the fire to try and defuse her husband yet again.

"What'd she mean by that?" Chelsea asked. She ripped a corner off the bag of marshmallows and popped two in her mouth.

"Hey, save some for the rest of us." Maddie snatched the bag away from her friend and tore into a marshmallow of her own.

All of a sudden a shout came from the campfire, answered a moment later by an even louder voice.

"I can't deal with that." Maddie sighed and rolled her eyes. "Wanna walk?"

"As long as we can take these bad boys with us."

"I don't think anyone will miss them." Maddie gave Chelsea a sneaky look and held out the bag of marshmallows. The girls scooped up their flashlights and headed into the woods, away from camp and Ed's raised voice.

They didn't say much as they walked. Their flashlight beams danced in front of them, illuminating odd strips of the forest. It looked so different at night, dark and impenetrable. What secrets did it hide?

Someone could be watching them and they'd never know. A chill tickled its way up Maddie's spine, and she couldn't keep her eyes from darting to every tree trunk they passed.

"Do you think that's what our moms were like?" Chelsea asked out of the blue.

Maddie pulled her eyes around and looked at her best friend.

"Like what?" she asked.

"Ed." Chelsea's lips thinned to that serious face Maddie knew well. "Or, like...any of them."

She trailed off and Maddie let her think.

"Do you ever wonder what our moms were *really* like?" Chelsea asked. "I don't have that many, like, concrete memories of mine. And my dad only ever has good stories to share when I ask about her. But that's not realistic. Our moms might be dead, but they weren't saints. What if—"

"What if what?"

Maddie tried to ease the worry on her best friend's face.

"What if"—Chelsea took a moment, steeling herself—"What if my mom wasn't who I think she was? What if she was a nightmare, like Ed? What if she was shrill or short-tempered? An alcoholic? What if she had an affair? Or daydreamed about leaving us behind and starting a new life? But then she got sick and—and she couldn't go through with it."

Maddie stopped walking and looked at Chelsea with real care. She loved this about her best friend, that they could talk about silly stuff like boys and what dresses they should wear to prom, but then also turn around and have truly serious conversations. That they could bring up their own doubts and insecurities and have someone there as a therapist. But also more than that, as a best friend who understood, who had experienced the same kind of devastating loss.

It was astonishing how a tragedy could make an entire school forget someone's most embarrassing moment. Almost as astonishing as when Maddie had woken up in the hospital those five years ago to find her worst enemy's beady eyes staring down at her.

Of course, Chelsea's eyes hadn't been beady. But back then Maddie had seen the devil in the girl. Good thing Chelsea had left her mean-girl days behind her, because in reality, her eyes had been giant and distressed and swimming with tears. Comforting and understanding. A friend when Maddie had needed one most.

Apparently, Chelsea's mom had died of cancer the year before, and she wasn't afraid to spell it all out for Maddie right there in the hospital room.

"Like it or not, you're stuck with me. We're sisters now. Maybe not by blood or even by choice. But tragedy chose us. It took our mothers from us, and now we have a bond that no one and nothing can break."

She'd reached across the hospital bed then and held out her pinkie. *"Sisters for life."*

And what could Maddie do but hook her finger with the girl's? However unsure she'd been that day, it'd turned out to be the best thing that had happened to her. She'd never forget how Chelsea had breezed into her life, how she'd made her feel welcome and not alone. Chelsea had been right. They were sisters, and nothing could tear them apart. They'd always be there for each other, no matter what.

"Chelsea, where's this coming from?" Maddie asked.

"I don't know." Chelsea didn't meet Maddie's gaze. "I guess I've been thinking it for a while but haven't really known how to say it. I just see all these other adults in real life and in movies and books, and they're all so complicated. They're good and bad and it's all mixed up inside them."

Maddie cocked her eyebrow, confused.

"I guess what I'm trying to say is that all these other adults I see— your aunt Julie and Mark and even your uncle Ed—they all have depth. Whereas all I have to remember my mom is a one-dimensional picture. *She was a good mother who loved me very much, but who died too soon of a terrible disease.*

"There's got to be more, but no one will tell me. Did she have a rock'n'roll streak growing up? Or did she ever dream of running away to Hollywood to become an actress? Or even simple things, like how did she and my dad first meet? Did she know he was the one at first sight?

"I'm tired of hearing about the cookie-cutter saint that my mother was." Chelsea was winding down, her voice losing its sharp edge. "I want to know about her flaws, too. But I think my dad's afraid those stories would make me love her less."

Maddie let Chelsea's words simmer. Then, in a quiet voice, she told her best friend about her own mother.

"I don't remember a ton about my mom, either. But I do remember she worked a lot. She missed most of my cross-country meets. One time she completely forgot to pick me up from a friend's house, and my dad was out of town with Charlie that weekend, so I ended up staying the night, using my finger as a toothbrush and borrowing my friend's clothes to wear the next day. It didn't even bother me that much. I was used to it. But the pitiful look my friend's mom gave me—that's when I knew it wasn't normal. It was something for me to be ashamed of.

"But the thing is," Maddie's voice grew brighter as she remembered the over-the-top birthday parties her mom would throw her and the movie nights they'd have twice a month, just the two of them, boys quarantined upstairs. "She did try. Sure, she worked a lot. But she worked because she had to. She wanted to launch her business, to follow her dreams, to provide for me and my brother and my dad so that we could be comfortable and happy. And we were...until—"

A tear trickled down Maddie's cheek. She remembered how she'd broken down at her twelfth birthday party, the knife shaking from her hand and splatting into the cake. Even with flecks of frosting dotting her cheeks, she'd only been able to think of her mother. All the birthdays to come without her. Maddie had bolted out of their backyard, eyes streaming, and run wherever her feet would take her. It was only when Charlie had shown up in the park—climbing to the top of the playground fort—that she'd lifted her head and realized where she was. She'd looked at him, and he'd known exactly what to do. He'd taken a seat next to her, and they'd sat quietly together, only getting up to go home when the sun had set completely.

Maddie moved to wipe her tears away, but Chelsea beat her to it.

"My mom wasn't perfect," Maddie sniffed. "But she loved me in her own way. If you want to know everything about your mom, you've got to push your dad for more stories. Look through old photo albums. See if she kept a diary. There's got to be something.

"And never forget that our moms were more than just good. They were brave. And fearless. And full of love. They were badasses. Who else would we have inherited those traits from?"

A smile flitted back to Chelsea's lips.

"You always know just what to say." She pulled Maddie in for a hug and squeezed her tight. "Thank you."

They hugged for a good minute, letting their tears dry.

"God, I really picked a weird place for a heart-to-heart," Chelsea said as she released her best friend.

Maddie giggled. She couldn't help it.

"Yeah. It's a bit creepy." Then a wicked idea struck her. She didn't know where it even came from. "Want to make it even creepier?"

Chelsea's eyes narrowed, her black pupils reflecting the light from their flashlights.

"How?"

Maddie reached out and grabbed Chelsea's flashlight.

"You're not afraid of Bambi, are you?"

She switched the flashlight off and then turned off her own, plunging the girls into darkness. A surprised squeal erupted from Chelsea. Maddie clapped her hand over the girl's mouth and everything went quiet. They stood there together and let the night swallow them whole.

Around them the forest slept, breathing in and out smoothly, an altogether different rhythm from that afternoon. Gone were the chirping crickets and cawing birds, the skittish rabbits and scurrying squirrels. The wind even seemed to have tucked in for the night. Not a tree branch stirred above them. Maddie looked up, peeking through the canopy of dark leaves. She spotted a few stars twinkling through the branches, the full moon looking down at her with its bright, waxen face. She closed her eyes and breathed in the night, letting its stillness overwhelm her.

Then she heard a hoot. An owl on the prowl. Her ears perked up as she listened for more. She heard a rustle of leaves, far away, then the bone-snap of a twig, a firecracker in the quiet night. Her eyes flew open. Her heart beat faster in her chest. She strained to see through the forest, to peer around the solid tree trunks surrounding them.

Another crack shot through the woods, and Maddie jumped. All of a sudden she could feel the forest's nightmares moving around her, pressing in. A path of goose bumps scurried up her arms. She heard something else—a jingle?

It couldn't be. Her mind had to be playing tricks on her. She tried to calm down. She shook her shoulders out and closed her eyes, listening intently.

A few seconds passed and nothing. Another minute, and still nothing. She started to relax. Then she heard it again, the softest tinkle of metal. Her eyes sprang open and she flicked on her flashlight.

"Did you hear that?"

"Hear what?" Chelsea sounded just as creeped out as Maddie, but she didn't seem panicked.

"I think I'm losing it." Maddie swung her flashlight beam around. "I could have sworn I heard—"

A rustle of leaves caught their attention. Maddie spun around with her flashlight. There was another rustle and then a bush started moving. Maddie's arm wobbled with nerves, the flashlight beam trembling in response. A figure emerged from the trees. Chelsea screamed, and

Maddie drew back her arm, ready to chuck Chelsea's flashlight at their attacker.

"What the hell?" Abigail shouted. She squinted as Maddie's flashlight tried to blind her. "Can you get that thing out of my face?"

"Sorry," Maddie sputtered, embarrassed by how frightened she'd been only three seconds ago. She lowered her arm. It might have been the first time she'd ever been relieved to see Abigail. "You scared us."

"What, you think I was some kind of big bad bear out to eat you?" Abigail smirked. "You can't honestly think that story was true. What babies."

"No." Maddie bristled, but she didn't have any better comeback. "What are you doing out here on your own, anyways? Smoking again?"

"No." Abigail made a face. But it wasn't a bad guess. The girl's hair had fallen out of its ponytail and red circles splotched her sweaty face. Her lips were a bright cherry red and swollen. Even if she wasn't high, she definitely looked out of sorts.

"Well then, what were you doing out there?" Maddie pressed.

"I was peeing." Abigail seethed. "Happy? I can't just go anywhere when someone could be watching. We're not all savages like you."

Maddie didn't buy it, but she let it go. Maybe Abigail had had too many beers. That'd explain the pee, at least. And her complexion.

"Let's just get back to camp," Maddie said, uneasy, her earlier courage gone. "It's spooky out here."

Chelsea and Abigail agreed, and the three girls made their way back to camp together. Maddie still didn't feel right, though, and kept shooting glances over her shoulder as they went.

Finally they got back to camp. Chelsea and Abigail broke away and joined the others around the fire, but Maddie held back. Apparently Mark and Ed's argument had died down and the group was ready for another story.

"I'll tell the next one." Maddie heard her brother's voice carry from the campfire. "Sit down, sit down. I think you're all gonna like it."

She took one last look over her shoulder, but didn't see anything. She turned away from the forest and walked over to the campfire. She sat down next to Chelsea and waited for Charlie to begin.

"It was a dark and stormy night. . . ."

Everyone groaned, but Charlie quickly hushed them and restarted.

"It was a dark and stormy night at the old hospital. . . ."

RED RAVEN

Lightning flashed and rain lashed relentlessly against the windows, but Nicholas didn't bat an eye as he rolled a hospital bed down the hall. He stopped and pushed the button to call the elevator. He started to whistle, a cheery tune, the one he'd heard playing on the radio when he and the new nurse intern had taken the time to get to know each other in the backseat of his car.

His pitch went sharp as he remembered Sadie. Her keen hazel eyes. The deep purple of her lips. It'd looked so unnatural, that color, like she'd just drunk a whole bottle of red wine. But the color was real, inherited from her mother and her mother's mother, and made her all the more alluring. He could have sat there in the backseat of his car for hours sucking on those plum lips of hers, but then the first drops of rain had fallen, bombs loosed from the heavens, their fat bottoms exploding with dull *thunks*. Sadie had jumped away and stared at him as if waking from a dream. Then she'd bolted, scurrying up the drive and disappearing back into the hospital.

In the rain-washed week since, they hadn't met up again. They'd passed each other in the hallways numerous times, though, this secret smoldering between them. It all felt inevitable to Nicholas, so he waited patiently—and hoped—for a second chance.

The elevator chimed brightly, the only thing besides Nicholas that the dreary weather hadn't managed to depress. The doors slid open and Nicholas pushed the hospital bed in.

"What floor?" He recognized that voice.

"Fourth, please."

Sadie punched the button for the top floor and the doors closed.

In the cramped car, the subtlest hint of rose tickled Nicholas's upper lip. He took a deep breath and remembered that smell—Sadie's smell. Her shampoo, since the nurses weren't allowed to wear perfumes or lotions. He opened his mouth to say something, but the elevator chimed again, the doors opened, and Sadie slid out. Nicholas could only stare as she went, disappointment churning in his gut.

Then, a flip of her chin-length hair. A look back over one shoulder. A smile and a wink. Acknowledgment. Finally. Nicholas didn't even stop to wonder what had changed. The disappointment rushed out of his system with one flush. His toes wiggled forward. It was all he could do to keep from racing after her right that moment.

"That's a look if I've ever seen one."

Nicholas glanced down and saw that his patient had woken up and was staring down the hallway after Sadie with a wolfish glimmer in his eye.

"I see you're feeling better today, Mr. Sadusky," Nicholas said, patting the elderly man on the shoulder.

"I feel good every day."

Nicholas ignored the lie, knowing that Mr. Sadusky couldn't remember his bad days, those when he'd sit in bed, his face a crumpled-up sheet of blank paper, his mind a thousand miles away.

"Tell me, are you seeing that young lady?"

Mr. Sadusky twisted around in his hospital bed, uncomfortable and slow. He peered up at Nicholas, honking nose and elephant ears, his features grown too large for his face.

"I—" Nicholas paused, considering. "I'm not sure."

"Well, don't dawdle. A girl like that—she won't be around for long."

Nicholas nodded. "Trust me, I'm working on it."

The elevator shuddered to a halt and spit them out on the fourth floor. Nicholas wheeled the hospital bed down the hallway while Mr. Sadusky talked on. Nicholas ignored the old man—most of what he said made no sense, anyway—and watched the downpour outside.

It was nearly six o'clock, almost time for supper, though no one could tell by looking out at the gray haze. A bolt of lightning crackled and illuminated the maelstrom. Nicholas could just make out the valley's walls rising up on both sides of the hospital. The mountains sheltered them from the worst of the gale, but they also cut them off from the rest of the world. On a clear day, it was a good hour's drive to the nearest town, but with the past week's deluge, most of the mountain roads had washed away. And if it weren't for their generator, they'd have lost power days ago.

"We're here," Nicholas pushed the old man into his room and quickly locked the bed into place. "They'll be by with dinner soon." And with that, Nicholas made his hasty escape, blocking out the octogenarian's parting advice.

"Nicholas," a voice shot out at him from down the hall. He stopped on the spot and backtracked.

"Yes?" He poked his head into one of the open offices.

"Come in. I have a few things for you."

Nicholas nodded and walked inside, taking a seat across from a gentleman in his mid-forties. The nameplate on his desk read *Dr. Hagen—Director*. He looked like the kind of doctor Nicholas would see on some afternoon talk show. He had that telegenic appearance—bright blue eyes, large shining teeth, his head covered by a forest of lush salt-and-pepper hair. Nicholas often wondered what the doctor had done to deserve this backwoods exile.

"Want some?"

Dr. Hagen had just finished pouring a finger of scotch in a tumbler on his desk. Nicholas waved him off. He liked to drink, but only the cheap stuff, what went down easy. Dr.

Hagen shrugged and took down the scotch in one gulp before pouring himself another.

"This damn rain," he lamented as he took a sip. "It's going to be the death of us all. We've got flooding in the staff halls. And now it looks like we'll need a new roof for this whole place."

The doctor sighed, already well on his way to drunk. Nicholas didn't know what to say.

"At least we got most everyone out this morning."

"Hmm?" Dr. Hagen hadn't been paying attention. "Oh—right, right."

The morning had been a nightmare of work, Nicholas moving patients up and down, loading them into vans and ambulances to be ferried down the mountain. His lower back still smarted. And they had two more patients to move the next morning, with just a skeleton crew.

"Sir, was there something you needed from me?"

"Sorry, I almost forgot." Dr. Hagen set his glass down. "I need you to check on the generator. Make sure we've got enough gas."

"That it?"

The doctor nodded to himself, his mouth back in his scotch. Nicholas turned to leave, but Dr. Hagen called him back.

"Oh, and can you check on Rick?" Rick was the other patient they still had to move in the morning. His room was just at the other end of the hallway. "Make sure he's ready for tomorrow. And that he's taken his meds."

"Will do."

Nicholas pulled the door shut behind him as the doctor finished his scotch and started to pour himself another. Better to let him pickle in private.

Boasting the longest stay at the hospital—patient or staff—Rick Ransom had been at the facility for nearly two decades. According to Rick's charts, he suffered from delusional episodes, though in Nicholas's six months as an orderly, he'd never witnessed one. Rick had to be the most mild-mannered patient they had, reserved and void of any emotion. Most days he spent alone in his room, quietly working on his paintings. Harmless. Rumor around the nurses' station had it that Rick's father was some mining tycoon who funded the entire hospital, all so that they'd keep his eldest son tucked away, unable to embarrass the family name.

Nicholas arrived at Rick's door and knocked softly. A few moments later, Rick's quiet voice invited him in.

"Everything okay?" Nicholas pushed the door open slowly. His eyes swept around the room. Even though it was the largest in the facility, it didn't look it, the way Rick had stacked and laid canvases against every wall and on every flat surface. He had to have fifty of them spread throughout the room.

"Looks like you're hard at work." Nicholas had spotted Rick's latest canvas, propped up on an easel in the middle of the room. The man turned, his round face expressionless and pale, his paintbrush aloft in one hand. He was a big man, with hulking shoulders.

"Just finished," he said, even quieter than before. "What do you think?"

"It's one of your best," Nicholas replied. How many times had Rick asked him this same question? And how many times had he responded with the same lie?

It wasn't that his paintings were bad. They were actually quite good. But Rick only ever painted the one thing, over and over and over again.

Nicholas's eyes moved away from the canvas and fell on Rick's side table. He spotted the man's medication.

"Did you forget to take your pills today?"

Rick squirmed atop his painter's stool. His eyes popped. Then they turned back to study his latest canvas, the firm lines and bold colors, a pictograph of a raven mid-flight.

Nicholas crossed the room and picked up the small plastic cup. He counted the pills and then shook them. They rattled around, like an owner calling a dog to dinner. Reluctantly, Rick pulled his eyes from his painting. He offered the orderly his open palm and Nicholas spilled the medication into it. Rick threw them back and swallowed down a nearby glass of water.

"All good." Nicholas brushed his hands together and threw the empty cup away. "We're moving you and Mr. Sadusky in the morning, so make sure you're packed."

Rick didn't reply, and Nicholas felt uncomfortable in the silence. His eyes moved away from the man's blank face and fell on a stack of canvases instead. His fingers hovered over the corner of a downturned one. Rick looked at him hesitantly.

Then there was another knock at the door. It opened and Nurse Ryann appeared, matronly in her too-big nurse's uniform and white orthopedic tennis shoes. She had a tray of food in her arms.

"Have a good night, Rick," Nicholas said, pulling his hand back as he breezed out of the room. "And don't forget about tomorrow morning."

The lobby was empty when he passed through it, the front desk unattended. He pulled a rain slicker from the coat rack and slid its cold, rubbery flesh over his shoulders. He peered through the front doors. Lightning flashed, and he could see just how quickly the rain fell, pelting the earth. He saw the barn about two hundred yards away. He hung his head and pushed out into the storm.

Water pelted him from all sides, even, as impossible as it seemed, from below. It only took a millisecond for him to get soaked through. His feet slid underneath him, his rain boots filling with water. The mud threatened to suck him under in patches, like quicksand, unrelenting once it got a hold. He battled through the soupiness, though, and managed to make it across the yard.

They'd modernized the barn in recent years, converting the horse stalls to storage and maintenance lockers, insulating and weatherproofing the whole thing. Nicholas could hear the generator back in one of the closets, droning a dull, steady chug as it pumped power out to the entire facility. Their main power lines had gone down three days ago, and the generator had been working around the clock ever since. Nicholas shuffled through his keys and unlocked the closet. A cloud of gasoline fumes greeted him as he pulled open the doors. He waved it away and knelt to inspect the generator. It needed a little more gas, but otherwise everything looked fine.

Suddenly, something pricked at the back of Nicholas's neck. The hairs on his arm rose to attention, sent a chill shivering through his body. Was he about to get struck by lightning?

He flipped around, and there, standing just inside the doorway was a phantom, black hood pulled up to hide its face like the grim reaper. Water ran off the figure. Two pale hands slid out of their sleeves, pushed the hood back. Nicholas's breath caught in his throat.

"What are you doing out here?"

"I was lonely," Sadie said, a sly smile playing across her lips. Her dark hair was raven black with wet, plastered to her forehead and cheeks like streaks of ink on paper. "Everyone else is gone, so I thought I'd say hi."

"*Only* hi?" Nicholas rose and walked slowly toward the girl.

"It's a good place to start, no?"

"I think we're already past that."

Nicholas stopped in front of Sadie, a head taller than her. He put his hand underneath her chin and tilted her face up to meet his gaze. He leaned in and kissed her.

This time, lightning did strike. His vision went white. He pulled her in closer and kissed her more deeply.

After a minute they parted. Sadie shivered.

"You all right?"

"Just a bit chilly." Sadie burrowed into Nicholas's arms.

"Well, come a little closer then." Nicholas pulled her in tighter and Sadie pushed him back away from the door. She looked up at him, that glint in her eye again. Mischief. Nicholas smiled back and pulled her into one of the storage stalls.

Sadie kissed him, and Nicholas kissed her back. They made out like that for a few minutes. Then an explosion crashed somewhere nearby, jolting the couple apart.

"What was that?" Sadie's voice came out as a raspy whisper.

"I don't know," Nicholas replied. "Maybe a bolt of lightning hit a tree."

Nicholas pulled out his phone and used it to find the light switch in the storage closet. He flipped it, but nothing happened. He tried it again.

"Shit," Nicholas cursed under his breath. "I think I know what just exploded."

Nicholas opened the closet door and immediately smelled a chemical stench curling through the air, tart with gasoline. The generator had ceased its chainsaw purr. He crept closer and shined his light on the dead thing, watching smoke waft off it.

"It must have blown," he called back to Sadie.

"Can you fix it?" She appeared behind Nicholas, nervously twirling a strand of her hair.

He shook his head.

"We'll have to wait until morning."

"I think that means we can go to bed," Sadie purred slyly. "To *my* bed, that is."

But a glimmer out the front windows had caught Nicholas's eye. A light in the fourth floor of the main building. It winked out just as quickly as it had come alive.

"We should probably go check on everyone." It took every ounce of responsibility in Nicholas not to jump at Sadie's offer. "Make sure they're okay."

Sadie frowned.

"Then we can go back to your bed." Nicholas smiled. "It shouldn't take long."

They made their way across the lawn to the main building. The door clanged shut behind them as they entered. Nicholas took off his rain slicker and shook it. It snapped and echoed down the dark, empty hallway. He hung it on the coat rack and helped Sadie with hers.

"It's creepy in here," Sadie whispered, shivering.

"That's just because it's dark." Nicholas flicked on his flashlight, and the beam shot down the hallway, burrowing a tunnel through the night. "Here, we'll have to take the stairs."

Sadie let Nicholas lead. When they made it to the top, they walked down the fourth floor hall and checked Dr. Hagen's office.

"I think the light was coming from his window," Nicholas whispered as he tried Dr. Hagen's door. The knob turned easily and Nicholas pushed it open. He swept his flashlight across the desk, but Dr. Hagen wasn't there.

"Hmm...he must have turned in for the night." Nicholas pulled the door closed again and took Sadie's hand. "Let's check on Rick and Mr. Sadusky."

They decided to check on Rick first. Their footsteps echoed down the hallway as they went. Nicholas could feel Sadie's hand shaking in his.

"There's nothing to worry about," he assured her as he squeezed her fingers.

Sadie returned the pressure and smiled to herself.

"That's odd," Nicholas said, staring at Rick's wide-open door. He dropped Sadie's hand and moved closer to investigate.

"Rick?" he called softly into the dark room. "Mr. Ransom? Are you in there?"

No one answered.

"You can stay out here if you want," Nicholas said.

"Don't even think about leaving me behind."

Sadie clung even closer to Nicholas. He could feel the goose bumps erupting up her arm. Nicholas edged into the room, eyes peeled for Rick. But he didn't see anyone. The patient wasn't in his bed or at his easel.

"Where is he?" Sadie's voice quivered.

"Probably in the bathroom. Or getting a glass of water." Nicholas rattled off a few excuses. "Or maybe he couldn't sleep and went for a walk. We should wait for him to get back, though."

Sadie didn't like the suggestion, but she didn't argue. Nicholas turned around and started to shuffle aimlessly through the rows of stacked paintings. Then his flashlight beam danced across the room and fell on Rick's easel. He'd started on a new canvas.

"That's different," Nicholas said, as he realized.

Sadie turned and Nicholas came over to get a closer look. He drew his fingers over the two swoops of paint—like a V, but with ends that mellowed out into elegant curves. A wing-span. A bird mid-flight. Rick's usual subject, but rendered in a new style. Nicholas's flashlight beam winked back at them, the canvas still slick, the paint a bold red. The way it was smeared across the canvas, energetic and primal, it looked like Rick had thrown his brushes out completely and used his fingers instead.

Nicholas inched closer to get a better look, and his toe knocked into something. He looked down and saw a plastic bag. He picked it up and weighed it in his hand. It looked like someone had been hoarding their medication. His brain didn't connect the dots, though. Instead, his eyes fell on a spot on the floor just out of reach.

"He must have spilled," Nicholas said, showing Sadie the edge of the pool of red paint. Nicholas walked toward it. "That's probably where he wen—"

The last word died on his lips. He lurched back and banged into the easel. The painting tipped and clattered to the floor.

"We—we have to get out of here."

Sadie's flashlight dipped to the floor, to the pool of red paint, and a scream clambered its way up her throat. Nicholas leaped up and clapped his hand over her mouth, forcing her to swallow the scream back down. He looked at her hard and willed her to understand.

If she screamed, Rick would find them. And if he found them, they'd end up just like Nurse Ryann—face-up in a pool of her own blood, a second mouth curled into a ghastly smile where Rick had slit her throat from ear to ear.

"We have to be quiet," Nicholas whispered with all the intensity of a shout. "And fast. Do you understand?"

Sadie's eyes squeezed shut. Nicholas could see tears dotting her eyelashes, could see her shutting down.

"We're going to make it through this."

He held her face in his hands and kissed her on the forehead. Her eyes winked open and she looked up at him for a good ten seconds before nodding. He took her hand and raced back into the hallway, his flashlight turned off, thankful for the storm and its lightning flashes to navigate by.

Nicholas didn't bother knocking when he got to Mr. Sadusky's room. He twisted the doorknob and rushed inside. But they were too late.

Nicholas couldn't stop Sadie's yelp this time as she saw Mr. Sadusky's lifeless body, his sheets covered in blood, his throat painted with the same second smile as Nurse Ryann. On the wall behind him, a fresh set of wings unfurled their grim feathers. Nicholas pulled Sadie back out into the hallway and started for the stairs. But before they'd taken even three steps, a noise clattered somewhere ahead of them. Nicholas spun around and pulled Sadie into Dr. Hagen's office, locking the door behind them.

"Get down," Nicholas ordered. "And don't say a word."

Sadie crouched and hid behind Dr. Hagen's desk as Nicholas frantically searched the room for something heavy, something he could wield in case Rick found them. His eyes fell on an umbrella and he grabbed it. He held it above his head with both hands like some kind of sword and waited right beside the door.

He could hear footsteps stumbling down the hallway. Nicholas closed his eyes and prayed they'd pass.

But they didn't.

They stopped right in front of Dr. Hagen's door.

The knob turned and then caught on the lock. Nicholas heard an exasperated curse under someone's breath, and then a ring of keys jangled. One ground into the lock. Nicholas re-gripped the umbrella. His heart pounded in his ears. The doorknob turned and someone burst into the room.

Nicholas only had a second to react. He recognized Dr. Hagen's shock of gray hair just in time. The umbrella came down but thwacked against the nearby bookcase instead of Dr. Hagen's head.

"My God!" Dr. Hagen nearly jumped out of his skin. He looked right through Nicholas, red streaks of blood running up his temples and into the edges of his gray hair. Nicholas quickly pulled him inside and pushed the door closed, locking it again. The doctor staggered to his desk, hands shaking. He sloshed some scotch into his glass and threw it back. He went to pour himself a second but accidentally knocked the bottle over, spilling it across his desk.

"Damnit," he shouted and threw his glass at the wall, where it shattered into a hundred little pieces.

"Dr. Hagen, calm down—"

But the doctor went on right over Nicholas, babbling to himself.

"Damnit! I was going places. I could have been the next Dr. Oz, for Christ's sake! What'd I do to deserve this? Wasn't coming to this backwoods hellhole penance enough? That kid overdosed on his own. I only wrote the prescription. I didn't force the pills down his throat."

"Dr. Hagen." Nicholas grabbed him by the shoulders and shook him. The doctor's eyes snapped around and he saw Nicholas for the first time. "What are you talking about?"

"Didn't you see?" Dr. Hagen spoke more calmly, though there was still a wild look in his eye. "He's snapped. Gone completely mad. He's going to kill us all."

Not the most official of diagnoses.

"But what happened? What changed?"

"He must have gone off his meds," Dr. Hagen sighed. He plopped down in one of his office chairs. "Red Raven is taking over."

"Red who?" Sadie piped up from behind the desk.

"It's from when he was a boy. He fell through an abandoned mineshaft and got lost. He wandered underground for two days all by himself. They'd given up hope, but then, miraculously, he found his own way out. But he wouldn't stop babbling on and on about someone named Red Raven.

"He was delusional. Dehydrated and starving. Traumatized. He swore he'd unearthed some spirit down there. And that it had led him out. But he had to repay it. Red Raven wouldn't rest until it got blood."

The storm howled outside and Nicholas jumped.

"He cut himself before they got him on the right drugs," Dr. Hagen explained. "But I guess now...now Rick's blood isn't enough. He needs ours to appease his inner demons."

"But that's crazy," Nicholas exclaimed.

"Not to Rick," Dr. Hagen replied. "To him, Red Raven is very real. We can't reason with him. And he won't stop until—"

"Until we're all dead," Nicholas finished for the doctor.

"Well, how are we going to get out of here?" Sadie asked.

"We'll have to run for it," Nicholas said. He looked longingly at his phone, knowing full well it was no help. But even if it could pick up a signal, no police car could get through this weather in time to save them.

"We can take my truck. It's parked just out front."

"Are you sure that's the best plan?" Dr. Hagen asked, nervously running his hand through his hair. "Rick's still out there. He'll be looking for us."

"It's the only chance we've got. We get out now while it's still dark, or we're dead."

The other two nodded in uneasy agreement, and Nicholas took the lead. He peeked his head out the door, straining to see both ends of the hallway. There'd be no flashlights on the way down. Absolutely nothing that could give them away.

Everything clear, Nicholas motioned for Sadie and Dr. Hagen to follow him as he slipped out of the office. They crept down the hallway, holding their breath every time their wet boots squeaked. They shot glances back and to the sides, expecting the possessed killer to jump out of every doorway they passed. They made it to the stairway, though, and started down.

In the tight stairwell they could do nothing to mask their steps. Each footfall rang out a hollow, metallic bong, like a clock tower tolling noon. Nicholas picked up his pace and hoped the storm would drown out the noise.

They made it to the third floor. Then the second. So close to freedom.

But as they rounded the second-floor landing, a clap of thunder shuddered through the building and the stairwell door flew open. A flash of lightning illuminated Rick's face, a bloody kitchen knife, at least eight inches long, gleaming in his hand.

Where had he gotten that?

Nicholas froze, fear rooting him to the spot. He'd never seen any emotion on Rick's face, but now the man looked down at him with the red eyes of a demon, his lips cracked wide in a mad smile. Rick's free hand reached out and he grabbed for Sadie.

Her scream jolted Nicholas into action. He kicked out, connecting with Rick's elbow and knocking Sadie free. He pulled her up and they started down the stairs, running now. But as Nicholas shot a glance back, he saw that Rick had managed to grab hold of Dr. Hagen.

The man struggled with his patient, but then Rick's hand darted forward, found purchase in the doctor's belly. The knife came out easily, dripping with fresh blood. Dr. Hagen looked down at his slick hands. Then he keeled over. Rick knelt quickly and pulled the doctor's head up, tugging at his thick mane of hair. His knife swooshed and a long slit opened up in Dr. Hagen's throat.

"Hurry," Nicholas shouted. It'd only taken seconds for Rick to dispose of Dr. Hagen, and now he was after them. Nicholas and Sadie rushed down the last flight of stairs and burst into the lobby. Sadie headed toward the front door, but Nicholas paused. He flung his back against the stairwell door just as Rick ran into it from the other side. The door banged, opened a crack, but then Nicholas managed to push it shut.

"What are you doing?" Sadie had stopped. "We've got to go. Come on."

Nicholas looked at her with a sad smile on his face.

"Here," he said. "Take my keys."

He tossed them to her as the door shuddered again. Nicholas's boots slid on the wet floor. He almost lost his balance, but he managed to stay upright and push the door closed.

"I'm not leaving you behind."

"Go. It's the only way. I'll hold him off."

The strain was evident in Nicholas's voice. His face squeezed in on itself as he combatted another assault from the other side of the stairwell door.

"Go! Goddamnit. I can't keep him back much longer."

Sadie didn't argue this time, but scurried up to Nicholas. She leaned in and kissed him on the lips.

"Thank you," she whispered. Then she was gone.

The stairwell door banged against Nicholas's back. It felt like Rick had a battering ram. Nicholas's feet slipped. He couldn't get any kind of leverage on the slick floor. Rick rammed into the door again and Nicholas felt his boots slide right out from under him. He toppled to the floor and Rick pushed into the hallway.

At first, the madman didn't see Nicholas. But he did see Sadie and started after her.

"No!" Nicholas roared as he leaped up from the floor and tackled the man. He had to save Sadie. He had to buy her whatever time he could.

Rick slammed into the wall, but managed to stay on his feet. He turned and leered at Nicholas. He brandished his bloody blade and sprang forward. Nicholas spun out of the way, but Rick grabbed his arm with his other hand and pulled him in close.

The hospital walls spun around them as they grappled. Nicholas clawed at Rick's wrist and tried to beat the blade out of his hand. He kicked blindly at the man's legs, knowing that he couldn't lose sight of the knife. He heard the front door bang open and sneaked a glance over Rick's shoulder. Sadie met his gaze for a second, tears running down her cheeks. Then she blew him a kiss and disappeared into the night. That's when Nicholas felt the sharp pain in his side.

He coughed, choking on the pain. He hadn't expected it to hurt so much. His hands flew to his side and he felt the blood, warm and wet. He stared down at his stained hands and then back up at Rick. The man's maniacal grin filled his vision. He watched as Rick stabbed him in the stomach twice more.

Oddly, it didn't hurt as much the second and third times. It almost felt good. Like a release. Nicholas's head grew light and he could feel his mind starting to detach from his body. He wanted to let go and float up and away.

But he couldn't. Not yet. He had to make sure Sadie got out. He shuffled forward and wrapped his arms around Rick's leg.

Rick peeled him off easily, though, and threw him back to the ground. Nicholas managed to crawl forward, using his last strength to block Rick's path, but Rick reached down and yanked his head back. His knife hovered for a moment and then sliced across Nicholas's throat.

As blood poured into Nicholas's mouth, he strained to see past the hospital doors, to hear the sound of a truck engine revving.

Nicholas's eyes blinked. He tried to fight the drowsiness, but he could only hold on for so long. As the world went black around him, he thought about Sadie. He prayed she'd gotten away as he watched Rick racing forward, pulling open the front doors and sprinting headlong into the rain.

EIGHT

PAIN STABBED INTO MADDIE'S SIDE, BRIGHT and sharp. She kneaded her hand against it and kept going. She breathed in and out, focusing on the rhythm, gritting her teeth at the same time.

Her lungs seared in her chest, the high altitude air so thin she couldn't get enough oxygen. Maddie's body begged her to stop, but she pushed herself forward, her feet flying underneath her, the forest a green blur around her as she raced through the trees.

She peeked over her shoulder and her heart jolted into her throat. It was still there, just a few strides behind her—the bear, tattered tutu flapping, bells jingling, teeth bared and dripping blood. She turned back around and sped up. She veered to the right and Bambi's claws left slashes in a tree instead of her back.

That had been close. But she couldn't let up now. She couldn't let it catch her. She had to get away. She had to run for her life.

Another minute passed and Maddie glanced back over her

shoulder. She blinked and the bear was gone. But now a man ran after her. He had a mad gleam in his eyes and a long, sinister knife in one hand. Blood covered his pale face and shirtfront, stained his fingers. He moved quickly for such a large man, almost as if he had wings, skimming across the forest floor. Maddie squinted and could see them now, sprouting from his back, slick and red, spun from the blood of his victims.

She broke into a flat-out sprint, leaping out of his reach at the last second. His knife cut through the air right as her wristwatch started beeping.

She glanced at the time and started to slow down. Her sprint became a trot and then a jog. Then she was walking, feeling the ache in her lungs, the side-stitch needling into her stomach. She took deep breaths and paced in a small circle, letting her body cool down, letting it start its recovery. She bent over and stretched her calves and quads. She looked at her time again. Not too bad. Especially given the altitude.

Looking back the way she'd come, she saw the phantoms of Bambi and Red Raven glaring at her. It was a game she liked to play with herself during her training runs. She'd imagine some monster chasing her, and it'd trick her brain into giving her an adrenaline boost.

Fight or flight. But in her case, flight always won. No one could catch her.

Usually she imagined herself running from zombies or something she'd seen in a scary movie—like Freddy Krueger or Ghostface—but this morning she'd had even better material.

She stuck out her tongue at Bambi and Red Raven. Better luck next time. They snarled and then evaporated. Maddie laughed to herself—they'd make good additions to her monster gallery—and then continued on her way.

As Maddie walked back toward camp, the sun streamed through the trees beautifully, lighting everything in a warm and wonderful glow. So different from the night before, when Abigail had nearly scared the piss out of her and Chelsea. But Maddie wasn't too mad about that now. She liked that feeling—at least she did when she knew her life wasn't actually in danger. She enjoyed the way fear crept up her spine and blew its icy breath against the nape of her neck, the chills that shivered through her whole body as her heart beat faster, as her pupils opened wider. It was kind of like runner's high, adrenaline flushing her system, intensifying all her senses.

There was nothing like a good scare, and her aunt and Charlie had certainly delivered with their stories last night. The real question was, would anyone be able to top them tonight?

The trees started to thin out, and Maddie could just see the sun's shimmer off the valley lake. She'd almost made it back to camp. Her stomach grumbled, and she wondered what they'd fix for lunch. She couldn't wait to pig out. That's when she heard voices, hushed and urgent, coming her way. She slid behind a particularly fat tree just as Charlie and Dylan broke through the tree line.

"I don't know why you're making such a big deal about this." Dylan's words trailed after Charlie as he stomped through the underbrush. Even anger couldn't dampen the girl's natural prettiness, her effortless beauty. She looked nothing like her devil of a younger sister, Abigail. But that might have been Maddie's own bias coming through.

"Can you stop and look at me? Please?" Dylan grabbed for Charlie's hand but missed.

"You don't know why?" Charlie spun on his heel and faced his girlfriend head-on. He spoke loudly now, abandoning whatever need for caution they'd had before. Maddie peeked out from behind the tree and watched them, knowing better than to interrupt. Her brother looked pissed, his face as red as a stop sign under his Giants cap. "You just told me you want to break up . . . how did you think I'd take it?"

"That's not what I said," Dylan tried to clarify, but Charlie talked over her.

"That's exactly what you said."

"No!" Dylan shouted back, stunning Charlie into silence. His mouth hung open, but he didn't argue.

"You never listen," Dylan went on. "I said that we should *think* about what's going to happen in the fall—you know, when we go away to different schools."

She sighed and crossed her arms. Then, seeing the sad look on her boyfriend's face, uncrossed them. She reached out and put her hand against his chest.

"I'm not saying that we should break up—just that we should think about where this is going."

"You and your thinking," Charlie said miserably. "You're always worrying. College is months away. We still have the whole summer together. Can't we worry about the future later? Can't we just enjoy today and tomorrow and next week? Together?"

"Oh, Charlie. I wish things were that easy."

"Why can't they be?"

Dylan closed her eyes and leaned into his body, resting her forehead against his shoulder.

"Because the future is coming whether you like it or not," she whispered.

"But that doesn't mean we have to worry about it."

"No. But we should prepare for it. Or at least talk about it." Dylan pulled away from Charlie and crossed her arms again. She sank into her shell as she continued talking. "You know I have a thousand things on my mind. My mom's been riding me for weeks now. I thought getting into her alma mater would get her off my back, but now she's telling me which classes to take and where I should live. She keeps trying to get me to meet up with her old sorority sisters. She wants me to be like a mini-Kris—majoring in business, coming to work with her at the real-estate firm when I graduate. She's already assuming that I'm going to intern with her this summer.

"I can't stand it. It's not me at all. I'm not her. And I don't want to be. But you know how she is . . . never lets anyone get a word in.

"And then there's you," Dylan rushed on before Charlie could get a word out. "You know, you've always been so good at living in the moment. Even when we were kids. That's something I've always loved about you. You make every minute worthwhile."

"You can't waste a single second," Charlie leaped in. "If there's one thing I've learned in the last eighteen years, it's that the future is unpredictable and will mess you up the first chance it gets."

There was a bitterness to Charlie's voice now, and Maddie knew he was remembering their mother. The fire. All the time he hadn't spent with her while she was alive.

"But *I* need to start thinking about the future," Dylan said. "About where I'm going. Where you're going. Where that leaves for us to go... I can't live in the moment forever."

"But Dylan," Charlie fished for the right words and came up empty.

"I'm not saying that we should break up," Dylan said. "I just want you to think about the future. To think about what you want. Whether we can make this work long distance."

"I want you," Charlie spoke quietly. He pulled Dylan in close and hugged her tight. "Nothing else matters, as long as I have you."

"Oh, Charlie." Dylan pulled away again and looked him in the eyes. "Can't you see that that's the problem? Don't you want something more?"

"I do."

"What?" Dylan challenged. "Baseball? Do you really think you can go pro? What's your backup plan?"

"I—I—"

Dylan leaned in and kissed Charlie on the cheek, saving him from his sputtering.

"That's what I want you to figure out," Dylan said kindly, lovingly. "And then we can see what makes sense for us."

Charlie stared stonily into the distance, not saying a word.

"I'm going to head back." Dylan broke the uncomfortable silence. "But think about what I said. Think about what you want."

She stood up on her tiptoes and kissed Charlie on the lips. "You know that I love you."

Then Dylan turned and disappeared back through the tree line.

Behind her trunk, Maddie squirmed. She hated seeing her brother so down, but Chelsea would certainly be happy to hear about it. Maybe her best friend would get her chance with Charlie. Finally.

Maddie held her breath and willed her brother to head off. But he stood there, staring off into the distance. Maddie looked at her watch, counting the seconds. When a couple of minutes had passed, she knew she couldn't hide out any longer. She tried to move quietly, but then a twig snapped under her foot and Charlie turned.

"Who's there?" Charlie called, spotting Maddie's back.

She froze. Caught. Her mind raced and finally landed on a plan. Though it only had like a ten percent chance of working. She turned around slowly and started shaking out her arms and legs. Panting.

"Oh, hey." Maddie acted surprised to see him. She pulled her earbuds out and put on her best tired smile. "Sorry, just finishing up my run. I didn't even see you there. Hope I didn't scare you."

"Nah." Charlie suddenly looked like himself again. "I was just out here thinking."

"Heading back?" Maddie asked, tilting her head in the direction of camp.

"Yeah. It should be about time for lunch."

Maddie nodded and followed Charlie. Neither spoke, though. Maddie could see her brother thinking hard. He didn't look happy.

"So." Maddie broke the silence. She had to cheer him up. Get his mind off his fight with Dylan. "You have to tell me…did Sadie make it down the mountain?"

"What?" Charlie blinked.

"From your story last night?" Maddie explained. "Did Sadie get away? Or did Red Raven catch her?"

"Oh, right." It took him a moment to remember. "Well, what do you think?"

Maddie thought about it. If it'd been her, she would have gotten away. She would have done whatever it took to make sure Nicholas's sacrifice hadn't been for nothing.

"I think she got away," Maddie decided.

"Maybe." Charlie grinned wickedly. "Maybe not."

"Not fair," Maddie punched him in the shoulder, relieved to see the spark back in her brother's eyes. He pushed her back lightly and they both laughed.

"Hey, what's happening over there?" Maddie asked as they got closer to camp. She pointed at the cluster of people just ahead. She could make out the back of Chelsea's head among them.

"Let's find out," Charlie said.

They headed toward their fellow campers, who were standing around a particularly big tree in the clearing. Maddie got there first and pushed through to see what everyone was staring at.

"What are you all—"

The rest of the sentence stuck in her mouth as she spotted Abigail up front, pointing frantically at the bark of the tree. Behind her, her father, Mark, paced back and forth, his eyes bulging, his hands pulling at his hair. He muttered nonstop to himself. He looked like he might lose his mind.

And for once, Maddie didn't blame him. She stepped forward, transfixed, and held her hand up to the tree trunk. She let her fingers brush against the wood, let them run along the grooves left there by three long slashes.

Claw marks.

"I found them this morning," Abigail said anxiously.

"I'm sure it's nothing," Ed said from the back of the group. Maddie hoped her uncle was right.

"I don't know," Maddie's dad replied, leaning in to get a better vantage point. "They look pretty fresh to me. And they're pretty big. Maybe a bear's."

Bambi.

Maddie couldn't keep the thought from popping into her head. But that was just a silly story her aunt had made up. Right?

Right. Maddie couldn't let it get to her. Mark was already hysterical enough for them all.

"What do you know about claw marks?" Ed pushed back.

"Well," Maddie's dad began to defend himself, but Caleb walked up just then.

"What are you all doing over here?" the guide asked.

Everyone got quiet, as if they were teens whose parents had just walked in and caught them raiding the liquor cabinet.

"BEAR!" Mark shouted when no one else answered. Caleb looked at him skeptically. "Bear! Bear! Bear!"

This was apparently the only word that Mark could say at the moment. But he said it with intensity as he gestured wildly at the tree. Finally, Caleb looked and saw what he meant. He moved in close and examined the marks. He pulled back after a minute.

"This could be anything," Caleb said decisively.

"But—but," Mark said as he craned his neck in, "look at those marks . . . it's clear as day . . . we're not safe!"

Caleb made a show of examining the marks one last time.

"It's really not a bear," the guide tried to reassure Mark, but the man whimpered still.

"Look," Caleb said flatly, perhaps ruder than he should have. He was tired of Mark's paranoia. "I've been taking people through these mountains for two years and never once come across a bear or mountain lion or whatever else you could possibly be afraid of. Trust me. Nothing's waiting to get you. We're safe."

Mark looked at the guide in disbelief, then back at the marks on the tree. He yelped and hurried back toward camp.

"What a pansy," Ed muttered under his breath with a chuckle.

"I hope you guys aren't worked up over this." Caleb turned to everyone else. "It really is nothing. And even if there was a bear nearby, it'd be more afraid of you than you are of it. It's not going to come poking its nose around our camp. Trust me."

Everyone nodded, wanting to believe their guide. He did have the most experience.

"So what's next on the agenda?" Maddie's dad asked, trying to change the subject.

"Well, I thought we'd have lunch and then I'd take you all on a hike," Caleb replied, ushering everyone away from the tree and back toward the center of camp, where sandwiches and chips waited for them. "I know this spot that has the best view of the valley."

"That sounds like fun," Kris said. "Maybe I can even convince my husband to come out of hiding."

She motioned at her tent, where Mark had disappeared in his fright.

"Mark, honey," Kris called. "Come out here. We're going to eat and then go on a hike."

There was a commotion in the tent, and then Mark poked his head out.

"A hike? In the woods?"

"Oh, come on, Mark," Ed teased. "Don't be such a wimp."

Mark blanched but stood his ground.

"I don't know..." He hesitated. "I might just hang back here."

"It'll be fun, Mark," Maddie's aunt Julie piped up, much kinder than her husband.

Mark still looked unsure, but Kris cut him off before he could protest anymore.

"You're coming on this hike. Get your pack ready and let's go."

Mark hovered indecisively for a moment and then disappeared into his tent.

"You've just got to be firm with him sometimes." Kris rolled her eyes and then smiled.

A moment later, Mark's tent flap rustled and he came out holding the long brown paper package Maddie had spotted him with the day before. She hadn't been sure what it was then, but now, by the way he carried it, she had no doubt. It wasn't a baseball bat at all.

Maddie's breath caught in her chest as Mark unwrapped the paper to reveal a gleaming rifle.

"Why the hell do you have that?"

Kris's voice turned shrill as it lost its earlier authority.

"It's for protection."

"Protection?"

"From bears! Wolves! Mountain lions!" Mark was adamant. His eyes looked a bit crazed. "You saw the claw marks. I don't care if *he* says it wasn't a bear, I know what my two eyes saw. There are dangerous animals out there. We're not safe."

"This can't be legal." Ed seemed more amused than worried. "Do you even know how to shoot that thing?"

"I took lessons. I have my permits." Mark pushed his shoulders back and tried to stand up taller. He swung the gun around to his other hand. Maddie flinched as the barrel's line of sight moved across her.

"Hey! Watch where you point that thing." Her dad looked pissed as he leaped in front of Maddie.

"The safety's on." Mark flashed the gun's trigger to prove it. "There's nothing to worry about. I told you, I know what I'm doing."

"Well, excuse me if we don't all believe you, Dad," Abigail snapped in her snottiest voice.

"Hey. What's all the commotion about?" Caleb turned back around. He'd been grabbing a sandwich and some chips. His gaze fell on the rifle, and his eyes flashed dangerously.

"What do you have there, Mark?" Caleb kept his tone even. "You know it's not hunting season, right?"

"I know," Mark spluttered. "It's so *we* won't be hunted."

"I thought we already went over this." Caleb sounded like a very patient preschool teacher down to his last straw. "There's nothing out there that's gonna hurt you."

"I saw the claw marks! We all did. You all heard that roar yesterday in the woods. So don't you tell me there's nothing dangerous out there."

"Nothing more dangerous than a lunatic with a loaded rifle and a hair-trigger finger," Ed quipped under his breath.

A nervous laugh threaded through the group. Maddie didn't find it so funny, though. Generally speaking, it wasn't the best idea to tease a man holding a gun.

"I'm not about to end up some mountain lion's lunch. And neither are my girls." Mark eyed Dylan and Abigail. He wasn't going to let anyone talk him out of this. "I've taken lessons. I have a license. I know what I'm doing."

"Come on, Mark," Caleb tried one last time. "You don't really need that."

"I'm not going without it." Mark stood his ground, and no one stepped up to argue with him.

"Fine." Caleb relented. "Just make sure you're careful where you point that thing. We don't want anyone's arm getting blown off.

"Everyone else, grab some food and we'll head out in twenty."

NINE

NO ONE SAID MUCH AS THEY walked through the woods, heading uphill. Caleb had tried his best tour-guide spiel, pointing out different trees and flowers and animal tracks, telling stories from the history of these particular Colorado mountains. But when no one seemed the least bit interested, he'd shut up and focused on the trail instead.

Near the back of the pack, Maddie and Chelsea walked together, a rare quiet moment passing between them. Maddie didn't feel much like talking. She knew everyone else was probably still thinking about those slashes on that tree. The alleged claw marks. Or maybe about Mark's rifle. But Maddie didn't have either on her mind. Instead, she couldn't stop thinking about her brother.

She shot a look forward and saw him walking with Dylan. She could tell things were still off. They weren't holding hands or touching at all. But they didn't look totally uncomfortable with each other.

A part of her wished she could eavesdrop on them again, but another part knew she'd already overheard too much that morning.

She hadn't told Chelsea about Charlie and Dylan's fight. The two weren't really broken up—yet—and Maddie felt like she owed them the chance to work things out before releasing the she-wolf that was her best friend.

She hoped Charlie was all right. That he and Dylan would work things out. Even if that meant she'd forever have Abigail as a sister-in-law. Maddie didn't even know if that's how marriages worked, but she'd put up with anything if it made Charlie happy. She sighed and bit her lip. She wished she could help her brother, but he'd have to figure this out on his own.

"He's really giving me the creeps." Chelsea had interrupted Maddie's thoughts.

"Who?" Maddie asked without thinking. Chelsea pointed off to the side, toward Mark, of course.

Everyone else had backed away from him, giving him plenty of space as he prowled through the trees, rifle clutched in both hands, eyes scanning the underbrush. At least he had a steadier hold on the gun now. And he had it pointed at the ground, like he might actually know what he was doing.

His eyes, though, buzzed frantically in their sockets. And that made Maddie anxious. Mark could barely walk straight for his nerves. He jumped at every twig snap and leaf shiver. Every bird that landed on a tree branch. Every squirrel scampering through the grass. It was a miracle he hadn't already blown a hole in some defenseless tree.

Out of one ear Maddie heard Caleb halting the group and speaking softly to them, drawing them together to peer through the trees at something. She pulled her eyes off Mark for a second and peeked over her shoulder. Caleb was pointing ahead at something large and brown and moving. Something furry.

Maddie glanced quickly back at Mark. He was oblivious to everyone else, still straining to see through the brush. He hadn't heard Caleb at all. She watched as he jerked excitedly. His eyes bulged in his head. He pulled the rifle up to his shoulder and aimed.

A deafening shot cracked through the woods.

TEN

JULIE'S SHRIEK FILLED THE ENTIRE FOREST. It eclipsed the echo of Mark's rifle shot as pandemonium broke out. In the middle of it all, Maddie stood surprisingly calm, watching the chaos unfold.

On one side Mark pointed through the foliage, hopping up and down, having a fit, demanding that someone notice him. On the other, everyone had frozen. Dylan and Charlie lay flat on the ground, hands thrown over their heads. Abigail and Chelsea had dived behind the nearest tree for cover. Julie stood straight up, her mouth wide open, wailing her head off.

"Is everyone okay?" Kris asked, the shock of the shot starting to wear off. "Abigail? Dylan?"

"We're fine, Mom," Dylan said, getting up from the ground slowly, unwrapping herself from Charlie's arms.

"Maddie?" Her dad's head swiveled around, looking frantically for her. She cleared her throat, but before she could say anything, Caleb stormed past.

"What the hell were you thinking?" Caleb was on Mark in a furious flash. He grabbed the rifle in one hand and pushed Mark. The gun came away easily as Abigail's dad stumbled back, tripped on a root, and fell.

"I—I—" Mark cowered on the ground, rendered speechless by Caleb's anger.

"You what?"

Everyone crowded around behind Maddie, keeping their distance from the guide as they watched.

"I—I—There was something in the forest. A wild animal. I saw it. There!"

Mark's hand quaked as he pointed into the woods.

"It was a family of deer, you idiot."

"Deer?" Mark wasn't getting it. "No—no—I saw it. It was big. Hairy. It was going to attack us."

"They don't attack people! They eat grass. I thought even you'd know that."

A crash came from nearby. Leaves and twigs crunched. Caleb turned away from Mark to look.

"Jesus." He muttered under his breath. "I guess you weren't lying when you said you could shoot."

Maddie peered after Caleb and saw something moving in the near distance. She focused. And then her hand flew to her mouth as she gulped down a sob.

It was the deer. Maddie watched as it stumbled, lost its balance, and veered into a tree like a drunk man. Its blood left a bright red smear on the tree trunk. Its hooves floundered as it tried to get back up. It looked so pathetic. So sad.

"Camp's that way." Caleb pointed back the way they'd come. His voice sounded tired all of a sudden. "Sorry. No more hike. I've got to take care of this."

It took the group a minute to realize what their guide had said.

"Here," Caleb thrust the gun out. "Make sure he doesn't kill anything else."

Maddie's dad stepped forward and gingerly took the rifle.

"But—but—I thought it..." Mark whined, trying to get someone to take his side. No one looked at him as the group turned and started back the way they'd come.

Maddie held back, though, curious.

She watched as the guide took a few calm steps into the woods, completely focused on the deer ahead of him. His hand fished in his pocket and he pulled out a knife. He flicked the blade open.

It was clean. Sharp. Dangerous. He switched it to his other hand and Maddie caught a glimpse of the initial *C* stamped on the handle.

Caleb paused as he got close to the deer. It stumbled again, lost its balance, and slammed into another tree. It collapsed to the ground. It didn't get back up this time.

Caleb approached cautiously. He knelt over the poor creature and pressed one hand down over its eyes. Maddie could see his lips moving in what could have been a whispered good-bye or a prayer. An apology.

Then his blade moved across the deer's neck in an easy, slicing motion. If Maddie had blinked, she would have missed it.

A second later, a red line opened up along the blade's path.

Maddie sucked in a breath, and Caleb looked up at her, his hands still cradling the deer's head. Blood covered his palms and shirt as tears stung Maddie's eyes.

Caleb continued to press down on the deer, holding the animal steady as it jerked feebly.

The deer convulsed one last time and then fell still.

Maddie turned and took off after everyone else. She couldn't handle any more. Whatever else Caleb needed to do, she'd already seen more than enough.

ELEVEN

"ABIGAIL!" MADDIE'S VOICE CARRIED THROUGH THE trees. "Abigail!"

"Abigail!" Chelsea took up the call, screaming it into the woods. She shouted a couple more times and then turned to Maddie. "I don't think she wants to be found."

Maddie grimaced and plopped down on a nearby rock. When they'd gotten back to camp, they'd realized Abigail had gone missing. But Maddie was actually glad Kris had asked her and Chelsea to go and look for the girl. She needed time to clear her mind. Maddie shut her eyes and pulled her knees in close, hugging them to her chest.

"I'd want to disappear, too, if my dad had just nearly killed someone."

"Thank God for having less-embarrassing dads," Chelsea said, trying to lighten the mood. She sat down next to Maddie and leaned against her. "You okay?"

"Yeah. I'm fine."

But was she? She looked down at her hands and saw they were still shaking. She quickly curled them into fists and buried them in her lap.

"It's okay if you're not," Chelsea said. "Because I'm not."

Maddie rested her head on Chelsea's shoulder, and the two girls sat there on that rock in the middle of the woods in silence.

"I've never seen that much blood before," Maddie eventually whispered. "It was all over the trees and the ground and Caleb's hands...."

Chelsea rubbed Maddie's back and waited for her to finish.

"And Caleb...he looked—" Maddie paused and tried to find the right word. "He looked so...broken."

The girls lapsed back into silence. Maddie couldn't get Caleb's face out of her head. The hollowness in his eyes as he'd knelt over that deer and delivered it to a quicker death. He wasn't as hot when he was sad. His dimple didn't pop out. His eyes didn't sparkle. Maddie wanted the other Caleb back—the uncomplicated, easy-to-crush-on version of him.

She shuddered again, thinking about Caleb cutting the deer's neck open. She wondered what it was like—to feel the life drain out and away. She looked down at her own hands.

Clean and innocent.

Could she have done it?

His knife had moved so easily through the skin and muscle. It wouldn't take more than a flick of the wrist. The slightest pressure.

"Did you hear that?" Chelsea's whisper broke through Maddie's thoughts. She picked up her head and listened. "There it is again."

She heard it this time, a rustling in the woods, getting louder. They must have found Abigail. Maddie turned toward the noise and waited for the girl to appear. She narrowed her eyes and tried to see through the underbrush.

Then suddenly Maddie heard a new sound, something tinkling ever so softly, ringing in time with the rustling. She recognized it immediately.

But it couldn't be. It didn't make any sense. She looked over at Chelsea, and this time the sound wasn't in her head. Her best friend had heard it, too. The rustling got closer and she heard the bell ringing out as plain as day. She reached down and found Chelsea's hand. She squeezed it tight. Neither girl moved. Whatever this was, they'd face it together.

The jingling got louder. Closer. Then, just as it reached a peak, it stopped.

Maddie sucked in a breath and held it. At the same time, her eyes strained to see past the trees right in front of her.

One second. Two seconds. Five seconds. Twenty seconds.

Time ticked away at an excruciatingly slow pace as Maddie waited for the worst.

Her mind wasn't playing tricks on her, was it?

She peeked over at Chelsea, who wore a similar look of unease.

No. She hadn't made this up. Her eyes flickered back to the trees, but she didn't see anything. She blinked, and then two men appeared.

A scream broke through Maddie's lips in one deafening outburst. Beside her, she could feel Chelsea screaming, too. The two girls clung to each other and shut their eyes.

But then, as Maddie's scream died down, she realized something. She flipped her eyes back open and looked at the two men again.

She recognized them.

And they weren't men at all. But boys. Two of her classmates, in fact.

"Hah!" Abigail whooped, coming out from behind the boys, laughing her head off. She had to steady herself against a tree to keep from falling over.

"God!" Chelsea swore, releasing her grip of Maddie and patting her own chest, waiting for her heartbeat to drop back to normal. "You almost gave me a heart attack."

"I think I *am* having a heart attack," Maddie said, her fingers pressed into her neck, feeling her pulse racing. "It's almost worse than when Abigail's dad shot at us."

"Wait," one of the boys chortled. "Your dad shot someone?"

"It's not funny, Jason," Abigail snapped, and the boy's grin disappeared from his face. "And for your information, my dad shot a deer. Not any of us. He's not a complete idiot."

"Just be glad it wasn't him you were sneaking up on," Chelsea quipped, having regained some of her composure. "Or you might have a few new holes in you."

Jason's face paled.

"What are you two even doing here?" Maddie pointed at the boys.

"Well, I asked my mom if Jason could come," Abigail explained in her usual, snippy voice, "but she said no. Even though she doesn't seem to have a problem with Dylan and her boyfriend spending the week together, doing God knows what every time they sneak off into the woods."

Having fights about breaking up was what they were doing, but

Maddie knew better than to mention that to Abigail. Instead, she pointed at the other boy.

"And Tommy's here because—?"

Tommy Meyers—a.k.a. Funyuns-breath—stood next to Jason. He'd come a long way since Maddie hadn't kissed him at that party all those years ago. He'd grown six inches and buzzed his hair short so that he looked ready to join the army. And he'd gotten muscles from playing on the Varsity baseball team. Maddie couldn't deny that he looked good. But that didn't mean she was any more into him now than she'd been five years ago in Chelsea's basement.

"He's been having a rough couple of months," Jason jumped in and defended his best friend. "I thought it'd be good for him to get away."

"And you two, what...let him watch when you start making out?" Chelsea couldn't help herself.

"Maybe Maddie can keep him company," Abigail cackled. Maddie wrinkled her nose at this. "Oh, right. You're saving yourself for Caleb. Let me know how that goes."

Maddie ignored Abigail's sarcasm and turned on the boys instead. A feistiness started to bubble in her blood.

"Why the hell are you trying to scare us?"

"Because it's funny," Jason replied, as if it were the most obvious thing in the world. "I wish we'd been recording it. Your faces were priceless. You had snot dripping out of your nose."

Maddie self-consciously wiped her face, which sent Jason into another fit of giggles. Tommy, to his merit, didn't seem as amused.

"It wasn't funny," Chelsea piped up, clearly pissed. "Where'd you even get a bell?"

Jason pulled out his cell phone and waved it in front of their faces.

"The wonders of technology. And a kick-ass sound effect app." He clicked on his phone and a bell rang. Maddie jumped, even though she could see him doing it.

"I've got all sorts of great ones here."

Jason clicked another button, and his phone growled like a wildcat. Then a gunshot cracked from it. And finally he had it fart at them.

"Hilarious, right?"

"Not one bit," Chelsea glowered.

"Wait." Maddie had a thought. "Then was that you with the tree, too?"

Abigail couldn't keep her glee hidden as she nodded.

"My idea. Jason carved the marks this morning before anyone was up. Pretty genius, right?"

"Um, pretty stupid," Maddie shot back, though she felt a wave of relief to hear that the marks were indeed fake. "You sent your dad off the deep end."

Abigail waved the accusation away.

"He was crazy paranoid before that. He always is. It was only a matter of time before he did something stupid."

"Well, whatever." Maddie didn't feel like arguing. "Playtime's over. We've got to get back. Your mom's worried."

"Let her worry. I'm having fun."

"You can have your threesome later," Maddie snipped, her patience breaking. "Say good-bye and let's go. Unless you *want* me to tell your mom where you've been disappearing to."

Abigail had her mouth open, but closed it quickly at Maddie's threat.

"Always a party pooper." She shot Maddie a truly hateful glower. "Fine. I'm coming. I'll see you boys later tonight, though." She waved flirtatiously at them and didn't wait for Maddie and Chelsea as she headed back toward camp.

"Maybe we'll see you later, too?" Tommy spoke for the first time. He looked at Maddie with hesitant eyes.

"Yeah—maybe," Maddie relented. Was Tommy Meyers flirting with her? She looked at him again, trying to decide. "But don't hold your breath."

She turned and followed Abigail. A bell rang behind her, but she didn't turn around. Instead, she raised her hand high in the air and silently flipped Jason off as she went.

TWELVE

A FIRE CRACKLED IN THE MIDDLE of camp, where Maddie sat staring into the orange flames. The sun had gone down an hour ago and the moon had risen to take its place, high and full in the sky.

Across from Maddie, Caleb sat by himself, his face expressionless. He'd spoken barely two words since coming back to camp. His arms had been covered in blood, and Maddie had watched as he'd cleaned up, taking his time scrubbing his forearms until they'd glowed a faint pink and carefully picking the dried blood from beneath his fingernails. She'd been so worried about him that she hadn't even been able to appreciate his abs when he'd changed shirts. Once clean, he'd disappeared into his tent, not even eating dinner with them.

But now he'd come out of hiding. He still looked grim, though, as he polished his knife against his jeans, every once in a while testing the blade with his thumb. He glanced up and saw her staring, but didn't smile or wink like usual. Instead, he grimaced and dipped his head right back down, worrying over his knife again. Maddie couldn't look at him any longer. It was too depressing. So she let her gaze wander.

Behind Caleb, Maddie's brother and Dylan sat together, sharing sips of a beer. They held hands and giggled softly into one another's ear. Charlie leaned in and stole a quick kiss. They looked so happy. Apparently they'd gotten over their fight that afternoon. Good thing she hadn't gotten Chelsea's hopes up.

Maddie moved on—she didn't want to pry—and spotted Bryan next, lying in the short grass all by himself. He wasn't drinking. Instead, he stared up at the night sky. Stargazing quietly. He looked peaceful in his solitude, though.

A rustling off to the right drew Maddie's attention. She turned and saw Mark emerge from his tent, the first she'd seen of him since the accident. He paused, swaying unsteadily on his feet. He fished in one of his many vest pockets and pulled out a flask, taking a long swig from it. He wiped his mouth and stumbled toward the fire, plopping himself down as he took another drink. He looked over at Caleb like he might say something, but then didn't, turning to Maddie and giving her a full-on crazy-person smile instead.

She flinched and pulled back. She hadn't realized just how messed up he was. His mouth gaped open like his jaw had come unhinged. His hair stood up in frazzled needles all around his head. His face was splotchy, his eyes puffy pink orbs of bloodshot veins.

He took another swig from his flask and let out a belch. How had he gotten so drunk?

She opened her mouth to ask if he was all right, but Mark's attention had moved on from her. She turned and looked over her shoulder, following his drunken gaze. The rest of the adults were standing and talking in front of the coolers, each drinking a beer. Uncle Ed had his arm around her aunt's shoulders as he told a story. His free hand swept through the air, big and brash, his beer bottle pointing as he spoke. He got to the punchline and everyone started laughing. Julie, especially, tittered into her beer. Uncle Ed pulled her in close and gave her a great smacking kiss on the forehead.

Maddie turned as Mark harrumphed loudly. The adults had heard it, too.

"Is that Mark?" Ed called out. "I see you decided to slink out of your tent."

Ed walked over and joined the close circle of the campfire. Maddie felt an uncomfortable prickle at the back of her neck. Everyone's attention had turned to her uncle. Even Bryan had sat up to watch his father.

"Don't shoot!" Ed threw up his arms in jest.

Mark mumbled a reply that no one could understand.

"What's that?" Ed shot back. Maddie noticed the danger in his half-drunk eyes.

Mark pulled himself up and focused on Ed's face. He spoke slowly and deliberately, this time managing to enunciate through his liquor-thick tongue.

"Go. To. Hell."

Her uncle's beer bottle smashed in the flames. He moved around the fire faster than Maddie thought possible and hauled Mark up by the collar of his shirt.

"You want to say that again?"

Mark's eyes narrowed. Everyone else stood back, frozen by how quickly things had turned.

"Screw you." Mark's words seethed with contempt. He ducked down and jerked out of Ed's grip, pivoting to one side and swinging his arm around.

In his drunkenness, though, he moved in clumsy slow motion. His fist swung high and unsteadily. Maddie watched as her uncle easily ducked the attack. The punch's momentum spun Mark around, and Ed pushed him hard, then pounced on him, arms pulled back, ready to sink his fists into Mark's soft belly flesh. But before Ed could land a punch, a shout interrupted him.

"Hey!" Caleb finally broke his silence. Everyone's attention snapped back to the fire where he stood, still holding his knife. Its blade glinted threateningly in the orange light. "How about we relax a bit? It's been a tough day for all of us. Let's not get crazy."

Maddie looked around the circle. The commotion had pulled everyone in. Dylan looked worriedly at her dad, laid out on the ground, while Bryan gave his dad a look of pure embarrassment. Julie shot them both murderous glares.

Ed, getting the hint, got off Mark. A few seconds later, Mark pulled himself to a sitting position, looking just as drunk but unhurt.

"That's better," Caleb said. "Now how about we all sit down and enjoy the night. I know a good scary story, if anyone wants to hear it."

Everyone nodded slowly, still uncomfortable, and moved to take seats around the fire.

"But I'm warning you," Caleb went on, a wicked glint in his eye, nothing playful about it, "what I'm about to tell you isn't a story like the other ones. It's something that actually happened to me."

THE MOUNTAIN PEOPLE

Caleb didn't know what he was looking at.

Well, that wasn't actually true. He knew exactly what the man had thrown at his feet, but his mind refused to process it, refused to translate the monstrosity into words.

"Beautiful, isn't it?"

The thing stared up at Caleb with black, lifeless eyes, its snout open, its jaw cracked and crooked.

Beautiful?

No.

But Caleb could think of plenty better ways to describe it.

Foul.

Gruesome.

Sad.

A waste.

"It's sick," a second man jumped in. "It's gonna look so good on your wall."

The second man reached over and bumped fists with the first. Caleb tried to keep from rolling his eyes. He reminded himself that he really needed the money.

He hated playing chauffeur to yuppies. They had no respect for the wilderness—or experience in it—with their shiny L.L. Bean gear that they'd clearly just taken the price tags off of. Brash and idiotic, they crashed through the woods like they owned it.

No, worse. Like it owed them something.

Caleb took one last look at the severed head on the ground and grimaced.

Hunting was one thing, but this—it left a bad taste in his mouth. They'd hacked away at the deer, leaving jagged flaps of skin and tissue where the neck should have connected to the body. Blood had also gotten into the fur and stained it.

The antlers were the saddest part, though. Caleb held out his hands and tried to estimate their length. Each had to measure at least a foot. The buck had lived a long life—until today. Caleb's hands balled into fists and he quickly stuffed them into his pockets.

A fly buzzed by and landed on the deer head. A second joined it.

"You'll want to get that on ice," Caleb spoke matter-of-factly. And then he turned away. He couldn't look at it anymore.

Behind him, the men scrambled into action. They didn't want their hard work going to waste. Jared—the first man, the one who'd actually killed the deer—bent and grabbed the buck by the antlers, dragging the severed head the rest of the way into their small camp. Meanwhile, Keith rushed to empty their cooler, throwing two six-packs of beer out on the ground.

"I don't think it's going to fit," Keith said, presenting the empty cooler to Jared.

"We can take the antlers off."

"But won't that ruin it?"

"Nah, that's why they have superglue," Jared assured his friend as he pulled out a pocketknife. He flipped it open to a saw blade and set to work.

Sweat started to drip down Jared's forehead. His arm looked like it was getting tired, but he still had a grin on his face, the adrenaline of the kill pumping through his blood. Caleb wished he could rewind the morning and wipe that grin off Jared's face. It was their last day in the mountains, and after a weekend of nothing, the wannabe hunter had finally gotten lucky. They'd been up in that tree stand for hours, sitting in silence, waiting patiently. Caleb had thought they'd come up empty-handed, and had been happy about it.

But then, just as he had seen Jared's head starting to dip with sleepiness, Caleb had heard a crunch down below and a deer had walked into the clearing. Jared and Keith had spotted it, too.

And the rest—well—the rest was history.

Caleb knew Jared wouldn't tell the real story. These men never did. Jared's first shot had missed badly, but he'd gotten a second chance because Keith's bullet had landed in the deer's haunches and practically maimed it. Jared had had time to aim, time for another shot, which had hit the deer right in the chest. The killing blow. And now this beautiful creature would live on, stuffed and mounted in Jared's office, a trophy to impress every client. And there was nothing Caleb could do to stop it.

"Shit, this is going to take forever." Jared stopped sawing and wiped his brow.

"Here." Keith popped open a beer and handed it over. "Don't want these going to waste."

Jared laughed and took the beer. Keith opened one for himself and the two men cheers-ed. They both took a swig, and then Jared got back to work.

"God, this cooler is heavy," Jared complained loudly. He dropped the handle and then sat down on its lid, panting.

Ahead of him, Caleb stopped, cursing the man under his breath. When they'd first got on the mountain, he'd told Jared to leave the cooler with the truck, but the man had insisted, hauling the thing with them for the two miles they'd hiked into the woods. He couldn't go a whole weekend without his damn beer. And now the men had chugged two six-packs between them in the last few hours. This was turning into a nightmare on top of a nightmare.

"Five minutes, then we've got to keep going," Caleb said, annoyed. He watched as Keith plopped down on the cooler next to Jared, looking just as uncomfortable as his friend. "And drink some water."

Caleb pulled his own canteen out of his pack and took a gulp, glancing back at the two men. Both had their heads cradled in their hands. Caleb took a little pleasure in seeing them in pain. Maybe they'd learn something from the hangovers.

"How much longer?" Jared croaked, looking only a few inches from death. Caleb smirked as the man jumped up from the cooler, hand clutched to his mouth. The splash came a few seconds later.

"Gross," Keith groaned, pressing his hand over his own mouth. Caleb ignored them, walking a little ways ahead. He paused and took another sip of water. He could hear the two men still groaning behind him. He shut his eyes and tried to block it out.

One more mile. He wished he could fast-forward through the next hour. He just wanted to get back to the truck, drive down the mountain, and never see these men again.

"Dude! You're dripping on my shoes."

Keith's disgusted cry broke through Caleb's thoughts. The guide sighed and turned back around. Better to get it over with. He walked toward the two men, but something caught his eye and made him stop. He hadn't noticed it earlier. He moved closer to get a better look.

There, on one of the trees, it looked like someone had carved a symbol into the bark. Caleb got closer and ran his fingers over the spot. It looked like it could have been drawn by a knife. Maybe it was to help mark a trail.

Or it could just be that an animal had worn its mark into the wood. A bird. Or squirrel. Caleb had seen that before. But never in this pattern. Whatever it was, it looked kind of like a pair of lightning bolts sitting side-by-side, two jagged lines zigzagging from sky to earth.

Caleb took a long look and then moved on. Another curiosity to add to these woods. He'd been bringing people up here for a year now, and still he hadn't seen it all. Nature never ran out of surprises. Or mysteries.

"Let's get going," Caleb called to the men.

Both men groaned.

"Only one more mile to AC," Caleb tried. This seemed to work as the two men got slowly to their feet, shouldering their packs.

"Keith, man, can you carry the cooler for a bit?" Jared pleaded with his friend.

"No way," Keith shot back without a second's thought. "It's not my head."

Jared tried but couldn't think of an argument. He looked down at the cooler.

"You better look damn impressive on my wall."

Then he bent and picked it up.

Caleb nodded at the two men and started walking. They fell in line behind him, moving slowly, walking with clumsy, exhausted feet. It only took about five minutes for one of them to ruin Caleb's quiet.

"Hey—um—" Jared tried to get Caleb's attention, forgetting his name. "Is it just me, or do you hear something?"

"It's just you," Caleb said without giving the question a thought. He was so close to freedom. Couldn't they just shut up and keep walking?

Jared stopped and dropped the cooler.

"It's nothing." Caleb heard the annoyance in his own voice. He whirled around on the men. "Let's go."

"I definitely heard something." Jared wasn't backing down.

"Look." Caleb no longer cared. He couldn't deal with these two anymore. "We're almost back to the truck, so just stop complaining, pick up your damn cooler, and keep walking."

Jared's chest puffed up. He crossed his arms and opened his mouth.

But instead of words, a metallic twang sang through the trees. Caleb watched in confusion as a flower bloomed against Jared's shoulder, dying his shirtfront red, its stem sticking out a good foot from Jared's body.

It took Caleb another beat to realize it was actually an arrow shaft.

Another second after that, Jared's scream tore through the woods.

Caleb whipped around, his eyes darting through the trees. Who was shooting at them? And why?

He heard another metallic twang and an arrow notched itself in a tree just inches from Keith's head. The man turned and stared at it with wide eyes. Then he took off running. He didn't make it far.

Another arrow whistled through the air and hit Keith square in the back. He collapsed to the ground in a heap, but quickly realized he wasn't dead. He threw off his pack, the arrow embedded in it, and scrambled back to his feet. He looked around wildly, backpedaling. One step. And then two.

On the third step, his foot found something hard. An iron clank crunched sickeningly, and a bear trap snapped closed, breaking Keith's ankle in one bite as it devoured his foot.

His scream was even louder than Jared's.

Caleb froze. He didn't know what to do. They hadn't covered ambushes in his wilderness-training classes.

A man emerged from the trees, crossbow in hand. A big, bushy beard covered his face with coarse, gray hair. Then another man appeared. And another. All three wore dirty clothes, tattered at the hems. They all looked like they could use a good shower. They moved threateningly through the woods, calm and confident, stalking their prey. Caleb could only raise his hands and pray they'd let him go.

The man with the crossbow came up on him and stopped. He scrutinized Caleb from head to toe. Caleb tried to hold the man's gaze, but he couldn't help curling his nose. A pungent odor seeped from the man's pores. It smelled like dirt and rotted flowers and bear piss all thrown in a bottle and shaken up. The man motioned, and the other two went to tend to Jared and Keith, but he stayed there in front of Caleb. He sucked on his lips, tilting his mouth this way and then that, as if in deliberation. He smirked and turned around.

Caleb held his breath. Had he really just escaped?

Then the man whirled back and Caleb felt a crack open up in his forehead. He fell down into the black chasm and lost consciousness.

Caleb groaned. It felt like someone had taken his head and broken it open like an egg, pouring his brains out in one runny yolk. His head lolled to one side and then back to the other. His nostrils flared, and a tangy smoke filled his lungs.

He took another sniff, and—like with smelling salts—his eyes twitched. His mind started to clear. He blinked twice and came to.

He tossed his head, looking all around. He could hear the woods alive out there—the crackle of a fire, an owl hooting, the droning song of cicadas—but he couldn't see anything. Black night enveloped him, pulled him down as he struggled to get to his feet.

Panic overwhelmed him. He fought harder to get up, but no matter how much he strained, the ropes around his shoulders held fast. The blindfold covering his eyes wouldn't budge.

Finally, Caleb gave up. He tried to calm down. Tried to keep his mind from racing. Tried to think.

He remembered the men in the woods. The leader with his wild, gray beard. His crossbow.

What had happened to Jared? Keith?

Someone whimpered on his right. Caleb turned his head.

"Jared? You there?" He whispered.

But he only got more whimpers in reply. Caleb was about to try again, but just then footsteps stirred the underbrush. They came right toward Caleb.

"Hey! What are you doing? Let us go," Caleb shouted out. He couldn't even tell if he was looking in the right direction.

No one answered him.

Instead, one of the men grunted, and then Caleb heard him bend down, untying, not him, but the whimpering man on his right.

There was a shout of protest. Cries for help. A struggle as the men pulled Jared to his feet. Their footsteps receded, and the shouts grew farther away. But they didn't get any quieter. Jared's screams echoed through the forest, deafening in Caleb's ears. Then a heavy *thunk* and the screams cut off altogether.

"Oh my god oh my god oh my god oh my god."

Caleb recognized Keith's voice on his left.

"They just killed Jared and they're gonna kill us next."

Caleb struggled to find something to say—anything that could help calm Keith. But what? Wasn't the man right?

"It's going to be all right."

The words felt empty in Caleb's mouth. A lie. But he had to say something.

"Like hell it is." Keith's voice had dropped back low. He'd given up.

Then the footsteps came back.

"Look, if you survive this, do me a favor." Keith spoke quickly. "Tell my mom I love her."

And then they had him.

Keith didn't scream. He remained silent as they dragged him away, his broken ankle making him worthless for walking. Caleb perked up his ears, trying to hear anything he could. But there was nothing—until the same sickening *thunk*.

Caleb shut his eyes under his blindfold and waited. He wasn't the type to pray, but what could it hurt to try?

The footsteps approached, slower this time. Caleb set his lips in a steely line and waited. He wouldn't show these men any fear. If he was going, he'd go dignified. He couldn't let a yuppie like Keith show him up.

Someone knelt in front of him and pulled the blindfold off his head. Caleb squinted, letting his eyes adjust to the night. Just a few inches away, the leader from before stared at him with unblinking eyes, his gray beard bigger than Caleb remembered. And dirtier.

They sized each other up without speaking, and then the man motioned and Caleb felt rough hands untying him and pulling him up. He didn't fight as they led him toward a campfire set up in a clearing about twenty yards from where they'd been bound.

As they pushed Caleb into the light, a shock ran through him. He'd thought it was just the three men, rogue hunters out for a better thrill than deer or bear. But this—

Well, he'd heard rumors, but he'd never thought they had any truth to them.

However, he couldn't ignore this. Couldn't ignore the faces, young and old, staring at him from all directions. The burly men with their rough, leathery hands, sunburned from a life spent outdoors. Or the women with their long tangles of greasy, matted hair. And the children, with their spindly limbs and pinched faces, freckles dotting their cheeks.

This wasn't a campsite, but a small village—a community.

The Mountain People really did exist.

The realization stunned Caleb, surprising as it was terrifying. If the stories were true, these people lived completely off the grid, by a law all their own. They knew the mountains so well that the authorities could never find them.

Caleb didn't have any more time to think about it, though, as the men guiding him forced him to his knees and pressed his face down against a giant tree stump. The wood was wet and warm. Caleb didn't waste any time thinking why.

The men held him tight. Out of the corner of his eye, Caleb saw a glint of metal, the flash of an ax blade.

He took a deep breath. At least he'd die in the wild, with trees all around and a sky full of stars looking down at him. He'd go with the crisp scent of pine in his lungs.

He blinked and tears ran down his cheeks. The mountain man's shadow fell across the tree stump. He raised his arms and Caleb shut his eyes tight. He waited.

The ax came down and *thunked* against the stump.

Caleb's eyes shot open. The campfire still roared beside him, its light flickering off the ax that had buried its blade into the stump two inches from his nose.

The men suddenly released him. Caleb got up slowly, unsure. The man with the gray beard stood in front of him. He spat at Caleb's feet and motioned to the other men again. One came forward, carrying Jared's blue cooler. He offered it to Caleb.

The guide didn't ask any questions. He just took the cooler in his trembling hands and went slowly, throwing cautious glances over his shoulder, making sure this wasn't some kind of trick.

He walked for fifteen minutes before he felt safe. Then he broke into a run, moving as best he could with the cooler in his arms.

It took him a while, but eventually he found a path he knew. In another hour, he'd made it back to the truck.

His body shook with exhaustion and fear. He set the cooler down in the bed of his truck and rubbed his shoulders. He stared long and hard at the lid of that blue cooler, knowing what was inside. He didn't want to open it, but he knew he had to.

Carefully, he reached out. His fingers danced nervously across the plastic. He gulped, and then in one quick motion flipped it open.

Caleb gagged. A sob escaped his mouth and he turned away. But the image stayed with him, seared into his brain. He'd never forget it—Jared's and Keith's eyes, frozen open in horror, the matching pairs of angry red lightning bolts carved into their foreheads.

No, not lightning bolts, Caleb realized. Antlers.

THIRTEEN

AN UNCOMFORTABLE QUIET HAD FALLEN AROUND the campfire, everyone trying to avoid Mark's gaze.

"But—but—that can't possibly be true." Mark's anxious assertion broke the silence. The color had gone completely out of his face. The story must have sobered him up a bit. Caleb only shrugged, though, giving nothing away.

But Maddie knew the story couldn't possibly be real. It sounded so over the top. So far-fetched. What would Caleb have even done with the two heads? And why would he ever come back if those same Mountain Men were still out there?

Still, Maddie had to admit there was a part of her that believed him. Or a part that wanted to believe him. There'd been something in Caleb's voice as he'd told his story. Something tragically authentic. Like the gruesome ordeal had been seared into his memory, all the details there, plain as day, every time he closed his eyes.

Wouldn't it be nice to have someone who understood? Someone who, like Maddie, knew the pain of never forgetting the worst day imaginable? Those images of her mother—of the fire and its suffocating, black smoke—they haunted her. And always would.

No. Maddie had to check herself. Caleb was a good storyteller, plain and simple. He probably pulled this story out for all of the groups he escorted through the mountains. He hadn't survived some near-death trauma. The Mountain People didn't exist.

She got to her feet in a hurry, needing a moment to get away and clear her head.

"Everything all right?" Chelsea asked, and everyone in the circle turned toward her.

"Fine." Maddie put a smile on. "Just wanted to grab a drink. Anybody else want one?"

"I'll take another beer." Charlie raised one hand to get Maddie's attention.

"I'll be right back."

Maddie retreated from the campfire light. She could hear the conversation starting back up, but she only caught the first few words before she walked out of earshot.

The cooler wasn't far, but Maddie suddenly felt isolated. She hadn't bothered to grab her flashlight. The eerie quiet of the woods wrapped around her like a blanket. She felt alone. And a little paranoid. She could see just ahead where the woods started. She stopped and peered into the black chasm.

What hid behind the dark foliage of those branches?

Crickets? Owls? Deer? Bears? The Mountain People?

She shook her head and kept walking. When she got to the cooler, she hesitated. It was blue, just like in Caleb's story. Her fingers danced nervously over the plastic lid.

Wait. Why was she being so silly?

Maddie rolled her eyes at herself and flipped the cooler open. Before she could reach in, though, she heard footsteps come up behind her. She jumped. A squeal escaped her lips.

"Oh, sorry," Caleb apologized. "Didn't mean to scare you."

Maddie blushed, thankful for the darkness.

"No worries."

She tried to act cool. She reached into the open cooler—no heads—and pulled out a can of ginger ale and a bottle of beer for her brother.

"Did you want something?" Maddie asked.

"Nope. Just needed to stretch my legs."

Maddie nodded, the cold drinks sweating in her hands.

"Can I ask—" Maddie hesitated, and then charged forward. "That story—the Mountain People—they aren't real, are they?"

She was embarrassed, but she needed to know.

"Just between us," Caleb looked back toward the campfire, "it's all made up."

Caleb winked at Maddie then. She was relieved to see his old self return.

"But—um—don't say anything. No need for the others to know."

"I won't tell."

Her face glowed warm in the dark. She liked having a secret with Caleb. And she liked knowing for certain that she didn't need to worry about some mysterious Mountain Person decapitating her in her sleep.

"So—uh—" fear out of the way, Maddie saw her opportunity to flirt some more and jumped on it. Chelsea would be proud of her. "What do you like to do for fun?"

She cringed at her own question. How pathetic. But it was all she could think to ask. She wouldn't tell Chelsea that part. Caleb's head snapped back around.

"Oh, I guess I like being out here the best," Caleb replied. "Out in the wild. That part of my story was true, at least. I've always liked nature, but really fell in love with these mountains a couple of years ago. I dropped out of college to start guiding folks. I'd live in these woods if I could."

"But wouldn't you get lonely?" Maddie tried to channel Chelsea as she put a bit of a purr in her voice.

"Lonely?" Caleb thought about it. "I mean, not really. I like being on my own."

"But—like—what about a girlfriend?" Maddie held her breath and waited for his answer. She felt reckless, exposed. And she kind of liked it.

"Oh—uh—well," Caleb got sheepish all of a sudden. He pushed his hand back through his hair. "Well, I guess if I found the right girl."

"And what would make her the right girl?" Maddie couldn't believe the words coming out of her own mouth. But she felt bold. Invincible. Like a superhero. Like *Mustang Maddie*.

"Well, you know, I'm twenty-two—" Caleb let the end hang loose, clearly uncomfortable now. "So probably someone more my age."

Mortifying. There was no other word to describe it. Maddie felt sick with embarrassment as her confidence drained out of her.

"I—I didn't mean—" Maddie cut off before she could dig herself deeper. Her cheeks were truly on fire now. She was so stupid. He must get this all the time. With every tour group he led.

"I'm—uh—going to head back." And Maddie shot toward the campfire, leaving Caleb alone at the cooler.

When she got back, Mark still looked like a ghost. He had his drink clutched close to his chest, but his shaking hands only splashed the whiskey on the ground. He jumped up the moment Caleb got back, which wasn't long after Maddie.

"I don't appreciate you trying to scare me like that," Mark slurred. "I want—I want an apology."

The guide blinked across the fire but didn't speak.

"I said—" Mark raised his voice, but his wife cut him off.

"That's enough, Mark," Kris hissed through gritted teeth, clearly embarrassed by her husband's antics.

"No." He ignored her for once. He stomped his foot like a child throwing a tantrum. "I demand an apology. Now."

Everyone's eyes shot to Caleb. Except for Maddie's. She couldn't look at him. But maybe this would make him forget the last five minutes—her monumentally failed attempt at flirting.

The two men locked eyes across the fire, daring the other to blink first. Caleb's jaw clenched, and a new set of shadows danced across his face. He wasn't going to cave.

"We're paying you," Mark hollered. "So do your damn job and show me some respect."

Maddie thought she heard someone gasp, but no one moved or spoke. The tension in the air built with each passing second.

Finally, Caleb flinched. But instead of answering, he turned and walked away.

This only made Mark madder. He stomped his feet and shouted every obscenity in the book. Maddie couldn't believe it. She'd never seen this side of him. His face turned bright red and his eyes bulged in their sockets, threatening to pop out of his head entirely. He even threw his cup after Caleb, though it didn't land anywhere near its intended target.

"Oh, come off it," Ed shouted, finally shutting Mark up. "Stop acting like a damn fool."

From across the fire, Maddie caught Chelsea's eye. Maddie couldn't deal with this circus anymore.

"We're going to bed," Maddie said, taking advantage of the lull and pulling Chelsea up.

"Bed?" Chelsea asked as Maddie opened the flap of their tent and pushed her in. "But it's not even nine o'clock yet."

Maddie zipped up the tent behind them and started rummaging through her pack. She kept her head down, hiding her embarrassed, red face from her best friend. But she turned back around as she pulled out a black hat and a flashlight.

"I know. We're not going to sleep."

"Then where—"

"Get your stuff."

Maddie unzipped the flap at the back of the tent and scampered out. Chelsea grabbed her own flashlight and followed. "I just got epically shot down by Caleb and am in need of a little ego boost."

"Wait. What? Caleb? Where are we going?" Chelsea asked again, and this time Maddie answered by pointing toward the woods. Chelsea spotted a flashlight beam moving through the tree line.

"Oh," Chelsea said. She knew exactly what Maddie had in mind. And she liked it.

"Hurry. We don't want to lose her."

And the two girls stole across the clearing, trying to catch up to Abigail.

FOURTEEN

"SO THIS IS YOUR LITTLE CLUBHOUSE?"

Maddie looked around, disappointed, but not surprised, by the sad state of Tommy and Jason's campsite—if they could call it that. It looked like a pair of eight-year-old boys had thrown together a secret fort.

Cute, except for the fact that these boys were sixteen.

All they had for light was a lantern that they'd set on a rock. And they didn't even have a tent, just a blue sheet they'd thrown up between two trees. They must have been sleeping elbow-to-elbow under that thing. Maddie wrinkled her nose at the thought of the smells.

At least they had some music playing. She tapped her foot to the beat and then was shocked when a commercial came on after the song. Not just a boom box, but a radio. Retro, but cool. Maddie could see that they had an ATV, too. So that explained how they'd gotten up the mountain so fast. Abigail must have told them where their campsite was before they'd come. Maddie was somewhat impressed. That took more planning than she'd thought Abigail had in her. She must have really wanted her boyfriend along for the week.

"It's called galumphing," Jason said, too satisfied with himself. "The man's man's answer to glamping."

"So you're cavemen now?" Maddie couldn't pass up the opportunity to poke fun at him.

"No," Jason bristled.

"We're bringing camping back to its roots," Tommy jumped in. "Dirt under your feet. Open sky above your head. Camping the way it's meant to be done—all natural."

He put on a thick French accent for the last word, and Maddie couldn't help but giggle. Wait. What was happening? Had Tommy Meyers actually made her laugh?

"You know, you can just admit that you forgot to pack a tent," Chelsea cut in.

"Well…that might also be true."

"Let's hope it doesn't rain," Maddie added.

Tommy pantomimed crossing his heart like a good Catholic boy and pointed up to the sky. When he finished, he looked back at Maddie, beaming.

"See, Maddie, this is exactly why we need you here," Jason said. "My boy Tommy has been moping for the last two months, but now you've got him smiling again."

Tommy's gaze flickered away, embarrassed, but Maddie kept her eyes on him. Maybe she'd written him off too soon. He could be funny. And he'd certainly grown up from his eleven-year-old dweeb self.

She looked at him now, at his close-cropped hair, his cheeks that looked pink even in the weak lantern light, his muscular arms extending out of his cut-off T-shirt. A Giants shirt, she realized with a start, the black-and-orange SF logo taking up the entirety of his broad chest.

The universe couldn't have given her a clearer sign. She swallowed and returned his smile.

"I'm bored," Abigail complained, which really meant *Why aren't you paying attention to me?* She plumped her lips and pouted at her boyfriend.

"Take a seat," Jason said, scurrying into action. Abigail rolled her eyes again and tapped her foot impatiently.

"Oh, right." Jason fumbled for a second before finding a sweatshirt, which he laid on the ground for his girlfriend. Abigail stepped over to it and did a little curtsy as she sat down.

"Sorry. That's the only one I've got."

"It takes more than a little dirt to scare us," Chelsea answered as she sat down. Maddie took a seat next to her. Jason smiled uncomfortably and then disappeared under the sheet. They could hear him rummaging around for a few seconds and then he reappeared, holding up a clear bottle.

"I've got vodka," he said merrily. "But—um—no mixers. Or cups. Oh, and pot!" He held up a half-smoked joint.

"No smoking tonight. I need a drink. Give it here," Abigail snapped. She took the bottle and drank from it. She wiped her lips with the back of her hand. She took a second sip and Maddie couldn't help thinking of Mark. Like father, like daughter. Maddie must have made a face, because Abigail caught her eye and glowered right back at her.

"Your turn." The girl shoved the bottle at Maddie, but she waved it off.

"What? You think we have cooties or something?" Abigail shot back indignantly. Pink splotches had already started to speckle her cheeks.

"I'm not five," Maddie replied, still not taking the bottle.

"Stop pressuring her." Tommy reached across and grabbed the vodka away from Maddie's face, taking a small swig for himself. "She's an athlete. Drinking is a no-no."

"That never stopped you." Abigail's words crackled. Tommy paused and then took another drink.

"Well, I don't have to worry about that anymore, do I?"

His smile dropped into a sour grimace, and an awkward silence fell among the teens.

"So…what exactly did happen…with the baseball team, I mean?" Maddie rushed to finish the question. She'd heard about Tommy getting kicked off from her brother, but he hadn't said much more.

"The coach and I didn't see eye-to-eye." Tommy said it softly, his jaw clenched. Maddie could tell it was still a sore subject.

"It was a bit more than that," Jason coughed, taking the vodka from his friend.

"What?"

Jason looked at Tommy with wide eyes. "You took a baseball bat to Coach's car. Knocked the side mirrors right off. Talk about swinging with your hips. It was impressive. Really. Too bad he called the cops on you, got you arrested."

Jason said this last bit into the bottle, losing his nerve under Tommy's stare.

"I'm gonna take a walk," Tommy said with a quiet intensity.

"You want a flashlight or something?"

Tommy didn't respond to Jason but took off, disappearing into the dark woods.

"Okay. Fine. Ignore me. See you in a bit. Hope you don't get lost." Jason finished the conversation as if his friend had actually responded.

"What a tool," he mumbled to everyone else.

"Let him mope," Abigail said. "Just means more vodka for us."

She snatched the bottle from Jason and took another drink.

"I—I'm gonna go check and make sure Tommy's all right," Maddie got up, surprising herself. She gave Chelsea an apologetic look and scrambled to her feet.

"So, what did you all get up to tonight?" Jason asked. Chelsea took the cue and jumped right in, telling Jason about the fight and Caleb's story. Maddie mouthed a thank-you to her friend and retreated, using her own flashlight to go after Tommy.

It didn't take her long to find him.

"Hey," Maddie whispered, crossing her arms at the last second, trying to make it seem like she didn't care too much. He turned and she saw the tension loosen in his face almost immediately. She studied that face, those brown eyes.

"So, how are you? Really."

Tommy sighed. He scratched his head and leaned against a tree.

"I'm fine...better now."

"What happened?"

"Do you really care?" Tommy asked. Maddie felt bad for him then. She knew what it felt like to be the talk of the school. The center of all the gossip. People only cared about the scandal. They blew it up and made it bigger and badder than in reality.

"I do care."

"Well." Tommy paused, taken off guard by Maddie's sincerity. "I mean, I was struggling for a month or so with my swing. But everyone goes through slumps. It's part of baseball. I guess Coach wasn't happy, though. He comes to me out of the blue one day and tells me I'm benched. And then he promotes some freshman into my starting spot."

He paused again and Maddie waited. She didn't want to push him.

"I guess—I guess I just lost it. My anger erupted, you know. I couldn't control it. I saw Coach's car there after practice, and I had a bat with me, and something inside me snapped. I blacked out.

"Next thing I knew, a couple of the guys were pulling me back. Coach's car was busted up. Windows broken. Mirrors knocked loose. Dents everywhere. Coach was there yelling at me. He probably would have throttled me if I hadn't had the bat in my hands still.

"Then the cops got there and put me in handcuffs. Threw me in the back of their car. I spent the afternoon in a holding cell."

Tommy stopped, worrying that he might have already said too much and scared Maddie off. But she leaned in and looked at him without any judgment in her eyes, and he forged on.

"Sitting in that cell, I—I had time to think about what I'd done.

And I felt terrible about it. How could I let my anger take over like that...let it ruin everything in one idiotic moment?"

Tommy looked up as if Maddie might actually have an answer for him.

"And that was the end of my baseball career. Haven't been back to practice since. Not that I have time for it anymore. I'm working overtime to try and earn the money to fix Coach's car. And my mom's on my ass. Livid. Says I've ruined my future. Says she's not going to let me live at home when I don't get into college because of my criminal record.

"And my dad's no help, either. Six months since the divorce and he's already got a new family all set up. Two perfect little stepkids who'd never take a bat to someone's car. He's practically forgotten me and Mom even exist."

Tommy got quiet again after that. How had Maddie not heard about this sooner? It had to have been all over school.

"That—that really sucks."

Maddie knew it sounded lame, but what else was there to say? It was hard for her to believe that Tommy had really taken a baseball bat to someone's car. He'd always been a bit of a dweeb. A cool kid, sure, but only because he made everyone else around him seem cooler.

"But you're doing better now?" Maddie asked hopefully.

"Yeah." Tommy hesitated, but then decided he could trust Maddie. "I actually started seeing a therapist. My mom said I had to—but it actually really helps. And your brother has been great, too."

Her brother? Maddie's mouth popped open in surprise. She hadn't known that Charlie and Tommy were close. Sure, they played on the same team, but it was a big team. She'd never heard Charlie talk about Tommy at all until a couple of weeks ago.

"Yeah. Didn't he tell you?" Tommy went on. "He's actually the one who picked me up from the police station after they released me. He's been going through some hard stuff lately, too, what with losing his baseball scholarship and all."

Maddie's eyebrows shot up her forehead and threatened to rocket to the moon. What was Tommy talking about?

"Shit." Tommy put it together quickly. "I'm sorry. I thought you knew."

"It's fine," Maddie heard herself saying. Her mind was racing, though. Why hadn't Charlie told her? They told each other everything.

"Really, it's fine," Maddie said again. Tommy had moved closer, a concerned look pinching his cheeks in. She looked up at him and bit her bottom lip. She could tell Tommy wanted to kiss her. And isn't that why she'd come out here? To forget about Caleb? She wanted to kiss Tommy. She wanted to show Caleb exactly what he was missing out on. But she couldn't stop thinking about her brother. Why had Charlie lied to her? Was this why things were off between him and Dylan?

"We should probably head back." Maddie flipped her flashlight around. "Chelsea's going to kill me as it is."

Tommy gave her one last hopeful look, but then nodded.

"After you."

FIFTEEN

MADDIE'S FLASHLIGHT BEAM LEAPED AHEAD OF her, showing the way through the dark forest as she and Chelsea walked back to camp. She had to admit that she'd had a good time with the boys. Shocking, really. But exactly what she'd needed after the day's series of disasters.

Abigail, however, had been intolerable. Her usual bitchy self. Maddie hated thinking it, but she'd actually felt relief when the girl had passed out, her head slumped against Jason's shoulder, a long thread of drool running down her chin and wetting his T-shirt.

They'd left then, after watching Jason tuck his girlfriend in, rolling her on her side and leaving a full water bottle by her head. This apparently wasn't a new routine for him. Good that Abigail had found a sweet boyfriend. Maddie prayed the girl would be back on her feet in the morning because she didn't actually want to have to explain Abigail's absence to Kris. That woman scared her.

"So, he just went apeshit on the coach's car?" Chelsea asked. Maddie had told her Tommy's story the second they'd gotten out of earshot of the boys, and it had taken her friend a while to process it all.

"That's what he said." Maddie nodded.

"Wow."

The two lapsed into silence then, their footsteps the only sound as they walked through the forest.

"It's kinda scary, isn't it?"

The thought had churned in Maddie's head for the last hour. She couldn't decide how she felt about the whole thing.

"I mean, scary that he lost his temper like that and got so . . . violent."

The word sounded heavy coming out of her mouth. Maybe too extreme. And a bit damning. But how else could she describe it? It *was* scary. *And* violent.

"Yeah," Chelsea thought about it. "But it's not like he was swinging the bat at someone else. Like, then it'd be *really* scary."

"Mmm," Maddie agreed, but not with much enthusiasm.

"You know how boys can be." Chelsea picked up her thought. "All that testosterone. It can mess with their heads. It doesn't mean he's a bad guy. Just that he had a bad day."

Maddie could tell her bestie was trying to downplay the whole incident, and she knew exactly where Chelsea was going with it.

"I'm *not* into Tommy," Maddie stated plainly.

Chelsea stopped and turned to Maddie.

"You sure about that?"

"Positive." Maddie rolled her eyes. "I was just trying to forget about Caleb. About my face-palm of a pickup line with him."

"You know," Chelsea wasn't letting it drop, "it's okay if you like Tommy Meyers. You could do a whole lot worse."

"Worse than a felon?" It sounded so bad coming out of Maddie's mouth. "Who in their right mind would crush on a guy who's gotten arrested?"

"I mean, I'm head-over-heels for my best friend's brother...who also happens to have a girlfriend," Chelsea admitted. "So what if Tommy got arrested? That doesn't mean he's a bad person. And that doesn't mean you can't crush on him if you want."

"I don't have a thing for Tommy Meyers," Maddie said again.

"I'm not saying you do. I'm just saying that you could—in theory—and it would be okay. I mean, it even sounds like he's remorseful and dealing with it and all."

"But it's *Tommy Meyers.*" Did Maddie really have to spell it out? "As in the boy who once had us at each other's throats."

Chelsea only shrugged as if she'd seen it all before. They'd buried that fight a long time ago.

"I don't have a crush on him," Maddie said one last time.

"Fine. Fine." Chelsea threw her hands up. "I get it. You don't like Tommy Meyers."

Maddie sighed.

"But just know that if you do start liking him"—Chelsea had to get in the last word—"I'm 100 percent here for it."

Maddie rolled her eyes.

"You done now?"

Chelsea smiled innocently, and Maddie couldn't help smiling back. The girls started walking again, chattering away. They were so distracted that they didn't even notice the eerie shadows springing up around them, the trees creating tall and hulking figures beneath Maddie's flashlight beam. They didn't stop and worry about invisible eyes peering out at them from the cover of dark. For maybe the first time that week, they felt at ease. Safe. Not the least bit frightened.

And then, out of nowhere, something banged in the night.

Maddie stopped and Chelsea nearly tripped over her. Maddie quickly said "Shh" and motioned for her to listen. Then, feeling brave, Maddie flipped off her flashlight and dragged Chelsea into the dark forest. She was tired of being afraid of every little thing that went bump in the night.

She moved slowly, picking her way through the underbrush. The moon was hidden behind a cloud, but her eyes had adjusted somewhat to the dark. She could make out roots and leaves on the ground, but only those directly in front of her. She focused all her attention forward, knowing that if she chanced a glance over her shoulder at her reluctant best friend, she'd lose her resolve and turn back.

Every few seconds, Maddie paused to make sure she could still hear the rustling. It had gotten louder. Whatever it was wasn't worried about staying hidden. Maddie pressed on. They were close.

A moment later, a grunt punctuated the night and Maddie froze. Another grunt. It sounded human.

She peered ahead and saw a faint glow. She kept moving. Slower now. Creeping through the underbrush. She knew what was happening, but she didn't know who.

A little clearing opened up in the trees just ahead. They were almost there. Maddie sneaked behind a big tree trunk and listened.

It wasn't just grunts and rustling now. She could make out a low murmuring, too, someone whispering a frenzy of out-of-breath words.

"I'm so sorry. I'm so so so so sorry. I was just so angry. And so jealous. The way he had his hands all over you. I couldn't take it."

"Shut up, Mark."

Maddie's heart leaped into her throat as she recognized the second voice. She edged her head around the tree trunk. She knew what she'd see, but she needed to confirm it.

A lantern sat on the ground in the little clearing, illuminating everything—Mark with Maddie's aunt Julie, both naked, her aunt's back pinned against a tree trunk.

Maddie heard Chelsea gasp, but even as grossed out as Maddie was, she couldn't turn away. It was clear this wasn't a new thing. But how long had they been sleeping together?

Mark's grunts came louder as Julie's nails pressed into his back.

"You're such an idiot, Mark," she gasped. "But you're *my* idiot."

Maddie couldn't watch anymore. She turned and ran, pulling Chelsea along behind her, no longer caring if anyone heard them.

At that moment, the moon finally came out and the forest grew suddenly lighter. Maddie looked back, hoping that neither adult would see them.

That's when she saw something—a familiar glint in among the trees. But she turned back around quickly and kept going. She wanted to get as far away from her aunt's affair as quickly as possible.

As they made their way back, Maddie and Chelsea moved on autopilot, neither girl saying a word. Both were still in shock. Maddie's mind raced with the truth she'd stumbled upon. She wondered if anyone else knew. Was that why her uncle had been so quick to throw down with Mark earlier? She wished she hadn't seen anything at all.

When they arrived in camp, everything was still, everyone asleep in their tents. The fire crackled softly, its embers almost dead. Maddie started when she saw Caleb still up, sitting quietly next to the dying flames, working away at his knife. She didn't say anything to him, though, as she and Chelsea slid past and into their tent.

The two girls climbed into their sleeping bags and exchanged one last look before turning in for the night, their look saying it all—that they'd never tell anybody about what they'd just seen.

SIXTEEN

THERE WAS A CRISPNESS TO THE air as Maddie came out of her tent the next morning, her legs buzzing with energy. Sleep had helped dull the shock of what she'd stumbled upon the night before, but the whole scene—Julie and Mark's naked bodies—still disturbed her. She couldn't quite shake the image of Mark's butt.

Luckily, she had spotted a new trail the day before, one she was excited to tackle now. A hard run would definitely help clear her mind.

Bending over to stretch a little, Maddie pulled out her iPod and began scrolling through her playlists. But before she could pick one, a shout came from the other side of camp. A second later, Mark's splotched face appeared.

If anything, he looked worse than he had the night before. Sleep hadn't helped clear his red-rimmed eyes or flatten his scraggly mess of hair. It also didn't help that he only had on a pair of boxer shorts and a shirt that'd come completely unbuttoned, revealing his disturbing paunch.

"Who did this?" Mark spun around in a circle, looking for someone to blame. Only Maddie, Caleb, and Charlie were around, though. Everyone else was still asleep. "This isn't funny. Who's responsible?"

"What the hell are you complaining about now?" Uncle Ed came out of his tent, fully dressed. Aunt Julie appeared right behind him, staying a few steps back from her husband. "Some of us were enjoying a quiet morning."

"It was you, wasn't it?" Mark pointed his finger and leaped toward Ed. "You trying to get back at me for last night? Punching a drunk man wasn't enough?"

"What are you talking about?" Ed grabbed the accusing finger and shoved it away.

"Don't play dumb."

As he said this, Mark finally pointed to what he meant. Maddie followed his finger and gasped. There, splashed onto the side of his tent, plain as day and red as blood, were two lightning bolts—a pair of antlers.

"This your idea of a joke?" Mark spit the question at Ed, but the other man didn't reply.

No one spoke for a good minute. They all remembered Caleb's story from the night before. Maddie turned toward the guide and tried to read his face, but Caleb had on a stony expression.

"You." Mark's attention turned to Caleb. "This was *your* story. Did you do this?"

Mark stared at Caleb, almost daring him to deny it.

"No," Caleb finally answered. "And I made that story up. The Mountain People aren't real."

The guide's eyebrows crinkled inward, as if it pained him to admit the truth. But Maddie could see the immediate relief as Mark's shoulders loosened.

"It must have been one of the kids playing a prank on you," said Kris, who had scrambled out of her tent after her husband's outburst, throwing out a theory that Mark happily latched on to.

"Yeah. Yeah. Must have been. But which one?"

He spun around and eyed his own two daughters first. They'd just pulled themselves out of their tent, and neither looked pleased. Maddie was surprised but thankful to see Abigail there, rumpled but standing on two feet.

"It wasn't us, Dad," Abigail snarled, her patience razor thin. Maddie imagined she must have a pretty bad hangover.

Mark turned to Bryan and Maddie next, but both of them just shook their heads.

"It's not blood, is it?" Aunt Julie had gotten closer to the tent and was eyeballing the antlers. She reached out her hand in curiosity.

"Don't touch it!" Mark lunged forward and snatched her hand away. "It might be diseased."

"Well, if it's ketchup, we'll know it's just a prank." Aunt Julie twisted out of Mark's grip.

"And if it's animal blood . . ."

Mark took off his shirt and draped it over the antlers.

"I'll clean it up," he announced. He eyed everyone, unembarrassed by his bare, flabby torso. "Just—no one touch it."

And then he disappeared back into his tent, leaving everyone else a bit confused in his wake.

"You kids didn't do this, did you?" Maddie's dad asked gently as he looked at his son.

"Wasn't us, Dad," Charlie replied breezily. Then he took Dylan by the hand and pulled her away toward the lake as the rest of the group broke up.

Maddie didn't know what to think. The appearance of the antlers was certainly odd. In Caleb's story they had been ominous—a threat. Had Abigail gotten the boys to prank her own dad? It seemed like something right up Jason's alley, just like the claw marks on that tree.

"He probably did it himself." Maddie's ears pricked up as she overheard her uncle grumbling. "Probably wanted sympathy points or something. He's a twisted man."

"Oh, stop that," Julie chastised her husband. "Why would Mark do a silly thing like that?"

"Why would he take a rifle into the woods and shoot a damn deer?"

Ed held nothing back. He looked at his wife, challenging her to disagree. Bryan rolled his eyes and walked away from his parents without a word.

"Where are you going?" Ed hollered after his son, but Bryan kept going without a reply. "Hey! I'm talking to you."

Ed started forward, his voice raised. His wife's hand shot up and pulled him back.

"Let him be."

"That boy needs to learn some respect. And he needs to man up."

Julie kept her mouth shut, but her hand stayed firmly on Ed's shoulder. After a minute she let him go and headed back to their tent. Ed stared after her, a weird look in his eye. Again, Maddie wondered if he knew—or maybe only suspected—what she'd seen in the woods the night before.

"What are you looking at?"

He'd caught her staring. She smiled and was thankful that he couldn't see inside her head.

"Just going for a run."

"Have you seen your dad around?" Ed changed the subject quickly.

Out of the corner of her eye, Maddie caught a flash of her dad retreating toward the woods. She looked back at her uncle and shook her head.

"Well, if you see him, let him know that there's something I need to discuss with him."

"Okay." Maddie didn't know what that could be about, but she didn't really care. She gave her uncle a little wave and jogged off.

When she got to the edge of the clearing, she paused, pulling out her iPod again. She spun through her playlists. She wanted something upbeat, something that would dispel the morning's strange mood. She hummed to herself as she scrolled, until finally she found what she wanted—*Boy Bands*. That would do the trick. But just as she started off into a jog, a movement in the trees caught her eye. She squinted and there, just twenty-five yards away, she saw where her dad had sneaked off to. And he wasn't alone.

Maddie shuffled a few steps closer, and she could see Kris's disapproving frown. The woman didn't look happy as she listened to

Maddie's dad. Was this the word he'd wanted? The horse ride up the mountain seemed so long ago.

"Kris, you've got to help me out," her dad pleaded. "I don't have the money."

"You've always come up with it before." Kris's answer came out cold.

"It's different this time. I'm running on empty. I've already double-mortgaged the house. And I've got two kids to raise."

"Don't give me that," Kris snapped back. "I've got two kids. And Mark's useless ass might as well be a third. Yet I still manage to find the extra cash each month."

Maddie felt bad for listening. Even frightened. Was she about to hear something she didn't want to know?

"And you didn't see me getting a million-dollar payout from Linda's life insurance," Kris finished her point, thrusting her finger into Maddie's dad's shoulder for extra emphasis. "Where'd that money go?"

"You know it wasn't anywhere near that much," Maddie's dad snarled back, an animal cornered. "And most of what we did get went right into the funeral and—"

"You had plenty left over that you could have put away," Kris cut him off. "But instead, you got back into gambling. I thought you would have learned your lesson. I'm tired of your excuses."

"You try burying a wife—the mother of your children—"

"You can save the sob story, Mitch. We all lived through it. I lost my best friend, too, you know."

"Yeah. And you got her company after."

"Don't even start with that. I bought out your wife's share years ago. Fair and square. You got good money for it. Above market value."

"And what's that money doing for me now?"

"It's not my fault you spent it."

Their voices had risen to shouts. Maddie wished she could turn her ears off. She started backing away, one step at a time, praying the two adults wouldn't see her. But then, all of a sudden, Kris glanced her way.

Maddie didn't know what to do, so she turned away, ignoring Kris's anxious wave. She pretended to stretch, faked that she was so absorbed in her music—that wasn't actually playing through her earphones— that she hadn't even noticed Kris and her dad having a very apparent and heated argument.

Out of the corner of her eye she could see that Kris had given up on flagging her down and was talking to her dad again. Their voices were lower now, but Maddie could still hear every word.

"Please. Please." Maddie's dad sounded pathetic. Defeated. "Please help me out. Just this once."

"I'm sorry, Mitch. I can't." Kris sounded firm. "But talk to him. I'm sure Ed will understand."

Maddie's heart thumped. Why did her dad owe Uncle Ed money?

"No. You're right," Kris responded to Mitch's harrumph of disbelief. "But maybe he'll give you an extension."

"Thanks for nothing."

Maddie's dad grimaced as if Kris had punched him in the gut. He pushed past her and walked deeper into the forest. He looked like he had some serious thinking to do. Kris turned and watched him go. After a moment, she headed back toward camp.

Maddie couldn't move. Her father's words echoed in her head.

They were poor.

Broke.

Penniless.

She tried, but couldn't shake the depressing revelation.

So she hit play on her iPod and bolted into the forest.

SEVENTEEN

THE MILES BLURRED BY, DISAPPEARING UNDER Maddie's flying feet along with the thoughts about her father—the argument, the worries, the things she'd overheard that she wished she hadn't. It was one of the reasons she loved running. She could disconnect from the world, unplug her brain and the negative thoughts churning away there.

It was a motion honed over years of drills and thousands of miles. Perfected so that when she ran she felt weightless. Her thoughts gone. Her body flying. Her brain high on endorphins.

She focused on her breathing, on her body's rhythms as she pumped her arms. She felt the familiar burn of exertion, the wind whipping her hair back. Her heart pounded, letting her know that she was alive and well. That she was powerful. As her feet hit the ground, her worries flew up and scattered in the wind. She wished she could feel this way all the time.

She rounded a tree on the other side of the lake and made her way back. She could feel her body tiring, but she didn't slow down. The pain drove her forward. She pushed along the last stretch of shoreline and then plunged back into the forest. She had only a quarter of the trail left—just under three miles.

Around her the trees crowded in, their trunks swishing by like she was riding in a car, counting the streetlight poles as they whizzed by. Out of the corner of her eye she saw something stir and then spring away in a hurry.

She wondered what it could have been as she continued on.

Her father? A bear? Another deer?

It came back to her then. In one flash. The blank stare in the deer's eyes. Blood seeping from a fresh curve drawn along its neck.

She picked up her pace, trying to push the image out of her head.

But it stuck with her. And then changed. She imagined opening a blue cooler and seeing a deer's severed head grinning maniacally up at her. Then it was her father's head. Uncle Ed appeared next, holding a knife, asking her for the debt her dad hadn't been able to pay.

She sped up again, careening through the trees now. She weaved through the forest like a downhill skier. She'd never gone so fast.

But she couldn't outrun her thoughts.

The image shifted again. Charlie looked up at her now, his eyes hollow, a pair of red, angry antlers slashed across his forehead.

No. Not Charlie. She didn't know what she'd do without him.

Her foot caught on a root and Maddie faltered. She tried to keep from falling face-first on the path, but she was too late. Gravity won. She lost her footing and pitched forward. She hit the ground hard and kept rolling.

The world spun around her, made her sick with dizziness. Instinct took over as she pulled her arms in to cover her head, tucking her legs under her the best she could. She tumbled another few feet and came to a stop, splayed there on the ground like a monster had just chewed her up and spit her out.

She lay there, her chest heaving, not daring to move. Her legs hurt, but maybe that was just from the run.

Slowly, Maddie lifted her head and peered down at her feet. She wiggled her toes and was happy to see them respond. She rotated her ankles. She bent one knee and then the other. Both legs ached, but they moved without a hitch. Everything seemed to be in working order.

She pulled herself upright and noticed the blood trickling down her right leg. She nervously wiped her knee, but it was only a shallow scrape under the dirt and blood. Nothing a Band-Aid couldn't fix. She tilted her head back and breathed an exhausted sigh.

She sat like that for a while, clutching her knees, trying to steady her breathing. Her heart pounded loud and fast in her ears. The fright of crashing into the earth had scared every other thought out of her head. She closed her eyes and let herself calm down. After a few minutes, she felt normal again. She got to her feet and looked around. Which way was camp?

Nothing looked particularly familiar, but she didn't think she'd strayed from the path, so she picked a direction and started walking. Ahead of her the path split suddenly. She didn't remember the fork, but then she had been running the opposite way earlier. She stopped and peered down each path. They looked the same to her.

Damnit. She hadn't gotten lost, had she?

She chose the left one. The lake was on that side. If she found it, she could find camp.

She walked slower now, scanning ahead in hopes of spotting something familiar. Then something caught her eye, off to one side of the path. Maddie got closer and bent down to examine it.

It was a boot. But how did someone forget their boot in the woods? Her mind flashed back to the night before—to Mark and Aunt Julie.

That was one way.

She picked it up. It was sticky with mud. She peered through the underbrush. Maybe she could find its missing partner.

Sure enough, about twenty feet away she saw the other boot poking out from behind a large tree trunk. She stepped off the path and made her way to it.

She didn't know why, but something didn't feel right. She looked at the boot in her hand and then at the one lying on the ground just ahead. A chill ran up her spine. She remembered the campfire stories from the past two nights. The terrible things that could happen in the woods.

Maddie shook the feeling off. Why was she being so paranoid? She kept going, focused on the boot. She got to the tree and bent down. She took hold of the boot and pulled, but it didn't budge. She tried again but only managed to lift it a few inches. Something was weighing it down. She turned and looked behind the tree.

A scream clawed its way up her throat and crashed through the woods. She screamed again and again. But no matter how loud she wailed, she'd never wake the bloody corpse lying in front of her.

EIGHTEEN

MADDIE BLINKED. THEN BLINKED AGAIN, PRESSING her eyes closed for ten full seconds. She had to be seeing things. But when she opened her eyes, it was still there in front of her. It wasn't a dream or her imagination or some post-run delirium.

It wasn't ketchup.

She gasped and dropped the boot. Blood stained her fingertips. She wiped her hand frantically against her shorts and then looked back down at the dead man.

His face was blanched white in the places that weren't covered in blood. His head was still attached to his body, thank God, but someone had sliced his neck open, a stroke that reminded Maddie of how Caleb had put that deer out of its misery the day before.

And then on his forehead—the antlers. The jagged lines had been carved carefully, a perfect match to the ones that had appeared on his tent that morning.

Mark.

Who could have done this to him?

Behind her, Maddie heard someone crashing through the trees. She spun around and there was Caleb, red-faced and out of breath. She ran into his arms and hugged him tight, forgetting about the night before, her bombed pickup line. She buried her head in his chest, warm tears trickling down her cheeks and staining his shirt.

"I heard your scream and got here as fast as I could." Caleb returned Maddie's hug. "Are you all right? What happened?"

"I—I—" Maddie couldn't speak. She took a deep breath and tried again. "I found him . . . after my run."

Caleb looked over her shoulder and saw Mark's body propped up against the tree. He pressed her head deeper into his shoulder, hugging her tighter. Maddie's whole body trembled in his arms. The shock was wearing off, and terrible thoughts were rushing into her brain.

What had happened to Mark? How much had he suffered? When had he been killed? And most importantly, who could have done it?

There was more commotion, and Charlie emerged from the trees, followed closely by Maddie's father. Dylan, Ed, and Bryan were right behind them.

"Oh, my God," Ed had spotted Mark first.

"Dad?" Dylan uttered in disbelief. She mumbled it again. And then shrieked it the third time. Charlie grabbed her as her legs collapsed underneath her. He set her on the ground gently and held her tight. He covered her eyes and murmured something in her ear.

"What happened?" Maddie's dad was the first to speak.

"Maddie found him." Caleb spoke for Maddie without loosening his grip on her.

"Are those—antlers?" Ed had inched closer to the body.

Bryan pushed his glasses up on his nose and peered in after his father. "I think so."

"Just like in—" Maddie's dad eyed Caleb in disbelief.

"My story." Caleb finished the thought for him.

"But you said—you said this morning that that wasn't real." There was accusation in Ed's voice.

"It isn't," Caleb confirmed.

"But the antlers on his tent," Maddie's dad sputtered. "And now this—"

"How do you explain it?" her uncle demanded.

"I can't."

"You can't?" Ed raised his voice. "It's *your* story. You're the only one who *can* explain it."

"Look." Caleb let Maddie go and turned on Ed. "I'm as much in the dark here as you. The Mountain People, that's just a stupid legend that you hear around the campfire all the time."

"So that means it could be real." Charlie joined the conversation, still holding on to a weeping Dylan.

"No," Caleb said, though there was less certainty in his voice now. "They can't possibly be—"

"Aren't most legends based on some nugget of truth?"

There was a weirdly optimistic note in Maddie's dad's voice. Faint, but there. They hadn't run into a soul out here in the woods. If the Mountain People didn't exist—well, then one of Mark's fellow campers had to be the murderer. And no one wanted to think about that possibility.

"We've got to get out of here."

Dylan spoke so softly that no one even heard her. She pushed away from Charlie's chest, a glazed look in her eye.

"We've got to get off this mountain!" She screamed it this time and everyone paid attention. "We've got to leave before they do the same thing to us!"

NINETEEN

FEAR RUSHED THEM THROUGH THE FOREST, Dylan's words echoing in their ears. Her frantic shrieks couldn't be forgotten. Someone had brutally murdered Mark. There was no getting around that. But no one paused to worry about who as they raced back to camp. If they thought about that, they'd have to admit that that *who* was still lurking out there somewhere. And that that *who* might just be one of their own.

Instead, they thought about survival. Of getting back to camp and calling for help on their emergency radio. It was their only way off the mountain. The tour company had taken the horses after the first day. The campers weren't supposed to have needed them for an entire week.

Breaking through the tree line into the clearing, they came upon an empty camp. A hook snagged Maddie's already pounding heart and wrenched it down into her stomach.

Where was everyone? And more importantly, where was Chelsea?

"Julie!" Maddie's uncle yelled for his wife. "Julie!"

Ed's shouts carried through the clearing, but his wife didn't immediately appear. That's when Dylan realized that her mom and sister were also missing.

"Mom! Abigail!" Dylan shrieked. Her desperate cries cut through the morning air. She kept screaming over and over, her voice quickly growing hoarse. She sank to her knees, and tears streamed down her beet-red face.

"Where—where is everyone?" Maddie turned to Caleb.

The look that Caleb gave her told her everything she didn't want to believe. But before he could speak, a loud metallic clang interrupted him.

It clanged again, getting closer, and everyone spun around to see Julie and Kris sprinting up from the lake. Between them they carried the big metal pot they'd made dinner in the previous night.

"What? What's the matter?" Julie huffed, seeing everyone's concerned faces. "Is everything okay?"

"Is Chelsea with you?" The words flew out of Maddie's mouth. Her aunt cocked her head to one side and looked at her oddly. Maddie thought she would explode if her aunt didn't answer her right that second.

"She's right behind us," Julie said.

And then Chelsea appeared, carrying a stack of plates. Maddie rushed to her best friend and threw her arms around her. She didn't care about the plates clattering to the ground or about how silly she might look. Chelsea was okay. That was all that mattered.

"What's gotten into you?" Chelsea yelped, taken by surprise and nearly falling over under Maddie's crushing hug. But before Maddie could respond, Kris's voice brought everything crashing back down around them.

"Where's Mark? He hasn't gone and shot something else, has he?"

Tension clogged the air. Not a single person laughed as Kris had expected. Instead, the adults all looked at one another, as if drawing telepathic straws on who would have to break the terrible news.

"Kris," Maddie's dad took a hesitant step toward her. He had his arms out in comfort, so different from what Maddie had witnessed just an hour ago.

A worried stitch creased between Kris's eyebrows as she started to realize that something was up.

"What's this about? Where's Mark? Did something happen to him?"

Maddie's dad hesitated. He shot an unsure look at Ed and Caleb. How did one deliver this kind of news?

"He's dead, Mom." Dylan blurted out the truth. "Dad's dead."

"Oh, honey. Don't be silly. Your dad's not—"

"He is! I saw it. His throat—there was blood everywhere—and antlers—" Dylan couldn't get it out fast enough.

Kris's hand flew to her mouth. Her eyes cast around the group, bewildered, until they finally landed on Maddie's dad.

"No," she muttered in disbelief. She tried to laugh it off as another prank. "Mark's not—no. That's silly. He can't be."

"I'm sorry, Kris." Maddie's dad's voice was somber, and Kris finally understood.

"But—but—" she stuttered. "How? Did he fall? Was it a bear?"

"Someone—someone—" Maddie couldn't imagine how hard this

was for her father. "Someone killed him. They slit his throat—and the antlers—the antlers from Caleb's story—they were there on his forehead."

Kris couldn't speak. Her mouth fell open and her eyes got far away and blank.

"I'm so sorry, Kris." Maddie's dad approached her slowly and put his arms around her. Kris stood there in his embrace for a moment, but then she squirmed. She pushed out of his grip in a hurry, anxiously patting at her hair as her eyes flitted around the group.

"I'll check the radio," Ed said, clearly uncomfortable. He took off toward the equipment shed.

"Good," Caleb said. "Leave a message with the park rangers. Let them know what's happened. They'll send help. Everyone else, get to packing. It shouldn't take them long to get here."

Everyone scrambled into action. Maddie watched as Kris pulled Dylan into a fierce hug. Tears ran down both of their cheeks. Maddie turned away quickly. She couldn't watch. But she couldn't block out their pitiful, sad crying.

In front of her, Aunt Julie looked just as torn up even though she didn't weep aloud. It was almost worse, though, this silent display of grief.

Caught between two mourning families, Maddie didn't know what to do. She should probably help her dad pack. But as she turned to go, the equipment shed door banged open and her uncle rushed out. A panicked look obscured his face, and he had something black and mangled cradled in his arms. It looked like he'd picked up some kind of roadkill, with fuzz and guts spilling out everywhere.

Of course, it wasn't an animal at all. But their radio. Someone had smashed it to pieces.

Ed looked stunned. His mouth hung open, but no words came out. One by one, they all turned and looked at him, as if sensing the moment, drawn to the devastating blow. They dropped their backpacks, hands flew to their mouths, and panic welled up behind their eyes as they realized what the mangled radio in Ed's hands meant.

They were stranded. Stranded on the mountain with a killer.

But before anyone could let this new fear loose, Kris's voice pulled them all back.

"Where—where's Abigail?"

Everyone turned from the broken radio and stared at Kris. She still had Dylan pulled close to her with one arm, but where was her other daughter?

"She wasn't here with you?" Maddie's dad asked. Kris shook her head frantically and then rushed over to Abigail's tent, clawing the flaps open. The girl wasn't inside. Kris turned back around, desperation in her eyes.

"I think," Chelsea swallowed as everyone turned to look at her. "I think I saw her walking into the woods. Maybe ten minutes ago."

"By herself?"

"Well, I think—I think she might have—" Chelsea faltered under Kris's frantic gaze.

"Jason's here," Maddie jumped in. Kris only blinked at her, though, as if she didn't recognize the name.

"He and one of his friends followed us up here," Maddie tried to explain. "They set up camp about a half-mile away. Abigail's probably sneaked off to see them."

This, Kris seemed to get. She blinked, and her eyes regained their focus. Her lips returned to their familiar stern set.

"Well, why are we standing around?" The edge was back in her voice. "Let's go find my daughter and get off this godforsaken mountain."

TWENTY

"I THINK IT'S THIS WAY," MADDIE said uncertainly, turning back to look at everyone else. "Or maybe…"

She stopped and tried to get her bearings. She spun around, but all she saw were trees, trees, and more trees. None of which looked particularly familiar.

A dull ache started knocking on her forehead. She felt frustrated. She couldn't think straight. It would have been hard enough to retrace her steps to the boys' camp, but then throw in Mark's grisly, lifeless body *and* the fact that someone had intentionally stranded them on the mountain…Maddie was lucky she could walk at all, much less lead everyone back to Tommy and Jason's camp.

But they needed to get to the boys—for more reasons than just finding Abigail. When Ed had discovered their radio smashed, they'd all whipped out their cell phones and tried in vain to get a signal. One bar and any one of them could have called down for rescue.

But they'd all come up empty.

Now, the boys' radio was their only hope, the only way they could alert the police, get someone up to help them before...before it was too late for them all.

Maddie didn't want to think about it, but she couldn't ignore the reality.

They were stranded, days away from civilization. Someone had murdered Mark and probably had more in mind for them. Why else smash their radio? The killer had to have a plan. And he wasn't done yet.

Maddie shivered at the thought. Was he out there right now? Watching them? Enjoying his game of cat and mouse? Who would he come for next?

The thoughts swirled above Maddie's head like vultures. They were dead if they couldn't get off the mountain, if she couldn't get them back to the boys' camp. She spun around again, but still, nothing looked familiar. Her head throbbed. She wanted to scream.

"I think it was this way."

Maddie nearly jumped out of her skin as Chelsea placed a warm hand on her shoulder and pointed through the trees.

"Th-thank you," Maddie whispered, feeling instantly better. She'd forgotten she still had her best friend by her side. Her sister, even if they weren't related by blood. They'd been through so much together. She reached up and gave Chelsea's hand a reassuring squeeze. Then she started walking again, leading the way.

A few minutes later, Maddie felt a wave of relief. She finally recognized something—the tree Tommy had been leaning against as he'd spilled his guts to her the night before. The one she'd almost kissed him under. Maddie picked up her pace. They were almost there.

"Tommy!" Maddie yelled the boy's name as she pushed through the trees ahead of everyone else. She opened her mouth to call for him again, but his name dropped off her tongue. Her mouth hung open as she took in the boys' camp—what was left of it.

She lunged forward, but someone threw their arms around her shoulders and pulled her back. She glanced up and saw her father, his lips set in a grim line. She turned back to the camp, and a whimper escaped her. What her eyes hadn't wanted to believe at first slowly sank in.

The camp wasn't at all like it'd been the night before. Someone— or something—had come through and ravaged it. Like a hurricane. Or maybe a bear.

Strips of frayed fabric littered the ground, like someone had taken a shredder to the boys' sleeping bags. Their pillows had been gutted, too, the stuffing strewn out across the ground, a fine dusting of snow covering everything.

Only it hadn't been a white Christmas. Not entirely.

Here and there patches of red flared against the ground. The blood had splashed against the trees, too, in long and violent streaks, like a Jackson Pollock painting. It clung to the bark, soaked right into the canyons of what looked like fresh claw marks.

"Over here," Ed shouted. He'd lumbered into the camp when everyone else had stopped. "I think I found something."

He bent and pulled at a lifeless lump of rags lying on the ground.

The boys' makeshift tent. Someone had ripped it down and balled it up. Patches of blood covered it, too. Ed gave the sheet a firm tug and the whole thing came undone in one tumbling motion. Jason's body flopped out onto the ground.

Maddie turned away, but not before she saw his face—the three long marks running from his forehead down to his chin, red and clotted, the only color blemishing his now unnaturally pale cheeks. She gritted her teeth and tried to keep her scream inside. But a sob still broke through the forest. It took Maddie another moment to realize it wasn't hers.

Pulling away from her father's chest, Maddie saw Abigail curled up tightly against a tree, her head bent low, her hands pressed over her eyes and ears. She rocked slowly back and forth as she cried.

For the first time in a long time, Maddie felt sorry for the girl. She must have gotten to the camp just before them, must have stumbled onto all this and crumpled in on herself.

Would Maddie have done anything different if she had come across her boyfriend's body? Not that she had one. But if she did...

And then it hit her. Where was Tommy?

Her eyes flitted around the trashed campsite. She scanned the ground and the trees. There was so much blood everywhere. Could it have all come from Jason? Maddie knew the answer, but she didn't want to believe it until she had proof. She kept looking, searching for any sign, any little thing that would tell her Tommy was somehow, miraculously, still alive.

"Over here."

Maddie heard her brother's voice and, without thinking, pushed out of her dad's arms. He tried to pull her back, but she took off, sprinting through the camp, bloody fluff sticking to the soles of her running shoes. She made for Charlie's voice, hopeful.

When she saw Charlie crouched low to the ground, she knew what her brother had found. But she kept going, running the whole way to him. She had to see for herself.

"He's gone," Charlie said quietly. A body lay at his feet, facedown, its limbs twisted to the side. Charlie's fingers pressed into the body's neck where there was no longer a pulse to take.

"It can't be," Maddie whimpered, knowing how pathetic she sounded but not caring. Because she didn't need to see the boy's face to know it was Tommy. She recognized his close-shaven head, the cut-off Giants T-shirt. She bent down and stretched out her hand.

"Don't," Charlie stopped her from flipping the body over.

"But—" Maddie started.

"It's nothing you want to see." Charlie cut her off gently, pulling her shoulders around and leading her back toward camp. "Trust me."

Maddie glanced back at the body one last time, lying so still, as if Tommy were only sleeping. But the blood told a different story.

A sharp pain squeezed her chest. Guilt, Maddie realized. He'd had a crush on her and she'd known it. She'd used him for the attention, to make herself feel better about Caleb. And now he was dead. She felt bad for not letting him kiss her. He'd waited five years for a second chance. Maddie would have let him kiss her ten times—no, fifty, Funyuns-breath and all—if only he were still alive.

She turned away from Tommy's body and tried to push the bitter thoughts out of her head.

"Come here for a second." Charlie bent down, pulling Maddie's face toward his, making sure their eyes locked. "I'm going to protect you. You know that, right?"

Maddie sniffed and then nodded.

"But you have to promise me something," Charlie went on. "Promise me that you'll do whatever I say. If I tell you to run, you run. No matter what. You save yourself. When you run, no one can catch you. Got it?"

Maddie nodded again.

"Promise me."

"I promise," Maddie said, and Charlie pulled her in for a hug.

"I'm not going to let anything happen to you, I swear."

"I know," Maddie mumbled into his ear. Because she did know. Charlie had always protected her. He'd never let her down. Not once.

"Did you find anything?"

Maddie lifted her head, but her father had meant the question for her uncle.

"Nothing," Ed huffed. He went back to kicking through the debris, and Maddie realized he was looking for the radio.

After another five minutes of searching, they had to give in to the sobering fact that the radio wasn't there. And neither was the boys' ATV. They wouldn't be getting the help they so desperately needed. They'd have to hike down the mountain on foot, a trek that would take them a couple of days.

As Maddie glanced around the bloody campsite, she saw her father standing nervously with Charlie, her aunt and uncle pulling Bryan in close to them and Kris cradling an emotionally spent Abigail while Dylan hovered at her shoulder. Caleb and Chelsea stood off to one side, looking lost and worried, the outsiders.

But in that moment, separated as they were, Maddie knew that the same thought ran through all of their heads.

Did they have any chance at surviving the two-day trip down the mountain?

TWENTY-ONE

MADDIE'S BACK ACHED FROM CARRYING HER pack. They'd been walking all day. Her swollen feet groaned with soreness. Her shirt and shorts had fused to her slender body, sweat dripping off her in disgusting streams.

But they couldn't let up, not with a killer somewhere out there. Everyone had seen Jason and Tommy's camp, their bloody, broken bodies. Another story come to life. Caleb had warned them about telling scary stories under a full moon.

But that was only a joke. This was—this was very real. Someone was after them, and no one wanted to see what the killer would do next. They had to keep moving. They had to stick together. They had to watch each other's backs.

Caleb led the way, while Maddie's dad and uncle brought up the rear. They moved in a tight line, Maddie next to Chelsea. Ahead of them, Kris and Julie walked carefully. In Mark's absence, they'd taken up his anxiousness. Their heads swiveled around like gyroscopes, frantically searching the woods for any threat.

Except it wasn't a mountain lion or bear they were looking for, but an altogether different type of killer. A smarter one. More cunning and cruel than any wild animal.

He had to be out there watching them. Following them. Waiting for his chance to strike.

Watching the two women gave Maddie a headache. Their paranoia was contagious. And the last thing she needed right now was a reason to be even more terrified. Instead, she glanced back and saw Abigail ambling along behind her. The girl moved unsteadily, like a zombie wandering through the woods. She walked quietly, though, absorbed in her thoughts, mindlessly following the leader. She wore a numb expression, the blank stare and slack jaw of shock. The red-rimmed and puffy eyes of someone completely cried out. Every few minutes Maddie would hear a sniffle and then a whimper. She'd always disliked Abigail, but now she felt sympathy for her fellow half-orphan. Abigail didn't have anyone she could talk to. Maddie nudged Chelsea and slowed her pace, falling back alongside Abigail. Chelsea got the hint and moved to the girl's other side.

"How are you doing?" Maddie asked, keeping her voice low.

Abigail turned her head slowly and stared Maddie down.

"How do you think I'm doing?"

Maddie flinched, as if Abigail had smacked her in the face. But she remembered her first few days in the hospital all those years ago—her own hostility—and she leaned back in, ready to try again.

"I—I'm sorry," Abigail said, beating Maddie to the punch. Her face fell and she awkwardly dropped her head to stare at the ground.

"It's okay." Maddie gingerly placed a hand on the girl's shoulder. "I know it's hard. I've been there, too."

Abigail looked up, and there was a glint of recognition in her eye.

"I almost forgot," she mumbled. "About your mom, I mean."

Maddie nodded, actually relieved that Abigail had forgotten. Maddie had always feared that her mother's accident would define her.

"How do you do it?" Abigail asked. "How do you get through each day without her?"

Maddie paused and thought about it. How *did* she do it?

"I guess—I guess I just keep running." Maddie knew it didn't make much sense. But it was true. Abigail still had a dazed look, though, so Maddie scrambled to find the right words.

"What I mean is—I—I just keep going. Sure, I still think about my mom every single day, and I miss her like crazy and wish she was still here. But I don't let her absence get in my way. I know she'd want me to live my life. So that's what I do."

It felt right as it came out of her mouth. But there was something Maddie had forgotten.

"Some days, though—some days still seem unbearable. Some days I need help. But that's why I surround myself with people I love. With people who love me."

Maddie's eyes flitted to Chelsea as she said this. Her best friend had gotten her through the worst moment in her life. She didn't know what she would have done if Chelsea hadn't appeared in her hospital room all those years ago.

"People who I'd fight the world to protect and who would do the same for me."

She thought of Charlie this time.

"I want you to know that you're not alone," Maddie went on. "We might have had our issues—but I'm here for you. I'll always be here for you. Chelsea, too."

Chelsea nodded and quickly placed her hand on Abigail's other shoulder. Between them, Abigail sniffed. A fresh set of tears leaked from her eyes.

"Thanks," she said, her voice nasally and wet. She took another moment to compose herself. "I'm sorry I've always been such a bitch."

"That's all in the past," Maddie waved it away and leaned her head against Abigail's shoulder.

It'd always been Maddie and Chelsea against the world. Ever since that day in the hospital. But now, as the three girls walked, their arms linked together, Maddie realized it'd be the three of them. Tragedy had just given them another sister.

"Everyone, hold up," Caleb called back to the group. They stopped, confused. "This is as far as we're going today."

"Are you crazy?" Kris's voice sounded shrill. She clenched her pack tighter around her shoulders as if it could protect her. "The sun's still up."

"We've got to make camp while we still can," Caleb explained. "We've got to get ready for the night."

"The night?" Julie didn't understand. "You don't expect us to sleep, not with whoever's out there trying to kill us."

"We need to rest," Caleb tried to reason with them. "Tomorrow's gonna be another long day."

"But—" Julie still couldn't grasp it.

"It'll be okay, honey." Ed placed his meaty hand on his wife's thin shoulder. "We'll set up a watch and take turns. No one's going to get us."

"Unless it's one of us who killed Mark."

Maddie barely caught the muttered accusation, and when she turned back to look at the others she couldn't tell who had said it.

"Right," Caleb said, taking the lead again. "We'll have a rotating watch. But first we've got to set up camp. Our tents can go over there. And there should be a stream nearby where we can fill our canteens and wash up. No fire tonight. And no flashlights. We can't risk giving ourselves away."

They stood frozen for a moment. No one wanted to be the first to move. It all felt like a really bad nightmare. Any second they'd wake up and Mark would be with them, freaking out about spotting bear tracks, which Caleb would examine and determine had actually been made by squirrels.

Maddie tried pinching her arm, but the painful sting only reminded her of their terrifying reality. She let her pack slide from her shoulders, and everyone got moving.

Her uncle and Bryan set to pitching the tents, while her aunt pulled out some cans of food to decide what'd make the best cold dinner. Caleb said he was going to the river, and Maddie decided she'd tag along. She needed to clean up. Her shoes were still covered in blood from Tommy's campsite.

As they set off, Charlie and Dylan joined them, along with Kris and Abigail. And then Maddie's dad. Maddie felt bad leaving Chelsea behind, but her best friend was tired and wanted to rest her feet.

As they walked out of camp, a sinking feeling punched Maddie in the stomach. She looked back at Chelsea sitting there on the ground, helping Julie go through the canned goods. Maddie couldn't help wondering if this would be the last time she'd see her best friend.

She turned back around and tried to shake the black thought out of her head.

Of course she'd see Chelsea again. They were both going to make it down this mountain *alive*. She kept this thought planted in her mind as she followed Caleb out of camp.

TWENTY-TWO

IT TOOK THEM A FEW MINUTES to find the stream, but once there, they spread out a bit along the bank and quickly knelt to fill their bottles and wash up. Maddie greedily gulped down the cool water. She hadn't realized how thirsty she was. She'd had no time to rest since finishing her run—since stumbling upon Mark's body. Her face felt grimy, her arms and legs sticky with dried sweat and maybe blood.

She didn't want to think about it. Instead, she pulled a bandana from her pocket and dipped it in the stream. As she wiped herself down, she listened to her dad and Kris talking. They sat a little downstream from her.

"Are you okay? I still can't believe that someone—" Maddie glanced up and saw the stricken look on her dad's face. "Well, just be glad you weren't there to see the body."

"Of course I'm not okay," Kris snapped back. "But I've got to be strong. For my girls."

Kris's gaze flitted upstream to where Abigail stared absently into the flowing water.

"They need me now more than ever. But you know what that's like."

"It's not easy."

The two adults fell silent and busied themselves with filling their water bottles.

"What I don't understand," Maddie's dad thought aloud, "is who could have done this. I mean, we don't really believe that these Mountain People exist, do we? Maybe it would make sense with Mark...but those boys—Abigail's friends—they didn't do anything to piss anyone off. Certainly not enough to—to—"

Her dad trailed off, unable to get the words out. But they buzzed in Maddie's head.

Words like *brutalized* and *dismembered*. *Gutted*. Words that were only ever used in horror movies and cop shows on TV. Not in real life. Certainly not in *their* real lives.

"But who else could it be?" Kris had taken a moment to respond. "One of us?"

It was clear that Maddie's dad didn't like the sound of that.

"I don't know. I guess. Maybe..."

Her dad looked at Kris expectantly. After a moment, Kris realized what he was asking.

"It wasn't me," she sputtered indignantly.

"Me neither."

The two relaxed. Then Kris picked up the conversation.

"How well do you know that guide? It was his story. Maybe he planned it from the beginning. He was pretty pissed when Mark shot that deer."

"But what about the boys? Did he even know they were up here?"

Kris shrugged, still thinking.

"Well, what about Ed?"

This seemed to resonate with Maddie's dad and he nodded as Kris went on.

"You know how he can be. That temper. I mean, he had Mark on the ground last night. Maybe that wasn't enough."

"Mmm," Mitch agreed. "I wouldn't put it past him. Especially with Mark and Julie sleeping together. A man like Ed—he wouldn't take that lying down."

A gasp spilled out of Maddie's mouth. She expected Kris to reach across and smack her dad across the cheek, but the woman's face only scrunched up in disgust as she nodded her head. So they had known. Maddie leaned in closer to make sure she didn't miss another word.

"My husband had his weaknesses," Kris admitted, the words clearly sour in her mouth. "At least if he was going to sleep with someone else's wife, he could have picked one whose husband wouldn't try to murder him."

Maddie's dad nodded absently, his mind still thinking.

"But that still leaves those kids."

"I don't know, Mitch," Kris said, exasperated. "I'm not a detective. Maybe he murdered them to scare us. Or to make sure we couldn't get help. Their radio was gone. And their ATV."

She rubbed her forehead and shut her eyes.

"What if..." her dad started, a new theory at work.

"What if we're trapped in some terrible, B-horror film come to life and there's a serial killer out there stalking us, waiting to pick us off one by one, probably tonight while we're all sleeping?" Kris finished, out of breath and panicky.

"It's not impossible," Mitch said grimly.

"Damnit, Mitch!" Kris let loose her frustrations. "Why'd you have to bring us up here? Why'd you have to get us all killed?"

Maddie's dad cleared his throat and stared out across the water. It took him a moment, but he finally answered Kris's question.

"Charlie wanted something special for graduation," he said quietly. "I thought it was the least I could do, getting everyone up here for one last trip together."

Mitch dropped his head and gazed into his lap.

"I'm sorry—I didn't mean that," Kris apologized, placing her hand on his shoulder. "I know what's happening isn't your fault."

"Isn't it?" Mitch said. Kris looked at him, a new, deeper fear rising in her eyes. "A bit like karma—"

"Shut up," she snapped. "Shut your mouth right this second. We swore never—"

"How are you holding up?" Caleb surprised Maddie, coming up next to her to fill his water bottle, and she missed the last words of Kris's conversation. She kept her gaze on Kris, though, watching as the woman jerked her bag up on her shoulder and then walked away from her father. Maddie wanted to scream. What had her father meant? And why had it spooked Kris like that? Did it have something to do with Ed and the money her dad owed him? They'd already argued about that once this weekend. Or maybe it had to do with the murders.

"I guess I'm okay." Maddie's voice came out rough and tired as she turned to face Caleb. "As good as can be expected."

"Don't lose hope," Caleb said, trying to lift her spirits. "The Mustang Maddie I know would never give up. She'd ride that horse to the end of the plains—"

Caleb cut off as a smile bubbled up on Maddie's lips. What she wouldn't give to go back to that first afternoon.

"You're gonna have one hell of a scary story for your next campfire—if we—" Maddie had tried to keep things light, but realized too late that she'd failed. Caleb's smile flitted away, his one dimple disappearing.

"We're going to get off this mountain," Caleb said, his face set, determined.

Maddie nodded, wanting to believe him, but finding it hard to in the face of everyone they'd already lost.

"Hey," Caleb said, pulling her back out of her grim thoughts. "I saved you once, and I promise, I'm going to keep you safe again."

Maddie stared into Caleb's blue eyes and saw them change, saw a steely gray wash over them.

"I know you will."

TWENTY-THREE

AS THEY WALKED BACK TO THEIR makeshift camp, Maddie couldn't stop her thoughts from racing. She couldn't get the image of Mark's lifeless body out of her head. And when she finally did, a picture of Jason and Tommy's shredded camp filled the void.

Blood and bodies.

She couldn't think of anything else. She was going to have a nervous breakdown.

"You okay?"

Her brother's voice penetrated Maddie's thoughts, a life buoy pulling her out of the black hole before it could crush her.

She snorted, even though there was nothing funny about Charlie's question. But how could she not laugh? What a ridiculous thing to ask.

Of course she wasn't okay. None of them were.

But what other way did he have to put it?

"I've been worse," Maddie replied. "How about you?"

"Same," Charlie agreed. He sounded tired.

"Actually, I have a question for you." Maddie winced as she remembered what Tommy had told her the night before. But she pushed through, trying to block out the boy's face, his broken body lying there on the ground. Maybe now wasn't the best time to ask, but she needed something to distract her. "Did you lose your baseball scholarship?"

Charlie's shoulders stiffened. His jaw clenched. Maddie thought he might freeze up like the Tin Man, but then he nodded. Once. Twice. And his shoulders slumped back down, his chin buried in his chest.

"It's nothing to be ashamed of," Maddie said quickly. "What happened?"

"They picked someone else to fill my spot."

"They can do that?"

"Apparently," Charlie said. "They told me I could try out in the fall, maybe get a walk-on spot. But I don't really see the point."

Maddie could see that Charlie didn't want to talk about this, but she pressed on anyway.

"Why didn't you tell me?"

Charlie shrugged.

"Does Dad know? Did you tell Dylan?"

"Dad knows," Charlie said. Was that a bitter note Maddie picked up in his voice? "But I haven't told Dylan yet, so don't say anything. Why would she want to stay with a college no-show."

"But you can still go to college—"

The words left Maddie's mouth before she realized they might be wrong. She'd never thought about money or not having it—until that morning. But now she knew they were poor. Or, at least, struggling. Maybe they couldn't afford to send Charlie to college.

"Just—don't worry about me," Charlie said. "And don't tell Dylan. This might be the last summer I have with her. I don't want to ruin it."

"Okay," Maddie said even though she didn't agree with him at all. She watched as Charlie sped ahead of her and caught up to his girlfriend. He slid his hand into hers and kissed her on the cheek.

Dylan wouldn't judge him for losing his scholarship. She wouldn't break up with him just because he couldn't afford to go to college. Would she?

When they got back to camp, the tents were all set up in tight rows. Maddie's aunt had pried open several cans of baked beans, each with a spoon sticking out of it. She'd also opened up a couple of bags of hot dog buns. Maddie's stomach grumbled. Dinner wouldn't be much, but at least it'd be food.

As they ate, gone was the chatter of the previous night. Everyone had closed ranks, each family circling up and casting a suspicious eye on everyone else.

Because who could they trust?

As much as Maddie wished it weren't the case, she knew the likelihood was that one of them had murdered Mark. And the boys.

Ed. Kris. Her dad. Even Caleb.

They were all suspects. They all had motives. And these people around her, these people who bullied their friends and had affairs—they were all capable of terrible things.

Her spoon scraped against the bottom of the can of beans and

Maddie looked down, surprised to see that she'd finished it. She looked over and saw that Chelsea had finished hers, too. Above them the sky had turned a bruised shade of purple. Night wasn't far away.

"Okay, we should be turning in soon." Caleb stood up, taking the lead again. "We need to set up a watch. I figure we should split into three shifts."

Bryan and Charlie volunteered to go first. Maddie's dad and Kris accepted the second shift alongside Caleb. And Aunt Julie and Uncle Ed said they'd take the last.

"Here." Caleb handed Mark's rifle over to Charlie. He'd made sure to grab it when they'd broken camp in the valley. "Do you know how to use it?"

Charlie looked uncertain.

"It's easy. The safety's here. Then just point and shoot. It'll give you a kick in the shoulder. But nothing you won't survive. It's already loaded."

Charlie took the gun. It weighed heavily in his hands.

"We'll wake you all in a few hours to switch out," Charlie muttered nervously.

"No flashlights. No loud noises," the guide reminded them all. He gazed out into the woods. Maddie felt the back of her neck prickle. Was someone watching them right now?

Charlie and Bryan nodded.

"Okay, everyone. Try and get some sleep. We've still got a lot of ground to cover tomorrow."

Maddie didn't think she'd get any sleep, but she followed Chelsea into their tent. The sun had almost disappeared below the horizon, and the stars were coming out. Maddie hovered at the tent flap and looked out into the woods one last time.

"It's going to be all right, Maddie." Charlie's voice surprised her. "I won't let anything bad happen to you. I promise."

"Thanks," Maddie mumbled. Even with her brother and Caleb looking out for her, she didn't feel so safe. She let the tent flap close and crawled into her sleeping bag.

TWENTY-FOUR

"PSST," MADDIE HISSED ACROSS THE DARK tent. "Are you still awake?"

A sleeping bag rustled, and Chelsea turned over to face her best friend.

"Yeah. I don't think I'll get any sleep."

"Me neither."

The two girls lapsed into silence. They could hear the crickets chirping outside, the soft murmur of voices and the rustling of a tent. It sounded like Charlie and Bryan had traded off watch. That meant it'd been, what—three, maybe four hours since they'd turned in? It seemed like an eternity. Maddie didn't know how she'd make it the whole night, especially if she couldn't sleep.

"Look, I wanted to tell you that—" Maddie began. She realized suddenly that this could be the last time she and Chelsea spoke. "That I'm sorry."

"Sorry?"

"Yeah. For inviting you on this trip. If it weren't for me, you'd be safe and sound in your own bed. Instead…who knows if we'll even make it off this mountain."

"I'd never want you to face this alone," Chelsea said, her voice low and warm. "You changed my life, too, you know. If it weren't for you, I'd be that same bitch who made your life miserable back in middle school. Hell, I'd probably be worse than Abigail."

They'd never talked about this before, though Maddie knew it all. Still, she perked up as Chelsea went on.

"But visiting you in the hospital that day—I don't even know why I went—but I'm so thankful I did. Getting to know you—it did more good than you'll ever realize."

"You changed my life, too." Maddie could feel her tears bubbling up. She wasn't going to cry, though. She didn't want to turn this into some sappy after-school special.

"And for the record," Chelsea went on in a firm, resolute voice, reaching out to take Maddie's hand and squeezing it hard, "we *are* going to get off this mountain. Look at everything we've already gotten through. Nothing has stopped us. We're survivors. Don't forget that."

Maddie nodded, squeezing her eyes shut. A few tears slid out and plopped against her sleeping bag. She let go of Chelsea's hands to wipe her eyes.

"You're right," Maddie squeaked out. "We'll fight to the end."

"Pinkie promise?"

Chelsea held her hand out, her littlest finger crooked. Maddie reached out and their fingers intertwined. A renewed strength welled up in Maddie. They weren't dead yet.

"Okay. We should probably try and get some sleep," Maddie said, reluctantly pulling her finger back from Chelsea's. "We're going to need it tomorrow."

Chelsea agreed and pulled her hand back, too. They stared at each other for another moment and then both rolled over in their sleeping bags.

"Good night," Chelsea said.

"Good night."

Maddie felt better as she closed her eyes. Safer. They'd never broken a pinkie promise to each other. Her shoulders relaxed and her breathing slowed. She began to dip into sleep. In and out, hovering along that fine line between the dream world and reality. Her head sank into her pillow and she was out. Still and peaceful.

TWENTY-FIVE

A SCREAM BROKE THROUGH THE NIGHT, long and shrill.

In her tent, Maddie jarred awake, her dreams shattered. She jolted up in her sleeping bag, a cold sweat breaking out over her entire body. Her heart pounded away in her chest. She felt like she'd just woken up from a nightmare. But she knew better. Her dreams had been a haven. She'd just woken up *into* the nightmare.

She scrambled out of her sleeping bag, relieved when she saw Chelsea doing the same next to her. At least her best friend was safe. But who was out there screaming? Maddie shoved her feet into her running shoes and rushed through the tent flap.

Chaos reigned outside, everyone struggling to get out of their tents, terrified. Ed had the rifle in his hands, nervously checking the safety over and over to make sure it was off.

"What was that?" Kris shouted as she came out of her tent. She had her flashlight in her hand and flicked it on. It lit up the night, falling on Julie first, her hands balled into tiny fists, her face flushed pink. "Did you see something? Why'd you scream?"

Julie's lips moved, but no sound came out.

"Spit it out," Kris yelled.

"It—it wasn't me."

Kris's face fell. She whipped around and stared at her daughters' tent. No one had come out of it yet. She took a quick step toward it but stopped when the zipper moved. Everyone got very quiet and watched as it slid down and Dylan tumbled out, her hair a tangled mess, her eyes big and worried.

"Mom," her wild eyes found Kris first, and everyone immediately knew what was coming next. "Abigail's gone."

"Gone where?" Kris asked, unable to process it.

Another scream tore through the night in answer.

No one waited for a discussion, to make a plan of action. Kris bolted into the forest first, Charlie a second later, heading in slightly different directions. Maddie dug her feet into the ground and then took off running, too, following after Charlie. She heard her father shouting at her to stop. That it wasn't safe. But she ignored him. She'd made a promise to Abigail that day. She'd never let Chelsea go without a fight, and she couldn't abandon Abigail now.

She tore blindly through the forest, praying she wouldn't trip on anything. She could hear Charlie's footsteps crashing through the underbrush ahead of her. She picked up her pace and tried to catch up to him.

Another scream carried through the trees, and Maddie corrected her course, plunging to the right. She felt a little like a bat, flying blindly through the night, using Abigail's cries as a guide.

Another scream and Maddie knew she was close. She slowed down and listened.

"Let her go!"

She heard her brother's voice and spun around in time to see him lunging at a figure hidden in the shadows. The two crashed to the ground and started wrestling. Maddie made a beeline for them, nearly running over a squealing Abigail in the process.

"We have to help him," Maddie shouted, desperate. But Abigail didn't listen. She didn't even slow down as she shot off in the opposite direction.

Maddie wasted a second watching her go, but a grunt pulled her back around. She saw her brother there sprawled on the ground, thrashing with the figure. The man wore all black. He even had a ski mask covering his face. But there was no mistaking the glint of metal as it flashed against the moonlight, the long hunting knife he held over her brother.

"No!" Maddie raced forward and shoved the man, using all her strength, every ounce of momentum. He stumbled backward and fell. Maddie immediately bent to help Charlie up. They had to get out of there. They couldn't defend themselves against that knife.

"Hurry," Maddie shouted, grabbing Charlie's hand, trying to pull him up. "We can outrun him."

"Maddie!" Charlie leaped up, wrapping his arms around his sister as he spun to put his body between hers and the attacker's.

Maddie yelped as she felt the blow. As the knife stabbed into Charlie, it pushed her back, almost sent her toppling over. Charlie gasped and let go of her. He turned and kicked at the attacker, managing to knock the man down at the knee but stumbling over in the process.

"Go!" he yelled. But Maddie couldn't move. She stood there, stunned, unable to lift her legs.

"Run!" he tried again, his voice weaker this time.

"I'm not leaving you," Maddie whimpered.

"It's too late." Charlie locked eyes with his sister. She knew that look, but she reached forward anyway. She pulled his face to hers, tried to get him up onto his feet. She'd drag him behind her if she had to. She couldn't go without him.

"You have to go *now*," Charlie said, pushing her hands away. Her fingers trailed through his hair and pulled his San Francisco hat off.

"But—but—" Maddie stammered.

Charlie wasn't listening to her, though. He'd staggered awkwardly to his feet, and turned to face the attacker. The man had recovered from the kick. He had his knife out, pointed dangerously at Maddie. It no longer flickered in the moonlight, though, as blood swam across the blade.

"Maddie," Charlie said between heaving breaths. "Remember what you promised. You have to run. You have to save yourself."

Maddie shook her head, not wanting to believe the words coming out of her brother's mouth. He smiled at her and touched his forehead in a final salute.

"I love you."

Then he turned back around and lunged at the attacker.

"No!" Maddie screamed.

But she didn't move. She couldn't. Tears streamed down her face as she watched Charlie fight—as she realized he was going to lose. She could hear it in his strained movements, his exhausted panting, how his feet crashed clumsily through the underbrush. Blood seeped from the wound in his back and pattered on the ground in drops like rain.

"Maddie," Charlie moaned, desperate, his jaw clenched as he held the attacker back. "Run."

And then she heard the heartrending groan, watched as her brother twitched and went slack. His head dropped and then his knees buckled. The attacker pulled his knife out of Charlie's stomach and quickly raised it, coming to finish her off next.

Her body reacted before her brain had the chance to think. She took off running. It was what she did best. She had to get back to their makeshift camp. There was safety in numbers.

Maddie ran without thinking, without looking back. If she kept going, the truth would never catch up to her, her brother wouldn't be gone, wouldn't be murdered.

"Maddie!"

She slowed down when she heard her name and stumbled into her father's arms without realizing it.

"Are you all right?" He hugged her tight and let her cry into his shoulder.

"Where's your brother?"

"Gone," Maddie moaned, the word catching on her halting breaths. "He's gone and it's all my fault."

She broke down then, collapsing into her father's arms. She cried and cried, holding her hands tight to her chest, gripping her brother's balled-up Giants hat like it was the most precious thing in the world.

TWENTY-SIX

THEY'D BEEN WALKING FOR HOURS, BREAKING their restless camp the moment the sun had peeked its first rays over the horizon. They slogged through the trees, their number diminished, everyone exhausted, their nerves frayed edges that the slightest snag would unravel.

Feeling empty and broken, like that horse had succeeded in stomping on her head that first day on the mountain, Maddie stared blankly ahead. She kept replaying the previous night's events, going over it and over it in her head until she started to doubt her own memories.

Abigail's scream piercing the night. Charlie running into the woods to save her. Maddie blindly and foolishly following after him.

What had she been thinking? Why had she thought she could help? Would Charlie still be alive if she hadn't gone after him?

He'd leaped at the attacker to save *her*. To give *her* time to escape. He'd pushed his body between hers and the knife, taken the blow that should have struck her in the stomach. He'd sacrificed himself. And now Maddie would never see him again.

A fresh set of tears trickled down her cheeks, but she didn't move to wipe them away. She wanted to feel like shit. She deserved it.

She hadn't slept at all after her father had carried her back into camp. Abigail had been there, her mother holding her close like she'd never let her go again. Everyone had stared at Maddie. But no one asked what had happened or where Charlie was. Her dad had put her on the ground, and Chelsea had scrambled over to her. She'd thrown her arms around her, but Maddie had shrugged them off. She wanted to be alone. She wanted to curl up and die, to be with Charlie again.

Quietly, her dad had gone around the camp telling them all that the attacker had gotten Charlie. He hadn't been able to piece together much from Maddie's ranting, but this he had understood. Just like he'd lost his wife, he'd lost his son. Dylan took the news particularly hard. Her face crumpled in on itself and a howl ripped out of her. She'd run into her tent then, burying herself in her pillow, though they could all still hear her muffled sobs.

Maddie had scoffed at that. Hadn't Dylan wanted to break up with Charlie? Why should she care so much now?

It was a bitter thought. But in the afternoon light, Maddie found it still true. She knew it wasn't fair, but she didn't care. *She* had earned the right to grieve. *She* had loved her brother the most.

Her head dipped and she felt another wave of tears coming on.

How had everything turned to shit so quickly?

Because losing her brother hadn't been the only bad news of the night.

About ten minutes after Maddie and her dad had gotten back to camp, Julie had appeared, shuffling into their broken circle, her flashlight loose in her hand so that it jumped up and spot-lit her face. She had a gash on her forehead and her left eye had already started to swell up. It'd turn black by morning.

Bryan had leaped to his feet and rushed to her.

"Are you okay? What happened? Did they attack you, too? Where's Dad?"

The questions spilled out of him, but Julie couldn't answer any of them. Not at first. Bryan had to sit her down and give her a drink of water before she calmed down enough to speak.

"He's gone," Julie finally muttered, her voice hollow, dead. Her mouth opened wide around the words, her bottom lip red and cracked open.

"The attacker got him, too?" Bryan didn't believe it.

"Hah," Julie cackled bitterly. "No one got your father."

"But your face..." Bryan trailed off, not understanding.

"*He* did this to me! I thought you'd recognize his handiwork by now. I tried to stop him from running, but he wouldn't listen."

"What?"

"He ran off by himself," Julie spit out. "Your father's a coward. He said he wasn't going to wait around and get killed with the rest of us. He took the rifle, too. Selfish bastard."

And now they were stranded on the mountain, defenseless, as a killer stalked them, picking them off one by one. Things couldn't get worse.

Maddie was so wrapped up in her bleak thoughts that she barely noticed Caleb pulling up short in front of her. They hadn't rested all morning. But now, as Maddie came to a stop, her stomach ached. She unzipped her bag and grabbed a granola bar and her water bottle. As she drank, she could vaguely hear Caleb saying they still had a ways to go, but that they'd made good progress that morning. Maddie recapped her bottle and pushed it back into her bag.

What was the point? It was hopeless, wasn't it?

Her mind cycled back to the night before, started over at the beginning again—following Charlie through the woods, watching as he grappled with the attacker, bought her time to get away, sacrificed himself for her.

Just like in his story, Maddie suddenly realized.

Had that girl made it out alive? Sadie? Charlie hadn't said.

Maddie looked down at Charlie's hat. She'd carried it balled up in her fist the whole morning. He'd worn it everywhere. Having it with her made her feel like she had him there, too.

She unrumpled it and stared at the SF logo, remembering her brother. His laugh and his smile. The way he'd always looked out for her, especially after their mother had died. A sad smile stretched across her lips and a tear slid down her cheek, dropping onto the fabric.

Maddie sniffled and blinked her eyes several times. She tried to shake the memories out of her head but lost her balance instead, stumbling, just managing to catch herself against a tree. As she hugged the tree, her sadness weighed her down. It urged her to let go, to slide to the ground and sink into the earth. No one could hurt her there. She couldn't lose anyone else.

"Are you okay?"

Maddie looked up and saw Chelsea's worried face staring down at her.

"I'm—I'm fine," Maddie replied, pushing off the tree slowly.

"Here, let me get that for you."

Chelsea bent over and retrieved Charlie's baseball cap, holding it out for Maddie.

"Th-thank you." Maddie took the hat from her best friend.

"It's not your fault," Chelsea spoke softly. "You know that, right?"

"Isn't it?" Maddie mumbled, playing with the hat, dusting it off.

"He wanted you to run. He wanted to protect you—to fight for you."

"And now he's dead...."

"But you saved yourself," Chelsea rushed to assure her friend. "You ran. You couldn't have done anything to—"

But Maddie wasn't listening. Chelsea was right. Maddie had always run. And Charlie had always been there to fight her battles for her. But what if...

Maddie remembered her brother's campfire story. Nicholas had urged Sadie to run. Told her to save herself. But what if Sadie hadn't listened to him? What if she'd stayed? What if she and Nicholas had fought Red Raven *together?*

Maddie looked down at Charlie's baseball cap. She saw the faded logo and knew what she had to do. She adjusted the strap and took a deep breath. She pulled the hat over her hair, the brim blocking out the sun, focusing her eyes on the path ahead.

It couldn't end like this. She couldn't give up. She couldn't let Charlie down.

She wiped her eyes. No more tears. She had to stop running and start fighting. She had to start saving more than just herself. She was getting off this mountain. Alive. And so was Chelsea.

"What's that over there?" Bryan asked suddenly. Maddie whipped her head around, preparing herself for another attack. But it wasn't a threat Bryan had spotted. In fact, it could have been the exact opposite. Maddie felt a jolt of hope as she looked at the cabin roof a little ways in the distance.

"Maybe they have a radio," Bryan said optimistically.

"Maybe," Caleb agreed.

"We should check it out." Bryan took off without waiting for permission. Everyone followed after him, buoyed by a new sense of hope. Maybe their luck had finally turned.

TWENTY-SEVEN

THEY CRASHED THROUGH THE FOREST, THE sudden, unexpected taste of hope making them lose their senses, forget their caution. Bryan led the way with Maddie taking up the rear. Could they really be saved? A part of her doubted it would be so easy. But there was the proof staring them in the face, the cabin coming into focus as they got nearer, one last tree line blocking their view.

Bryan pushed through the trees first, Kris and Caleb right behind him. Maddie was about to push through herself, but a sudden cry rooted her feet to the ground. It rattled through her bones.

She gulped as a second wail cut through the trees. She knew it'd been too good to be true. But what had happened? What new monstrosity waited for her on the other side of those trees? How many tragedies could she witness? How many bodies did she have to find before she broke?

Another scream scratched its way into Maddie's ear. She took a deep breath and steeled herself. Then she pushed through the trees. What was one more body?

"Jesus Christ." Maddie's dad's breath whistled through his teeth. He was only a few steps in front of Maddie, blocking her view. Cautiously, Maddie walked up behind him and peeked around his shoulders. Everyone had fanned out around one side of the cabin.

But what had scared them all? Maddie pushed past her dad.

"Maddie, no!"

He tried to grab her by the shoulder, but Maddie's gasp told him he was too late.

There was so much blood.

Her knees shook. Bile surged up her throat, hot and poisonous. It spilled into the grass where Maddie expected it to smoke and steam. She dry-heaved a couple more times before getting it under control. She wiped the corner of her mouth with the back of her hand and looked up.

Blood was splattered across the cabin wall—two dark-red stains arcing up and then back down.

"Wings—" Maddie whispered to herself as the realization broke over her. She turned and looked back at her dad. He looked equally astonished.

"It—it can't be," he murmured. He ran a frantic hand back through his hair but left his thought unfinished.

A body leaned against the cabin wall underneath the bloody wings, its throat slit from ear to ear, the skin on its head peeled back, its scalp missing. Flies buzzed around the fileted skull. That hadn't been in

Charlie's story, but it was clear this was the work of Red Raven—or a Red Raven copycat.

Julie let out a new shriek and then began sobbing uncontrollably. She tried to cover her face with her hands, but her tears fell fast. Maddie's dad pulled her close, and Maddie noticed Bryan crouched down near the cabin wall, sitting only inches away from his father's brutally butchered body.

Ed hadn't gotten away after all.

Maddie willed her legs to move, and she inched forward. The shock of her uncle's bloody body had started to wear off. She joined the rest of the group near the cabin wall.

"I'm so sorry, Julie," Kris said. The women had both lost their husbands now.

"I guess it's safe to assume there won't be a radio in there." Julie turned away from her husband's body. She'd managed to pull herself together a bit.

"I would guess not," Maddie's dad said. "But at least we have our rifle back." He reached down and picked the gun up off the ground, checking its ammunition chamber. "Only one bullet left."

"Small miracle," Kris muttered. It was all starting to get to her. She looked ten years older after just one night, her hair frayed at the ends, the wrinkles on her forehead and around her eyes deep crevices.

"How could this happen?" Maddie asked no one in particular, knowing there was no answer.

That was when Bryan finally made a sound.

His grunt came out as half-sob, half-hiccup. He didn't turn to face them but only held up a hand, a hunting knife sitting on his open palm. He must have picked it up off the ground near his father's body. Maddie stared hard at it, taking in every detail. It was covered in blood, with errant strands of hair stuck to it. Bryan shifted it slightly in his hand and she saw it—an odd flourish on the handle. A flourish that she recognized.

"But that—that's Caleb's knife," she muttered in shock.

TWENTY-EIGHT

NO ONE DARED MOVE. OR BLINK. Or even breathe. Maddie's words had sucked all the oxygen out of the forest.

She racked her brain, trying to think. Had she seen Caleb the night before, when Abigail's scream had woken them all? Could it have been him out there in the forest, attacking her brother?

She couldn't remember. Damnit. It'd been dark and everything had happened so fast. She'd raced off after Charlie without a thought. And the attacker had worn a ski mask. It could have been anybody.

Bryan's hand went limp and the knife fell with a thud.

Then chaos erupted.

In a whirl of thrashing arms Maddie's cousin clawed his way up from the ground. He ducked his head and launched himself at Caleb. Their bodies collided with a ferocious crash, and the guide fell to the ground a second later, Bryan on top of him.

His fists rose and fell frantically as he tried to pummel every inch of Caleb's face. Bryan ripped at Caleb's blond hair and tried to scratch out his eyes. There were no rules to this kind of fight—only survival.

Maddie winced each time Bryan landed a punch. Not Caleb. Not his beautiful face.

But why was she rooting for him? What about his bloody knife?

Bryan had surprised Caleb when he'd tackled him like a linebacker on steroids, but Caleb was stronger. And he knew how to fight. As soon as he'd hit the ground he'd pulled his arms up to protect his face. Bryan's blows were hitting him, but none were landing squarely.

"Get off me," Caleb tried to shout over the volley of punches. "It wasn't—"

But Bryan's attack trampled his words.

The younger boy was breathing hard, though. Sweat started to splotch his face. His glasses slipped down the bridge of his nose as he wore himself out. Meanwhile, Caleb still had plenty of fight in him.

Between punches, Bryan paused for a second to push his glasses back up his nose. It was reflex, and all the time Caleb needed.

The guide thrust his torso forward, a sit-up with such force that it sent Bryan flying backward and onto the ground. Caleb scrambled to his feet. His hair mussed, a small line of blood dribbling from one corner of his mouth. Other than that he didn't look too banged up. Bryan, though, had crumpled into a disheveled mess. His glasses were twisted and barely fit on his face. Bruises and scrapes covered his knuckles. Caleb looked down at the boy with a menacing stare.

"Listen to me." Caleb's voice came out powerful and angry. "I didn't kill anyone."

"Stay right where you are."

The shout came from Maddie's dad.

"I'm trying to tell you," Caleb spun around to face Mitch. "I didn't—"

But the words died in his throat as he spotted Maddie's dad, the rifle trembling in the man's unsteady hands, pointed directly at Caleb's chest.

"I said, don't move."

Caleb's hands went up in surrender.

"Let's be careful now, Mitch. You don't want to do something you'll regret."

Maddie didn't know how Caleb could speak so calmly. Her dad had a gun pointed at his chest. And he didn't look like someone who could be reasoned with. Not right now.

"Not another step." Maddie's dad shook the gun's barrel at Caleb and he stopped inching forward. "That's your knife, isn't it?"

Caleb's face looked pained in admitting it, but he knew he couldn't lie.

"And how do you explain it getting out here, if you're not the one who killed Ed? Killed them all?"

"I—I—" Caleb grasped for a reason but couldn't come up with one. "Someone must have stolen it from me."

Maddie's dad pursed his lips and then farted through them.

"That sounds awfully convenient."

"I—I can't explain it. But I didn't kill them."

"Right. Just like you didn't kill Mark or those poor boys. My son."

His arms shook less as he rattled off Caleb's victims. He gained confidence as he got used to the gun in his hands, the certainty he felt in

Caleb's guilt. He still had a crazy look on his face, though. He was wired, like he'd gulped down six cups of coffee one after the other. His shoulder twitched, and Maddie yelped, sure that her father was about to fire.

"Come on now, Mitch," Caleb pleaded. "I would never hurt you all. You can put the gun down and we can talk this—"

"Shut up!" Maddie's dad was really cracking up now. "You're not going to kill anyone else."

He raised the gun the rest of the way to his shoulder and stared down the barrel at Caleb, bringing the guide squarely into his sights.

"Dad!" Maddie tried to get his attention. "Dad, listen to him."

But her father didn't hear her. He was going to shoot, and Maddie couldn't stop it. She screamed and turned away as she saw Caleb lunging forward, a last, desperate attempt to save himself. His fingers hovered inches from the gun, but he wouldn't get there in time.

The rifle exploded with an earsplitting roar. Maddie shut her eyes and prayed for it to be over.

Only when the gunshot's echo had died did Maddie ease her eyes open again. She looked at the ground beneath her, at her feet planted flat, her knees hovering just over the laces of her running shoes. She extended her legs and rose from her squat. She didn't want to look, but she had to. She turned and saw her dad standing in the same spot, gun still in his hand—pointed up into the trees.

Wait. That didn't make sense.

Maddie looked at the gun again and noticed that a hand gripped the barrel, forcing it up.

Caleb's hand. Maddie's breath caught in her lungs. The guide was still standing. He'd managed to get there in time.

"Shit!" Caleb screamed out, breaking the tension. The shot had also shaken Maddie's father out of his mad frenzy. He didn't seem so enthusiastic now.

Caleb's hand smoldered as he let go of the gun. The metal had scorched his entire palm when it had gone off. He shook it out now and continued to curse.

"What the hell? You were really going to shoot me? I told you I didn't kill anyb—"

But before Caleb could finish, Kris rushed in and yanked the gun from Mitch's hands. She raised it above his head in one swift motion, bringing the butt down with a crack against the guide's forehead.

Everyone looked on in shock as Caleb crumpled to the ground.

"What? He's a murderer," Kris explained.

TWENTY-NINE

MADDIE COULDN'T HELP STARING AT CALEB'S uncon-
scious face. A giant bruise had bloomed on one side of his head, a
patch of dried blood scabbing over in his hairline, where Kris had
smashed him with the butt of the rifle. Maddie wanted to reach out
and touch his swollen face, to clean him off with a cool cloth. But she
didn't dare.

He was a murderer—at least that's what everyone else seemed to
think. They were over on the far side of the fire right now, deciding
what to do with him.

Maddie didn't want to believe it, but she couldn't ignore the evidence. It wasn't much, but it certainly made Caleb look bad.

He knew the mountains the best. He could have slipped back and
forth, even in the middle of the night, and they wouldn't have noticed.
He'd also been furious with Mark. Maybe the deer incident had set
him off. He'd heard all their campfire stories. It wouldn't have been

hard for him to bring them to life. To terrify them all as he picked them off one by one.

And then there was his knife. Its decorative *C* and bloody blade screamed his guilt.

How could he have done it? How could he have murdered all their friends?

"Maddie." Abigail startled her, saying her name softly. "Can I talk to you?"

Maddie turned. Even in the flickering firelight the girl looked pale. Unwell. Maddie had barely noticed Abigail that day. The girl had been attached to her mother's hip, silent. When Maddie had caught her eye, Abigail had turned away quickly each time.

"What is it?"

"I—I wanted to apologize," Abigail began.

"Again?"

"No, I—" Abigail's eyes dropped down to her hands and she fiddled with her fingernails, scratching at the dirt underneath them.

"What is it?" Maddie snapped, losing her patience.

"I wanted to explain," Abigail began uncomfortably, "about why I was out in the woods last night when—when Charlie saved me."

"Oh," Maddie realized with a start. Her fingers flitted to the brim of her hat. "But that wasn't your—"

"I went out into the woods last night because I wanted it to be over. I wanted—I wanted to be with my dad. And Jason. I didn't want to be scared or sad, or to lose anyone ever again. I was trying to find the stream. It would have been a peaceful end, floating away, disappearing under the current.

"But then—*he* found me instead. Once he had his arms around me," Abigail shuddered and corrected herself. "Once *Caleb* had his arms around me, everything in me screamed to live."

Maddie only nodded, letting Abigail finish what she had to get out.

"And then—and then your brother showed up and he saved me. And I ran away. I left him behind to die. And I'm *so* sorry for that."

Abigail blurted the last bit out in one go. She winced, waiting for Maddie's anger.

But Maddie couldn't be mad at her. She couldn't be mad because she understood. She'd felt the same crippling depression all morning. The same survivor's guilt.

"It's not your fault," Maddie said, looking Abigail directly in the eye, making sure she understood her sincerity. What she didn't say was that it wasn't *Abigail's* fault because it was *her* fault. Maddie had let Charlie down in those woods, too.

"Th-thanks," Abigail stuttered, though she didn't look very relieved as she shuffled away, back toward her mother and sister. Maddie had tried her best to absolve the girl, but Abigail needed to forgive herself if she truly wanted to feel better.

A groan escaped Caleb's lips, and Maddie snapped around in time to see his head loll from one side to the other. She leaned in closer. She could see his eyes probing against his closed lids.

Suddenly, Caleb jolted forward. Maddie fell back in fright. But before the guide could reach her, he came up against his bindings and was flung back into the tree they'd tied him to. He strained against the rope two or three more times before giving up. Then his eyes finally popped open and he spotted Maddie.

"Wha—what happened?" His voice croaked softly. He closed his eyes as if to take a nap but opened them again almost immediately. "My head—ugh—it's killing me."

Maddie didn't know what to say, and so just stared at him.

"So thirsty. Do you think—could you get me some water?"

Maddie could hear the dryness in his voice, the way his tongue stuck as he took raspy breaths through his mouth. She hesitated and then scurried a few steps away, where she grabbed her water bottle from her pack. She looked back over her shoulder. No one had noticed that Caleb was awake. Even Chelsea had missed it, so exhausted by the day that she'd fallen into an uneasy sleep, her head resting against Bryan's shoulder. Maddie turned back around and approached Caleb tentatively. She poured a few gulps of water into his mouth without saying a word.

"Tha—" Caleb coughed up some of the water before swallowing another gulp. "Thank you."

Maddie smiled at him and was about to say something when Kris's voice rang out.

"He's awake."

Maddie spun around, looking guilty, and saw Kris and her father rushing over. She backed away in a hurry.

"So you're finally back with us." Kris's voice dripped venom. "You killed my husband and Ed and poor Charlie. Even those boys out in the woods, my daughter's friends. Why?"

Caleb replied with two simple words.

"I didn't."

"Stop lying!" Kris raised her hand but Maddie's dad reached up and grabbed her wrist before she could strike.

"I think he's already been hit hard enough. Let me try."

Kris bristled at the interruption but stepped aside.

"Come on, Caleb." Maddie's dad bent down so that he could look Caleb directly in the eye. "You were furious at Mark. We found your knife under Ed's body. You did this. So let's stop pretending."

Caleb looked away, and Maddie's dad pressed on, his questions coming one after the other as Caleb refused to answer any of them.

"Why'd you kill everyone? Mark, I can kind of understand. Even Ed. But those boys? Charlie? Was it your plan all along? To lead us out into the woods and then pick us off one by one? Did you think it was funny, torturing us like that? Torturing them?"

Caleb hadn't said a word since he'd first asserted his innocence.

"Enough of this."

Kris leaped forward and pushed Maddie's dad out of the way. She squeezed Caleb's face between her hands, pressing her nails into his cheeks, digging her index finger into the wound at his hairline. Caleb shouted in pain.

"Stop it!" Maddie couldn't take it anymore as she screamed at Kris. "You're hurting him."

"He killed them, Maddie." Kris turned to face her, but her fingernails still dug into Caleb's face. "My husband. Ed. *Your brother*. He doesn't deserve compassion. He's a murderer."

Kris underscored her point by digging her fingers harder into his head.

"Why'd you do it? Why'd you kill them?" she screamed.

Maddie backed off, trembling, more afraid of the wild glint in Kris's eye than Caleb, bound and defenseless.

"I—didn't—kill—anyone!"

Caleb reasserted his innocence, and Kris savagely tossed his head back against the tree. She turned from him and walked over to the fire. She wasn't done yet. She bent over and picked something up off the ground. She held it over the flames for a few minutes.

When Kris turned back around the thing caught the light and gleamed dangerously. Even from where Maddie sat she could make out the *C* on its handle. Kris took four quick strides and had Caleb by the hair. She jerked his head back. His neck strained but he didn't fight her grip. He stared her in the eye, unafraid.

"Maybe we should do to you what you did to my husband."

The knife hovered an inch above Caleb's forehead. He didn't seem to take Kris's threat seriously, though. Until she brought the searing flat of the blade down on his cheek.

The scream was horrible. Feral. Caleb jerked forward, but his restraints held fast.

"No!" Maddie cried again. This time she ran toward Kris, trying to grab the smoldering knife out of her hand. But her dad scooped her up, holding her back.

"Confess," Kris shouted, her voice raw and wild. But Caleb didn't speak. "Then I guess we'll have to give you a taste of your own medicine."

Kris repositioned the knife in her hand and yanked Caleb's hair back even harder this time. She brought the knife's tip down on the guide's forehead and made three slow, excruciating cuts.

Caleb's cries were even worse this time. Even Maddie's hands couldn't block them out as she squirmed in her dad's arms, struggling to get free.

"Still don't want to talk?" Kris gave the guide one last chance and then carved a second antler into his forehead. Once Caleb's howls had died down, she pulled back and admired her handiwork. "Not too bad. Though maybe I made them a little bigger than the ones you gave Mark. My mistake."

Maddie didn't know how Caleb remained conscious. His face was swollen and cut up almost beyond recognition. The guide closed his eyes and tucked his chin into his chest as he whimpered. He was defeated, all the fight beaten out of him.

But still, he didn't confess.

"I think I'm going to be sick," Dylan spoke up. Her skin had lost its color, and she held her stomach like she really might vomit on the spot. "I need some air. This is all—this is all too much."

"Honey, don't—" but it was already too late. Kris's words fell unheard as Dylan staggered off into the dark woods. The knife shook in the woman's hand, the spell broken, and she let it drop to the ground.

"Let her go," Maddie's dad said as he released his own daughter. "We've got our killer. She'll be fine. I'm sure she won't go far."

Kris nodded, reluctant to see Dylan disappear. She turned and Maddie caught her gaze. The mania had disappeared from the woman's eyes. Maddie hadn't known Kris had it in her. Wherever it'd come from, though, it had gone. She looked broken and weak now. She stared right through Maddie, lost in thought, and then turned to speak to Maddie's dad again.

"Am I going crazy?"

"No." He didn't sound so sure, but what else could he say?

"It's just," Kris paused and looked at her shaking hands. "Mark and

Ed are dead. Charlie. He almost got Abigail. *He* did this. Why won't he admit it?"

Maddie watched as her dad wrapped Kris up in his arms. There was an intimacy between them that she'd never noticed before.

"He's a lunatic, Kris. You can't try and understand him."

Kris sniffled and then wiped her nose on Mitch's shirt.

"You know what's sad," she started, pulling away slowly, "for a while I thought you'd killed them. I mean, when I saw Ed—that seemed a little too convenient."

"I would never."

"Oh, don't act so innocent. We both know what you're capable of. You would—if the right opportunity presented itself."

"Well, I didn't," Maddie's dad bristled. He let his arms drop to his sides.

"I guess that's something good in all this," Kris said, as if saving the situation. "No more Ed means no more blackmail."

"Means we can finally bury our past mistakes for good," Mitch grimaced.

"Maddie." Someone was whispering her name. She turned, knowing it'd be Caleb. "Maddie, you've got to help me."

She could barely keep her eyes on him. But she couldn't turn away, either. Two rivulets of blood ran down from the matching antlers on his forehead and merged into one stream between his eyebrows. The blood continued down his nose and into one eye so that he had to squint to see her.

"I'm innocent." His voice was a croak as he pled with her. "All you have to do is cut me loose."

Maddie looked down and saw his knife lying where Kris had dropped it. A few inches closer and Caleb would have been able to hook his foot around it and free himself.

"I didn't do this. You have to believe me." Caleb's tears trickled down his cheeks, falling from his blue eyes and mixing with the blood from his forehead. "Only you can save me. Be brave. Be my Mustang Maddie."

She froze, remembering that first day on the mountain, how he'd leaped in without a second's thought, risked his own neck to save her. Had that really been only a couple of days ago?

"Please. They're going to kill me."

Didn't she owe him? A life for a life?

But no. *He* was the killer. *He'd* murdered her brother. She couldn't forget that.

But why deny it? Why not confess?

Maddie didn't know what to do. She was frightened. Saving him could mean killing them all.

She crawled over and picked up the knife, balancing it in her palm. Caleb's blood dripped off it and into her hand. She wiped it on her shirt, polishing it like she'd seen him do around the campfire.

"That's it," Caleb whispered. "Now just bring it over here and cut me loose."

Maddie hesitated but then started toward Caleb.

"What are you doing?" Chelsea's voice startled Maddie, and she almost dropped the knife. She turned to meet her best friend's gaze.

"What are you doing?" Chelsea asked again, eyeing the knife suspiciously. "He's a murderer, Maddie. He killed Charlie."

Maddie stood frozen for a moment, trying to work out the thoughts spinning in her head. Finally, she answered her best friend as simply as she could.

"Did he?"

She was doing the right thing. She was certain of it. Her gut told her he was innocent. And if that was the case, then that meant the real killer was still out there. They'd need Caleb if they wanted to survive.

The rationalization played on a loop in Maddie's head as she turned away from Chelsea and focused back on the guide. She leaned against the tree to get a better angle and held the knife over Caleb's restraints.

But right at that moment, a crash sounded out in the woods. Maddie jumped, her heart back in her throat. The knife clattered out of her hand as she turned away from Caleb. She strained her eyes against the darkness, looking out the way Dylan had gone.

There was another crash, leaves crunching and branches snapping, the thud of something heavy hitting the ground. Then a piercing scream filled the woods.

Maddie froze. She looked to her dad and Kris. Both of their faces had gone white with fear. They stared at Caleb and then out into the woods, trying to put it all together. Their mouths opened in gaping *O*s as they realized—the killer was still out there.

There was another scream and the two adults snapped back to themselves. They looked at each other with wide eyes and then rushed off into the night.

THIRTY

JUST AS SUDDENLY AS THE NIGHT had filled with commotion, the woods went eerily quiet. Maddie strained her eyes to see something—anything—through the darkness. The silence was so much worse than the screams.

Silence meant death.

"No. No. No. No. No."

She tried to fill the void, hoping the noise would help calm her down.

Her heart pounded, nonetheless. Her breaths came in short huffs. Sweat soaked through her shirt. She couldn't lose her cool. She had to think. What would Charlie have done?

He would have rushed in and tried to save his girlfriend.

But that hadn't worked out for him. So what should Maddie do?

The realization hit her with a shocking certainty. She should free Caleb.

They'd need everyone if they wanted to survive. They couldn't run anymore. It was time to face their attacker head-on.

Maddie spun around and ran back to Caleb's tree. Chelsea was still there. Her best friend rushed forward, grabbed her hand, and squeezed it with all her strength. Fear flooded Chelsea's eyes. *Was this really it?*

Maddie felt the finality of the moment, too, and returned the pressure. They'd gotten through a lot over the years, but this—this seemed like more than they could handle. This felt like it could very well be the end.

But then Maddie remembered the previous night. Their pinkie promise. They'd sworn to fight until the end. And that's just what she was going to do.

A log cracked open in the fire, and Maddie jerked toward it. The flames danced before her eyes, filling her vision as she caught a whiff of the smoke. She shook her head and turned back toward Caleb. She had to find that knife. She had to free him.

She knelt down in front of him, her hands scurrying across the ground, searching for the knife.

"Where is it?" she muttered under her breath, losing her cool, growing more desperate and frustrated with each passing second.

"It's over there," Caleb croaked. His voice surprised her. Maddie looked up, her nose only inches from his. Her gaze slid across his face, puffed up and crusted with blood now, the antlers vicious trenches dug into his forehead. Her breath caught in her chest as she saw the burn on his cheek, the waxy red patch of seared flesh. Her nose tingled and she swore she could smell it, the pungent odor of burnt skin. Her lungs seized up. Her vision tunneled and she was back in that parking lot five years ago.

She couldn't move. She was frozen to the spot. She couldn't bend her arms or take a step. She couldn't even blink. The fire burned so brightly in front of her.

Her mom was in there. She was going to die if Maddie didn't do something.

Maddie willed herself to take a step forward. Then another. She was brave. She could do this.

With a sickening crunch, she watched as the office roof caved in, as a swirling tornado of smoke and ash crashed into her, clawed up her nose and down her throat.

She couldn't breathe. She collapsed. She wanted to cry, but no tears came out. She wanted to scream for help but couldn't make a sound. She felt weak and sleepy. This was all a bad dream. Maddie's eyes blinked shut, and the world went black as she let her mother die.

"Maddie!"

Caleb's voice shattered her nightmare.

"Maddie, look at me."

She turned. She tried to look brave, but her bottom lip quivered nonetheless.

"We're not dead yet," he said fiercely, still tied to the tree, still bleeding from his forehead.

Maddie didn't know what it was exactly, but something in Caleb's voice gave her hope. He was right. Her mother and Charlie might be dead, but she and Chelsea and her dad and her aunt and cousin—even Abigail—they were all still alive. They could still survive.

She wiped her eyes and pressed her lips together with determination.

"Help me find the knife," Maddie ordered. She took Chelsea's hand and pulled her best friend down as the two scoured the ground.

Maddie wasn't going to let it happen again. She wasn't going to let anyone else die, not without doing something. She was stronger now. She could save them. She could save all of them. Her fingers flitted back to Charlie's hat, and she felt his spirit buoy her.

"I know I dropped it somewhere over here."

"It's there." Caleb nodded.

Maddie was closest and scooped it up. She tried to cut the rope, but it was harder than it looked. The blade was sharp, but the rope was tough and her hands kept slipping.

"Almost there," Maddie grunted in frustration as she sawed desperately at the rope. She just had to get through one cord and it'd all come loose.

"AHHHHHHHH!"

A banshee's shriek cut through the night, the first noise in the last few minutes. It rattled around Maddie's ribcage and down her arms, knocking the knife out of her hand once more.

The scream was so loud. So close. Maddie looked toward the fire but saw only Julie there with Abigail and Bryan.

Then she saw it. A hand appeared at the edge of their camp and clawed its way into the circle of light, the slender fingers madly digging into the dirt.

Slowly a head followed. Dirt and blood matted her hair down, but Maddie would have recognized that blond helmet anywhere. She gasped as Kris crawled into the light, one of her eyes swollen shut, a nasty cut opening up her cheek.

"Help—me," Kris croaked. The effort of her last scream had shredded her vocal cords. She tried to say something else, but her voice failed her.

The shock of the woman's appearance wore off, and Maddie started forward but then stopped in her tracks. Her eyes grew big as a figure loomed up behind Kris. It bent down and yanked the woman's head back. Kris didn't even have time to turn and look at him as his knife flicked across her throat.

Blood poured out of the cut, warm and wet. It splashed on the ground, gurgled in her lungs. Maddie watched as the woman convulsed a few times and then fell still, just like Caleb's deer had.

But Maddie didn't have time to think about that as the killer calmly stepped over Kris's body, confident as he looked at all of them, his face shrouded in a black ski mask. His knife moved through the air, landing on each of them as he took his time in picking out his next victim.

As his knife reached Maddie, he stopped. But instead of coming after her, his fingers moved to his face. He peeled the ski mask off of his head, and Maddie gasped.

Tommy? But he was dead.

THIRTY-ONE

THIS DIDN'T MAKE ANY SENSE. MADDIE stared at the killer's face—*Tommy's* face, his close-shaved head, his wicked little smile that had almost made her swoon just two nights before—and her brain couldn't process it.

She'd seen him dead. Seen his bloody body, his San Francisco T-shirt filled with holes, and soaked in red.

But no, this was definitely him. And he'd definitely just killed Kris.

"Miss me?" Tommy hadn't taken his eyes off Maddie.

"But you're—you're—" Maddie stuttered.

"Not so dead after all."

"You bastard!" Abigail shrieked, surprising them all as she threw herself at Tommy.

The fight only took him a second to handle, though, as he caught her balled-up fists neatly in his hands and tossed her aside like some rag doll. She fell to the ground but scrambled right up, lunging for him again.

This time Tommy didn't play nice. His knife flicked, a serpent's devilish tongue, and Abigail yelped. She fell back clutching her stomach, watching in disbelief as blood seeped out of her, soaking her shirt and hands.

"How could you?" Abigail mumbled as she gasped for air.

"I've done a lot of things these past few days," Tommy replied coyly. "You're going to have to be more specific."

"How—how—" Abigail started, but she could barely get it out. She was losing her strength fast. Her knees wavered underneath her and then she collapsed to the ground. But she didn't lose her thought. "How could you murder your best friend?"

"Jason?" Tommy asked, as if this had been last on the list of things Abigail could have meant. "That was easy. Not hard killing your best friend when you despise him."

"But—" Abigail's last words died on her tongue as she sank the rest of the way to the ground. This seemed to shake Julie out of her paralysis, and she rushed forward to hold the girl.

But it was too late. Abigail lay there, unmoving, and Maddie knew she wouldn't be getting up again.

Another broken promise. Another person Maddie couldn't save.

"Don't look so sad. It doesn't suit that pretty face of yours."

Maddie's eyes snapped up and found Tommy's. He was playing with them now. With her. But maybe she could use that. She couldn't give in yet.

"Should I be thanking you?" Maddie asked, her voice shaking as she tried to get him talking.

"A little bit of recognition wouldn't hurt," Tommy replied. "You did hate her, after all."

Around the campfire, everyone—Bryan, Julie, and Chelsea—stood frozen. No one dared move, knowing that it'd mean Tommy's knife if he caught them. They didn't have anything to fight back with. Mark's rifle lay useless near the fire, the last bullet shot up into the air hours ago.

"I didn't hate her," Maddie said, her mind racing. She had a plan. She just had to get to Caleb's knife and finish cutting him loose. It was their only hope.

"Yes, you did. No use in lying about it now."

"But why?" Maddie tried to keep him distracted. "Why'd you kill so many people? What'd any of us ever do to you?"

"Hmm…" Tommy smiled wide, like he might gobble Maddie up in one bite. This was it. Her chance. And Maddie wasn't going to waste it. Not this time.

She pounced, throwing herself to the ground and grabbing Caleb's knife. She whirled back around and cut at the guide's restraints. But Tommy was already there, moving lightning fast around the campfire, his hand on her shoulder, pulling her back.

Maddie didn't think. She used his strength against him and spun around. The knife flashed in her hand, sliced through the air, through clothes and flesh. Tommy yelped and Maddie pulled her arm back for another slash, but he grabbed her by the wrist. He squeezed and now she was the one wincing.

"You're quicker than I thought," Tommy wheezed. "And more annoying."

He tightened his grip on her wrist and forced the knife out of Maddie's hand.

"You won't be needing that anymore."

He tossed the knife into the dark woods. But Maddie hadn't given up. Not yet. She dug her teeth into the back of Tommy's hand. He let loose a volley of expletives as he tried to shake her off. When she wouldn't budge, he smacked her across the face, knocking her away.

"What's going on?"

Maddie's heart leaped in her chest as her dad rushed back into the circle of light. Tommy hadn't gotten him. Did that mean Dylan could still be alive, too?

"It's Tommy," Maddie squealed out, pointing at him.

Maddie's dad looked at her with confusion. But then her words slowly started to sink in. He spotted Kris's bloody body lying at the edge of the campfire. He saw the slap mark starting to bloom red across Maddie's cheek, the knife in Tommy's hand.

"What the hell are you waiting for?" Caleb screamed as he strained at his ropes. "Get him."

"You bastard. Stay away from my daughter."

Maddie's dad charged around the campfire and launched himself at Tommy. Maddie just barely managed to jump out of the way as the two collided and went rolling across the ground. Tommy lost his grip on his knife, and it bounced away toward the campfire.

It wasn't a fistfight like before with Caleb. Mitch and Tommy wrestled on the ground, a sloppy, frantic scuffle. Mitch had his arms wrapped around Tommy's chest and squeezed him as tight as he could, but Tommy managed to get an arm free and pounded on the older man's back.

Eventually, Mitch had to let go. But he didn't stop fighting. He couldn't stop, not when his daughter's life hung in the balance, too. Mitch head-butted Tommy and then sat on the teen's stomach, pinning him to the ground.

"Get—off—me!" Tommy shouted. He squirmed underneath Mitch's weight.

"You're going to pay for what you did." Mitch leaned down and hissed in Tommy's face. "You're not going to hurt anyone else—you—you—lunatic."

Tommy only smirked and then spit in the older man's face. Mitch jolted back in surprise, which gave Tommy enough space to wiggle loose. He punched Maddie's dad in the crotch, and Mitch howled fiercely, rolling off of the teenager.

Both scrambled to their feet and were on each other again in a second. They grappled with each other, pushing and pulling, trying to knock the other to the ground. Tommy lunged for Mitch, but somehow Mitch managed to get out of the way in time. Tommy stumbled a few steps past him, and Mitch moved in from behind, taking Tommy under the arms and forcing him into a headlock. He had the upper hand, finally.

Maddie watched the whole fight in amazement. In her head she rooted her dad on, just like he would have cheered for her at one of her races. She didn't even know he knew how to fight. But he had Tommy where he wanted him now. The boy's face started turning blue. They were saved.

But just when Maddie thought it was all over, a crack shot through the night. Maddie's dad started, and Tommy managed to get loose from his chokehold. He backed up quickly, retrieving his knife from the ground. He rubbed at his neck with his other hand, the color returning to his face, his wicked grin back.

What was that? What was about to happen?

A shuffling of approaching feet made its way to the campfire and everyone turned to look as a handgun appeared at the edge of their camp, followed by a second figure dressed in all black.

Only this time, the man didn't have a ski mask on. He had, however, also returned from the dead.

"Charlie?" Maddie gasped under her breath.

THIRTY-TWO

THEY WERE SAVED. MADDIE COULDN'T HELP beaming. Not only had Charlie survived the attack from the night before, but he'd tracked them down. He'd come to rescue them. To rescue her.

"Get him, Charlie," Maddie shouted. She pointed her finger at Tommy and waited for her brother to turn his gun on the teenaged murderer. "He killed Kris. And Abigail, too."

But her brother didn't respond. Instead, he surveyed them all, holding his gun level. Absolutely calm. As Maddie watched him closely, waiting for him to leap into action, a dangerous gleam crossed into his eyes. Only then did Maddie stop to think.

Where had Charlie gotten a change of clothes? Hell, where had he gotten a handgun? Why hadn't he turned and shot Tommy already? Why wasn't he saving them?

"I'm afraid I'm going to have to disappoint you, Maddie," Charlie said coolly. "I'm not here to save you."

The pieces clicked in Maddie's head. It all became clear.

There were two of them. Two murderers.

And *Charlie*—Charlie was one of them.

Maddie couldn't believe it. All her courage evaporated in that second of realization. She shrank back into herself. She'd thought she could be brave, fearless like she'd always imagined her mother had been. She'd thought she could save them all.

But this—Charlie—a murderer. It was more than she could handle.

She backed away until she felt a tree against her back. She let her legs go and sank to the ground. She couldn't speak. She couldn't move. She could only watch and listen as the world broke apart around her.

"But—but—you're dead—someone attacked you—last night," Mitch sputtered, trying to put everything together. "Maddie saw you die."

"It's amazing what you can get away with on a dark night," Charlie said. He lifted his shirt and angled his torso to the side to show that there was no wound on his back where Maddie had seen him get stabbed. "The same stuff we used for Mark's tent. Looks real, doesn't it?"

"I—I—I don't understand."

"Look at him," Tommy quipped. "I think his head's going to explode. He can't process that his son's a murderer."

"What father could?" Maddie's dad snapped. He turned back to his son. "Charlie, this isn't you. You didn't do this. You didn't kill Mark and Ed and those boys."

Charlie stared down the sight of the handgun. He didn't flinch. He didn't even blink. No one else moved, either, the teen killers holding court, their weapons drawn and ready to strike down anyone who so much as coughed.

"Don't forget Dylan," Charlie smirked, nodding back toward the woods. "To think, she wanted to break up with me. What a silly girl."

The coldness in Charlie's voice told the whole story. Mitch's face cracked down the middle. It broke open like a shattered mirror.

"And I'm not done yet."

Charlie's handgun swept around the campfire and came to rest on Julie.

"No!" Bryan yelled, leaping in front of his mother, throwing his arms out to protect her.

"Move out of the way, Bryan," Charlie said testily. "She deserves this."

"She doesn't."

"She abandoned you!" Charlie shouted. "For so many years. She let your dad rule over you. Let him beat you. How many times did you wake up with bruises? A busted lip? A ringing in your ear that wouldn't go away?"

Maddie could see her cousin struggling with each of Charlie's words.

Was it true? Maddie knew Uncle Ed had been tough on his son, but had he really beat him? Had it really been that bad?

"Now's your chance," Charlie said, quieter, talking solely to Bryan. "You can right his wrongs. Get even. Join us. All you have to do is move aside."

Bryan raised his head and his round glasses caught the light, winking across the campfire at Maddie. And she remembered.

It was the same flash of light as when they'd first set up the tents. And then again in the woods when she'd stumbled across Mark and Julie having sex.

So he'd seen it all, too. He'd known about the affair.

"Move out of the way," Charlie repeated himself, "and we'll let you live."

Bryan stood there, frozen, his glasses hiding his eyes in a sheen of white light. His feet shuffled underneath him, and then his head dipped. His shoulders fell solemnly, decisively.

"No," Bryan muttered, raising his arms back up.

"You don't owe her this," Charlie said in disgust. "She let it happen. She let your dad beat you. She could have left. She could have gotten help. But instead, she ran into Mark's arms? She's a slut. And a terrible mother. She doesn't deserve to live. Now move out of the way."

Bryan's arms shook but he held his ground.

"Please," Bryan whimpered. "Please don't do this."

"Suit yourself."

And Charlie fired.

Bryan groaned. Blood gurgled from his mouth, and then he collapsed. Julie wailed and scrambled toward him, pulling his head into her lap. She ran her fingers through his dark hair. His round glasses caught the firelight and winked one last time.

"And now it's time for you to join your husband." Charlie spit the words at his aunt's feet. He lifted the handgun again and fired. Julie's crying cut out suddenly as she slumped over, her forehead coming to rest against her son's. Charlie didn't seem a bit moved, though.

"Why—why are you doing this?" Mitch's voice shook as he tried to understand.

"Why?" Charlie looked at his father in disbelief. "You want to know why?"

"Yes." Maddie's dad balked at being mocked.

"Someone had to take out the garbage," Charlie spit out viciously. "Cheaters and liars. *Murderers*. They all deserved what they got."

"But Mark—and the antlers—" Maddie's dad sputtered, still trying to make sense of it all, still trying to find a way to believe that his son hadn't killed all those people, even though he'd just seen Charlie shoot Julie and Bryan point-blank. "The Mountain People—"

"Stories." Charlie cut him off. "All stories that *we* brought to life."

"Don't look so shocked," Tommy chimed in. There was a lilt in his voice. He was toying with Maddie's father. "The stories made the cleanup fun. And it freaked all of you out. I could barely keep it together when you came across our camp and found Jason's body. And the whole time you thought I was dead, too."

Tommy performed a little jig in his excitement.

"I only wish my dad could have been here, too. But he'll get what's coming—him and his shiny, new family. I'd love to carve a pair of antlers into their foreheads."

"But don't worry, Dad," Charlie cut in, pulling everyone back to the moment. "We didn't forget about you. In fact, we saved the best story for last."

"But—but what did I do?" Mitch's dad wondered aloud, which was the absolute wrong thing to say. Charlie's head snapped to the side in disbelief.

"I should shoot you right now for saying that," Charlie snorted. "What did *you* do? WHAT DID YOU DO?"

Charlie shouted the words at his dad, his anger bubbling over for the first time.

"You have the nerve to play innocent? Still? When I have a gun pointed at your head?"

Charlie shook with anger, but his firing arm remained steady.

"You think I know about everyone else's indiscretions—their affairs, their child abuse—and I don't know what you did? What you *and* Kris did? You think we'd have done any of this if we didn't know that?

"Why do you think Uncle Ed had to die? Sure, he was a bully and an asshole. He beat his son and wife. But that's not even the worst of it."

Charlie paused, flashing with rage still.

"Are you listening over there, Maddie? I don't want you to a miss a single detail."

Maddie's whole body shook. She didn't want to hear what her brother had to say. But he didn't give her a choice as his anger carried him on.

"Ed was blackmailing you," Charlie yelled at his father. "He'd found out about you and Kris. What you'd done. You'd think he would have gone to the police. But no. The scumbag didn't care about justice. He wanted to make an easy buck.

"If I'd found out that my sister had been murdered, her killer sure as hell wouldn't have gotten off so easily."

Maddie froze as she realized what Charlie was saying.

"You don't know what you're talking about," her dad protested. He had a wild look on his face.

"Don't I?"

"No. No. You don't."

"Then why don't we have any money saved up? Why couldn't you afford to pay for college after I lost my scholarship?"

Charlie dared his father to come up with an answer, any excuse. But the man could only sputter, his face growing red, sweat beading his forehead.

"How pathetic," Charlie scowled at his father. "To think you almost got away with it. But when I lost my scholarship and you didn't have the money for school, I knew something was up. I started poking around and found out all your dirty secrets.

"Why do you think I asked to go on this camping trip?" Charlie laid it all out.

His father looked up at him and began to understand.

"I've known about you for months. About what you and Kris did."

Charlie's eyes flashed dangerously.

"And now, finally, it's time for you to come clean. No more secrets. No more lies. It's time for you to confess. It's time for you to tell your daughter what you did. To tell her how you and Kris killed our mother."

THIRTY-THREE

MADDIE'S WORLD HAD UNRAVELED AROUND HER. She tried desperately to grasp at the threads and keep them from pulling apart, but Charlie's accusations tore at her.

Her mother had died in a fire. A terrible, *accidental* fire. Maddie had witnessed it all. Her dad hadn't been there. He couldn't have killed her. He wouldn't have.

It was the *fire*.

The *fire* had ruined everything. Faulty wiring. Or just horrible luck. Not her father.

"It's time you heard the truth, Maddie," Charlie said. "Tell her."

Maddie's gaze slid to the side and met her father's. Tears filled his eyes. His face had turned bright red.

"I didn't—"

"Stop lying," Charlie growled. "Confess and we can be done with this."

He pulled the hammer back on the handgun for emphasis.

"I—I—I—"

Her dad's face fell, and Maddie could see the years of fear and sadness and regret suddenly weighing him down.

"I never meant to hurt her. You have to believe me. She wasn't supposed to be there."

Maddie sucked in a breath. She shook her head as tears bubbled up in her eyes, too.

It couldn't be. She didn't want to hear it. She covered her ears but then felt hands prying hers away from her head.

"You can't run away from this," Charlie said to her. He still had the gun trained on their father as he pulled Maddie up and led her closer to the fire. Out of the corner of her eye, she saw that Tommy had grabbed Chelsea, too, keeping her from interfering.

"You need to hear this," Charlie went on. "You need to know what he did."

Maddie trembled. The last five years of her life were coming undone.

"Kris came to me," her father sputtered, his face pathetic, streaming with sweat. "She—she had some bad business deal that she needed to make disappear. A fire would destroy the paperwork. But she needed help. And she knew I needed the money.

"I was in debt back then. I had—I had a gambling problem. I didn't know how I was going to come up with the money. And then there was Kris, offering me a way out. We'd torch the real-estate office and collect the insurance. We just couldn't tell your mother. She didn't know about the bad deal or my gambling problem."

Maddie's dad paused, but Charlie kept his gun pointed at his father's head and gestured for him to continue.

"It was supposed to be simple. We weren't going to get caught.

"But then, that night the police called and I was sure they knew we'd set it up. I panicked. I began making up excuses. And then—and then they told me they were calling to inform me that my wife had died. She'd been killed in a fire."

Mitch stared blankly into the dark woods, unable to look his daughter in the eye as he confessed, lost in the past, lost in that night all those years ago.

"When I realized that I'd killed my wife—your mother—I called Kris. I freaked out over the phone. We had to come clean. But Kris talked me down. She convinced me that the best thing to do was to say nothing. Let the police figure it out. It was their job, after all."

He shook his head, remembering his mistake.

"I lived in fear every single day. Every time the phone rang or someone knocked on the door, I was certain it'd be the police, ready to storm in with an arrest warrant.

"But as each day passed, the police didn't come. And the guilt slowly became easier to live with. After a couple of months we knew we'd gotten away with it. They'd officially closed the case. The insurance payout came through."

"Except that Uncle Ed knew," Maddie whispered. She didn't know why this was what she chose to say. There were a thousand other things she could have said.

"Right," Maddie's dad said somberly. "Somehow your uncle found out and blackmailed us."

No one spoke as Mitch's words sank in. He was a murderer. And a liar.

Maddie's ears burned with the truth. She couldn't look at him. She had almost died in that fire. Would he have confessed then? If he had killed both his wife and his daughter?

"I didn't mean to do it." Mitch groveled for his life. "I never meant to hurt her. I swear. It's been torture, keeping it a secret all these years."

"Torture?" Charlie turned on his father. "Torture? You think getting away with murder is torture?"

He gripped Maddie's arm tighter and shoved her in front of their father's face.

"Look at your daughter. Look at what you've done to her. And you think *your* life's been torture?"

Maddie squirmed in Charlie's grip as he laughed cruelly.

"Please, please, please," Mitch begged. "Please don't shoot me. Not like this. Not in front of Maddie. Please, show some mercy."

Charlie smirked and then looked down at his sister.

"What do you think, Maddie? Does he deserve to live?"

"What?" She startled out of her daze. Did she really have a say in this?

"Do you think he deserves to live? Or die?"

"Maddie." Mitch shifted his attention. "Listen to me, honey. You don't want him to do—"

"Shut up!" Charlie barked. "You've had your chance. Now let her decide."

The night grew quiet, the campfire crackling behind them as Charlie asked the question one last time.

"Maddie, do you want him to die?"

Charlie's words echoed in Maddie's ears. Was it really up to her?

Her father had lied to her for five years. He'd killed her mother. And he'd gotten away with it all. Did someone like that really deserve forgiveness?

But how could she pass judgment? How could she sentence someone to death? He was her father. The only one she had.

But he was also a murderer.

She didn't know what to do.

"Well?" Charlie waited for her answer.

Slowly, she shook her head. Did she really want to be like her father? Like her brother?

"No," Maddie said clearly, making sure her brother understood. "I don't think he should die."

Reluctantly, Charlie lowered his gun. Relief washed over Mitch's face. His daughter had spared him. Maddie trembled in her brother's grip. Had she made the right decision? Could it really be that simple?

"Hmm . . ." Charlie reconsidered Maddie's decision and then in one fluid motion raised the gun back up and shot his father in the leg.

"You're right, Maddie," Charlie shouted so she could hear him over their father's howls. "We shouldn't kill him just yet. After what he did, he deserves to suffer."

THIRTY-FOUR

MADDIE SQUEALED AS HER FATHER WRITHED on the ground, howling like some felled animal. The bullet had gone right through his shin, shattering it in an instant. He wasn't going anywhere on his own. She tried to get loose, to go to her dad and help him, but Charlie held her tight, his grip a vise she couldn't break free of. Out of the corner of her eye, she could see Chelsea fighting against Tommy as well, her best friend having just as little luck.

"Look at him, Maddie," Charlie said, pulling her around so that she couldn't help seeing her poor father. "You deserve to see this. This is justice. Five years in the making."

Maddie squeezed her eyes shut, but she couldn't block out her father's pained screams.

"I said look at him," Charlie shouted, jerking her arm. Reluctantly, Maddie opened her eyes. She saw her father there on the ground, whimpering now, an animal knowing its time had come.

"You don't have to do this," Maddie whimpered. "It's not too late, Charlie. You don't have to kill him."

"He's a monster," Charlie spat out. "He brought this on himself. It's time for him to get what he deserves."

Charlie let Maddie go, and then stomped closer to their father. He bent down and shined his flashlight directly into the man's eyes.

"Oh, don't act so pathetic. You're not dead yet."

And then Charlie grabbed Mitch by the scruff of the neck and hauled him up to his feet. A groan escaped the man's mouth.

"Please—please—you don't have to do this, son." Maddie's father squeezed the words out between pained breaths. Fearful tears ran down his cheeks.

"Ah, there's the dad I know," Charlie toyed with the man. "Sniveling. Useless. Mom was always stronger. It should have been you in that fire."

He let go of his father, dropping him like a sack of potatoes. Maddie watched it all, crawling away slowly, terrified. Her arm hurt where her brother had grabbed her. She could see the red outline of his fingers still there on her skin. She wanted to turn and run away. To escape all of this.

Fight or flight. Her legs were tired but strong. Charlie would never be able to catch her in these woods, not if she got a head start.

If she ran now, she knew she could get away. She could make it back down the mountain. She could survive.

But what about Chelsea?

Maddie's eyes flitted over her shoulder and she saw her best friend still struggling in Tommy's grasp.

No. Maddie couldn't leave. If she left, Chelsea wouldn't make it. And Maddie had a pinkie promise to keep.

"You're not going anywhere."

Maddie's shoulders tensed. She spun back around, but Charlie had meant the words for their father, who hadn't managed to crawl far. Her brother was already on him, bent low to look him in the eye. He took his handgun and rubbed it against his father's face.

"See how he squirms, Maddie? Pathetic, isn't it?"

"Stop it," Maddie cried, but fear rooted her to the spot, kept her from running to help him.

Charlie only laughed as he made a show of placing his finger around the handgun's trigger. He pushed the barrel right up under his father's chin, felt the man's pulse racing.

"Any last words?"

Tears flowed down Mitch's cheeks. His teeth chattered uncontrollably as he shook his head. He squeezed his eyes shut and prepared for the end. Charlie pressed the gun deeper into his neck. His finger danced against the trigger.

But he didn't pull it.

Instead, he stood up. He ran his fingers backward through his hair, leaving a streak of blood on his forehead, though Maddie couldn't have told you whose.

"A bullet's too easy," Charlie chided his father. He took a step back and then spun around and kicked the man in the stomach. Mitch's eyes bulged as his breath shot out of him.

Charlie fished in his back pocket and pulled out a little canister. It looked like a flask, but Maddie knew it must contain something worse than liquor. She watched with wide-open eyes as her father tried one last time to get away from Charlie, to escape the inescapable. Charlie only shook his head.

"Didn't we already do this?" he asked solemnly as he tipped the canister over his father's head, dousing him with its contents. "You burned my mother. Now let's see how *you* like the fire."

The gas's chemical stench seared Maddie's nose. She didn't want to watch, but she couldn't turn away as Charlie threw the canister down and took two steps back toward the campfire. He reached in and lifted a single, smoldering stick from its fiery bouquet. He turned back around and held it up like a torch.

The flame danced in front of Maddie's eyes, so small but so powerful. It hypnotized her. She couldn't turn away as Charlie lowered his hand slowly, making sure his father saw.

"This is for Mom."

Charlie touched the flame to his father's shirt.

"No!" Maddie shouted. But it was too late.

The fire leaped from the stick, snaking across her father's body, gobbling up the gasoline and growing larger, but also hungrier. The flames raced up his arms, taking bites out of his clothes and hair and flesh.

Maddie watched, petrified, as the fire spread, engulfing her dad in a white-hot blaze. He shrieked and squirmed on the ground, his nails scratching at his shirt, trying to get it off. When that didn't work he tried rolling in the dirt.

But the fire had already grown too large. There was no escaping it.

Her father's screams grew rabid. He hollered at the top of his lungs, knowing his end had come but fighting it nonetheless. Maddie couldn't bear to hear it. But Charlie remained unmoved, standing steadfast just out of reach of his father's burning body.

The death cries grew weaker as the seconds passed. They sank into a pathetic mewl and then died down altogether.

Through squinted eyes, Maddie watched her father's body smolder. The heat of the fire still pressed against her face, the smoke filling the air with the acrid smell of burning flesh, but her father wasn't with them any longer.

Maddie's eyes pricked, but no tears fell.

Another minute passed and Charlie finally moved. He turned around to face Maddie. His skin had turned bright red from the heat of the blaze and he practically glowed. He reached out his free hand and touched Maddie's cheek. She flinched, but he held her there. Maddie heard a commotion behind her and turned to see Tommy pushing a reluctant Chelsea over to join them.

"Shh," Charlie whispered to both of them. He spoke smoothly, his voice calm and unworried, like he hadn't just poured gasoline over his father's head and set him on fire. "You don't have to look so scared. Everything is going to be okay now. There's just one more thing that—"

But whatever that one thing was, Maddie and Chelsea didn't hear it as a grunt echoed through the night. They turned their heads just in time to see a blur racing toward them, moving impossibly fast. It took Maddie another second to realize that that blur was Caleb. Somehow he had managed to break through his restraints. He'd finally gotten free.

THIRTY-FIVE

CALEB FLEW AT THEM, BUT BEFORE he could reach Charlie, Tommy had thrown Chelsea to the ground and flung his body in the way. The two collided and crashed to the ground. Caleb yelled out as he attacked the younger boy, his voice primal, a wild animal making one last desperate fight for survival. He balled up his fist and punched Tommy in the face, breaking the boy's nose in an instant. Caleb grabbed Tommy's head between his hands and smashed it against the ground.

Once. Twice. Three times. Maddie counted all the way up to six. She winced with each crunch of impact.

"Stop it!"

The surprise of Caleb's escape wore off as Charlie pushed him off of Tommy.

But it was too late. The boy wasn't getting up. Caleb had shattered his skull, splattered blood and brains all over the grass.

Caleb rushed toward Charlie next, but the teen saw him coming. He spun the gun around and shot Caleb, hitting him in the thigh. The guide stumbled and then went down, his berserker strength spent.

"You bastard!"

Charlie kicked Caleb in the stomach. Then in the face. He kicked and kicked and kicked. "We only kept you alive so we could blame it all on you. We've been planning this for months, ever since I picked Tommy up from the police station, and now you've gone and ruined everything."

Charlie stepped on Caleb's leg where he'd shot him and relished the wild cry of pain.

"You've outlived your usefulness."

He looked down at the guide and smiled. He took aim for the final shot.

"No!" Maddie shrieked. She rushed forward, but she didn't go for her brother and the gun. Instead she went for Caleb, throwing herself on the ground, shielding his body.

"Move out of the way, Maddie."

"No! He didn't do anything," Maddie wailed. "You don't have to hurt him."

Charlie paused. For the first time that night, he looked concerned. Conflicted.

"Don't you see that he has to die, Maddie?" Charlie explained it to her as if it were something obvious. "It's part of the plan. We need someone to blame."

Behind her, Maddie could hear Caleb taking labored breaths. She wanted to turn and see how bad it was, but her brother pulled her attention back forward.

"Don't you see," Charlie went on. "They *all* had to die. Every one of them. They were bad people who needed to be punished."

"But he's not bad," Maddie shouted back. "He's innocent. He saved me. He's a good guy."

"*I'm* the good guy." Charlie shook his fist and beat it against his chest. "*I'm* the one who got his hands messy. The one who brought about justice for our mother. For you."

"But that doesn't mean you have to kill Caleb."

Charlie only shook his head, keeping his gun raised the whole time.

"They're gonna want an explanation when we get down the mountain," Charlie tried one last time to make it clear for his sister. "They're gonna want a suspect. Someone to blame."

Maddie shook her head. She didn't want to hear what her brother had to say.

"Caleb did *all* of this," Charlie spelled it out for her. "He planned it *all*. From the beginning. He was a psychopath. A lunatic. He brought us up here and smashed our radio. He picked us off one by one."

Maddie shook her head again. She closed her eyes and tried to block out her brother's lies.

That wasn't what had happened. It wasn't true. Caleb didn't do any of those things. He was innocent. A hero. He'd tried to save them when he could have easily bolted into the woods and gotten away. He'd risked his life for them. She tried to block out Charlie as he pressed on.

"Caleb was the one who sliced Kris and Mark's throats. He scalped Ed. He dismembered that boy in the woods. He shot Bryan and burned our father alive."

Charlie paused, a wicked smile on his face. Did he actually believe he'd get away with this? Did he actually believe that Maddie would go along with him?

"But he didn't get us," Charlie went on. "We managed to stop him. To put an end to his killing spree. We survived."

No. No. No. Maddie closed her eyes and tried to shut out her brother's words.

"Maddie?" Concern crossed Charlie's face. "Did you hear me? Do you understand me? We can still go back to a normal life."

A snort shot out of Maddie's nose. She'd tried to keep it in, but failed. Had he truly lost it? How could he expect her to just go back to a normal life with him? How could she ever trust him again?

Yes, their dad had done terrible things. But that didn't give Charlie the right to go on a killing spree. To murder their friends. Their family. She couldn't go back to watching Sunday Giants games with him and pretend that nothing had changed.

"No." Maddie shook her head. "I won't lie for you."

"No?" Charlie arched an eyebrow and took a step closer, the gun still in his hand.

"No." Maddie said it again, but with less certainty this time. Her eyes watched the gun carefully.

"It wasn't supposed to end like this," Charlie lamented. "We were supposed to get away together."

Charlie shook his head in disappointment. He sighed, looking put out.

"I was hoping you'd make this easy. But now—now we're gonna have to do things the hard way."

Charlie retreated a few steps. And then his hand shot out and grabbed hold of Chelsea's arm before the girl could move. He pulled her up from the ground and nestled his gun into her messy tangle of hair.

"If you don't move out of the way and go along with my story, Chelsea's not going to make it off the mountain with us."

The world narrowed right in front of Maddie's eyes. Her head spun like she'd stood up too quickly, and she thought she might pass out.

Then she screamed.

THIRTY-SIX

"IT'S UP TO YOU, MADDIE," CHARLIE said, holding the gun tight to Chelsea's head.

"Don't hurt her," Maddie begged, desperate.

"You're not leaving me much of a choice." Charlie frowned at his sister. "It's Caleb or Chelsea. You can't have both."

Maddie stared at her brother, lost for words. What had happened to him? He had always protected her. Had always been the best brother.

But this—this wasn't that Charlie. She didn't recognize him. The crazy look in his eye, the way he talked so breezily about killing everyone they knew. How he wanted to shoot Caleb, too, and then frame the whole thing on him.

Where was the brother who had always looked out for her, who helped her set up her tent and hugged her close whenever something frightened her?

With a start, Maddie realized that brother was gone. And she knew better than to trust a word that came out of this Charlie's mouth.

She dropped her eyes as she tried to buy some time, tried to think of something, a plan that could save all three of them. Her gaze wandered across the ground. She jumped as her father's body came into focus. The flames had died down, leaving behind an unrecognizable corpse, raw and red, the skin mottled.

"Maddie." Charlie's voice broke through her thoughts. Her eyes flew back up to find her brother's face. "It's time to decide. Chelsea or Caleb."

"But—but—" Maddie fumbled for words. She didn't have a plan.

"It's okay."

The croak came from behind Maddie. She glanced over her shoulder and saw Caleb struggling to sit up. He wore a pained look on his beaten and bloody face. Maddie couldn't even make out the antlers on his forehead from all the blood. He nodded to her and smiled, that one dimple still managing to poke up out of his swollen face.

"But—but—I can't." Maddie fumbled for words.

"It's okay," he croaked again. And Maddie understood. This was the only way. She stretched her arms out and hugged him tightly, hoping the gesture would be enough, praying her gratitude would translate. She let go of him and got to her feet slowly. Her legs shook underneath her, but she turned to face her brother.

"I'm happy you've finally come to your senses," Charlie said, a smile breaking out over his face. He moved the gun away from Chelsea's head and let her go. She stumbled forward and then ran into Maddie's arms, hugging her tight.

"Are you okay?" Maddie whispered, her hands pushing Chelsea's hair back, her fingers wiping the tear tracks from her best friend's cheeks. Chelsea sniffled and nodded. She buried her nose in Maddie's shoulder and kept crying.

"We're not done yet, Maddie." Charlie's words startled the two girls. They turned around to face him but kept a tight hold of each other.

"Here," Charlie said. He held out the gun for Maddie. "Take it."

What? She stared at her brother. She didn't understand.

"Take the gun, Maddie." Charlie shook his hand. "Take the gun and shoot Caleb."

Maddie looked down at Caleb's broken body and then back up at her brother. That hadn't been part of their deal. She couldn't shoot Caleb.

"Take it!" Charlie shouted it this time. "Prove that you're with me."

He held the gun out for Maddie and waited.

"I can't," Maddie's voice wobbled.

"You can," Charlie assured her. "And you will."

With his free hand, he reached around his back and pulled a hunting knife from his belt. The blade flashed dangerously in front of Maddie's eyes as he pointed its tip at Chelsea.

"Okay. I'll do it."

The words rushed from Maddie's mouth as she reached forward. Anything to keep Chelsea safe.

"Careful now," Charlie warned, pulling the gun back. "Don't try anything. There's only one bullet in there. So make sure you don't miss."

Charlie opened his palm back up and offered the gun to Maddie. She looked at it for a few seconds and then lowered her hand, taking it. Charlie quickly pulled Chelsea in front of him, a human shield. He rested his hand on her shoulder, the blade of his knife pointed out, ready to slash the girl's throat at the slightest wrong move on Maddie's part.

Maddie looked down at the gun, weighing it in her hand. It was heavier than she'd thought.

"Maddie," Chelsea whimpered, "don't worry about me. You don't have to do this."

"Shh," Charlie hushed the girl, pressing his knife closer to her throat. "Maddie can make her own decisions."

He turned his attention back to his sister.

"Now, just take a deep breath. Hold your arm steady and aim. It'll be over for him quick. He'll barely feel a thing."

Shaking, Maddie looked at the gun and then back up at her brother. Her eyes pleaded with him to change his mind, but he only nodded forward, waiting for her to finish the job, to prove her loyalty to him.

She gulped down a sob and turned back toward Caleb. Mark's deer flashed in her mind. It'd had the same helpless, sad look in its eyes when Caleb had eased it to a quicker death. Was this so different?

"We're waiting on you, Maddie." Charlie tsked. "Prolonging it won't make it any easier. Now raise the gun and take aim."

Maddie followed her brother's instructions this time. She held the gun in both of her trembling hands as she brought it up and pointed it at Caleb's chest.

"Now pull the trigger slowly," Charlie said. "You don't want to jerk it."

Maddie's pulse drummed in her ears. The gun slipped in her hands as sweat poured from every one of her pores. She didn't want to do this, but she had to. Charlie had left her no other choice. He would kill Caleb if she didn't. And then he'd kill Chelsea, too. Maddie couldn't let that happen. She couldn't lose everything in one night.

"Mustang Maddie," Caleb croaked, startling her out of her thoughts. "It's okay."

She looked up and focused in on his face. That face so handsome underneath all that blood and dirt, those cuts and bruises. The face of a hero.

The gun felt suddenly still in her hands. She swallowed and took a deep breath. She readjusted her grip on the gun and took aim.

Slowly, she pulled the trigger, a silent apology flitting from her lips.

The gun fired, louder than Maddie had expected. She jumped back. Her eyes popped as she saw a splotch of red explode against Caleb's chest. The guide grunted and then fell forward, his face crashing into the ground.

The gun shook in Maddie's hands and she let go of it like it was a hot iron burning her fingers. She watched as it dropped to the ground and tumbled away.

Behind her, Charlie let Chelsea go and the girl stumbled, falling to the ground as well. He sheathed his knife, a smile beaming across his face as he pulled Maddie to his chest. He pressed her head against his shoulder and hugged her close.

"You did it," Charlie said proudly. "I didn't think you had it in you, but you did."

He pushed out of the hug and looked at Maddie, the campfire flickering in his pupils. He seemed calmer all of a sudden. Less crazed. More like the brother Maddie knew.

But he wasn't.

Maddie's eyes flickered to the ground. She saw Chelsea lying there where she'd fallen, too exhausted to pick herself back up. She looked spent, almost too weak to lift her head.

Maddie turned back to her brother, his hand outstretched, waiting for her to take it. He could rationalize it all he wanted, but in the end, he'd killed all those people. Their friends. Their family. She could never trust him.

He was just as bad as—no—much, much worse than—her father.

Maddie lowered her hand and took Charlie's. She leaned in close.

"I love you," she whispered and felt his body relax into her.

She pulled him in closer, hugged him tight. And then she planted her feet, using all her strength to push her brother away. She watched as a look of surprise blossomed on his face. She let go of him and he stumbled backward a couple of steps. His heel snagged on a rock, and he lost his balance. His body tipped back and he was horizontal with the ground, poised somewhere between floating and falling.

Maddie watched as gravity took hold and her brother's body crashed down, landing right in the middle of their campfire.

A shower of sparks and flames erupted. The fire sputtered, threatening to go out as Charlie rolled around and tried to get up.

No. Maddie couldn't let him get away. She dropped to her knees and scurried along the ground. She'd seen it earlier. But where had it gone?

There. She spotted the canister. She grabbed it, hoping her brother hadn't used all the gasoline on their father. She leaped back to her feet and threw the whole thing into the fire.

At first, nothing happened. Maddie started to panic. Her brother was almost back on his feet, his screams filled with fury. He had his arm out, ready to grab her and pull her in, too.

But then the canister exploded. The fire blew up in Maddie's face, knocking her off her feet. A curtain of flame erupted and enveloped her brother, bringing him back to his knees, setting him on fire from head to toe.

Maddie struggled to her feet and hobbled over to Chelsea. She collapsed right next to her best friend, leaning her head on Chelsea's shoulder. They sat there on the ground together and watched the fire build, watched as it regained strength, devouring Charlie's shirt and hair, his flesh.

"Help me!"

Charlie's plea came out raw and desperate. Maddie's hands shook uncontrollably in her lap.

What had she done?

Her fingers flew to her head and played along the brim of the Giants cap. *Charlie's* Giants cap. She lifted it off her head and studied the logo.

She looked into the fire. Looked at her brother one last time. Then she tossed the cap into the blaze and watched as the campfire finished Charlie off.

This was what it was like to burn. This was how her mother had died.

After a couple of minutes, Charlie stopped moving, and the fire started to die down. Maddie counted another sixty seconds and then exhaled.

It was over. Finally. She'd saved them.

She nuzzled deeper into Chelsea's shoulder. She could hear the girl's soft, steady breaths. Tears speckled her cheeks as she whispered into her best friend's ear.

"We made it."

Chelsea smiled wearily and pressed her head against Maddie's. Somehow, they had survived.

A sudden grunt pulled them out of their stupor. Maddie's eyes flitted to the fire, panic rising in her chest.

But Charlie's body was still there, smoldering in the flames.

Maddie heard the grunt again and spun around. How could she have forgotten? Her eyes swept the ground and she saw Caleb moving.

"Oh, my God," Maddie shouted. She rushed forward and bent down, helping Caleb pull himself upright. "I'm so sorry."

"You meant to miss, right?" Caleb winced and pressed his shoulder. Maddie could see the wound seeping blood where her bullet had hit him. Thank God, her nonlethal shot had been on target.

"I'm just glad you played along," Maddie said.

Caleb laughed, but it quickly turned into a groan.

"We have to get help," Maddie said. Chelsea had already stumbled over and joined them. "He's lost a lot of blood."

"But how?" Chelsea wondered aloud, starting to panic. "He's too heavy for us to carry."

Maddie looked around, as if she'd find a phone or ambulance that they just hadn't noticed before.

"I'll have to run for it," Maddie decided, realizing it was their only option, the fastest way they'd get help for Caleb.

"But what if you get lost?" Chelsea asked. "What if you hurt yourself?"

"I'll be back soon. I promise," Maddie said, determined. "Just— just make sure he holds on."

Chelsea nodded and pulled Maddie in for a hug.

Maddie took one last look at her best friend. Her sister. The only family she had left. Then she turned on her heel and bolted into the night, running faster than she ever had in her life, running to save Caleb.

EPILOGUE

THE HOSPITAL BUZZED WITH ACTIVITY, MONITORS beeping, gurneys clattering and phone messages paging over the loudspeaker. In a corner of the waiting room, two girls sat by themselves.

"Do you think he'll be okay?" Maddie asked, worrying her bottom lip between her teeth. After they'd cleaned her wounds and stuck an IV in her arm, the nurses had given her an oversized pair of sweats to wear. They'd given Chelsea the same, but her father had arrived at the hospital shortly after they were admitted and brought her pajamas from home.

"I don't know," Chelsea spoke quietly, not raising her head to look at Maddie.

"I'm sure he'll be fine," Maddie said absently, more to assure herself than anything.

The two lapsed back into silence.

"We got him to a hospital," Maddie went on nervously, getting to her feet. She started pacing back and forth. "They can fix bullet holes, can't they? Modern medicine and all."

She let the thought drop, her mind racing back to the flashing lights and the doctors' shouts as they'd wheeled Caleb into the emergency room. That'd been about five hours ago. She still didn't know if he'd survive.

"I—I thought we were going to die up there," Chelsea mumbled, ignoring Maddie's question. "I thought—I thought I was going to lose you."

Maddie stopped her pacing and turned to look at her best friend. Though cleaned up now, Chelsea still looked damaged. Broken. She saw the tears welling up in the girl's eyes.

"But you—you saved me." Chelsea's words came out wet, and Maddie rushed forward, pulling Chelsea into a hug.

"We saved each other," Maddie whispered. "I couldn't have done it without you."

The girls held their hug for a long time, both crying now. Neither could actually believe that it was over. That they had gotten off the mountain. That they had survived.

"I don't know what I'd do without you," Chelsea pulled away first, her hands flying to her face to wipe away the tears.

"I'm never going to leave you," Maddie said. "Like it or not, you're stuck with me."

Chelsea giggled, remembering those same words she'd spoken to Maddie five years before.

"Together forever. Pinkie promise."

And Maddie held out her finger, waiting for Chelsea to take it.

"Pinkie promise."

The girls clasped hands and pulled into an even tighter hug.

"Excuse me," a voice interrupted them. "Is one of you Maddie Davenport?"

Maddie lifted her head and stared up at the doctor.

"That's me."

"Caleb's out of surgery now," the doctor went on. "And he asked to see you. Both of you."

A smile broke over Maddie's face. She looked excitedly at Chelsea and then back at the doctor.

"What are you waiting for?" She leaped to her feet. "Let's go."

The doctor gave her a strange look but then led her and Chelsea out of the waiting room. They walked a few minutes and then the doctor stopped, pointing them into a patient's room. Maddie and Chelsea rushed past him, then came up short as they spotted Caleb lying in his hospital bed.

Even through the bruises and cuts and bandages, Maddie could still see his bright blue eyes shining. They sparked as they caught sight of her. She rushed forward and took his hand, smiling as he squeezed hers back.

"There she is," Caleb whispered, his voice hoarse and barely there. "Mustang Maddie. My hero."

ACKNOWLEDGMENTS

FIRST OFF, I WOULD LIKE TO thank my family. My mother and father (Linda and Richard) always encouraged me to read as a child. Without their support, I wouldn't be where I am today. I'd also like to thank my dad for being an awesome beta reader. He knew Maddie before anyone else and gave me invaluable insight as I went along the scary road of writing a novel. My brother, Christopher, and his wife, Mandi, were also always there to bounce ideas off of.

For their encouragement, I'd like to thank Allary Montague, Megan Frost, and Terrell Bostic. They've been my biggest cheerleaders throughout the years. I'd also like to thank Kyle King, who made sure I was always well fed as I wrote.

It was the opportunity of a lifetime, getting to work with James Patterson. He saw potential in my book, and I can't thank him enough. Maddie's story wouldn't exist without him. Also, gigantic thanks to the entire JIMMY team. Aubrey Poole was a dream of an

ACKNOWLEDGMENTS

editor. Sasha Henriques, Jenny Bak, Tracy Shaw, and Stephanie Yang all helped make this book a real thing that I could hold in my hands. Thank you to Sabrina Benun and Alexis Gilbert. To Sean Comstock, Erinn McGrath, Florence Yue, Elizabeth Guess, Katie Tucker, Kathryn Rogers, and Ned Rust. Also to the entire sales team at Hachette! I've worked alongside most of them for years and am so thankful to have gotten to publish my first book with them.

ABOUT THE AUTHOR

SHAWN SARLES was born and raised in a small town in western Kentucky. After graduating from Wake Forest University, he moved to New York City. He has lived there and worked in the publishing industry for almost a decade. *Campfire* is his debut novel.

For
EVELYN McCALL BROWN
My wife and companion for more than two decades

PREFACE

ROUGHLY THREE YEARS have elapsed since work was started on this project. Doing research in and writing about Colorado's early history, with particular reference to the mining period, has been an immensely satisfying experience. Several time blocks during vacations, many, many weekend jaunts, and not a few holidays have been spent in relocating and exploring these early towns by Jeep, on foot, and occasionally on snowshoes.

Two rather annoying frustrations have persisted throughout the preparation of the volume with regard to the selection of places to be included. In some instances there are rather good pictures of towns, but insufficient or conflicting information has precluded the writing of a chapter. There are other locations where a veritable wealth of information exists, but apparently no photographer ever recorded how the place looked for posterity. In no instance has a town been included without pictures. Likewise, in no case have I included towns that I have not visited personally.

In duplicating the angles from which the early photographs were made, wide-angle lenses were used far more than optics of a normal focal length. Due to the growth of trees, changes in the terrain, and for other like reasons, several fine old pictures could not be matched and were therefore excluded. For those persons interested in photography, the pictures were made with Leica equipment, using green or yellow filters in most cases. The film was Plus-X. All prints were made on Luminos enlarging paper.

A word of special gratitude is due to my wife, Evelyn, and to our two children, Diana and Marshall, for their patience during many long trips to remote locations, and for their help in the identification of photographic angles. Thanks should also go to Dianne Zahller, Kathleen Brandel, and Evelyn Brown for typing all of these chapters. Freda and Francis B. Rizzari gave generously of their time, ingenuity, and understanding by proofreading the completed manuscript for errors and omissions. Virginia McConnell checked the historical accuracy of my chapters dealing with the South Park towns. Arthur Abe and Jessie Bingham assisted with technical photographic problems. Fred and Jo Mazzulla were most generous in supplying a large number of early photographs from their superb collection. Many additional pictures were secured from the fine collections of Richard A. Ronzio, Francis B. Rizzari, Jack Thode, Malcolm E. Collier, George A. Dumont, and Velma Churchill. The photographic library of the State Historical Society of Colorado and the Western History Department of the Denver Public Library filled a number of other photographic needs with rare old pictures.

Erl Ellis, Allison Chandler, Joe Tomsick, Harry Simcox, George Dumont, and many others furnished me with information by letters, tape recordings, and personal interviews. Mrs. Enid Thompson, Mrs. Laura Ekstrom, Mrs. Kay Pearson, and Mrs. Louisa Ward Arps spent many long hours and were of tremendous assistance to me in researching information at the library of the State Historical Society of Colorado. Mrs. Alys Freeze and her staff at the Western History Department of the Denver Public Library also devoted a great deal of time to my many requests. Mrs. Opal Harber, James Davis and Mrs. Hazel Lundberg were particularly helpful.

Finally, in alphabetical order, the following references were used in the preparation of this book. The *Alamosa Journal* for February 28, 1884; the *Boulder Daily Camera* for March 8, 1946, and August 13, 1953; Samuel Bowles, *The Switzerland of America* (New York: Samuel Bowles and Company, 1869); the *Canon City Mining Gazette* for August 23, 1882; the *Carbonate Chronicle* for February 27, 1939; the *Central City Register-Call* for April 26, 1897; the *Colorado Business Directory* for 1885 and 1877; the *Colorado Graphic* for October 29, 1887; the *Colorado Miner* for September 14, and 21, 1878, February 1, March 29, and August 2, 1879; the *Colorado Mining Directory* of 1883; George Crofutt, *Grip-sack Guide to Colorado* (Omaha: The Overland Publishing Company, 1881); the *Denver Daily News* for February 3, 1883, and March 15, 1884; the *Denver Post* for February 11, 1899, October 28, 1900, December 19 and 31, 1941, October 23, 1954, and November 17, 1957; *The Denver Republican* for February 4, 1867, January 17, 1882, June 25, 1893, May 17, and September 9, 1897, February 3, and 4, 1899, January 2, July 20, and August 6, 1900, January 23, and September 29, 1901; *The Denver Times* for December 16, 1874, November 1, 1881, December 31, 1896, August 16, 1898, January 4 and 25, February 4, 6, 9 and 21, May 13, June 28, October 22, and December 21, 1899, October 30, 1900, January 19 and November 28, 1902; the *Denver Tribune* for December 20, 1880; John L. Dyer, *The Snow-Shoe Itinerant* (Cincinnati: Cranston and Stowe, 1890); the *Eagle Valley Enterprize* for April 12, 1940; Perry Eberhart, *Guide to the Colorado Ghost Towns and Mining Camps* (Denver: Sage Books, 1959); the *Elk Mountain Pilot* for July 18, 1935; the *Fairplay Flume* for July 17, 1879; Frank Fossett, *Colorado, Its Gold and Silver Mines* (New York: C. J. Crawford, Printer and Stationer, 1880); Don and Jean Griswold and Fred and Jo Mazzula, *Colorado's Century of Cities*, published by the authors (Denver: 1958); the *Gunnison News Champion* for November 30, 1939; Frank Hall, *History of Colorado*, four volumes published between 1889 and 1895 by the Blakely Printing Company of Chicago; Ernest Ingersoll, *Knocking Around the Rockies*

(New York: Harper and Brothers, 1883); Sidney Jocknick, *Early Days on the Western Slope of Colorado* (Denver: Carson and Harper Company, 1913); David Lavender, *The Big Divide* (Garden City: Doubleday and Company, Inc., 1948); and *One Man's West* (Garden City, N.Y.: Doubleday and Company, Inc., 1956); *Leslie's Illustrated Weekly* for March 23, 1899; Virginia McConnell, *Bayou Salado* (Denver, Colorado: Sage Books, 1966); L. L. Nunn, *A Memoir* (Ithaca, New York: The Telluride Association, 1933); the *Pueblo Chieftain* for May 16, 1955; the *Rocky Mountain Miner* for October 11, 1902; the *Rocky Mountain News* for November 14, 1860, February 6, May 4, and October 19, 1867, June 9, 1877, April 10, September 24, and November 16, 1880, August 12, and December 12, 1881, January 13, and October 17, 1882, March 18, and 21, 1883, October 10, 1891, July 12, 1897, January 1, and January 28, 1898, and March 10, 1958; the *San Juan Prospector* for July 2, 1887; Marshall Sprague, *Money Mountain* (Boston: Little, Brown and Company, 1953); and *The Great Gates* (Boston: Little, Brown and Company, 1964); the *Steamboat Springs Pilot* for April 17, 1936; the *Summit County Journal* for August 14, 1936, and November 19, 1937; Warren and Stride, *Cripple Creek and Colorado Springs Illustrated* (Colorado Springs, 1936) the *Wason Miner* for December 12, 1891; Frank Waters, *Midas of the Rockies* (Denver: University of Denver Press, 1949); Albert N. Williams, *Rocky Mountain Country* (New York: Duell, Sloan and Pearce, 1950); George F. Willison, *Here They Dug the Gold* (London: Readers' Union, 1952); and last but far from least, Muriel Sibell Wolle's magnificent and monumental *Stampede to Timberline* (Boulder, the Author, 1949) and *The Bonanza Trail* (Bloomington: Indiana University Press, 1953).

By far the most trying problems in the preparation of this book were encountered in my efforts to disassociate fact from fiction, folklore, and downright deliberate errors. In one instance, the son of a former publisher of the *Animas Forks Pioneer* admits that his father often made up his own news stories to fill the columns and sell papers when news was short. Likewise, even first-person accounts of pioneer happenings, early mine production figures and population statistics—to name just three—vary widely from source to source. In all instances my work has been the often impossible task of finding out what really happened.

In no instance have I knowingly presented events as facts without good authority, or have I intentionally colored what happened by my own literary style or ideas of what might have been. Whenever a "story" has been included, it has been labeled as such. For all unresolved statements and figures that have eluded careful checking, and for any other errors, genuine or imagined, that may vary from what the reader has seen or heard, the author apologizes in advance. In several cases within these chapters, the truth has been stranger than fiction.

R. L. B.

INTRODUCTION

SINCE THE PUBLICATION of *Jeep Trails to Colorado Ghost Towns* (Caxton, 1963), I have often received letters from and been confronted by many persons who have neither the desire nor the audacity to own or operate a four-wheel-drive vehicle. Nevertheless, these same people express a profound interest in Western history, an incidental concern with the mining period, and a specific fascination with the mystery associated with our ghost towns. With only minor variations in their approach, the desire has almost always been expressed for information about ghost towns and early mining camps that can be reached on a weekend or single-day outing in the family sedan, or perhaps this coupled with a very short, easy hike.

The idea seemed appealing to them, and to me, and a file of materials for possible inclusion began to grow during the preparation of another book (*An Empire of Silver*, Caxton, 1965). Serious work started on this project in October of 1964. A wide variety of communities with interesting histories grounded in the mining period were considered. Some, like Leadville and Central City, were rejected as being too obvious. Others were deleted due to my failure to find enough interesting material that could be documented in the text, to geographical conditions, to the present status of the site, or to changes in routes—to name just a few.

Although most of the towns in this book were selected for their accessibility, a smaller number of prime places where a four-wheel-drive vehicle is needed for access have been included just to keep things interesting. I might add, however, that a hike to these locations is not out of the question.

Seeking the locations of Colorado's myriad array of true ghost towns is often a frustrating experience. The multiplicity of old and unlabled mountain roads or trails may lead you up countless blind alleys, and it may require hours or even days for you to reach your destination—and this only by the complicated process of elimination. Often these "freeways" wind about in all directions at once and a compass actually becomes more useful than your road map, or the directions from natives. And then, assuming that you finally do get there, your town may have been totally obliterated by the natural environment indigenous to our Colorado mountain winters. The history of most early Colorado mining camps is liberally punctuated with an extremely high incidence of their destruction by rockslides, snow avalanches, fires, mud slides, and a few floods. Assuming that a given camp may have escaped, to a degree, the rigors of these destructive forces, its remains must still somehow survive contemporary Colorado's high mountain winters.

Woodstock was obliterated when a train, approaching the western portal of the Alpine Tunnel, started a snowslide which took the lives of fourteen of the town's seventeen inhabitants who, unfortunately, were in the right place at the wrong time. A mud slide buried Brownsville, just west of Silver Plume. Three mud slides thus far have submerged parts of Marble and the end is not yet. Three fires and two Hollywood motion picture companies on location have left a sadly depleted shell of once attractive Rosita. Snow avalanches terminated the life of Tomichi and were so common in southwestern Colorado that the "white death" became the most dreaded single aspect of living in the San Juan camps. Rockslides interrupted the way of life at Eureka with a frightening degree of regularity. Colorado's history is replete with many other similar examples but these few should suffice to make the point. What one may or may not find at any given location may change radically from year to year or, in a few instances, from day to day.

Searching for ghost towns may also be rewarding. There's a real thrill in store when one tops a ridge or rounds that last curve to find an abandoned town spread out below in some remote meadow. It's a silent and empty place now with streets overgrown by grass and weeds. Tiny fenced yards, once proudly kept, are now filled with restless, ugly spheres of sagebrush. Once upon a time, hundreds (or thousands) of people like ourselves lived here. Now there is no one.

By way of providing a modicum of background material against which this book is to be read, I'd like the reader to consider with me a series of four questions which, it is hoped, will enrich and enhance your enjoyment and appreciation of what has been attempted in this book.

First of all, what is a ghost town? There are many definitions. Some insist that the only true ghost town is one that is completely gone; a town like Parkville or Quartz, that simply is no more. Some academic objections have been raised with reference to labeling as ghost towns those locations where buildings still stand, even though no population currently exists. To many of us, an empty town that is not all that it used to be, qualifies as a ghost town. Various other sources have included in their definitions those towns that are only partly ghost or empty, but which have small numbers of people living in some of the structures within the community. Accepting this last definition would allow inclusion of Leadville, Central City, Cripple Creek, and a variety of similar communities. One author said, "A ghost town is a shadowy semblance of its former self." Obviously, there will be borderline cases within whatever definition you accept. My own ideal example is a town completely abandoned by all business and permanent residents, preferably with buildings still standing. Oriental City, Dyersville, or Animas Forks would qualify here.

Second, how does a community become a ghost town?

Probably the greatest single cause was repeal of the Sherman Silver Purchase Act in 1893. Destroying the basic economic value upon which the community was built inevitably destroyed the purpose for its existence. Pegging the price of gold at thirty-five dollars an ounce wiped out many towns early in the present century. With rising costs of mining equipment, unemployment insurance, higher taxes at all levels, union wages, social security and other similar items, the price of gold is nevertheless still only thirty-five dollars an ounce. This largely negates the efforts of an American mining industry and there are almost no new mining towns being started.

In 1861 the Civil War brought about a collapse in the speculative mining boom, depopulated the towns, and resulted in a decided chill that developed between Eastern risk capital and Colorado deep-mining ventures. High transportation costs for travel over difficult terrain killed the otherwise promising camp at Ruby. Floresta became a ghost town when there was no longer a market for its fine anthracite coal. A similar ending engulfed Coal Basin, and the railroads were taken out in both instances. Today, huge trucks haul coal down over the old grades from Coal Basin and a measure of prosperity has returned to the industry, but the town will probably never be rebuilt.

By no means were all early towns built as a result of mining, or died as a consequence of it. Eastonville expired when the railroad was abandoned and its taxes no longer supported the town. Jefferson was once a big railroad shipping point for sheep and South Park hay. The same circumstances applied to the now extinct town of Michigan. Bent's first stockade was abandoned after only two years 1826-28) when it was discovered that it had been built in the middle of a no-man's-land between hostile Ute and Arapaho territories where no Indians dared venture for purposes of trade. Robinson, a beautifully preserved gem among ghost towns, was buried under the vast, ever-expanding dump of the Climax Molybdenum Company. Montgomery is in a watery grave at the bottom of a reservoir storing water for Colorado Springs. Marble faded when its product became too expensive. In Vermont, quarries were more accessible and, therefore, transportation costs were minimized. Later use of synthetics hurt the market for marble in both states. The previously mentioned mud slides were no help.

Wagon Creek and Garland City on the Denver and Rio Grande Railway, expired when the line was extended to Fort Garland. Wagon Creek, in fact, lasted only six months. Trail City, in eastern Colorado, folded when the great cattle drives stopped concurrent with the end of the open range cattle industry. Many twentieth-century ghost towns were created on the Colorado and Kansas prairies in the 1930's. Mainly, a town dies from lack of business.

Some towns went out of business by becoming a part of another community. In Gunnison County Irwin and Ruby got themselves annexed and ceased to exist as separate entities. Recen and Kokomo joined forces after a fire destroyed the latter. Old Congress Town and Red Mountain were abandoned due to location. Both apparently merged later into Red Mountain Town in a new location just off the top of Red Mountain Pass. Then in 1892 the town burned. Again in 1896 the fire laddies were called out as history repeated itself. Red Mountain, however, rose once more from its ashes. A destructive forest fire nearly finished the job in 1937. Rosita also had three fires. No Colorado mining camp worthy of note escaped the ravages of at least one fire. In some instances, fires became a stimulus to accelerated growth—Nevadaville being a case in point. At other times they became a secondary reason contributing to abandonment.

A better road which was bladed into Leavick from the Fairplay side hastened its destruction by vandals. Conversely, the wretched road into Carson has left us a well-preserved town. Notoriety is sometimes the downfall of a town. Following the publication of a fine illustrated article in a Denver paper about the old Victorian two-story house at Rosita, vandals burned it to the ground that next weekend. A few towns have been burned by the Forest Service as fire hazards. Bowerman was founded on a hoax and died following the exposure.

Third, where are the ghost towns? Most seem to have been founded up nearly every little creek where gold and silver were thought to exist in paying quantities. The mining towns were in the mountains, often high up since gold and silver deposits were forced into seams and faults during the prehistoric period when volcanic pressures wrinkled the earth's crust and formed our Rocky Mountains. Where there are no mountains, gold is not likely to be found except in the form of placers which have washed down via stream beds which in turn are fed by lofty melting glaciers which erode away the high canyons.

Fourth, and last, are any new ghost towns being created today? The answer is very definitely, "Yes. Como is dying from a combination of the mining collapse coupled with railroad abandonment. The original Dillon had to be abandoned when Denver built its new reservoir. A new town was built on higher land and took the old name. New highways have isolated some communities and left them to wither away on old vines. Henderson and Bayfield are two examples. Neither is dead yet by any means, and who knows what tomorrow may bring? Depletion of oil reserves in the Denver-Julesburg basin will undoubtedly cause some population shifts here as it did in Oklahoma and Texas.

It has long been the hope of this writer that one of these towns might be set aside and preserved, perhaps as a state park, at some time in the near future. Massachusetts has its old Sturbridge, Virginia has restored both Williamsburg and Jamestown. Since our mining period ranked high on any list of priorities responsible for bringing people here in large numbers, what could be a more fitting monument than a well-preserved mining camp to show future Coloradoans how people lived during the nineteenth century in the Centennial State? A possible choice might be St. Elmo, which is centrally located, accessible, scenic, well preserved, endowed with adequate water and sufficient space for a park and campground. The mining period is unique in Colorado history. Its priority in time and its short life combined to furnish most of the true ghost towns.

In the meantime, tread easily on your visits to the past. The old relics are fragile and tinder dry. Vandalism, a carelessly discarded match, or a thoughtless act may erase these historic and interesting places forever.

R. L. B.

CONTENTS

𝄾

ILLUSTRATIONS

GHOST TOWNS
OF THE
COLORADO ROCKIES

1.

ALMA

SLOWLY THE LAST warming rays of the setting sun fanned out behind the majestic peaks of the as yet unnamed Mosquito Range. In their place a high-altitude chill spread across the Bayou Salado. It was a typical evening in late June of 1844 and the party of men who had just made camp were busily building fires to ward off the cold. Presently their leader returned from tethering his mount and sat down to record entries in his log by the flickering firelight. John C. Frémont, erstwhile pathfinder of the early West, was only thirty-one years old. Now he was on the return leg of a trip to California, having been charged with mapping the territory from the South Platte River to the Pacific Ocean.

Some minutes after darkness had enveloped their camp, the mournful howl of a distant timber wolf shattered the mountain stillness. Frémont is said to have remarked that at some time in the future, even this very spot would probably be settled. He further speculated that the forlorn animal had merely scented the path of progress and was doubtless raising his voice in protest. Already, a band of Utes had started camping on Sacramento Flats nearby, and now a band of whites was busily tramping the alpine meadows.

Within the brief span of white man's recorded history, the Bayou Salado, now known as South Park, had experienced many explorers prior to Frémont. Among others, it was well known to such men as Jim Bridger, Zebulon Pike, Lancaster P. Lupton, and Jim Beckwourth. Under the circumstances, Frémont's prediction had a better-than-average chance of proving to be accurate. Ultimately, a whole series of camps grew up in the neighborhood, largely as satellites of Fairplay and Alma. Some legends insist that Fairplay was actually built over the site of the Frémont campsite.

Park County was established by an act of the First Territorial Legislature when it met in 1861.

Alma seems to have had its beginnings in the very early seventies. Hall's *History of Colorado* states quite positively that it was established in 1872. J. B. Stansell and Abram Bergh put up the first house in town for a Mr. James who had kept a general store at Fairplay. James also planned to open a branch at Alma. His wife, Alma James, is often mentioned as the source of the town's name. From another quarter we hear that several other ladies in town all shared the same given name and that the settlement was called after, "All the Almas in town."

Before going into the contracting business, J. B. Stansell had been an early partner of Joseph Higginbottom at Buckskin Joe. After he had completed the James home, he also built a large ore storage building of rough log construction. By that time Alma was booming and by 1873 it already boasted a population of five hundred people.

Initially, the impetus for the establishment of a town at this point came from the discovery of placer gold. Both placer mining and extensive hydraulic dredging were tried here. Huge ugly piles of smoothly polished boulders still bear mute testimony to this most destructive of all mining methods. Dredging is now mercifully outlawed in Colorado. As time passed, the gold search was expanded to include silver, copper, and lead. All of these metals were found near Alma. Among the better known properties were the Dolly Varden, Sweethome, Fanny Barrett, Sacramento, Silver Gem, Moose, and Security.

*Looking west toward the Mosquito Range, this early photograph
shows Alma at the height of the mining boom.*

Alma today appears to be fully as large as it was in the old picture above

Alma's location proved to be an extremely fortunate one. In 1879-80, silver discoveries were made at a number of locations on the slopes of Mount Lincoln and Mount Bross, both of which are 14,000-foot-class peaks. Alma was built almost at the base of these two adjacent mountains where Buckskin Creek flows down into the Middle Fork of the South Platte River.

George Crofutt, energetic chronicler of early-day Colorado communities, also visited South Park and recorded that Alma had one sampling works, a newspaper called the *Alma Eagle*, the St. Nicholas, the Southern, and several other hotels, and twice-daily stagecoach and mail service to and from the surrounding communities. He also recorded its proximity to other camps as being twenty miles from Breckenridge, five miles from Fairplay, and only seventeen miles from Leadville. This latter distance involved a crossing of lofty, rocky, Mosquito Pass which tops the rugged range to the west at an elevation well in excess of thirteen thousand feet.

On March 23, 1937, long after it had passed its prime as a mining camp, Alma fell victim to that most common and most destructive scourge of mountain boom towns, the fire. Here, as in so many camps, the blaze seems to have started from an overheated stove located in the back room of the Budd and Beck Recreation Company, a beer parlor. The time was about 4:00 A.M. Only the bank at Alma was of masonry construction, all the rest were frame buildings. As a result the business section was virtually destroyed. Overall damage amounted to fifty thousand dollars.

It now seems likely that a chance spark from the stove was fanned into flame by a fifty-mile-an-hour wind that had been blowing across South Park. Within a few minutes the structure was ablaze, destroying a pool hall and the Williams Barber Shop which were also housed in the Budd and Beck Building. Next door, Clark's Restaurant caught fire and in turn ignited the Red and White Building. A grocery store went next as the blaze spread along the town's single business street. When an automobile dealership went, this was the greatest loss in the fire.

In 1937 the population of Alma was about five hundred. The town had no fire department of its own. Five miles away, the Fairplay Fire Department heeded the call for assistance and sent their equipment. By that time most of the damage had been done and little could be accomplished beyond preventing any further spread. Since Alma had no community water system, the people depended upon wells. To further complicate things, Buckskin Creek was frozen solid. The same high winds that had whipped the flames also blew down the telephone lines that night.

When the fire broke out again in the center of town, a bucket brigade tried but could do little beyond concentrating on saving the rest of the village. Surprisingly, much of Alma still stands today. Some new construction has gone up in places over the old scars.

Alma is one of the simplest of all places to find, and excellent roads enter it from two directions. From Denver, U.S. 285 will take you southwest through South Park to Fairplay. Alma is five miles to the northwest on State Highway 9. From Dillon and Breckenridge, State Highway 9 comes across scenic Hoosier Pass and south into the town.

Alma was of considerable importance in the gold and silver mining history of Colorado. Here, even in the early days, miners washed huge fortunes from the earth. The Alma district, however, was never a hard-rock country. In many instances, precious metals were placered from the creek beds by the same men who had panned the waters of Cherry Creek near Denver. By any measure, the Alma district is a region notably rich in memories.*

---

* In this same general area, see also Buckskin Joe, Fairplay, Puma City, Quartzville, Montgomery, Leavick, and Sacramento.

2.

ALPINE AND ALPINE TUNNEL

FOR MANY YEARS Colorado had not merely one but two communities called Alpine. Since they are reasonably close together and are now ghost towns, each will be treated in this chapter. Our first Alpine was, and still is, about twelve miles west of Nathrop, southwest of Buena Vista on State Highway 162, a very good dirt road. Today, only a few original cabins and the ruins of the smelter remain. Summer cabins now dominate the area about one mile off the present road.

Although the first house was built at Alpine in 1877, the town was not incorporated until two years later. For many years its population hovered around five hundred people. In the course of the town's growth, the Tilden Smelting and Sampling Works moved into Alpine and erected a fair-sized mill. Colonel Chapman, who owned and operated the plant, employed about forty men. In an incredibly short time the Tilden was processing thirty tons of ore per day. Among the better producing mines which contributed to the welfare of Alpine were the Tilden, Livingston, and Britenstein. Ores from these properties averaged from fifty to one hundred and twenty-five dollars per ton.

Alpine was located along the track of the beloved narrow-gauge Denver, South Park and Pacific Railway. Incidentally, the fare from Denver in those days cost $12.85. When George Crofutt visited the town he said that it consisted of "A number of stores, hotels, restaurants, two saloons, and other buildings." The hotels were called the Arcade and the

Badger. Crofutt was conservative on the subject of saloons; there were twenty-three. Within the town's short life span, a newspaper developed, the *True Fissure*. Alpine lost out to St. Elmo when the owner-editor chose to migrate upstream and publish in the new location.

Three banks took care of all financial demands at the town. George Knox opened a school at Alpine in 1881. One source tells us there was never a church in the town, while another insists that one church was built and did flourish for a time. Since Alpine had gained a rather rough reputation for itself, this single church among those twenty-three saloons must have seemed as out of place as a cow on the front porch.

Suddenly Alpine went into a slump from which it never recovered. Actually, its life span was extremely short. When St. Elmo was booming in 1882, most of the people from Alpine simply packed up and moved on to the newer town. For years afterwards, the town held only memories and a couple of hermits. Lady Zabriskie and Napoleon Jones were the two inhabitants. Mrs. Zabriskie is alleged to have been a Polish princess and highly intelligent. She once wrote a scholarly treatise on minerology in which she said that Colorado was full of uranium and molybdenum. In it she predicted that these resources would become extremely valuable. Alpine was not her only home. At one period in her life she lived in a house beside the railroad depot in St. Elmo.

Mrs. Zabriskie seems to have been one of the most singularly migratory of recluses, moving in or out of empty cabins here, at Romley, and up at Hancock. In the latter town, one of the few remaining buildings, which was at one time the town saloon, is sometimes referred to as Mrs. Zabriskie's cabin. As time passed, both these people became more and more reluctant to give up their memories of the past.

Quite apart from any sociological reasons or considerations for their actions, Jones and Zabriskie continued to wander about the empty townsites of Chalk Creek for many years after all of the other residents had gone. It would be pleasant if a happy ending to this story could be reported but outside of fiction this rarely happens to those who have been so hurt by the world that they feel impelled to live apart from the rest of society. In 1930 the county commissioners brought out their frozen bodies for burial.

From then on, Alpine gradually became the property of Bird Fuqua who began acquiring land in Chalk Creek Gulch in connection with Hortense Hot Springs. When a good road was bladed up the valley, her efforts to preserve Alpine were frustrated. Sheep and cattlemen took refuge at will in the old buildings. Those who cared were unable to cope with the vandalism that good roads tend to bring. Thus, in an incredibly short time, Alpine was systematically stripped of most of the few remaining cabins that still stood in the old town.

Our second Alpine was really known as Alpine Tunnel and was only a few miles away and can be reached from a point near the other Alpine by taking either Hancock or Williams Pass. Both are Jeep roads that start up from the old ghost town of Hancock. A third trail follows the railroad grade out of Hancock to the east portal of the Alpine Tunnel. From there, a short hike across twelve-thousand-foot Altman's Pass will put you in the second Alpine. A simpler approach became a reality during the summer of 1964 when Gunnison County bridged Quartz Creek just a mile from Pitkin. It is now possible to drive all the way to Alpine Tunnel over what was formerly a hair-raising Jeep road.

The town is 167.7 miles west of Denver, built at an altitude of 11,546 feet. At the eastern end of the redwood-lined, 1,805-foot-long Alpine Tunnel was a settlement called Atlantic. Immediately adjacent to its western terminus stood the town of Alpine Tunnel. Its story is inextricably tied up with that of the pioneer railroad bore. Since 1879, ex-Governor John Evans had been putting money into the project. His goal was to allow the Denver, South Park and Pacific to extend its rails into Gunnison.

Bids for construction of the tunnel were let in November of 1879. Actual work was started in 1880. Serving as engineer for the project was another Evans, James A., who had cut his railroading eyeteeth on General Grenville Dodge's Union Pacific. Construction began at 11,600 feet, almost directly beneath Altman's Pass. Here the trouble began.

Construction workers were offered free transportation by the Union Pacific Railroad if they would agree to work on the tunnel. Before the job was completed in 1881, some ten thousand workers had come and gone. Most averaged two to three days before the altitude got them down. In the beginning, the laborers were housed in a series of six crude log cabins which stood above the tunnel's west portal. By the time the job was finished, it had cost a staggering sum in excess of $242,000. Three problems account for the cost— loose stone, underground water, and decomposed granite. Costly twelve-by-twelve beams of California redwood timbering were brought in to shore up the whole shaky proposition.

From the west portal, the Alpine station was just a half mile south. Although winter snow and cold had enveloped the site, a huge stone enginehouse was built during the worst part of 1881. That same season saw the completion of the telegraph shack and the installation of an "Armstrong" turntable and a switch. Later, a 29x56-foot stone section house was put up beside the enginehouse. A tent city appeared at the site and sheltered the laborers during construction.

Work on the Alpine Tunnel ended just a few days before Christmas of 1881. The bore was completed and the job was done. Historical events apart, bad luck continued to dog the project with heavy winter snows that required construction of 150 feet of protective snowsheds at Atlantic and another 650 feet of this costly construction a third of a mile away at Alpine Tunnel. Unlike most railroad tunnels, this one had no ventilation problems. Harsh winds whipped across Tomichi Pass, through Brittle Silver Basin, and kept the bore clear of smoke every hour of the day and night.

But bad luck was still at hand when the first narrow-gauge train whistled into Gunnison in September of 1882. The Denver and Rio Grande had beaten them with rail connections into town over a year before.

By January 1, 1886, the structures at Alpine Tunnel consisted of a stone section house, 29x56 feet, a 54x153-foot enginehouse, a 14x16½-foot bunkhouse, a 10x16-foot storehouse and a 10x18-foot washhouse. Inside the enginehouse stood a 4x14-foot coal bin and a water tank that held 9,516 gallons. All of these structures were built of stone and were located on the east side of the tracks. On the west side there was a wooden telegraph office, first used as a section house.

In the strictest sense of the word, Alpine Tunnel probably would not qualify as a town since it was never incorporated. What its actual status was is a question still being debated. It was listed as a station stop where meals were served. For many years it was a passing stop for trains and their crews often slept there. A siding of 1,350 feet was installed along with a fifty-foot turntable and a turntable siding that stretched out for 212 feet.

Beyond the town, two huge rock palisades were constructed in 1881. Both were built above Brittle Silver Basin to keep the tracks from sliding down the steep, rocky mountainside into Quartz Creek. They held the tracks up but didn't keep the tremendous snowpacks in place. In March of 1884 one of the trains whistled while approaching Alpine Tunnel, starting a snowslide that came roaring down the almost vertical mountainside. Before reaching the bottom of the valley, it had swept away the town of Woodstock which, for a short time, had been clinging precariously to life in a tiny meadow below the tracks.

*In 1906 Alpine still had a few buildings and the stage
still ran along the road above Chalk Creek.*

*At the west end of the railroad tunnel, the town of Alpine Tunnel may be seen in this
old picture made from atop Alpine Pass. This was, of course, actually Altman's Pass.*

When a fire swept Alpine Tunnel in 1906, all of the buildings were destroyed. Since no mortar had been used, heat from the blaze caused the stone structures to collapse. By September of that year a new boardinghouse had been built at a cost of $1,701.58. It saw little use. Suddenly, in 1910, the tunnel caved in. A work crew inside it was overcome by coal smoke gas and four or five (the accounts vary) lost their lives. Without a clear passage for the air, natural ventilation meant nothing. These were the only casualties ever to occur at the Alpine Tunnel. Miraculously, no life was lost at any time during the construction period.

From then on, the tunnel was never reopened. Although the cave-in was disastrous, other reasons compelled the management to close out this phase of their operation. For one thing, heavy snow removal during a large part of the year had far exceeded all cost expectations. Quite apart from any physical difficulties, the tunnel route simply had not paid off as anticipated. Contributing to this was the fact that both the Colorado Midland and the Rio Grande now had lines running across Colorado. Beyond this, a rockslide came down across the tracks that same year just below Alpine Tunnel, between it and the first palisade.

Shortly afterwards the tracks were torn out and Alpine Tunnel was dead. The caved-in boardinghouse, the telegraph office and remains of one stone building may still be seen. Historical events apart, the rest of the town is little more than a memory.*

---

* In the same general area, see also Pitkin.

The historic palisade of the Denver, South Park and Pacific Railway

The abandoned right-of-way still offers a thrilling Jeep ride

3.

BONANZA

Bonanza is nestled among the Cochetopa Hills, which vary in altitude from nine to twelve thousand feet. The general topography of the section is comprised of a main gulch running north and south. Through it flows a small stream known as Kerber Creek. From the center of town, Copper Gulch runs to the east. Nearby are Squirrel and Rawley gulches which formerly held some of the heaviest producing mines.

The history of Bonanza is much the same as that of a score of other camps created as a result of the Leadville excitement. Claims were worked as early as the 1870's. Following this, a continuous round of individual miners and prospectors passed through the valley on the way to the Gunnison gold rush. After discovering surface croppings of silver-bearing lead ore many of the gold seekers became silver miners.

In the spring of 1880, Pete McCardo and John Stansbury were making their way up the San Luis Valley, looking for a shorter route across Marshall Pass to the Gunnison country. Along Kerber Creek they found oxidized quartz in such quantities that it became comparatively easy to find the original vein in the hillside. They checked off a claim which they named Exchecquer. As the ore was quite heavy in sulphides, the refining process became extremely expensive. At that time the cost was thirty dollars a ton. A report of this rich discovery resulted in a stampede to Kerber Creek. Within two years five thousand people were scattered throughout the hills.

Four towns, named Exchecquerville, Sedgwick, Kerber City, and Bonanza were quarreling for preference. Inevitably only one of these could survive in such close proximity. As time passed, the growing and expanding Bonanza gradually absorbed the other three.

For a time Exchecquerville held out against all odds, thinking that it might continue to exist as a separate entity since it was built up around one of the very best and oldest mineral properties.

The Exchecquer Mine was still one of the finest in the camp. It was being vigorously worked by Rathvon and Co. Three tons of rich ore were shipped almost daily to the smelters. A large crew of men was employed and only limited housing held up the company in hiring more. The ore was a free smelting type of good quality that was often able to be shipped without sorting. Work on the Exchecquer began early and continued until late in the life of the camp.

In 1900 the Exchecquer Mine became the realization of a long-deferred hope. The owners had then been working the mine for many years on a sporadic basis until they came into a body of high-grade ore that promised to make it a good producer once more. That same year there were nearly two hundred men working in the immediate vicinity of Bonanza.

The settlement was officially incorporated as Bonanza City in 1881. New prospectors climbed the hills, explored the gulches, sunk shafts and drove tunnels, hoping to find rich, gold-bearing veins. In many shafts the prospectors passed over low grade silver ores that were to await treatment under modern, cheaper methods at a later period in time.

At the turn of the century, Bonanza had two principal streets, both of which were lined with creaky boardwalks. Twenty thousand inhabitants, according to one source, quenched their thirst in forty saloons. Such numbers made the town wild and wooly enough to require a United States deputy marshall, in addition to the efforts of a large police force, to maintain law and order.

During this entire period, Bonanza had no formal religious institutions. The late Dr. S. E. Kortright, pioneer physician and assayer at Bonanza, once recorded the answer he gave to a question about churches in Bonanza. The doctor replied that they never had one and then quoted the following:

> We have no churches there to confine
> The God that's with us all the time
> The mystery of these hills you see
> Are evidence of divinity.

To this day the town has never had a church.

Bonanza had its own fire department, bank, and a smelter built to reduce ores that did not carry lead. It was, consequently, a failure. The town enjoyed about all of the usual conditions of life that went to make up a typical mining community, including the enevitable visit by ex-President Ulysses Simpson Grant, whose itinerary included a seemingly endless number of Colorado's booming mining camps.

Bonanza endured its share of claim jumping, lynching parties, riots, and murders. An Irishman named John O'Hara was killed by a Negro musician named Forbush. "Bush," as he was more familiarly known, was a former Arkansas man who could pop off the head of a squirrel with the greatest of ease. During Reconstruction days he had been a member of the Arkansas Carpetbagger Legislature.

After a quarrel developed with O'Hara over some unknown offense, he met the Irishman on the street one day and deliberately shot him. Properly aroused, the Irish element in the camp organized and hastily prepared for a lynching. One man, later prominent in Denver business circles, agreed to go after the murderer. "Bush," meanwhile, had barricaded himself in a log cabin. The volunteer lawman left his team at the foot of the gulch, waiting to transport the culprit to the jail at Saguache. Shortly the Irish lynchers also assembled near the team and waited patiently for the arrival of the two men.

When the one-man vigilante party approached the cabin, he found the long barrel of a revolver protruding from between the logs. "Bush, I want you! Hand me that gun," ordered the gentleman. Being astonished at such audacity, the killer meekly complied. Descending the trail, "Bush" heard sounds on the path below and both men suspected the worst. His captor promised the Negro safety if he would obey orders.

Forbush was told to go up Kerber Creek, over the hills, and then to Saguache as fast as he could travel. A few moments later the mob saw only one man descending the hill to calmly inform them that the prisoner was safely on the way to town and that there would be no lynching. At the trial a verdict for acquittal was returned and Forbush disappeared. In later years he led a delegation of colored men from Arkansas to Washington, D.C., to assure Grover Cleveland of their support in the campaign, which resulted in President Harrison's election.

Bonanza was no single-mine camp. A complex labyrinth of mineral properties was scattered up and down the sides of most of the nearby gulches. The Empress Josephine was the most important mine of the camp. In the early days its production ran high in tellurides and one carload yielded twenty thousand dollars. The first owners sunk a shaft and burrowed in the vein without method, order, or system. With depth, the cost of operation grew too heavy and disaster came when the extravagant management spent its profits as fast as they were realized.

The Empress Josephine yielded minerals worth something like $200,000 during the Bonanza boom. It consisted of a shaft 300 feet deep, with several drifts along the vein. A new shaft was driven to a depth of 420 feet where further developments were stopped by a flow of water encountered at that point. No existing pumps could contend with its volume. Explorations with a drill at the bottom of the shaft revealed the ores lying in a true fissure vein close to the shaft. The existence of a larger body of ore below seemed likely.

In later years the new owners of the Empress Josephine had their own way in Bonanza. The company purchased scores of cottages at twenty-five dollars each, only to tear them down for the lumber. Having its pick of the best property in the district, the company often made its own prices on anything it cared to purchase. The old ranchmen in the district hauled quantities of building stone, supplies, lumber, and coke. They later worked in the mines which the company was putting in condition for operation. It cost the company sixty thousand dollars to repair the damage done to the Empress Josephine by the reckless and extravagant operations of the original owners.

Another of the prosperous mining properties was the great Bonanza Mine itself, owned by the Hon. Irving Howbert. Howbert later pioneered in the history of the Cripple Creek district. In January of 1900 he raised $3,500,000 for construction of the narrow-gauge Short Line from Colorado City up around Pikes Peak to Cripple Creek. At its peak the line carried fifty-four trains a day. At Bonanza, however, he built no railroad.

One of the richest strikes was made by James Downman and James Kenney who found the Rawley lode. Since it first went into production in 1880, this single mine has shipped more than six million dollars' worth of ore. Production was retarded somewhat by the closing of the American Smelting and Refining Company. The Rawley Tunnel was started in 1911 and was completed a year later. In size, it was an eight foot wide bore, seven feet high and six thousand six hundred feet long. In later years the Rawley was sold to Mr. W. P. Lynn, of Denver. When it was sold in 1881 it brought a record price of $100,000 to its original owners.

The Eagle Mine was owned and operated by the Lucrative Mining Company of Colorado Springs. A test carload, just as it was extracted from the vein without sorting, was sent to the smelter. Returns showed nearly $1,000 for this ten-ton lot.

Capt. W. B. McKinney was the founder of the first newspaper at Bonanza, the *Enterprise*. Its type all arrived at camp in January of 1882 and the press itself came along shortly thereafter. The town then had a daily paper that was greeted with pleasure and no little anticipation by all Bonanzaites. One early item from the new chronicle said that:

W. C. Knowles, the Silver Creek murderer will surely be hung. This will be the first legal hanging in Saguache County and no doubt will be looked forward to with the usual interest.

All of the following items were gleaned from the pages of the *Enterprise* during the single month of June in the year 1882. They reveal not only some intimate glimpses into the life of people in a mining camp, but something of the intricate gyrations of a highly individualistic six-months-old newspaper as well.

The only lady-like way for a woman to ride in Bonanza is side saddle.

Everything that is now transpiring in our district inspires all our hopes as bright as the Star of Bethlehem, making each resident think that Bonanza is the new Eldorado on which the light of Aladdin's magic lamp has fallen, turning rocks into diamonds and mountains into gold.

The smelter started up on the fourth of January and the results have since been most satisfactory indeed. Each five days three carloads of bullion have been turned out and the energy and perseverance of its owners is deserving of the highest praise. The reverses that were met were very grave but the determination of Mr. O. W. Kelly overcame every obstacle and his ultimate success is shared by every man, woman and child in the Kerber district.

It has commenced snowing here lately which looks a little odd to us as we have had a perfect springtime up to the first. We now expect a little snow, however, intermingled with a little cool weather. This is considered the worst month of the year.

Rumor says that Dewey Dorn will soon take unto himself one that will share his joys and sorrows alike.

A party of Bonanza gallants went down to Sedgwick a few nights ago for the purpose of serenading their "ladie loves." All managed to get back safely but two have since been confined to their beds, one with frozen feet and another from too free an indulgence in his "ardent." Phil O'Rourke says they should remember the fate of the three little flies and never indulge in luxuries, especially on a winter night in the mountains.

Bonanza has more pretty girls than any other town in the state to its age.

Billiards and ten pins are the chief sources of amusement to our young men.

A rather novel wedding took place at the Cannon House a few mornings ago at Bonanza. The groom was Mr. Ike Doffelmeyer and the bride was Miss Henrietta Loy. The novelty was that the nuptial was celebrated at six in the morning which is indeed an early hour for a native of Bonanza to rise.

A second newspaper, the *Bonanza News,* flourished for a time but it was neither as colorful nor was it as successful as the *Enterprise.*

As the years passed by, rich discoveries around Ashcroft and Aspen drew the attention of capitalists away from Bonanza. The town began to dwindle in size until only a few families remained, still loyal to their faith in the future of the camp.

Miners who remained at Bonanza turned ranchmen to support their families while occasionally getting out a little ore which yielded them small profit. Among the seventy once-prosperous mines, only a few continued active in later years.

Gen. W. S. Rosencrans had learned of this near-deserted camp from a friend. After investing a small sum, he gained control of the Empress Josephine and eight other properties. After he interested a number of his wealthy New York friends in his enterprise, a company was formed. Engineers were sent out to Bonanza to reopen the mines and to get out the rich ores still believed to exist there. The New York syndicate spent money for three years in an attempt to reverse the trend of history in this district which was all but forgotten by the rest of the world. Their holdings amounted to two hundred acres of ground with a clear title.

An examination of a mineral map of Colorado will show that the Bonanza district is located on a mineral belt that is thought to extend all the way from Cripple Creek to Creede. Mining men still hold a theory that the gold belt is continuous throughout that entire area. This idea came in for considerable attention when reports of the operations of the New York syndicate were made public.

The possibility of the wealth of another Cripple Creek or a second Aspen seemed just around the corner. Old mine-owners began receiving letters from people who wanted to lease properties in the Bonanza district. County records at Saguache were searched to prove titles on property that had been neglected for more than ten years. During this last excitement over two thousand filings were recorded. Many of the old claims had been allowed to go by default during the previous decade.

Eventually, the rising costs of producing low-grade ores depleted the town. In 1900 there were only one hundred people still there. To further complicate matters, large numbers of beavers had invaded the idle mines, crawling down the shafts. In some cases they penetrated as far as two miles underground, gnawing the timbering and endangering anyone who ventured down that far. Three decades later their number had swelled to the point where trappers were brought in to rid the shafts of the unwelcome rodents.

In 1937 a fire destroyed almost the entire business section and damaged a number of houses and cabins. None of the structures has been rebuilt. In recent years lessors have continued to work the Rawley property. The decline in copper,

lead, silver, zinc, and gold mining has contributed to depletion of the town. In 1950 nearly $240,000 in precious
metals was produced as compared with $21,859 in 1953.
Children from Bonanza now use the Saguache school. The
9,465-foot-high town now has an assessed valuation of
$16,490 with one of the very lowest municipal mill levies
in the state.

In 1955 the Whale Mine showed outstanding assays of
uranium and was reopened for production of this and other
ores. The Warwick was also reopened the first week of May
and the few remaining residents were optimistic that these
two properties would bring back the good old days.

Today, mining is still going on at Bonanza. This, along
with the large number of summer people who have converted the old structures to fine summer cabins, now make
up the main basis of Bonanza's seasonal economy.*

---

* In this same general area, see also Crestone and Turret.

An early photograph of Bonanza on Kerber Creek

Bonanza still has many of its original buildings

4.

BOREAS

At various times during our history, quite a large number of Colorado communities have claimed the distinction of being the highest in the United States and, in some cases, the world. For many years Waldorf, at 11,666 feet above sea level, claimed to have the highest post office in the country. During the Cripple Creek boom in the 1890's, Altman often boasted that it was the highest incorporated city in the civilized world, a distinction that actually belongs to La Paz, Bolivia. Currently, Leadville claims to be the highest municipality in the United States and calls itself the "cloud city." Although the foregoing by no means constitutes an exhaustive list, it will show some fairly typical examples of this highly elevated classification of civic pride.

One other member of this exclusive fraternity was Boreas, the subject of this chapter. Boreas was one of the claimants within the post office category. Actually, its claim was a relatively valid one, during its short life, since its elevation was 11,498 feet above sea level. Although the climb to Boreas seems like a comparatively short one, it is well to remember that you are already well above nine thousand feet when crossing South Park prior to beginning the gradual ascent of Boreas Pass.

Throughout its history the town that was constructed on its top was inextricably tied up with the pass itself. In the beginning it was alternately known as both Hamilton and as Tarryall Pass. Quite commonly many important roads took their names from those nearby settlements which they might serve. Both of these names came from very early mining camps in South Park, each of which is now gone. Shortly after Breckinridge (the original spelling) grew to prominence, the pass assumed its name, switching its allegiance to the western side of the divide.

It should be made clear that in this early phase, the pass was hardly more that a footpath. To supply the miners' wants, burro packtrains and foot travelers carried supplies over the range in 1859 and early 1860. Many records exist which describe how men skied over the range during these first two winters. Each new discovery made the need for improvement of the road more apparent.

Instead of waiting for a benevolent bureaucracy to do their job, men from both sides rolled up their sleeves and hacked out a crude miners' road by August of 1860, enabling wagons to get their supplies across the ridge. From that time on, it was widely used for a variety of purposes, including regular stagecoach travel for more than a decade.

When faced by the need to gets its rails into the fabulous silver camp of Leadville before its competitors, the Union Pacific Railroad pulled James Evans off his job as supervisor at the Alpine Tunnel. Evans and his crew of track layers began work in the spring of 1882. Construction was started from the Como side with rails being put down over a 3½ percent grade which did not follow the old stage road in every instance.

Perhaps, at this point, it might be well to note that this was not a standard-size railroad. Instead, it was a narrow-gauge branch of the Denver, South Park and Pacific, designed to connect the towns in South Park with the gold-producing facilities around Breckenridge (the later spelling), before going on to Leadville.

By June, construction crews had completed an amazing twelve miles of rails and ties from Como across the top. Building the last ten miles to Breckenridge involved an incredible drop of 1,925 feet in that short distance. Their task was a difficult one and the job was not completed until late in 1882. All too frequently, work and maintenance gangs were driven back by timberline blizzards and the biting, marrow-chilling cold. Since few obstacles can successfully buck the march of progress, the time finally arrived when the last tie and iron were carefully fitted into place and the job was done.

Nevertheless it soon became clear that their problems had just begun. Before reaching the top, sturdy little narrow-gauge locomotives were often called upon to plow their way through mountain-size drifts while on their way from South Park to Breckenridge. At other times the mountains of snow grew too large, swept high by the raging velocity of fierce timberline winds. Before trains could run, the slides and drifts menacing the road had to be shot down. The latter part of January was often the most difficult time. On one occasion operations had to be suspended for most of the latter part of the winter, and the first train did not reach Leadville until the following May.

In the course of attempting to operate and maintain a railroad across this particular section of windswept tundra, both workers and passengers endured biting cold, penetrating winds, and often real physical hardship. Because of the awful winter blasts, it seemed appropriate to rename the pass once more, this time in honor of Boreas, the ancient deity of the North Wind.

It was now absolutely clear that winter operations would be a problem. Often it was next to impossible for crews to keep the line open for more than a few miles beyond Grant. At such times nearly all commercial ventures were shut down at Como, with the notable exception of its five saloons where stalled train crews fell avidly under the influence of the grape and the grain. Under these circumstances, few trainmen complained of the inclement weather.

The tiny hamlet of Boreas was constructed exactly on the top of the pass, 11,498 feet above sea level. Its purpose was to serve the railroad and to provide shelter for crews and visitors to this remote part of Colorado. Through its fortunate geographical location, the town became the most important stop on this singularly most important route, capable of carrying people from Como to booming Breckenridge and Leadville.

Inevitably, a large number of log cabins were built at the site along with a few of the usual commercial structures. During its peak years, Boreas was a fair-sized town, although population estimates vary from the believable "few hundred" to the ridiculous.

Facilities for the Denver, South Park and Pacific included a stone enginehouse which also contained company office space and a two-room telegraph facility. Outside, one might see the very necessary turntable; necessary because it would have been next to impossible to turn a locomotive around on the apex of an alpine mountain pass. Nearby stood the inevitable above-ground water tank and a six-hundred-foot-long snowshed. The snowshed had doors only on the Breckenridge end. Old accounts reveal that they were very difficult to open when snowdrifts had piled up against them. Inside this latter structure was a depot where Mr. M. J. Trotter, an early-day agent, held forth and performed the usual functions indigenous to such an establishment.

Letters that went out of this "highest post office" told with almost monotonous repetition of the full terror of being marooned in horrible snowstorms, and of temperatures that went down to sixty degrees below zero. On one occasion the people at Boreas were snowed in for an incredible ninety days during which no trains were able to reach the station from either side. When supplies dwindled below the danger point, two men made a frantic effort to reach Como. Shortly after noon they started out over the awesome white wasteland on snowshoes. Nearly everything they attempted was futile and their frozen bodies were found along the trail during a search which was attempted the next day. Food was finally brought in from Grant by using horse-drawn sleighs after a semblance of a trail had been broken through the drifts.

Once, during the winter of 1898, a Boreas resident attempted a winter walk from the snowbound town on the top to Como. His mission was made all the more urgent by the fact that his wife was ill and medical help from Denver was deemed essential to her recovery. Regrettably, no trace was found of him until the following summer when the drifts melted. His body was on the eastern slope, between Halfway and Tarryall. When the remains were excavated, it was noted that his suitcase was opened and a number of his papers had been scattered about. It was thought that he had been preparing to build a fire to ward off the freezing cold. The fate of his ailing wife was not recorded in any of the sources utilized in researching this chapter.

Without a doubt the most bizarre happening in the history of Boreas involved the Phineas T. Barnum Circus train. The story has all the elements for a delightful musical comedy except the music.

Shortly after it had played at Denver, the circus train crossed Kenosha Pass and huffed its way across South Park to Como. In the course of trying to reach Leadville, it became stalled about three miles below the town of Boreas. Seemingly no amount of steam was capable of carrying the ponderous cargo of wild animals over the crest. Since the line, at this point, consisted of only a single track, all other traffic from both sides was effectively blocked as the sun went down and darkness began to descend.

To add chaos to confusion, the lions grew hungry and started roaring. In desperation the elephant keeper offered to remove his huge animals from their car, allowing them to push against the rear of the train. Frantically, the engineer is said to have replied, "Anything to get to Leadville." Carefully the pachyderms were arrayed behind the last coach.

A part of old Boreas is visible at the left while a snowshed dominates the foreground of this early picture.

Very little of old Boreas can still be seen at this high, lonesome, and windy location

Impatient little knots of people gathered to watch hopefully as the strange hookup was arranged.

Almost simultaneously, the brakeman released his iron shoes while the caretaker uttered an impressive string of Arabic oaths. Up front, the shrill whistle split the darkening sky. From the rear of the train, a powerful snort was heard as the strange procession actually began to move.

When the top was reached, a few Boreas residents are said to have taken a hasty pledge of alcoholic abstinence, but Leadville got its circus anyway.

For today's visitor the ride to Boreas is a beautiful little jaunt. From either Como or Breckenridge, take the good graded road and simply drive to the top of the range. In autumn, this is one of the few places in Colorado where red aspens may be seen. In an incredibly short time, most of the original structures have fallen down or have been carried away. Only a few of the masonry buildings are still there, sitting bleakly above timberline on the cold and inhospitable tundra. The rest of Boreas has slipped away into the shadows of time.*

---

* In this same general area, see also Como, Dyersville, King City, Tarryall, and Hamilton.

5.

BROWNSVILLE

DURING MY RESEARCH for this chapter, two different spellings for the town's name were encountered with amazing frequency. Brownville or Brownsville, take your choice, since both forms seem to be accepted. When a miner named Brown found a paying lode here in the late 1860's, a mountain and a gulch were named for him, but the development of the town came about more slowly. It seems to have been started in the 1870's as a construction town for workers on the Atlantic and Pacific Tunnel.

Although regarded sometimes as a suburb of Silver Plume, Brownsville boasted a population of about six hundred people who gradually began to work in the nearby mines during the day, returning to the town that housed, fed, and entertained them at night. Prominent among the residents were large numbers of Cornish miners and their wives, often called Cousin Jacks and Cousin Jennies.

This was a happy town, built along a single main street. It had the usual saloon, a restaurant called the Fox and Hounds, about a dozen houses, a large boardinghouse, an Odd Fellows Hall, a smelter, and a slag dump that consisted of a huge pile of ground-up bones, purchased from the nearby slaughterhouse, which was used to flux the ores. The village was located at the foot of Brown Mountain, in a direct line with Brown Gulch. High above it at an elevation of 10,451 feet was the great Seven-Thirty property.

In many ways the history of Brownsville is tied up with that of the Seven-Thirty Mine. Facts concerning its beginnings are nebulous. Most sources credit its discovery to Clifford Griffin, an Englishman allegedly of noble ancestry, whose past in the old country was shrouded in mystery. Another version tells us that Clifford was not the discoverer. Instead, his brother Heneage is said to have purchased an interest in the Seven-Thirty from Jack McDonnel, who is also credited with being the original discoverer. Seemingly, Heneage, in an attempt to rehabilitate his younger brother, arranged to bring him West.

Although little was actually known about the background of the Griffin brothers, rumors, of course, were most plentiful. Many shared several points in common, and the story went something like this. Clifford Griffin had been engaged to an extremely beautiful girl, also of royal lineage. True to the melodramatic nineteenth-century tradition, his fiancée just naturally had to be a most attractive physical specimen. In all such stories, plain-appearing girls were as scarce as hiccoughs at a prayer meeting. At any rate, her dead body was found in his room on the night before their wedding. There are already many embellishments upon this story and newer ones will doubtless appear with time.

There have been some extraordinary blind spots within British justice when it comes to malfeasances among the nobility. Thus, in an incredibly short time, Clifford was on his way west. Shortly after his arrival in Colorado, he either discovered the Seven-Thirty lode or was taken under the protective wing of his older brother. Heneage planned to exercise his moral guidance but the press of duties in a new mining camp afforded him little time.

In the course of events, Heneage made Clifford superintendent of the Seven-Thirty, in an effort to keep him interested and occupied. He seemed to like the new job well enough but never lost his air of sadness. Although he built himself a cabin on the side of lonely Columbia Mountain, he was unable to wipe out the memory of the tragedy he had left behind in England.

For many years the mines on Sherman and Brown mountains had followed the practice of blowing their starting whistles in chorus at 6:30 in the morning. Shortly after the Griffin brothers acquired their mine, by whatever means, they decided that the earlier hour was a completely uncivilized time for going to work. From then on their whistle blew an hour later. In the course of time, their mine became known as the Seven-Thirty from this consequence.

The Seven-Thirty was rich in both gold and silver and seemingly the veins grew wider as the shafts went deeper into the earth. From then on, the Griffin brothers became the wealthiest mineowners in the camp. Clifford spent most of his time at the mine but there were times when he came down to the saloon at Brownsville, sang songs, and beat upon the bar with the miners.

But regardless of his personal popularity and the money that had come his way, the emotional burden that he bore became too much for him. People at the mine noticed that he had started to dig what appeared to be a grave, hewn out from the tough granite. This type of rock was often quarried at Brownsville and was frequently labeled as the world's toughest. Suddenly Griffin began to share his melancholy feelings with the camp. Being an accomplished musician, he emerged from his lofty cabin each evening at dusk to render haunting and sad melodies on his violin. Such performances continued far into the night to the cheers and applause of his appreciative audience far below in the town. Workmen and their families would gather each night in the fold of the gulch, listening to the music. At the end of the strange concerts, their cheers could be heard rolling through the canyon.

One summer night, following a pause in the usual concert, listeners in the valley heard the unmistakable sound of a shot. Rushing up the mountain, they found Griffin face down, stretched out in the grave he had dug. The bullet had apparently gone through his heart. Inside his cabin they found a note requesting that he be buried in the tomb he had dug. Since he was already in it, this seemed like a reasonable request under the circumstances. His older brother saw to it that the last wish was carried out. Just a year later, a monument was placed over the body as a lasting memorial. It can still be seen high on the mountainside but it takes a hike to reach it. Before leaving for England, Heneage left a sum of money to provide flowers for the site on special occasions.

For many years the huge dump of the Seven-Thirty grew until it completely filled Brown Gulch at its elevation. A small culvert was installed to carry the annual flow of water under the dump and on down toward the South Fork of Clear Creek. In the spring when the snows melted and the rains came, this culvert was sometimes not large enough to carry all of the flow. Surplus water came up to the top of the dump, cascaded over the edge, and slowly saturated the whole mess. As all of these thousands of tons of mountain became thoroughly soaked, they began to move.

Sometime in the 1880's a heavy rain swept the area for days and loosened the great tailings piles of the Seven-Thirty, the Brown, and the Dundenberg. A small segment slithered down the gulch toward Brownsville. All was quiet for a while until the next segment came down in June of 1892. This slide buried a few homes, part of the old Brownsville Hall, and the town saloon, which was occupied at the time by relaxing miners.

A still larger mass moved down three years later, on June 15, 1895. This time the huge Seven-Thirty dump completely gave way, squished down the mountainside, and demolished the Lampshire Boarding House in the town. Again things seemed to calm down for a while and most people appeared to have forgotten the dangers of living where they did. Later that year, the largest of all the slides struck Brownsville. This time, in addition to the Seven-Thirty dump, several of the mine buildings also went. The Griffin cabin, blacksmith shop, and ore house were carried away. More serious than before, this was a rockslide. Grumbling down Brown Gulch, the boulders devolved upon the town. Luckily, the roaring mass lost its momentum before reaching the mill.

Although the town was now pretty thoroughly inundated under tons of debris and slush, the elements seemed not to be content merely to let it go at that. There was still more to come. In June of 1912, the air was suddenly filled with a sound like muttering thunder. It was the same warning that had evacuated Brownsville and the adjoining village of Silver Plume seventeen years before. After a look up the mountain at the mass of moving rock, most women, men, and children lost no time in leaving.

Suddenly the muttering became a deafening roar as a gigantic river of stone came tumbling down Brown Gulch. Rapidly it spread over the town, burying everything that had escaped before. Down went the beautiful hotel with its grand piano. Miners' cottages, with all the worldly possessions of the occupants, were torn asunder. Two railroad cars, loaded with quarrying granite, were tossed about like children's toys. In the course of total destruction, the mud came again.

People came from miles around to watch the mud flow slowly down the mountainside. Most eyewitness accounts reveal that none of these slides was an instantaneous event. Some of the more imaginative have stated that they could hear the piano tinkling under the slide as the mud and rocks slithered slowly over the keys. This, of course, gave rise to the myriad rumors that men had been imprisoned by the slide. Both stories are almost equally unlikely. First of all, the tumult and noise would have obscured any sounds from a piano. Second, only a rare mental type ("The captain must go down with his ship") would remain at his instrument while being slowly drowned in a muddy ooze. Historical events apart, this is the stuff of folklore. Due to the slowness of a mud flow, it is difficult to believe that anyone could have been accidentally caught there. Likewise, the rumor that an entire train, filled with people, was caught by the slide, is also unfounded.

Gradually a rounded mound took the place of the village. It still stands today, a great rock pile about a mile and a half west of Silver Plume along the course of Highway 40, seemingly as out of place as a saloon in a new church district. On the opposite side of the road is a deep pit. These are the only remains of what was once the town of Brownsville.*

* In this same general area, see also Silver Plume, Fall River, North Empire, Gilson Gulch, and Freeland.

Brownsville, on both sides of Clear Creek, as shown in half of a stereo pair

Brownsville today, as taken from atop the old mud slide

6.

BUCKSKIN JOE

THE TINY COMMUNITY of Laurette, which later became known as Buckskin Joe, has no connection whatever with the reconstructed pioneer village on Highway 50 which now bears its name. The two should not be associated in the mind of the serious student of history. As an attempt to duplicate a pioneer Colorado settlement, the recently established Buckskin Joe is now very much alive, is lots of fun, and has a picturesque name which offers a wide degree of appeal. The original town today is a very dead place indeed. Only a few dilapidated buildings, scattered foundations, and a very extensive cemetery remain to mark its location or spot in the sun.

Facts and legends have become so entwined here that it is already difficult, if not impossible, to determine what is the truth. Many stories still exist and their number is growing, but few authentic records are now extant. That the community first was called Laurette is disputed by no one. How the town got its name is something else again. In one version, Laurette appears to have been a contraction of the first names of Laura and Jeanette Dodge, members of the family of Horace Dodge, part owner of the nearby Phillips Lode. Another story identifies Laurette as the sweetheart of Joseph Higginbottom whose preference for aboriginal wearing apparel caused him to be known in the mountains as Buckskin Joe. The man himself is also something of an enigma. One source says that he was a mulatto. With this as a starter, he was subsequently identified as a Negro. Some other sources insist he was neither. Even his family name has come in for a share of confusion. To date, I have encountered spellings ranging from "Higginbottom" through "Higgenbottom" to "Higginbothan."

The chronology of Buckskin Joe ranks it among the very earliest of Colorado mining camps. Most, though by no means all, accounts credit Higginbottom with the initial discovery of lode gold along the banks of what is now called Buckskin Creek. Just how he did it and under what circumstances is anybody's guess. Without doubt the most theatrical version tells of Joe being on a winter hunting expedition in the valley. Different accounts tell how he sighted a bear (unlikely in winter), a herd of deer, or a large elk, and prepared to shoot. At the moment of discharge, or just before, he is said to have slipped on the snow, causing the shot to go wild. The game animal was promptly forgotten since the errant bullet grazed the side of a nearby hill, laying bare a surface vein or lode of rich gold deposits. Since this same story has shown up on at least four separate occasions in other Western states with names and places changed, its authenticity is certainly open to question. In still another version the hunting episode is credited to a pioneer named Harrison.

Some other accounts have Higginbottom making the discovery, but by more conventional means, while a few fail to mention him at all, or merely identify him as an early trapper and resident of South Park. At any rate, the Phillips Lode, a tremendously rich producer, became the mainstay of the town's economic life and a population of about one thousand eventually formed the nucleus which became a new town. As Laurette grew and prospered, more and more of the "Pikes Peakers" gravitated into South Park until a peak population of five thousand souls was reported to have settled there. Considering the size of this valley, the latter statistic is certainly open to question. For the entire district, including Montgomery and Mosquito, it may have been realistic.

All too frequently the census taker got carried away with his own importance and counted the same highly migratory people on more than one occasion. This circumstance was not always intentional.

The miners never completely adjusted to calling their town Laurette and from the earliest times insisted on Buckskin Joe. The change was seemingly made official in the early 1860's, when a post office was opened there by Horace and Augusta Tabor. At this time the Tabors were still casting about from camp to camp. The great wealth that later made the name of H. A. W. Tabor synonomous with the Silver Dollar was still a long way off. The Tabors were not newcomers but had arrived in Buckskin Joe early in 1861 from either Oro City or Montgomery—the accounts differ. Having operated a general store in their previous location, the Tabors lost little time in conforming to their previous calling. At this time the Henry Webber family, good friends of Horace and Augusta, also lived at Buckskin Joe. Here young Henry Webber and Maxcy Tabor attended school. The original Tabor store, or a reasonable facsimile thereof, was moved down to Fairplay some years ago and now stands in their restored pioneer village called South Park City.

The way of life in Buckskin Joe differed but little from that in other contemporary mining camps. People from a wide variety of backgrounds gravitated to the town: conspicuous among them were gamblers and others of their fraternity, including fifty women from "all walks of life." A fairly extensive red-light district flourished on the outskirts at one end of the camp. A variety of saloons, billiard halls, three dance halls and a brass band that played on the street corners helped the argonauts to pass their off hours. Two men, named Stansell and Harris, seem to have been responsible for having set up the first stamp mill in the narrow valley. In partnership with a man named Bond, Stansell and Harris also had a bank at Buckskin Joe. About a dozen mills were operating at the peak of the boom. In addition to the more conventional and efficient means of ore extraction, several crude arrastras were also in use. One of these, quite well preserved, may be seen in the edge of the creek just west of the townsite. While there are those in South Park who feel that this particular device dates from the period of Spanish exploration in the 1600's, I feel that its state of generally good preservation would date it more logically with the boom at Buckskin Joe.

During the winter, flights of stairs were cut in the banks of deep snow to assist the residents in entering and leaving their buried cabins. By 1861, there were two hotels, fourteen stores, and a bank building where most transactions were handled in gold dust. A large log building, erected in 1861, became the first courthouse in Park County and was distinguished by its huge stone fireplace and chimney. Soon thereafter, this structure became the seat of Park County. As the town grew, a terminal stagecoach station was built at Buckskin Joe and the Dan McLaughlin Stage Line carried passengers, freight, and gold to Denver. The student of history may recall an 1863 invasion by the Confederate guerrilla Reynolds gang which sought Colorado gold to further the Rebel cause. Loaded with gold from the Phillips Lode, the Buckskin coach was robbed at McLaughlin's station just east of Fairplay. Since the raid failed when the Rebels were scattered by a crossfire of pursuing posses, many legends have grown up around the $40,000 in gold the gang is alleged to have buried high in Handcart Gulch. Quantities of spurious maps now exist to guide the gullible who want to dig up a fortune from old Buckskin Joe.

No accounting of the early life at Buckskin Joe would be complete without at least a superficial retelling of the story of Silver Heels, a "dance hall girl" who was easy on the eyes and of easier virtue. So many versions of this story have been bandied about that truth, again, will probably never be extracted from fiction. An opera which attempted the story moved the locale from Buckskin Joe to Central City.

In two other versions the Silver Heels family name was given as Keller and as Josie Dillon, respectively. Actually, her identification was never established.

Most versions, however, agree on the following aspects of the story. First of all, the name Silver Heels was derived from her preference for wearing silver-heeled slippers when she plied her trade as an entertainer in the dance halls. Having a pleasant, cheery, personality, the girl soon became a great favorite among the miners.

Prior to the introduction of widespread public health vaccination programs, smallpox regularly took a frightening toll of human life in the mountain mining camps. These epidemics are easily documented by the prevalence of headstones for small children found in overgrown ghost town cemeteries where large numbers died in the same year. Buckskin Joe was a victim of one such epidemic.

Some say that Spanish herders from the San Luis Valley brought the disease into the camp with their herds of sheep, driven up for sale to the miners in the spring of 1861. Large numbers of the Buckskin residents were affected and flat on their backs. Mining nearly came to a standstill and business houses generally closed their doors. In one story it has been reported that only two nurses from Denver heeded the tragic cry for assistance. One of the first to die was Silver Heels' lover. Since hospitals in this era were little more than pesthouses, it is probably fortunate that no such institution was ever established at Buckskin Joe. The afflicted miners had no choice except to ride out the storm in their cabins.

Silver Heels, temporarily out of a job since the dance halls were closed, rose superbly to the challenge in the finest tradition of a slightly tarnished Florence Nightingale. For months on end she tirelessly nursed both miners and their families. She washed their clothing, cooked their meals and tidied up their cabins. This deliberate exposure through such a massive frontal attack once more proved the futility of defying the law of averages. Silver Heels, too, became a victim of smallpox. Following her recovery, a pockmarked complexion ruled out the possibility of a return to her former profession.

To show their gratitude for all she had done, the miners took up a collection which amounted to about four thousand dollars. Senator Edward O. Wolcott, when he heard about it, added another thousand of his own. Silver Heels, however, could not be found. In the best tradition of the theater, she took her few possessions and quietly left the camp for parts unknown. Not even a forwarding address was left behind.

In subsequent years there were periodic reports of a heavily veiled woman who appeared from time to time in the cemetery, placing flowers on the graves of the 1,861 smallpox victims. Sentimentalists chose to believe the veil hid smallpox scars and that these were nostalgic visits by Silver Heels. Today, one of the nearby mountains behind Alma bears the name of Mount Silverheels.

Late in 1865 the rich lodes began to show signs of exhaustion. Huge granite walls were found on all sides of the deposits and for a time tragedy was forestalled by operating the mines as stone quarries. By late 1866 the town was empty and the county seat was moved to Fairplay that year. One source makes the statement that Buckskin Joe was emptied in a single day and a night. Statements of this sort make superb copy but are hardly likely.

Visiting Buckskin Joe involves a very short and quite pleasant drive on a well maintained dirt road. From Fairplay, drive northwest on State Highway 9 to Alma. Near the center of town, turn west or left off the pavement onto the dirt road that follows Buckskin Gulch and drive two miles. Since so few authentic landmarks remain I would suggest that you refer to the photographs accompanying this chapter and merely drive until the peaks line up in proper sequence above the valley. As you approach the townsite a smaller dirt road leads off to the right into the trees and terminates at the cemetery. When last seen there was a "cemetery" sign at the fork. The actual location of the town was in the meadow to the right of the main road and about fifty yards beyond the road to the cemetery. Nearby is a road leading off to the left and ending at an old mine, possibly the Phillips. Along this road, on the right side is a badly dilapidated building which was pointed out to me as being the old Silver Heels Dance Hall. This structure is not visible from the main road. Although I feel that both these latter identifications are open to question, they were made by a person with long residence tenure in the district. The arrastra is on the left side of the main road, about a mile beyond the townsite.

Buckskin Joe was one of the earliest "Pikes Peak" boom towns to mushroom into existence in the early sixties as hordes of prospectors explored the hills in ever-expanding waves. Gold was the object of their search, and when the rich lodes were exhausted they moved on, leaving little behind to mark their brief stay.*

---

* In this same general area, see also Alma, Fairplay, Puma City, Quartzville, Montgomery, Leavick, and Sacramento.

Buckskin Joe, as it was photographed by George Wakely in the 1860's

The site of Buckskin Joe a century later

7.

CAMP BIRD

BY SOME HISTORICAL ALCHEMY of fate, the territory around the Camp Bird Mine was rather thoroughly explored during the late 1870's, but the greatest discovery of all was overlooked until 1895. George Barber and Bill Weston located the Una and Gertrude, two good silver claims, a full two decades prior to the gold discoveries by Andy Richardson and Tom Walsh. Weston and Barber sold their mines to the Reed brothers, of Ouray, in 1880. That next year, the Reeds resold both properties for fifty thousand dollars. Although the claims were good, the upper reaches of Canyon Creek had such a formidable reputation for snowslides that most prospectors shied away from the area. After the silver crash of 1893, the region declined on its own. Neither the Gertrude nor the Una was worth working under the circumstances.

Then, in 1895, Andrew Richardson, a scout for Thomas F. Walsh, uncovered the Camp Bird Lode. In another version, Walsh himself explored the old Gertrude property and made the discovery unaided. Most accounts, however, favor the Richardson location story. In any event, Walsh bought up the old claims for twenty thousand dollars. By 1900 he had spent close to a half million dollars both in buying up other nearby tracts as they came onto the market and in making improvements upon the properties. As a result of the silver crash, the price was down. Few people other than Walsh and Richardson suspected the presence of gold in the Imogene Basin. Incidentally, both this basin and the high Imogene Pass that went over to the Tomboy and Telluride were named for Richardson's wife. The Camp Bird name came from the thieving Canada jays that allegedly pilfered Tom Walsh's lunch one day while he was prospecting.

Walsh was a native of Ireland. He migrated to this country at the age of nineteen and worked as a carpenter. Near Golden he helped to build the Colordo Central Railroad, working as a member of a construction gang. At heart he was a frustrated prospector. During his career he mined at Del Norte, at Deadwood, South Dakota, in Central City, at Rico, and he also took part in the great silver rush to Leadville. For a time, principally after 1896, he operated a smelter at Silverton. He first entered the Imogene Basin in 1895.

After buying up the neighboring claims, Walsh first reworked the old dumps. When he dug into the Camp Bird, his first samples ran $3,000 to the ton in gold. Over the years, the Camp Bird placed among the top three gold mines in Colorado. It produced from $3,000,000 to $4,000,000 annually during its peak years. Total production figures that have been given out place the Camp Bird's overall production at between $30,000,000 and $50,000,000.

At the head of Canyon Creek, but below the Imogene Basin, a settlement grew up and assumed the name of Camp Bird. All things considered, the town covered about nine hundred acres. There were many small white frame homes with gabled green roofs. A fine little school was built and used well into the present century. The post office was served from Ouray, six miles down Canyon Creek. After a very brief period, a general store also went into business at the site. By far the largest structure in town was the huge red mill with a sloping roof to prevent having to lift the ores. Packtrains and ore wagons plied their way up and down the narrow shelf road between Ouray and Camp Bird. In winter, horse-drawn freight sleds took over the hauling of supplies and ores.

Two or three miles above the town, at the end of an aerial tram, was the actual mine itself. One story tells us that there was a second red mill up there by the mine. To shelter the three hundred or so men who labored in the deep shafts, a huge three-storied boardinghouse was built. In his superbly written book, *One Man's West*, David Lavender gives a vivid and fascinating firsthand account of life in the Camp Bird boardinghouse. Despite the precarious location, it had electric lights, steam heat, modern plumbing, marble-topped lavatories, and a reading room. In one room, a highly individualized general store was run. In winter, the men tunneled in and out of their quarters and to and from the mine proper. Later, this boardinghouse burned and a new one, equally ornate, replaced it. It even had hot showers. Unfortunately, the second one was nearly destroyed by a snowslide. As the crow flies, the Tomboy Mine was only five to six miles away from the Camp Bird. Both properties were linked by under-the-range tunnels.

By 1902, Walsh had personally taken out something in the neighborhood of $2,500,000. That same year he sold out to a British syndicate, called the Camp Bird, Ltd., for $5,200,000. By 1902 he was already a millionaire. His daughter, Evalyn Walsh McLean, acquired the fabulous Hope Diamond and most of the ill fortunes that are alleged to have accompanied it. In better times, she became the leading social hostess in our nation's capital while Warren Gamaliel Harding was living at 1600 Pennsylvania Avenue.

Meanwhile, back at Camp Bird, life went on after a fashion. The nearly vertical walls of Canyon Creek had made this one of the most dangerous spots in Colorado. Over the years, many deaths have resulted from snowslides. Most of the slides run on the same courses, year after year, and are known. Many have even been named. Among these the Water Hole has been consistently regarded as one of the most treacherous. When it ran in 1909, four men and sixteen horses were killed. Another time it roared down onto the road to Camp Bird and snuffed out the lives of five men and twenty-three horses. Most frequently, the slides run in the spring after warm weather has promoted a certain amount of melting and shifting of the great masses of snow and ice on the peaks above. Generally the drivers cut new trails over the tops of the slides and transportation went on. Hardly a winter has passed without mishaps of some sort on this vital but dangerous road.

When costs rose in 1916, the Camp Bird closed down for a while. After reopening, it declined again during the great depression of the 1930's. In a search for paper profits, President Franklin D. Roosevelt boosted the price of gold to thirty-five dollars an ounce. With this shot in the arm, operations were resumed once more and have been pursued, with varying intensities, ever since.

Your tour to Camp Bird begins inevitably at Ouray. Near the south edge of town, U.S. 550, the Million Dollar Highway, begins its switchbacked climb out of the amphitheater. Barely beyond the town, a dirt road branches off to the right. This is State Highway 361. Two forks, barely fifty yards or so apart, confront you almost at once. At the first, go right and cross the bridge over the Uncompahgre River. At the second you should turn left. The right turn here, incidentally, goes into Box Canyon, an area well worth seeing if time permits. As your car grinds its way upward, visualize, if you can, the pioneer drivers and stagecoach passengers desperately clinging to a swaying and creaking wagon. Covered with dust, they gazed vertically downward into the awesome depths of the canyon. Six miles later, you will arrive at Camp Bird, situated slightly to your left where the vertical walls widen out into a circular basin. Here, in sight of the town, another road forks off to the right and goes on up to Mount Sneffels and Yankee Boy Basin.

From Camp Bird, permission must be secured if you want

to go on for the last two miles to the site of the original mine. On this last stretch, a Jeep or a horse or a pair of sturdy hiking boots is required. Since people often behave unpredictably and because liability laws are written as they are, the management has been understandably reluctant to permit access to the Imogene Basin. Nevertheless, this is a magnificent area, a fine place to come and enjoy the unmatched scenic beauty and historical significance of a bygone era.*

* In this same general area, see also Dallas City, Ouray, and Silverton.

In 1912 George Beam photographed Camp Bird and its reduction mill

Vastly changed but still operating, the Camp Bird is an interesting place

8.

CAMP FRANCES

FOR AN ENGLISH TEACHER, life at Camp Frances would have been frustrating indeed for this was a community of a rather confused gender. In researching the chapter, I found nearly as many references to "Camp Francis" as there were references to "Camp Frances." I shall use the latter form since it seems to predominate, but we will probably never be sure whether the namesake of the town was masculine or feminine. However, one story has it that the community was named for the youngest daughter of William P. Daniels, founder of the town and president of the Ni-Wot Mining Company.

Camp Frances was started in the early 1890's and was operated by a syndicate that developed a series of well-paying mining properties in the vicinity. The Big 5 Mines Company employed about one hundred men and had control of some eight hundred acres of land. Under this single management, such mines as the Adit, Ni-Wot, Columbia, and the big Dew Drop at the head of the gulch, were operated. All of their combined ores came down to the town by way of the Adit Tunnel. Processing was carried on in the huge Dew Drop Milling Company plant or the even larger Big 5 Mill on the side of the gulch below the town. From the stream bed, the huge mill extended for some distance up the hill. The Big 5 powerhouse, with its huge black smokestack, stood nearby. Beside it there was a stone powder house, a portion of which still stands. Just up the hill, almost in the edge of the trees, was the red-pointed mining office building with a huge Arabic numeral "5" painted on the outside wall.

A close friend of mine recently excavated a spot near the door of this building and recovered quite a number of well preserved and rather attractive crucibles.

Throughout most of the 1890's there were about two hundred people in residence here. Most of them were employed at the Big 5 or Dew Drop mills. Before long it had a post office and a few business structures. The *Colorado and Southern Railroad Guide* for 1901-2 lists the T. J. Cox General Merchandise Store at Camp Frances. Before the turn of the century about fifty cabins had been built there. Despite the nearness of Ward and its excellent educational facility, Camp Frances decided to have its own school.

At the head of the gulch, near the Dew Drop Mine, the Colorado and Northwestern Railway built a station house. This line is more frequently remembered as the Switzerland Trail. On this particular branch, the tracks ended at Ward. In winter the train crews were always hard pressed to keep the tracks clear of snow all the way to Ward. After each storm, workmen shoveled out the snow-filled cuts. On April 24, 1901, a tragedy occurred. A double hookup was pulling a string of cars up the valley toward Camp Frances. As they gained altitude, the snows grew deeper until they were confronted with huge drifts blocking their track. Several times the engineer backed off and bucked into the big piles of snow. When they seemingly could go no farther, the coaches were uncoupled and left on the track. Both engines now went on ahead, bucking the drifts.

Some doubt exists about what happened next. Whether the snowslide started accidentally or whether it was precipitated by the concussion and noise from the two locomotives is uncertain. In any event a slide was started which carried both engines—and the men on them—down the gulch. Two firemen, the brakeman, and the conductor were killed. Several others were injured in the fall but recovered to tell the tale.

The location of Camp Frances is fourteen miles west and

three miles north of Boulder. From the other direction it is just a mile south of Ward. Several dilapidated cabins and a greater number of foundations still mark the site. On down the hill toward the stream are the mill foundations and a stone wall from the powder house. Slightly apart and up the hill is the Big 5 office building. Across the gully from the remaining cabins is an old bathtub, standing alone on the barren hillside. An open pipe protrudes from the earth nearby and keeps this fixture filled with cold running water. Surely nobody in Camp Frances was enough of an exhibitionist to have used this as a very public community bath; but what else could it have been? A watering trough, perhaps?

To see what remains of Camp Frances drive southwest out of Ward on State Highway 160, a fine paved thoroughfare that is known locally as the "peak to peak highway." At a point about one mile out of Ward, look for a rather large gravel pile on the left side of the road which now blocks the old trail down the side of the hill into the valley containing Camp Frances. Although there is one spot a bit farther on where it is possible to put a Jeep down over the bank, it is smarter to park by the gravel and walk from there.

Just follow the valley down until you see the scar that was once the old trail. It winds down past the bathtub on your left, the cabins to your right, and on down over the bank to the mills by the stream. Going back out, the distance to the highway is less than a mile but the grades look steeper than when you came down. At this altitude, several stops to rest and catch your breath will make your trip to Camp Frances a more pleasant one.*

---

* In this same general area, see also Eldora, Salina, and Tungsten.

Here, at the lower end of Camp Frances, we see a Colorado and
Northwestern train and some of the Big 5 mine buildings.

Just the old grade of the railroad, the large mine dump, and the Big 5 office
building serve as points of comparison with the above photograph.

9.

COMO

LIFE AT COMO began during the summer of 1879 when it became the newest in a series of end-of-the-tracks tent cities, put up to shelter construction crews that were busily laying tracks for the Denver, South Park and Pacific Railway across South Park. This was the era of the great silver rush to Leadville. Before the railroad was completed, migrants from Denver rode the trains to Como, then transferred to stagecoaches for the ride across South Park and over Mosquito Pass to the silver bonanza. Traffic headed for Leadville also included heavily loaded packtrains, big freight wagons, and people with packs on their backs. At one time Como was piled so high with provisions and freight that shipments had to be stopped until the town could be cleared. The population is said to have risen to six thousand during that first summer. This total was swelled somewhat when the last remaining residents from the old gold-mining town of Hamilton also moved down into Como.

This original Como was actually down in the meadow at the later site of King Park. When the railroad built a station three miles away in 1879, the people moved there and the town that grew up around this new facility became the present Como. Beginning in 1880, the original tent city site became King Park or King City. George W. Lechner laid out the second town after he had discovered a rich vein of lignite coal nearby. The first Lechner coal discovery dates back to 1871. Taken as a whole, the vein averaged from seven to ten feet thick. For several months he hauled loads of coal to Fairplay where it brought ten dollars per ton. Later, he sold his mine to the railroad. Several coal properties were found within the radius of a few miles. In addition, there were gold mines to the west. It will be recalled that the early gold camps of Tarryall and Hamilton were only a mile or two west of the present town. Off in this same direction, the unmistakable signs of dredging may still be seen with tremendous elongated ridges following the riverbed.

As business from the railroad grew, so did Como. Daily trains, some of them four-engined freights, huffed their way up over the eighty-eight miles from Denver. The town became known as a division point, with one branch carrying trains over Boreas Pass to Breckenridge while the other went to Gunnison by way of the Alpine Tunnel. A lunchroom was built and operated by the railroad at Como. By far the most prominent feature among the railroad facilities here was a huge roundhouse, built with partly frame and partly masonry construction. Within a few years, between fifty and one hundred men were employed in this facility. To assure smooth operation, repair shops were also located at Como.

For many years, starting in April of 1879, the South Park Coal Company, which also operated the King Mines, furnished the railroad with a ready supply of fuel. Their King Coal Mine was located about a mile and a half north of the railroad station. As with most coal mines, underground gases caused explosions, sometimes with fatal results. Worst of all was an explosion in the King Coal that snuffed out the lives of sixteen miners. The peak year for coal production was 1884.

Quite apart from the initial rush that brought thousands to live and work at Como, the average population hovered around five hundred to six hundred people. Most of them were of Italian extraction. In fact, their nostalgia for the northern Italian region around Lake Como resulted in the selection of the town's name. Labor troubles once erupted late in 1879 when Chinese miners were brought in from Fairplay. Infuriated, the Italians banded together, girded their loins for battle, and ran the Chinese out of town. Having been deprived of a good fight, they then proceeded to beat up the man who had brought the celestials to Como.

Over the years four hotels flourished at Como. They were the Kelly Hotel, the Como House, the Gilman Hotel and the Montag House. During the early days three newspapers were published at Como, through the simple expedient of a name change. First came the *Como Headlight*, a weekly that became a permanent fixture between 1883 and 1904. Later, its name was changed to the *Record*. Beginning in 1879, Como also had a school. It continued to operate until 1948. Children from the town are now bussed to Fairplay. Three churches, a Methodist, a Community, and a Catholic, also served the residents.

Streetlights, illuminated with gasoline-fired lamps, were used after 1900. No electricity reached Como until the REA extended lines into the town in 1963. Among the commercial enterprises serving Como were several saloons and gambling houses, many restaurants, and a number of meat markets and grocery stores. Como's heyday extended through the 1880's and 1890's. At one point the residents underwent delusions of grandeur and the name was kited to Como City, but it failed to catch on and was soon dropped. Several professions were represented among the residents of Como. There was a resident physician, a dentist, several attorneys, and one busy and prosperous undertaker. The cemetery was just beyond the town, on a windswept hillside above the road to Boreas Pass.

For many years Como had an extensive business district. There were several clothing stores, candy shops, a tobacconist, at least one drugstore, a lumber yard, two Chinese laundries, a dairy, some barbershops that offered fifteen-cent haircuts, a dry-goods store and a couple of stables. Many of these succeeded abundantly until after the turn of the cen-

Looking across South Park. The town of Como reposes in the foreground while a narrow-gauge train of the D.S.P. & P. passes in the middle distance.

From the same vantage point, many of Como's original structures are visible

tury. Then in 1909 a series of disastrous events began, forecasting the decline of Como.

First came a fire that destroyed the railroad shops. Although some parts were saved, many jobs were eliminated and the fire-damaged sections were not replaced. When the railroad abandoned all attempts to maintain their winter schedule through the Alpine Tunnel in the fall of 1910, it cut the population of Como by nearly two thirds as additional jobs were eliminated. Shortly after that the roundhouse was closed. In the course of 1911, the rest of the railroad shops were also closed. No less of a contribution to the decline of Como was a fire in the roundhouse during 1935, started by sparks from the stack of a locomotive. Once again the damaged part was not replaced. Two years later, in April of 1937, the Denver, South Park and Pacific, which by now through a series of reorganizations was the Colorado and Southern, abandoned its line across the entire high alpine park. With support from the railroad withdrawn, the exodus began in earnest.

To see Como today, drive southwest out of Denver on U.S. 285 across beautiful Kenosha Pass to South Park. A few miles past Jefferson, you will see a black and white sign pointing to Como, barely a mile north of the paved highway. U.S. 285 may be followed with equal facility to South Park from other parts of the state.

Fortunately, Como has been spared the final indignity of becoming a ghost town. Here, at an altitude of 9,796 feet above sea level, this alpine-ringed community now has a second lease on life. Gradually activities other than mining and railroading have taken over. Many of the fine, tight little houses have now become pretty summer homes. The old cemetery, now enveloped in sun-dappled groves of green and yellow quaking aspens, affords a strikingly beautiful final resting place for the pioneers who lived the history of Como.*

---

* In this same general area, see also Boreas, Dyersville, King City, Tarryall, and Hamilton.

10.

CRESTED BUTTE

FOR SEVERAL YEARS prior to the existence of Crested Butte, mineral prospecting forays had been carried out in the immediate vicinity. A few paying placers had been worked from time to time in nearby valleys. In the spring of 1879, the settlement that was to become Crested Butte was laid out by Howard Smith, who brought in the first sawmill. His chosen location was the broad, open valley at the confluence of Slate and Coal creeks. Although hard metal production was the primary attraction, large coal deposits were also found in this early period.

By the end of the year, population figures had grown to encompass a total of almost 250 people. During 1880, the settlement expanded and included some fifty houses and a number of tents which sheltered around two thousand souls by the end of the year. Most Crested Butte residents were of Austrian, Italian, and German extraction, people who had come to the valley directly from their native Europe. Since we humans characteristically transfer elements from our former culture to any new environment, these people recreated familiar conditions in their new home. Being strangers in a new country, they sought happiness and security by sharing their problems and by raising their families in an Old World atmosphere.

To a degree Crested Butte became a supply center for other mining endeavors in the vicinity. Prospectors, experienced miners and their supplies, passed through here on the way to other nearby camps. A total of thirty-three businesses, including three saloons and at least that many livery stables, flourished to cater to the needs of incoming migrants who sought the gold, silver, iron, zinc, and copper lodes. Formal incorporation became a reality in 1881.

Despite the fact that it was almost completely surrounded by mountains, the altitude of Crested Butte was still 8,888 feet above sea level. Inevitably, this meant long and difficult winters. For about six months of the year, heavy snows still blanket the townsite. Residents, then as now, use skis and snowshoes. Old records are replete with stories about going cross-country over the fence tops. Even the mail was carried on skis.

In the early days many Crested Butte residents found it necessary to get out at night and push the snow off their roofs to keep their houses from buckling. As time passed, the later structures were built with sharply pitched roofs, often surfaced with metal, so that deep winter snows might slide off without crushing the structures. Even the clotheslines were strung considerably higher than average, often being attached to pulleys from second-floor porches out to poles in the yard that might be as much as twenty feet tall. Because of the snow depth, a housewife might not be able to get into her backyard for months at a time.

Since indoor plumbing was still far off in the future, the more necessary sanitary facilities at the Butte were constructed with two stories. In summer, the lower levels were used. During winter's icy blasts, people snowshoed out to the second story. Regrettably, no examples of these most original innovations still exist.

Miners who spent the winter in the valley carried dynamite sticks wrapped around their legs under their trousers. This kept the explosives from freezing while the man was on his way to work. One additional condition of life justifies this practice. When a miner had to cross a potential snowslide area, a few sticks could be placed on a long pole for detonation. The resulting concussion was sure to loosen the snow, causing the slide to run and thereby avoiding the avalanche.

To provide better access to the district, men from Aspen, Ashcroft, and Crested Butte hacked out a difficult wagon road over Pearl Pass in 1882. In this way they could facilitate the movement of equipment and supplies from the end of the railroad at Crested Butte to the Aspen district across the range. Prior to that time most supplies were packed in on the backs of burros. In this town, as in so many mining camps, a herd in excess of two hundred of these animals could be seen standing in the street, waiting to be loaded with supplies for the nearby mines. Such sights were extremely common in the days when Crested Butte was the commercial center for this entire region. On mules and in wagons, supplies were carried up to the Esta Mine at Pittsburg, to the Painter Boy and Silver Jewel in Washington Gulch, to the Silver Knight at Gothic, and to the tremendous Forest Queen at Ruby-Irwin.

Three hostelries served the needs of the transients. These were the Forest Queen, the Crested Butte House, and Mrs. Sanger's Hotel. Even with their combined facilities, there were never enough rooms to accommodate the many outsiders in addition to the regular people of the town. By February of 1882, the Elk Mountain Hotel had been completed and was widely advertised as being the best in the country. Notable among its claims to fame were an indoor system of hot and cold running water, three indoor "water closets" and three bathtubs. The latter accommodations were made possible by a pressurized water system which had to be hand pumped by the kitchen help.

The fourth estate arrived in town very early in the game. In 1880 the first of two newspapers, the *Crested Butte Republican*, began publication. A second paper, the *Elk Mountain Pilot*, started life elsewhere. It was conceived at Rosita, in Custer County, during the summer of 1879. J. E. Phillips was the publisher. When he heard that George and Harry

Cornwall had reserved a free lot to be given to the first newspaper at their new town of Ruby-Irwin, Phillips decided to move. Since town lots at that location were bringing anywhere from $100 to $5,000, he had little to lose.

His paper was a "first" and continued to be published until it was discovered by some presumptuous clerk that the townsite was actually seven miles inside the Ute Reservation. Under these conditions there could be no legal rights or titles to any of the town lots. Although Ruby-Irwin went right along its merry way, Phillips grew apprehensive and began casting about for a wider, deeper, and safer rut.

Crested Butte, only a few miles to the south, seemed to be a growing town—and legal, too. Its central location had the advantage of being able to provide circulation for his paper to a variety of the surrounding camps. Prospects were further improved by the fact that rail connections had already reached the camp. In the face of all of these compelling reasons, the editor decided to pack up his type and presses for one more move. On May 2, 1884, the *Pilot* was moved by bobsled over the entire distance of eight miles and Crested Butte found itself with two newspapers.

During 1883, Crested Butte really boomed. In October the city hall was completed. That same year saw their school buildings and a church added to the mushrooming village. On December 7, 1881, Crested Butte watched breathlessly as the first hand-cranked telephone was installed in their town. After a very brief period, several more "talkies" were in service there to speed up communication to the nearby mining camps.

Gaslights fascinated everybody when they were first installed. Some residents admit setting their alarm clocks so they could get up at night, turn on the light, and just sit there watching it burn. At first, the local plant suspended operations after 10:00 P.M. From then until 5:00 A.M., the consumers were forced to use candles or kerosene lamps.

When the community water system was completed in 1883, everyone rested more easily.

Nearly all of the larger mining camps set up elaborate protection organizations against the threat of fire. The Crested Butte Hose Company No. 1 consisted of several nimbled-footed men who boasted that they never gave a fire an even break. They once chalked up a record of thirty-five seconds for the regulation contest. On July 4, 1901, an eleven-man team from Crested Butte defeated a team from Gunnison by a single second. Although the team of "Fire Laddies" from the Butte was made up of men who could individually sprint a hundred yards in ten seconds the competition was frequently so close that seconds and even fractions of seconds became all-important.

The years 1882 and 1883 were the town's best. Although gold and silver production began to drop off, the void was more than filled by stock raising and by a coal-mining company which began developing coal mines close to the town. Properties in the valley produced not only a high grade of bituminous, but had the only large source of anthracite west of the Pennsylvania fields. From this series of mines, coal was shipped to the steel mills of the Colorado Fuel & Iron Company in Pueblo. Just outside the town limits of Crested Butte, a battery of fifty ovens was put into operation to burn the coke needed in the production of steel.

Coal became the greatest economic strength of the town. Well within the corporate limits, there were several producing mines. Equally promising outcroppings existed in the surrounding region and along the hillsides above Anthracite Creek. Among the best-known mines were the C. F. & I., the Peanut, and the Bulkley.

Without a doubt the worst single catastrophe in the region's history was the gas explosion in a mine up Coal Creek during February of 1884. Shortly after the morning work crew had entered its shaft, an explosion snuffed out the lives of fifty-nine men. Only eleven of the workers who were in the mine at the time managed to escape. Since most miners in most camps of this period were young and just starting out in life, only six of those who were killed were married. Most were Civil War veterans. The mine in which the disaster occurred had a shaft which penetrated the hill to a depth of 1,300 feet.

When they had been recovered, more than half of the bodies were buried in a special, isolated plot in the Gunnison cemetery. When faced by the need to transport the remains to their final resting places, a path was cleared through six feet of snow on the flats between Crested Butte and Gunnison. In one case, a mother attempted to keep the bodies of her two sons by packing snow around their caskets. Her desire to preserve them was prompted by several attempts to get word to her husband who was mining in the White River country near Meeker. For about a month she sent frantic messages. When her husband could not be found, she took the bodies East for burial. Quite apart from the tragedy, mining at Crested Butte went on. The town was booming then and it continued to do so for many years.

The evolution of transportation here followed along in the usual pattern. Use of burro packtrains, mentioned earlier, constituted the crude beginnings. At a later time, the Sanderson Stage Line came into the valley and even made an overnight stop at Crested Butte. In 1882, the Gunnison and Crested Butte branch of the Denver and Rio Grande Railway was extended twenty-seven miles into the town. Winter conditions were hardly conducive to a routine kind of operation. In the cold months of 1888, trains were snowbound in Slate Cut for seventeen days. Sometimes they were able to get through by using an engine with a rotary plow in the lead, followed by a wedge plow on the front of the regular passenger train.

During February of 1900, a snowslide in Slate Creek Canyon caught the noon train at a point about four miles below the town. Several cars were nearly reduced to matchsticks and mail delivery was delayed for several hours. Railroad operations on this run were interrupted with methodical frequency by accidents of this type during most winter seasons.

After enduring these conditions for what must have been a truly frustrating sequence of winters, the good people of Crested Butte held a mass meeting on February 22, 1909. For the previous seventeen-day period, no trains had reached their town. A resolution was drawn up condemning the Rio Grande Railway for failing to cope with the long blockade of snow which had cut them off from the outside world.

In this document the citizens not only condemned the railroad—they pledged themselves to a work program designed to open the road. Footing the bill became the forte of the Bank of Crested Butte which offered a sum of one thousand dollars upon completion of the work. The offer was conditional upon the company's willingness to give the assistance of its local crews and engines without charge.

At the turn of the century, the Colorado Fuel & Iron Company was shipping almost 1,200 carloads of coal and coke from Crested Butte each month. On many of these runs, the narrow-gauge Denver & Rio Grande freight lines had passenger coaches attached to serve travelers commuting to the several nearby towns. Earlier, the Denver, South Park & Pacific had tried to reach Crested Butte ahead of the Rio Grande by building through South Park, across the Arkansas Valley to Buena Vista before going through the mountains at the Alpine Tunnel. Having encountered 1,806 feet of loose material instead of the expected granite, a million feet of California redwood timbering was used to reinforce this section. In the chapter which deals with Alpine, this story is recounted in more detail. Tragically, it lost the race to Gunnison and Crested Butte by a year.

At some point in its history, almost every mining town was burned out totally or in part. Prior to 1890, Crested Butte had only the discomforts of the usual epidemics to worry about. At various times the town was swept by pneumonia, smallpox, scarlet fever, and diphtheria. Due to a lack of community funds, regular fire hydrants were not installed until 1889-90. Here it was a case of too little and too late. In any case, the hoped-for protection was not available when the first big fire broke out on the night of January 25, 1890.

A family, living in the second story of the Edwards building, had gone away. Their children were left behind with an overheated stove. Although the children were saved, a total of sixteen buildings went up in flames before the fire ended its rampage. Most homes in Crested Butte were built close together. Wet blankets were hastily applied to the tinder-dry roofs and nailed up against the exposed walls to curb the flames.

Curiously, the hydrant system was completed in the spring, just as many of the burned buildings were being replaced. Eventually, three fire companies were organized. Being volunteer groups, they kept pace with the times and often appeared in public demonstrations. Three years later, almost to the day, another fire was discovered. The date was January 8, 1893, and temperatures had dropped to forty degrees below zero. As fires go, this one was about par for the course but it did not destroy the town.

In this, as in so many mining camps, disease and fire were not the only sources of peril. For about a week prior to June 12, 1899, swollen streams threatened to spill over their levies on the edge of town. The banks of the creek along the western edge of Crested Butte gave way. Before the people realized what had happened, nearly the whole town was swept by water and had been reduced to a state of chaos.

In the business district, the first store to be flooded was the large and prosperous Colorado Supply Company. It was completely swamped, as were several other business houses. Down at the end of the block, the Glick Brothers store suffered a similar fate and was left virtually standing in a lake.

Across the street, the Axtell Lumber Company caught its share of the flood when the crest came pouring in against the post office next door.

Early that evening, those residents who lived along First Street, the thoroughfare nearest to the creek, moved out with everything they could carry. Shortly after dark, several onlookers noticed that a tremendous pile of driftwood had become lodged on the First Street bridge. To prevent loss of the bridge from the growing accumulation, dynamite was used to dislodge the mess. In the meantime several men had been detailed to watch and to work along the bank in an effort to contain the water and avoid any further spreading. All odds, however, were against them that night.

When the bank gave way, the surging torrent literally poured out of the breaks. Although relays of men worked in the water until the wee hours of the morning, it was touch and go at best. They ripped out culverts and bridges to assure the greatest possible flow of water, thereby preventing any further flooding of nearby homes.

When morning came, the streets everywhere presented a scene of wreckage. In the flooded business section, where water had slopped over from the swollen creek, sidewalks had to be elevated several feet above street level so that customers could walk "high and dry." Despite this, the regular street crossings everywhere were flooded. Even after the water had receded, there was deep mud to be contended with over much of the town.

At four o'clock on the morning of May 9, 1901, flames broke out from an overheated stove in the back room of Bruces' Saloon. Joining the "hooch emporium" on the west and sharing a common wall, the Colorado Supply Company's big store, now dried out from the flood, covered a space in excess of five thousand square feet. Quickly the fire spread to the roofs of both buildings. Despite efforts of the fire companies to contain the blaze at these points, it was soon a raging inferno. Nearby, Mrs. Lovelace's Notion and Confectionary store was wiped out. The Lovelace family, still asleep inside, had a narrow escape and saved only a few items of clothing, hurriedly grabbed up in their flight.

At this point the hardest fight of the day was made against further encroachments by the flames. A vacant lot allowed room for a determined effort by the fire laddies. Close to the vacant site was Otto Matsekey's jewelry store and beside it stood a large dry-goods house. Despite all efforts to save them, it began to appear that both of these buildings would go.

From then on, things started looking up. Fortunately for all concerned, a slight change of direction in a gentle breeze saved some of the structures and allowed the men to attend to the fire raging on the west side of town. Here it had already spread to the large Schainer Building, then occupied by the owner of a highly combustible hay and grain store. It was not until this structure had been entirely gutted and Young's Confectionary Store, next to it, had been badly damaged, that the flames were finally brought under control.

In the overall picture, the greatest loss was suffered during destruction of the Colorado Supply Company. Just a month earlier, this same store had experienced a nighttime fire which was, fortunately, discovered in time. The blaze was extinguished with only a slight loss. Since oil-saturated gunnysacks were found, there was little doubt as to the fire's origin. Since the second fire had originated in the same building and since oiled sacks were also found in several places to assure success, the overheated stove theory became somewhat suspect. In this as in so many other instances, the loss was only partially covered by insurance. Damage to stocks in this business alone exceeded thirty thousand dollars.

Beyond this, events on that incendiary front lay dormant until February 8, 1963. That night, the mercury dipped to forty degrees below zero and another fire was discovered. Summoned by the town alarm, firemen assembled to combat this latest threat to their town. Tragically, when they attached their hoses to a series of new fire hydrants, it was discovered that the whole system was frozen tight. Failure of the town's water system was nothing new. On December 28, 1939, it was shut down by a particularly bitter freeze, leaving the people dependent on Coal Creek and a few small wells.

In the 1963 fire, an entire block of business buildings tumbled in flames before volunteers brought in explosives and blew up Al Miller's furniture store with 150 pounds of black powder. Although the concussion definitely snuffed out the fire, it also shattered nearly every window in town. Without windows at forty degrees below, some folks playfully changed the town's name from "Crested" to "Frosted" and dropped the *e* from the second name.

So, gradually, activities other than mining have altered the economic base of Crested Butte. Coal mining was reduced to a trickle when the Colorado Fuel & Iron Company shut down its big operation on May 29, 1952. Directly as a result of the mining slump, the Denver & Rio Grande branch line was discontinued. Quite commonly, a town dies for less important causes than these. Miraculously, Crested Butte began to gain in popularity as a winter sports center. Some optimistic people think it is well on the way to becoming a favorite stop for summer tourists as well.

With ski resorts, a major revolution has transpired in what was once on the way to becoming a depressed mining area. Old Crested Butte, with its tin roofs, gingerbread-trimmed homes, and false-fronted business houses, stands in striking contrast to the ornate new lodges with red carpets, plush swimming pools, and vast panoramic picture windows.

By January of 1965, all ideas of becoming a ghost town were forgotten when the population more than doubled in the winter season. During the past winter, about 650 people filled 20 chalets and 5 lodges, not counting weekend people. About a dozen new businesses have started up in the past few years. In summer, saddle horses and pack animals may be rented by those who like to ride or fish in the nearby Elk Mountains and adjacent canyons.

For the visitor who would like to view a town in process of transition from the old to the new, Crested Butte is simple to find. Drive to Gunnison on U.S. Highway 50, turning north at the traffic light in the center of town. From this point a fine paved road goes all the way through Almont to Crested Butte, a wonderful spot to relax and unwind from the tensions imposed by city life.*

---

* In this same general area, see also Crystal City, Marble, and Scofield City.

An early photograph of Crested Butte when it was still a thriving coal camp

Crested Butte is now an exciting ski resort

11.

CRESTONE

THIS VERY ACCESSIBLE and beautifully located town experienced not just one but two separate booms. Life at Crestone was further complicated by conflict over ownership of the mines, brought on by arguments over title to one of the original Spanish land grants.

During the 1870's the first settlers began to move into this area while searching for precious metals. In 1879 fairly good prospects were unearthed and a small migration converged upon the lower slopes of the Sangre de Cristo Range. Since people need to have places in which to live, construction of the town began almost at once. Unfortunately, the early hopes for rich mineral returns failed to materialize as the diggings grew deeper and the booming prosperity of Crestone slowed to a grinding halt.

Economic affairs in the town hobbled along on a day-to-day basis until a promising quantity of free-milling gold was found in 1890, bringing on a second boom. During the 1890 prosperity the town was built. The usual variety of saloons, general stores and one hotel soon appeared. A railroad spur which reached the camp from Moffat provided better access and improved transportation facilities for the ores, mining supplies, and for the people. By 1900 the population of Crestone had reached a total of two thousand before the free gold pinched out when deep working was attempted.

One of the other factors affecting the destiny of Crestone dates back in European history. In 1823, King Ferdinand of Spain granted a very large land tract to some of his subjects in the New World. After winning its independence from Spain, Mexico recognized the rights of the family of Don Luis Maria Cabeza de Vaca to the original grant. As first conceived, the land included even the city of Las Vegas, New Mexico. In exchange for this latter region, the family accepted four new ranch sites. One of these consisted of 100,000 acres of prime rangeland in what is now Saguache County. When this whole region changed hands again following our war with Mexico, the United States also recognized the legality of the cessions as constituted.

Trouble developed when gold was found within the grant. Five towns grew up along the twenty-five-mile-long mineral vein which extended from the lower slopes of the Sangre de Cristo Range. Exercising their prerogatives, the owners threw out the miners and took over the rich mines themselves. Since Crestone was situated within the northeastern edge of the Luis Maria Baca Grant, the only alternative was for the community to pack up and move. The town of Liberty, once called Duncan, also got its orders to relocate at this time. Incidentally, to resolve any confusion, the name Vaca became Baca somewhere along the line and, despite the discrepancy in spelling, both names refer to the same family.

On March 21, 1901, W. J. Keim, the badman of Crestone, was placed in jail after building a dam across a high creek, cutting off the water supply of all six hundred of the people who lived in the town. Crestone derived its water supply from the mouth of North Crestone Creek. In November of 1900, Keim built his dam in the creek two miles above the town to secure a supply of ice. The ground near the dam was porous and the water soaked into the earth instead of going over the crest of the dam. As a result, the creek went dry. All residents of Crestone who had no wells were in trouble. Wails of protest from the townspeople fell on deaf ears. Keim defied the entire thirsty community for a total of four long, dry months.

Since laws governing such actions were rather inadequate at the time, the better legal minds of Crestone began investigating loopholes that might offer them some legal recourse. One suggestion that was made advocated prosecuting him for causing the deaths of thousands of fish. As the stream was state property the case was clear and Keim was arrested.

Deputy Game Warden Henry Moss and his deputy district attorney arrived from Denver to prosecute the culprit for the cruel mass murder of great quantities of innocent denizens of the deep in a watery concentration camp. The case was tried before Justice Lawrence at Crestone. A guilty verdict was almost a foregone conclusion. Keim was fined twenty-five dollars and costs and put under two hundred fifty dollars bail. Ten days were allowed for him to tear out the dam.

Keim swore at the judge before leaving the courtroom, and promptly found his bail raised and himself in jail. Residents of Crestone put their shoulders to the wheel and decided to tear out the dam themselves. Moss and his deputy were wined and dined by the grateful people of Crestone. In recognition of their services, both Denver men were made honorary members of the town's board of trade.

The experiences of Walter E. Perkins, of Crestone, read like a panorama of life in the several mining camps located along the rich mineral vein that paralleled the mighty Sangre de Cristo Range. Perkins was the town postmaster from 1900 to 1940. His memories of the area spanned some of the district's greatest years. His first work with the mail service found him in the capacity of postmaster at Liberty, another nearby ghost town. One man still lived at Liberty in 1940. Perkins was at Liberty during the forceful eviction of unhappy miners by U.S. marshals. He remained there until most of the other residents had left the town.

At another time in his career, there was an appointment as postmaster at Duncan, still another name for the same

near-extinct ghost camp. John Duncan, originally from Indiana, was the source of the town's name. An extremely
hospitable man, Duncan was both the first and the last towns-
man of that settlement. Any guests in the Duncan home
were liberally supplied with hot biscuits, bacon, eggs, and
other substantial foods.

John Duncan's most amusing characteristic was his enthusiasm for big words, most of which he used incorrectly.
He once told a visitor, "I intend to build an addition on here
for the hostility of my guests." When a friend called on
Duncan, he noticed a fine new dictionary and inquired if
he could borrow it. "Oh, take it," said Duncan, "I've already read it."

Life in the little town of Duncan saw both good and bad
times. The killing of several persons, however, shook the
townspeople. Once a man named Jim Stuart was killed by
a mild-mannered prospector named Charles Thompson. Two
women, a Mrs. Boyd and a Mrs. McFadden, were also killed
at Duncan but details surrounding their cases seem to be
conspicuous by their absence.

Today, Crestone is the only surviving town located along
the once-rich mineral belt. A small permanent population
swells in the summer and shrinks when deep snows begin to
blanket the San Luis Valley. The drive to Crestone is a particularly easy and rather pleasant one over a fine highway.
Drive north from Alamosa on Highway 17 or south from
Salida on U.S. 285 to Mineral Hot Springs where Highway
17 begins. From either direction, drive to Moffat where, at
the south edge of town, the road to Crestone branches west.
Although narrow, the grade is good and it's an easy jaunt
into the town.

Along the way, you will pass the entrance to the Baca
Grant. Several old ghost town sites are found within its
boundaries but permission is required before entrance. A
short distance farther along will bring you into Crestone,
a particularly beautiful location. Behind it, the horizon is

dominated by Crestone Peak, 14,291 feet high, Humboldt Peak, and the Crestone Needle. Both the hiker and the photographer will find much to recommend this region.*

---

* In this same general area, see also Bonanza and Turret.

This old photograph of Crestone shows the town at its peak as a mining camp

Today Crestone still has a small resident population

12.

CRYSTAL CITY

ROUGHLY TEN BUILDINGS still stand in the town that once boasted a population of five hundred in 1880. The town's name was allegedly derived from the consequence of its location on the upper reaches of the Crystal River nestled in the heart of the Elk Mountains. Although there are references to the Crystal River in the early 1880's, it was officially known as Rock Creek until the early 1900's. In its heyday Crystal supported two hotels, a barbershop, general store, saloon, and pool hall. Its residents made up the working force for about seven nearby mines. Crystal had its own post office, plus a very popular and quite exclusive male retreat known as the Crystal Club. Crystal City was formally founded sometime in 1880. During most years the average population at the town still hovered around five hundred. The fourth estate made its presence known with two newspapers, the *Crystal River Current* and the *Silver Lance,* which were published in the town at various times.

The first prospectors entered the Crystal Valley in the 1860's, but development of its mineral resources waited nearly two decades. Curiously, the exploration of this beautiful area did not follow the logical route north from Glenwood Springs and Carbondale. Instead, the first road in, which was hardly more than a trail, came south from Crested Butte through Gothic and across Scofield Pass. This is by far the most difficult means of access and it is still a Jeep road.

When John K. Hallowell, a geologist, published his findings in 1883, he described veins of zinc, iron, galena, and copper sulphides among the hillsides above the river. His report contributed to the small rush that converged on Crystal City. Throughout the years the camp remained primarily a silver-lead-zinc producer. Gold was never a prime factor in its economy.

The winding road to Crystal twists narrowly up the canyon over the old grade of the Kirk and Shaw Stagecoach Road from Marble. It followed the grade for six miles, past Lizard Lake, to the town. Nearby are some of Colorado's most beautiful summits: Sheep Mountain, Hagerman, Mineral, and Crystal peaks, Beam, Treasury, and Whitehouse mountains. In the course of its travels through the valley, the Crystal River crosses three counties. From the point where it is first seen near Carbondale, it lies in Garfield County. Farther up, it flows through Placita and Redstone in Pitkin County. In the high country around Scofield, Crystal City, and Marble, its upper reaches lie in Gunnison County.

On May 17, 1889, the *Denver Illustrated Sentinel* reported that Crystal City lay in the heart of the most heavily mineralized belt ever looked upon by prospectors or developed by miners.

Crystal may be reached by way of McClure Pass, just east of Paonia, or by Highway 133 just south of Glenwood Springs, by way of Redstone and Marble. From Crested Butte, hikers, horseback riders, or those who own Jeeps, will enjoy the trip through Gothic, over Scofield Pass, and then steeply down to Crystal.

Roads leading to and from the camps were hardly more than wide trails twisting around and over the mountains. Being ledge roads, they were subject to frequent rock- and snowslides. Those miners who chose to stay through the winter were snowbound for many weeks at a time.

By 1899 the only businesses listed in the directory were a general merchandise store and one newspaper. At the turn of the century the *Denver Post* maintained a correspondent at Crystal City. In February of 1900 a dispatch was carried out on snowshoes. Crystal was snowbound again. The stage road through the canyon between it and Marble was under from ten to fifty feet of snow. Using snowshoes, the mail carrier, Fred Johnson, had been able to get through only once during the previous week. Supplies would be exhausted within another week, according to the dispatch, unless the road could be opened up. In addition, several of the mines would probably be forced to close down and send the workers outside on snowshoes.

Usually, when a severe storm hit, the residents had little choice except to wait it out. At its conclusion, a force of fifty men took to the drifts to shovel out the road wide enough to allow a train of packhorses to bring in supplies. Sometimes snow tunnels were dug. They usually lasted long enough to bring in supplies from the terminal station at Redstone.

Serving the valley in this and in many other ways was the Crystal River and San Juan Railway. All communications between Crystal City and the mines were carried out on snowshoes. Drifts around the various buildings in camp often reached as high as the eaves. The 1900 storm was regarded as the worst ever to hit the Elk Mountains. Despite heavy suffering, no lives were lost. Few among the people who had lived there took any chances. They knew only too well that weather can change and that warm days bring snowslides roaring down nearby mountainsides.

Crystal City was a rich producer of silver, lead, and zinc until well past the turn of the century. The panic of 1893 killed Crystal City. Although the Lead King property continued a schedule of limited production well into the twentieth century, it was not enough. At the Chicago World's Fair of 1893, ironically the same year the Sherman Silver Purchase Act was repealed, Crystal was represented with a fine display of rich silver ore from the nearby Black Queen Mine. In 1913 its last ores were shipped. Transportation difficulties, as much as anything else, contributed to Crystal's

Collection of Fred and Jo Mazzulla
In this early picture of Crystal City, the Town's main street
is visible in the center background.

Collection of Robert L. Brown
An unusually lush growth of trees now precludes an exact match of the above picture.
Note the same mountain above the roof of the powerhouse building
on the Sheep Mountain Tunnel.

decline. By 1915 the town's population was down to eight. From then on it has had its ups and downs. For example, in 1916 it was back up to seventy-five, with two hotels, a store and billiard hall (why that combination?) in operation.

Getting to Crystal City today is comparatively easy when compared with conditions that were prevalent only a decade ago. State Highway 133 now has been paved nearly all the way from Carbondale to Marble. In recent years the old stage road from Marble to Crystal City has been improved enough to allow it to be used by conventional cars.

Summer residents of Crystal have restored many of the once-empty cabins, making them into fine houses. Nearby, the Outward Bound School brings additional people into the valley. Between June and October, there are still signs of life in this remote but beautifully located hamlet.*

* In this same general area, see also Marble, Scofield City and Crested Butte.

13.

CUSTER CITY

WHEN GEORGE ARMSTRONG CUSTER was massacred in eastern Montana in June of 1876, the United States took his memory to heart and American folklore acquired a new hero-martyr. All over the country streets were renamed and statues were dedicated. New communities like Custer, South Dakota, and an infinite number of schools adopted the vastly appealing name of the "Boy General" (actually a lieutenant colonel at the time of his death). Here in Colorado, the legislature, with a remarkable show of restraint, waited nearly a year after his death before vaulting onto the bandwagon.

From November of 1861 until 1877, the Wet Mountain Valley had been the southern portion of Fremont County. Then, on March 9, 1877, political surgery took place among the legislators in Denver, creating the new Custer County from this most handsome 720 square mile piece of real estate. Before this political subdivision took place, the Wet Mountain Valley had enjoyed a most distinguished series of rendezvous with history. It was first occupied by the Ute Indians. In 1806 Lieutenant Zebulon Montgomery Pike led his far-famed expedition across the valley and over the Sangre de Cristo Mountains. Among Colorado's earliest settlers was a group of trappers who moved within Hardscrabble Park in 1843, a circumstance frequently singled out with considerable pride by a later generation of Colorado historians. John W. Gunnison is known to have scouted the Wet Mountain Valley during his ill-fated search for an acceptable railroad route across the Rockies in 1853. Ranchers, the first of a hardy breed, found their way into this area in 1869. It was this land, rich in tradition, that became Custer County.

For the next quarter of a century, things were quiet on the General Custer front, and his memory was allowed to lie dormant. Then, in 1902, it started all over again. Near Querida, well within Custer County, a new town named Custer City was founded. Viewed in retrospect, the whole enterprise seems to have been started on speculation of the most spurious sort. Although two mine shafts were dug, no ore was ever shipped from Custer City. The entire setup was a stock deal and came dangerously close to being a hoax. Nevertheless, a fairly ambitious town plat was laid out and public relations were undertaken to attract people.

A community water system, with three-quarter-inch pipes laid under the ground, was installed. At strategic spots in the meadow, fire hydrants protruded along the streets-to-be. At the east end of town there was a ball diamond for interested parties. The Custer Mining and Realty Company opened an office in town. They were also responsible for the two mines that, hopefully, would justify the town's existence. As names for their mines, the company chose "Toledo" and "First Colorado." As a crowning touch, a fine statue of General Custer, with sword in hand, was installed in the fenced town park.

According to the *Rocky Mountain News* of June 10, 1902, quite an impressive ceremony was held in connection with the unveiling of the statue. Governor Orman, Colorado's chief executive, and ex-Governor Adams came to Custer City to attend the memorial services held later that month. On June 25, the exact anniversary of Custer's death, the memorial service was observed. There are rumors that Custer's widow visited the town a year later but no evidence exists to substantiate or disprove the story.

From a location standpoint, Custer City was in a good spot. The original road from Rosita to Querida passed through the eastern end of the town. Although a newer but

Custer City, showing the statue of General Custer in the center background

By 1966, Custer City was no more. The statue base has been moved and is visible at the extreme right of the picture.

poor dirt road now connects these towns, the ruts of the original trail are still to be seen where they crossed the high meadow. Nearby, in an eroded cut, a section of the pipe from the water system is visible. Down the hill toward Querida to the north, one of the old hydrants, now rusty from disuse, reposes on the ground. Originally, the statue itself sat on a three-stage base. Two stages of this foundation are still up there. A hole in its top and the outline of the metal base of the statue are still exposed to view.

The actual location of Custer City was on the hilltop just a mile south from Querida. To get there, take State Highway 115 south from Colorado Springs to Florence. Then drive south on State Highway 67 to Wetmore. From there turn southwest on State Highway 96 to either the Rosita or Querida signs. Both towns are south of the paved road a few miles and are connected by a passable dirt road. Assuming that you go to Rosita first, then turn north toward Querida. On top of the hill south of Querida, the last hill you drive down in order to enter Querida, look for a gate on your left with a trail turning off to the west. Follow the ruts, preferably on foot, through a gate to Custer City, a half mile away. An alternate route may be taken from Texas Creek, on U.S. Highway 50, east of Salida. Turn South at this point and take State Highway 69 to Westcliffe, Silver Cliff, and Querida to Custer City. The townsite is now on land owned by Mr. Joe Tomsick, of Querida. Common courtesy dictates that you get his permission and close his gate if you choose to see the relics of Custer City.*

---

* In this same general area, see also Silver Cliff.

14.

DALLAS CITY

FOR MANY YEARS the beautiful Unaweep Valley had been passing the time as a peaceful, pastoral, cattle-raising area. Shortly after the 1879 spring thaw, a small prospecting party made its way into the valley and put up a camp at the place where Dallas Creek flows into the Uncompahgre River. Within a few days they had discovered some rich gold placers along the riverbanks. From then on life was never quite the same for those who had settled there.

Once again, as with so many other new mineral discoveries, grossly exaggerated reports were spread and an impatient crowd came surging up from the south. Before it was over, the rush had depleted the populations of both Ouray and Silverton. Since no preparations had been made to accommodate this local nineteenth-century counterpart of the population explosion, those who had come got busy at once and threw up a hastily erected assortment of tents and ramshackle log and brush huts.

Someone recently called attention to a peculiarly American behavior characteristic by stating that whenever a group of Americans get together, they inevitably do three things. First of all they form a committee, the purpose of which can be determined later. Second, they choose a name for themselves or their group. Third and last, they try to elect someone as a member of Congress. Almost immediately these gold seekers faithfully carried out the first two of these steps. The name chosen for their disorganized slum was Unaweep. But regardless of the squalid condition of their surroundings, it was soon decided that Unaweep wasn't grand enough. True to form, another committee of the unqualified was appointed by the unwilling to do the unnecessary and Unaweep took on the grand sounding designation of Gold City. Someone should have told this group that a camel is nothing more than a horse that was designed by a committee. In any event, they ought to have spent more time placering and less time meeting because the deposits played out and Gold City was already dead by August.

When 1880 rolled around, some people had gone back again and had resettled beside the old gold placers. As more people came, a new town was platted that same year and it was to be known as Dallas. In this case the name was chosen to honor George M. Dallas who had served as Vice-President of the United States in the administration of President James K. Polk. A new firm called the Dallas Mining Company was formed to pursue further mineral investigations. Quite apart from any earlier reasons for the founding of a settlement at this point, its fortunate geographical location made it a logical spot for a major stage and wagon station on the new road to the West.

An eighteen-mile toll road had been built, running north along the San Miguel River to Placerville. This was another project of the incredible Otto Mears. From that point the grades were cut steeply up Leopard Creek to and over the divide, then through the Paradise Valley to the new station at Dallas. In some instances, maps of the period showed this location as Dallas Station, a designation that also persisted into its railroad period. Corrals were built to hold the large numbers of oxen, horses, and mules that were being used to pull the heavy freight loads along this road. Scarcely less significant were the several Concord coaches which hauled both passengers and mail over the same route. The trip took all day.

In the 1880's, population figures fluctuated between one hundred and two hundred people. To care for the needs of these early settlers, there were two general stores, two hotels (called the Placer and the Dallas), a saloon, a meat market and various other commercial enterprises. In 1884, Dallas kited a bit of status and became Dallas City. A private telegraph line was strung all the way over to Telluride. Once during a bank robbery it was cut in order to facilitate the escape of the miscreants.

When Dallas City acquired its own post office in the 1880's, mail came in directly instead of being hauled in from other communities by stagecoach. However, no postal service is any better than the personnel who operate it and the spoils system apparently dumped a couple of real gems at Dallas City. On May 13, 1899, the newspapers reported that Mrs. Carmichael, postmistress for the past ten years, had been arrested by United States authorities when her accounts were found to be four thousand dollars short, due to embezzlement. Also caught in the same net was Mrs. Emma J. Smith who carried the strange title of "Postmistress of the Dallas City Bank." Apparently Mrs. Smith was not as adroit as Mrs. Carmichael since her accounts were short only three thousand dollars, accomplished through the ingenious device of false cancellations. Although the firm members of Smith and Carmichael were arrested, subsequent issues of the local papers failed to report on the disposition of their cases. For some reason, Dallas City lost its post office on October 31, 1899.

When the Denver and Rio Grande Railway built through the valley in 1887, the hopes of Dallas City were high for a while, then word leaked out that the railroad planned to bypass construction in the town and build a city of their own a couple of miles or so to the south. This became Ridgway, established in 1888, and named for Superintendent Robert M. Ridgway of the D. & R. G. heirarchy. Although the Rio Grande also had high hopes for their operation at Dallas City, the people who owned the land in question put an exhorbitant price on it. As a result, only the right-of-way was used and a small station was put up. Their main installation was built at the much more receptive Ridgway.

From the west, Otto Mears was extending his Rio Grande Southern Railroad into the Unaweep Valley. In many instances his tracks were laid over the grades of his earlier toll road. The Rio Grande Southern was incorporated in October of 1889 and work was started the next year. By December of 1891 the job was finished and the tracks had reached Ridgway. From there passengers could transfer to the Denver and Rio Grande for Ouray or Montrose. Mears, too, had planned to build through Dallas City, but once again the asking price for land seemed too high and Otto built across the valley to the south. Two years later the Sherman Silver Purchase Act was repealed, the Rio Grande Southern went broke, and the Denver and Rio Grande was appointed as the receiver. In its earlier days the town had served as a stage station. Later it was a mining camp. Now it had become a railroad town of sorts and the Rio Grande officials shortened its name to just plain Dallas in 1890.

As Ridgway boomed, Dallas declined. Most of its residents straggled down the valley to find steady work and to establish homes in the newer town. By 1899 there were some six hundred people at Ridgway while only sixty diehards still stuck it out at old Dallas. By 1900 Dallas was already a ghost town.

At this writing, only the old railroad grade remains to remind us that a town once existed here. South of Montrose, U.S. 550 runs down the valley to Ouray and points south. Just north of the cutoff to Ridgway, a county dirt road leads to the west through rich farmlands. Barely below the pavement, the dirt road crosses a bridge above the river and passes the railroad ties on its way up a hill. Roughly a half mile past the top of the rise, look off to the south. There in the midst of this tilled field was the site of Dallas City, a town that led three separate lives in its day. Now the clock has run full cycle and the land has been returned to agrarian uses, just the way it was before placer gold was found here in 1879.*

---

* In this same general area, see also Ouray, Silverton, and Camp Bird.

Dallas City once stood on the flats north of Ridgway. This earlier photograph,
like most, does not record the background mountains.

Note the line of cliffs and hills in the middle background. These formations correspond
with those shown in the photograph above, pinpointing the site of the former Dallas City.

15.

DYERSVILLE

THE STORY OF DYERSVILLE is tied up in many ways with the life of the Reverend John L. Dyer, most notable of the early-day circuit riders. Despite his avowed Methodist leanings, he was far better known as "Father" Dyer. For many years, during the early part of the mining period, his mountain circuit covered Park City, Buckskin Joe, Breckenridge, and Fairplay.

Dyer was born in Ohio in 1812. His inspiration to preach seems to have come from a revival or camp meeting. He attended no theological school and was, therefore, never formally ordained. Prior to his decision to migrate westward, he gained experience in his calling by serving as a circuit rider in rural Minnesota. During the initial Pikes Peak gold rush he joined the westward-bound migrants. Incredible as it may seem, he walked all the way from Omaha to Denver.

While on a trek into the mountains, he was invited to preach for the miners at Buckskin Joe. Somehow, this engagement became a regular part of his early obligations. Each week Dyer walked from Denver to Buckskin Joe to conduct services. Being without adequate funds, he spent two and a half days on the road each way in order to save the ten-dollar stagecoach fare.

Like so many early-day men of the cloth, Father Dyer was forced to augment his meager income from the offering plate with another job. As a mail carrier he regularly packed quantities of weekly letters on his back as he made the various stops along his preaching circuit. Although he later built churches at both Fairplay and Breckenridge, his early sermons were delivered wherever he found people who would listen. When faced by the need to bring his message to the Argonauts, Dyer preached in saloons, gambling houses, tents, and in the streets. In winter he carried the mail on snow-shoes as he faithfully made his appointed rounds. For many years he was a beloved and familiar figure in the mining camps of the high Rockies.

In 1879, when Dyer was sixty-seven years old, he was placed in charge of the Breckenridge district where he built the quaint little edifice which still stands and is known as "Father Dyer's Church." A variety of unsettled conditions indigenous to most mining camps created an environment which was largely unfavorable to keeping up a religious society.

By late 1879, Dyer had begun to 'feel the pressure of his long years of overwork. He requested and was granted a superannuate leave. With his wife, Dyer made arrangements to live permanently at Breckenridge. Another of the periodic Summit County mining booms had just started. Within a year the excitement had passed and not even speculation in town lots was profitable. Following a fire, the town actually went into a temporary decline.

Since the Colorado Conference of the Methodist Church was unable to render him any financial help, most of his time was spent in work for wages. Most residents of the mining camps were financially embarrassed much of the time. Father Dyer felt and often said that a preacher had the right to earn his living at outside work if he could not get it by preaching. He also felt strongly that no clergy-man had the right to leave his congregation, regardless of conditions that had to be endured. He often preached three and worked the other four days of the week. In actual fact, he earned far more from his "moonlighting" labors than as a clergyman.

Since he was very well acquainted with the Colorado

Rockies and no stranger to mining, John Dyer was in constant demand as a claim locator. When deep snows blanketed the valleys, he went out on snowshoes in search of promising mineral leads. According to accounts given in *The Snow-Shoe Itinerant,* his autobiography, he was paid rather well for his efforts.

During the year 1880, the Dyers took in two boarders named Candell and Thompson. Although Father Dyer's practical knowledge kept him in demand as a locator he often gave his services to deserving young men. The two boarders seemed to fit into this category. In the spring of 1880 they sought his counsel. Both men were nearly out of money and had barely enough to cover their board bills for a few more days.

After securing tools, all three men set out up the mountain in waist-deep snow. When the trail ended, they broke their own path through the drifts, carrying picks, shovels, tents, and blankets. Dyer, despite his years, seemed to thrive on this kind of activity but the two inexperienced boys found it a tough climb. Reaching a likely spot, Rev. Dyer showed them where to dig and all slept in a three-foot prospect hole that night. Next day several trees were cut and a log pen ten or twelve feet square was erected. The structure served as a stopping place and was just tall enough to stand up in.

From their first prospect holes the two men took about three dollars a day. Later, with Father Dyer, they lined up a claim on some nearby ground together. In addition they also continued to prospect for themselves throughout the summer. At one point Thompson located some promising float samples and followed them up to the grass level where he sunk a ten-foot hole. In a short time he threw out over a hundred pounds of rich gray copper, worth about five hundred dollars to the ton. He promptly staked a claim measuring 150 by 1,500 feet.

Not realizing its value at the time, Thompson sold a one-fourth interest in his find to a man named Parkinson for a

mere one hundred dollars. It now appears that he would
have sold the remainder for $250 but the prospect failed to
show up with the money. When its true worth became
known, Thompson became secretive about his location. Dyer
suspected that the find was on one of his own earlier claims,
staked out three years before. A shovel had been left to hold
his tract.

When the two men compared notes, they left to check the
locations at once. Both the shovel and the old corner stake
were found. Although the claims did not overlap, Dyer was
pleased to note that vacant ground existed on both sides of
the new lode. Quickly he staked one claim to the south
and four more to the north of Thompson's workings. Both
men were very pleased with the initial showings of the lode.

Since he had never done his own assaying, Dyer took several pieces of the ore to Breckenridge with him. The assayer became quite excited and inquired where the samples
had come from. Father Dyer, now no longer a young man,
had little enthusiasm for the physical rigors of hard-rock
mining. Futhermore, he felt that the church building project
was more worthy of his efforts at this point. In exchange
for an interest in the property, the agitated assayer agreed
to do the work for him. Within the next week, on-the-spot
tests were made and a contract was drawn up.

Ultimately the Dyer and Thompson claims were merged.
One evening the Dyers sent for Thompson. When he came
into their home they told him they had heard of his offer to
sell out for $250. Their advice was that he ask for more.
Mrs. Dyer quoted platitudes and told him that it is easier
to fall than to rise. Her suggestion was that he should ask
for one thousand dollars. Thompson left at once for a meeting with his prospective buyers. They accepted and gave
him one hundred dollars on a "10% down and the rest in
60 days" deal. Looking reflectively at the hundred dollars,
Thompson said this was the first time he had ever seen this

much money all at once. Parkinson's fourth interest was purchased for five hundred dollars with 10 percent down.

The ore was not very rich, ranging from low grade to some that assayed a thousand dollars a ton. Several cabins were erected by the stream and the tiny settlement that grew up there soon took on the name of Dyersville. By far the best mining property became the Warrior's Mark Mine, approximately a half mile above the settlement. Father Dyer built a rough log cabin in the town for use by himself and his family. He began construction in January of 1881, cutting and hauling his own logs. The completed structure was seventeen by seventeen feet and stood a story and a half tall. There were two levels, two doors, and a shingled roof. By February 19 the Dyers had moved up the last of their goods from Breckenridge, six miles away. A slab for livestock was constructed later.

When summer came a superintendent and fifty men went to work on the Warrior's Mark. Between seventy-five and eighty thousand dollars were taken out in six months of work. Three million dollars' worth of stock in the mine was sold. It paid one dividend. Father Dyer took ten thousand in stock for his part interest. He had little faith in mining stock and once wrote that most of it was issued for three times its actual worth. He further stated that the average lode is beaten by directors, clerks, presidents, treasurers, bosses, and superintendents, all on pay. If this fails to cripple the venture, there are always mismanagement, wire-working, whiskey, cards, and fancy women. Dyer eventually realized a profit of two thousand dollars.

A lawsuit over fraudulent assays did little to inspire faith in the Warrior's Mark. Later the property was leased to an operator who had managed to secure more than half of the stock. Here, as elsewhere, the town was depopulated when the vein pinched out. John L. Dyer outlasted his town by some years and lived to a ripe old age of eighty-nine. His death occurred in 1901.

The ride to Dyersville is one of the prettiest and most rewarding trips in Colorado when the brush of autumn has spread vivid colors across the mountains. From Como a good dirt road leads northwest and follows the old railroad grade up through a series of cuts and across filled and long-abandoned trestles. At the top of the range it becomes Boreas Pass. On both sides of this crossing are patches of aspen that turn red as well as yellow, making for some extraordinary picture possibilities. When crossing from the Como side go over the crest and start down the other slope toward Breckenridge. Not far below the top one finds a huge mill on the right side of the road. Almost directly across from this structure is the beginning of a trail leading off down the hill in a generally southwesterly direction. A Forest Service sign placed at this intersection indicates that the road provides access to both Pennsylvania and Indiana creeks. Being essentially a no-nonsense road, whoever built this one must have assumed that its purpose was to reach the foot of the hill with as little ceremony as possible. Consequently some grades are quite steep and have naturally been eroded away, leaving a V-shaped trough in the center. Although I have never seen conventional cars down here, this does not mean that those with good clearance and adequate power could not get out again. My own preference has been to drive this section in a Jeep. Before reaching the bottom of the gulch, watch very carefully for an extremely dim trail leading off to your left and angling back up around the hill you just came down. The trail is somewhat more visible about twenty-five yards from the road at the point where it enters the trees. You are now very close to Dyersville. The trail leads around and down to the creek bed and one cabin. On the opposite side are a few more structures. This was Dyersville. At one time there was a bridge here but it has been gone for a long while. The creek is shallow and has a good rocky bottom. It may be easily driven in a Jeep or crossed on foot by stepping from rock to rock.

The roofless log structure on the left was the Dyer cabin. Beginning once more on the town side of the creek, the old trail heads uphill again and terminates at a large dump. This was the Warrior's Mark Mine, in which Father Dyer had a financial interest. All surface buildings are gone now but there are some huge holes for the unwary. During the fall of 1964, a huge tree fell across this trail to the mine. With this out of the way, the ride up to the mine is a very easy one.*

---

* In this same general area, see also Boreas, Como, King City, Tarryall, and Hamilton.

This is the sheltered, wooded site of Dyersville

*Here is the likeness of Rev. John L. Dyer which appeared
in his autobiography, The Snow-Shoe Itinerant.*

16.

ECLIPSE

IN 1894 THE GREAT GOLD BOOM was in full swing in the Cripple Creek District. Before it was finished, production figures would make this the second greatest gold camp the world had ever known. In the midst of all this activity, a construction crew in the heart of Victor's business district went almost unnoticed. These workmen had been engaged to put down the foundation footings for the newest and finest hostelry in the district, the new Victor Hotel. Situated almost in the middle of the business district, it would be handy to the stores, and one railroad nearly passed its front door.

Day by day, the blasting and excavation continued. Then, quite suddenly, a most unexpected thing happened. One of the workmen drove his pick into what he had thought would be solid rock. Instead, he opened up a rich vein that paid out over a million dollars in dividends before it closed. Here was the beginning of the fabulous Gold Coin Mine. The fortunate owner was one J. R. McKinnie. Actually, this type of find was not unusual in Victor. The Strong Mine was right behind the railroad station. Many people put shafts down in their backyards and got rich without even leaving home. It was not without justification that Victor was often referred to as the city of mines. Victor was actually built right over the top of miles and miles of underground shafts and tunnels.

When development of the Gold Coin got underway, a monumental problem faced the owners. With a mine in the center of a major metropolitan area, what does one do with the tailings pile or dump? Their answer was not only unique, it resulted in the founding of the new town of Eclipse. First of all, a pioneer bore was cut straight through Squaw Mountain. Next, it was enlarged to become a tunnel of respectable proportions. One source calls it the United Mine Tunnel while another refers to it as the Columbine-Victor Tunnel. Both names could be correct and were possibly just used at different times. In any case, the bore was completed in 1899.

Around the opposite end of Squaw Mountain, at the point where the tunnel emerged, a huge mill was erected. H. E. and Frank M. Woods, Cripple Creek capitalists and owners of the Golden Crescent Water and Light Company at Gillett, had put up the money. The Warren Woods Company was also involved in the partnership. Called the Economic Gold Extraction Company, this huge mill was one of the earliest attempts to use the chlorination process to refine gold in the Cripple Creek District. Unrefined ores from the Gold Coin Mine were trammed from Victor, through the 3,700-foot-long tunnel that pierced Squaw Mountain, running directly into the mill. Inside, huge roasting furnaces were fed by crude oil that was being shuttled up on the Florence and Cripple Creek Railroad from the petroleum fields near Florence.

Boasting of a three-hundred-ton daily capacity, the huge Economic Mill covered a good part of the hillside. At the other end, the Gold Coin operated night and day, yielding thirty thousand tons of ore yearly. When Victor's fire destroyed its frame shaft house, little time was lost in replacing it with a similar one of brick construction. On one of his visits to Cripple Creek, Teddy Roosevelt looked aghast at the huge installations on both sides of Squaw Mountain and pronounced it "bully." The date was 1901 and everything was fresh and new. If any ugly thoughts about trust busting crossed his mind while viewing the huge plant, Teddy kept them to himself.

Below the mill a string of houses and business structures

grew up along the bottom of the gulch. Somehow the name of Eclipse became attached to the small settlement. It was a single-street community, stretching out in a generally up-hill direction from the mill. Many of the employees found it convenient to live near their work. Such people accounted for a majority of the population of Eclipse. Nearby, close to the head of the street, was the lower terminal of Dick Roelofs' aerial tram from the Cresson Mine. After passing through nearby Elkton, the cables terminated in the Midland Terminal Railway yard at Eclipse. In addition to the two railroads already mentioned, the town was also served by the Low Line Electric cars as they ran from Cripple Creek to Victor.

When the inevitable fire engulfed the mill in 1908, it spread to the town and much of it was destroyed. For some reason, or collection of reasons, neither the Eclipse nor the Economic Mill was ever rebuilt. The availability of other and more efficient processing plants may account for some of it. Its extremely close proximity to the larger community of Victor was no doubt a contributing factor. Curiously, in 1915, an operator secured a lease and reworked one of the old dumps below the mill. His efforts yielded ten thousand dollars in gold, left behind by wasteful processing methods.

There are many reasons why a town dies. Eclipse seems to have expired chiefly from the inefficient techniques employed by the industry that was its chief source of income.

State Highway 67 begins at Divide and terminates at Victor. Just a mile northwest of Victor one may see the huge foundation of the Economic Mill below the highway. To the right, running along the spine of the gulch, are a few rock foundations of the town. For a better view, go on another mile or so around the loop and look back at Squaw Mountain and the tremendous perforated foundation. Eclipse was a town that enjoyed a very brief priority in time. Its demise, or eclipse, was sudden, and its return to nature is nearly complete at this writing.*

---

* In this same general area, see also Elkton, Gillett, Goldfield, and Mound City.

An early view of the Economic Gold Extraction Company Mill at Eclipse

Today, the empty site of Eclipse lies below the highway between Victor and Cripple Creek

17.

ELDORA

LIKE SO MANY CAMPS that belong logically to the latter phases of Colorado's mineral mining boom, those events that paved the way for the establisment of Eldora go back to a far earlier chronology. There had been some small-scale prospecting activities in this neighborhood as early as 1860. Some limited successes led a few of the more fortunate to form the Grand Island Mining District in March of 1861.

At the beginning the district included a section of land about sixteen miles long by four miles wide. From Castle Rock in Boulder Canyon, it included everything westward to the crest of the Continental Divide. On the south, its limit was the northern boundary of Gilpin County. Due to the Civil War and a collapse of the speculative mining boom, little actual work was done for more than a decade.

A series of discoveries, beginning in May of 1875, heralded the prospect of better days for the district. While prospecting near the Arapahoe Peak, C. C. Alvord uncovered the great Fourth of July Lode. Barely three months later, the Alvord Placer was located. Their locations were about five miles west of what was to become the village of Eldora, on the north fork of Middle Boulder Creek. Not far away, as the crow flies, was the great Caribou Mine, located by Sam Conger in 1869. For many of the early years, the district realized considerable financial support from this source.

Curiously, the two Alvord placers were both potential gold producers but little actual work was done on either of them. Yet the Caribou, just two and a half miles away on the north side of Eldorado Mountain, became a rich silver camp. For nearly two decades life in the valley of Middle Boulder Creek remained almost static. But when the wheel of fortune finally stopped on its number, it was not silver but gold that made Eldora spring to life. Although the Huron Lode was found in August of 1887 and the Clara Lode, on Spencer Mountain, became a reality just two years later, it remained the task of the Happy Valley Placer to begin the real boom. John H. Kemp and seven associates from Central City laid claim to a tract of about five hundred acres along Middle Boulder Creek on September 5, 1891. Since a few log cabins had already appeared in the valley, the Kemp party decided to go ahead with a survey for a townsite. In 1892, their task was completed and the area was divided into building lots. At that time the settlement was known only as Happy Placer.

With the increase of new arrivals, the little hamlet started to grow. Within a few months it began to assume some semblance of a budding town and the residents effected the first of several name changes. With pardonable civic pride, the name of Eldorado Camp was chosen. In this, as in so many other similar instances, there was a conflict. California already had a town of the same name. The job of dispatching the mails now became infinitely more complicated for the postal department. To facilitate better reception of their letters, the miners agreed to drop the word "Camp" and call their town Eldorado. When the town was incorporated on March 9, 1898, it was under this latter name.

In the meantime a minor revolt was brewing within the ranks, headed by one A. L. Tomblin. In April of 1897 a group of new arrivals, backed by Nebraska capital, organized themselves with the purpose of surveying a townsite of their own on ground already taken up by the Happy Valley Placer. They chose a tract of 320 acres which included the land already occupied by the new town. Since the ground was not valuable as a mineral location anyway, they argued, the original locators had no right to it. Actually, this was not entirely true since their proposed plot also extended up the side of the mountain for several hundred feet behind the town. Curiously, a number of lode claims were being actively worked on the slopes at that time. Also conveniently overlooked was the fact that the greater part of the land which they proposed to incorporate had been occupied for months by several miners' cabins.

Opinion in the town was divided into two rival factions and matters began to look serious as the dispute grew hot. When faced by the need to save his claim, Kemp took out a petition in opposition to the townsite scheme, reminding people that his was the earlier claim and that the new plot was actually covered by his placer claim. A large majority of the miners signed with Kemp.

In the midst of claims and counterclaims, the dispute was heard in May of 1897 before the Registrar of the General Land Office in Denver. After weighing the evidence, a decision was rendered in favor of the outsiders. Within a few days the (un) Happy Placer people appealed the case. In the course of time, the original decision was reversed and the Kemp group lost no time in completing their own town plot and embarking upon the sale of their lots. When the final two letters were dropped from Eldorado, the town assumed its present name.

With problems of legal ownership settled, Eldora began to enjoy a small boom. Early in 1898, a rich strike was made in a mine called the Enterprise. It had the distinction of igniting the fireworks that really set off Eldora's boom. A great stampede of new arrivals began to find its way up the valley and the town grew up almost overnight. Although one source reports that not a single saloon existed in 1897 many things were due for a change.

Quite suddenly, Eldora found that it had mushroomed from a sleepy little hamlet of prospectors to a fair-sized city with a population in excess of one thousand by the latter

1890's. Like most other new camps, the people here were poor. Living at an altitude of 8,600 feet was not easy. In winter, snow retarded their work. There was little money or influence available for interesting the right people in the outside world in what they had found or about its value. Most of the early residents were honest, hospitable, and industrious, barring consideration of the attempt by Nebraskans to jump the claim of the Happy Valley Placer.

Geologically, Eldora's mining properties were in a sulphide belt, although streaks of tellurium had been found in some of its outcroppings. There were also several large deposits of low-grade ore near the camp which could be treated profitably if mills were erected. Hundreds of new claims were located on almost any ground that was available, regardless of its mineral indications or lack of them. By far the greatest number of new locations filed were on Spencer Mountain. Among the better properties were such mines as the Virginia, Virginia Bell, and the Bird's Nest.

During 1897, the Mogul Tunnel was completed near the foot of Spencer Mountain. W. C. Andrews and N. B. Bailey constructed a fifty-ton-capacity mill at the foot of Ute Mountain, about a mile west of town. Although designed to take advantage of the chlorination process, it was never a success. Business from the huge tonnage that had been expected from the Mogul Tunnel failed to materialize.

Quite apart from the town itself, the great Eldora Mine was down the valley about four miles west of Nederland. Its deepest shaft reached a depth of only 110 feet. At the beginning, its owners took out a ton and a half of ore that assayed one hundred dollars to the ton. Fortunately for them, large and well-defined veins were found near the surface.

Along both sides of Middle Boulder Creek, from water level to the crest of the mountains, shafts and tunnels were being driven. Although the slopes were precipitous, footpaths provided access to some rather unbelievable locations. Most

of the incurable optimists in the lower valley were filled with
the belief that their own individual prospects were certain
to become paying mines. One local assayer made the statement that the relative values obtained for these depths were
unusually high. According to him fifteen to twenty-five
dollars from a four-foot hole were common returns.

To supply the wants of the miners, new buildings were
going up on all sides in the town which became not only
a residence center but the principal source of supplies for
most of the mines. Although commercial structures took on
the dignity of false fronts and stylish windows, the log cabin
remained as the favorite type of dwelling for most people.

Both the Goldminer and the Mines hotels were fine places
to stay. In addition, there were several well-kept boardinghouses where prices were moderate. Despite the earlier boast,
eleven saloons now flourished in Eldora. In time the inevitable newspaper and a bank also found their way up the valley.
For the pioneers who sought entertainment and enlightenment, there was a photographic gallery, a free reading room,
and in later years there were two ladies clubs. A Methodist
church seems to have been the first to be built in the town
but other denominations soon followed their example. A
single public school employed two teachers and boasted
an average daily attendance of one hundred children.

Considering the seamier side of life for a moment, most
kinds of gambling were allowed in the appropriate establishments. For those who could or would not conform, Eldora had a sturdy little jail which originally stood at the rear
of the Goldminer Hotel. Later it was moved to another location across the creek. In the course of time, a fair-sized
red-light district also grew up. Inevitably, one of these took
the name of "Bon Ton." In view of the existence of all these
organized institutions of dissipation, it seems incredible that
the town had no cemetery. Even today, there are no burial
grounds at Eldora.

Other real or imagined needs of the townspeople were

*A typical stagecoach, drawn by six horses, was a common
sight on the main street of Eldora.*

With the same mountain backdrop, Eldora today presents a far different picture

served by a number of stores. Particularly outstanding was the N. M. Mills General Store which was truly general. Here one could choose from an array of merchandise including clothing, butter, beef, dynamite, prunes, and rubber boots. Well before the close of the boom, a well-equipped drug-store, a hardware establishment, several bakeries, and an assay office found it profitable to set up shop here. Later, of course, a telephone exchange strung its wires across the valley to serve some of the more status-conscious settlers. Over the years, several physicians settled here to care for the sick, the injured, and the hypochrondriacs who lacked even the solace of a cemetery.

For many years, transportation into and out of the valley had been a hodgepodge. With the completion of a road from the Nederland end of the valley, a horse-drawn stage-coach was used. From the other direction, a twice-weekly stage crossed over from Central City. Four more lines came up from Boulder, using canopy-topped Concord coaches in summer. Four- or six-horse hitches were used to draw the load. Necessarily, passenger and mail service were erratic at best. When a post office was established in 1897, these fa-cilities improved. By the turn of the century, daily mails came up from Boulder. Freight and lumber outfits also used the route, once described as one of the best mountain roads in the state.

Many of Eldora's mines had started to experience hard times around the turn of the century. Some people saw a railroad extension as the solution to their problems. Town officials encouraged the construction of tracks by the Colo-rado and Northwestern which had already built a line else-where in Boulder County. The company was assured that the mines here could furnish two hundred tons of ore per day for shipment over the rails if they were to reach Eldora.

At the Fourth of July property, in the northwestern part of the district, improved machinery was installed and a three-thousand-foot bore was completed. Management at the

Mogul, and at other mines, hoped that the railroad would provide a remedy for what had become their very sick industry. By late 1904, tracks had been laid from Sunset, around Sugar Loaf Mountain and Glacier Lake, to terminate at Eldora. Operations began on New Year's Day, 1905. The hoped-for millenium did not transpire. Mining troubles were far too serious for pump priming. Actually, the ores had played out at about the turn of the century.

On all sides the mines began to close down. Employees at the Bailey Mill staged a riot when the management missed a payday. Mr. Bailey was smoked out of his house and shot. Little time was lost in putting his mill to the torch. What remained went into receivership, to be torn down and sold for salvage in 1916. By that time Eldora was nearly a dead camp. Some people held out, but population for the whole district in the 1910 census had been reduced to about six hundred people. By 1917, all except a few individual operations had been shut down.

When the railroad reached town, it had practically ended the stagecoach business. One company attempted to recoup its losses by operating a fleet of Stanley Steamers to Eldora in 1914. Two receiverships, the last in March of 1909, nearly stopped the railroad. In the course of reorganization, the company reappeared as the Denver, Boulder, and Western Railway. Its operations continued in a sporadic manner until a severe flood destroyed the right-of-way in July of 1919.

Since fire seems to have been the greatest nemesis of all Western mining camps, the one that damaged Eldora should be mentioned here. It broke out at roughly nine o'clock on November 28, 1902. A defective flue in the second-story stove at the Miller residence was its source. Extinguishing the fire was made more difficult by a harsh wind that fanned the flames from structure to structure. Final loss was estimated at $15,000 and a slightly scorched school building. By comparison with fires such as the ones that destroyed Rosita and Cripple Creek, this was not a severe blaze since the whole town was not destroyed.

Gradually, as the years passed, activities other than mining came to be the basis for Eldora's economy. Today, a fine ski center flourishes at Lake Eldora. Within the town, many of the old cabins have been converted to use as picturesque summer homes. The handsome scenery and easy access to hiking, camping, and picnic facilities are likewise assets to the community.

Eldora is located twenty-two miles west of Boulder and just nine miles east of the Continental Divide. Sulphide Flats is an elevated plain, roughly a mile square. Just beyond its eastern edge is the town of Nederland. The old settlements of Cardinal and Caribou are situated short distances beyond its northern boundaries. Highway 119 will lead you into this country from either Boulder or Black Hawk, while Highway 160 comes down from Ward. An excellent dirt road leaves Highway 119 and turns west just a few miles south of Nederland. Following along its three-mile course, you will enter the rather wide U-shaped valley of Middle Boulder Creek in which Eldora will be found. If you spend some time here, you will likely agree that the original Happy Valley was a most appropriate name.*

---

* In this same general area, see also Salina, Tungsten, and Camp Frances.

18.

ELKTON

When Grover Cleveland instigated repeal of the Sherman Silver Purchase Act in 1893, Colorado's shattered finances nearly scraped the bottom of the barrel. Fortunately for most residents of the Silver State, gold was almost immediately discovered at Cripple Creek in the cone of an extinct volcano. In its entirety, this story has been superbly chronicled by Marshall Sprague in his magnificent book *Money Mountain*. This book also details life in the multiplicity of little towns, such as Elkton, that once flourished during the Cripple Creek excitement. Before it was over, total production figures had made this the second greatest gold-producing district the world has ever known. Over the long haul, it was surpassed only by the Witwatersrand in the Transvaal of South Africa.

Quite an amazing array of notable persons was associated with the Cripple Creek District in its heyday. Bernard Baruch, late advisor to many recent American Presidents, worked in the Bull Hill mines and once defeated the boxing champion of Altman in a wild bare-knuckle melee that should have made the Marquis of Queensberry spin in his tomb. Tom Mix once worked here as a cowboy and later as a bouncer for a Bennett Avenue saloon. Groucho Marx at one time drove a grocery wagon in Victor. Texas Guinan began her musical career by playing an organ at the Sunday school in Anaconda. Lowell Thomas was born in Victor and graduated from high school there. The late Ralph Carr, one of our ablest state chief executives, also grew up in Victor and worked on the newspaper there. Bill Dempsey and brother Jack worked as muckers in the Bull Hill mines. When Jack was killed in a mining accident, Bill took his name and went on to become World's Heavyweight Boxing Champion. Another heavyweight champion, Jack Johnson, also worked as a Cripple Creek mucker in the Portland Mine.

When William Shemwell made his way up the side of Raven Hill, the Cripple Creek boom was already well underway. Shemwell was a former blacksmith from Colorado Springs with no known previous mining experience. Since gold formations here defied every known theory of mining, it was not at all unusual for the inexperienced to show up to dig with hoes and pitchforks. In one instance two druggists from Colorado Springs threw a hat in the air and filed on the spot where it fell. The result was the Pharmacist Mine which sold for a half million dollars.

Shemwell dug a hole near the head of Arequa Gulch, part way up Raven Hill. Although some gold was found, he could not foresee that his property would become the second largest producer in the district. One set of figures places total production from the Elkton at $50,000,000 while another says it was $45,000,000. Either figure represents a tremendous quantity of gold.

Shemwell took in a couple of partners. One of these was a colored man who gave him a mule to cover his share.

When the time came to register his claim, the ex-blacksmith found that he needed a name for the property. Thinking back over his labors on Raven Hill, Shemwell recalled having seen a pair of bleached antlers lying on the ground a short distance from his shaft. This coincidence seemed to suggest as good a name as any other and the name Elkton Mine was born.

Arequa Gulch had seemed an unlikely spot for a mine but conventional rules were abandoned here in wholesale lots. In the early days this had been the site of the original Womack Homestead. It was "Cowboy Bob" Womack who had located the first claim in the old crater, giving initial impetus to the whole Cripple Creek rush. Later, Horace Bennett and Julius Myers, Denver real-estate men who owned the property, subdivided the land and sold lots for $320,000. Historical events apart, the gulch had originally been named for a prospector of Italian extraction named Requa. His verbal attempts to master the English pronunciation of his own name caused others to indulge in a good-humored mimicry and the valley where he put up a cabin became "Arequa" Gulch.

In the meantime William Shemwell had given a half interest in his discovery to a pair of Colorado Springs grocers who had grubstaked him to the tune of a $36.50 grocery bill. When mineral production went up, Sam and George Bernard lost interest in their groceries, bought out Shemwell and his partners, and assumed active management of the Elkton. Next they hired Ed De La Vergne, an important name in the Cripple Creek story, to take over the operation. De La Vergne was the man who helped out when the Post Office Department refused to accept Fremont as a name for the first camp in the crater. It was his suggestion that it be renamed Cripple Creek. Before production declined after 1916, the Elkton had produced $16,200,000 from the depths of its 1,700-foot shaft.

Within a comparatively short time, a cluster of cabins and a few homes of dressed lumber began to go up on the steep hillside above the mine. Transportation facilities were not particularly good as yet and it was far more convenient for the miners to live close to their work. By the time of the 1900 census, there were 200 people at Elkton. In 1904 the population had grown to 2,500 people and the peak was reached when 3,000 had settled there by 1905. Despite this, the town was never platted; it just grew up and spread out on its rocky hillside at an elevation of 9,692 feet above sea level. In general, the town grew up around the mine.

A large part of the population increase at Elkton can be

explained by the fact that as the community mushroomed, it gradually absorbed its smaller neighbors. Arequa (sometimes called Requa), Beacon Hill, and Eclipse were all taken in or annexed by Elkton. In addition a further growth stimulus was provided by another penetration into the depth of the unpromising Cresson shaft. The Cresson was located about a mile above the Elkton, in the gulch between Raven Hill and Bull Hill.

J. R. and Eugene Harbecks, of Chicago, owned the Cresson. In 1915 they hired Richard Roelofs, a mining engineer, to survey their property. What he found nearly blew the roof off! In a state of high apprehension he insisted on taking Hildreth Frost, company attorney, and Ed De La Vergne of the Elkton down with him as witnesses. Roelofs led them into a 1,200 foot underground vug or cave. Its dimensions have been given as being 20 feet high and 30 feet in diameter. From another source we find that it was 40 feet high, 20 feet long, and 15 feet wide. In either case it was fabulous since the walls were lined with gold crystals, refined by nature to such a point of purity that reduction or milling were not always required.

Forty thousand dollars' worth of gold was scraped off the walls during the first week. To prevent high-grading or other popular forms of robbery, vault doors were installed on the mine entrance and the miners changed clothes after work. Whenever an ore shipment was loaded onto the trains, armed guards rode along to assure its arrival at the destination. Sealed boxes were also used to facilitate safer local transportation of the gold. From the depths of the Cresson came one world record carload which was worth a milloin dollars. Before they were done, the Cresson shaft had been dug to a depth of 2,400 feet. Total production amounted to $49,000,000.

Dick Roelofs built an overhead tram from the Cresson vault doors to the railroad station at Elkton, a mile down the gulch. In 1914, Albert E. Carlton purchased the Cresson for $4,000,000. It was worked well into the present century. In 1904, labor wars enveloped the entire Cripple Creek District. At issue were the usual questions of wages and hours. The Western Federation of Miners wheeled out their heavy artillery in the person of Harry Orchard, a professional assassin. Deep inside the Vindicator Mine, he set off a dynamite charge that took the lives of two supervisors. At Independence, he dynamited the railroad station, killing and injuring a number of nonunion men who arrived home on the late train. In an attempt to restore peace, the governor called out the state militia. One of the hastily improvised military camps was at Altman. Another one was in Elkton. Both of these towns were hotbeds of unionism. In the end the unions lost out and their members were herded out of the district at gunpoint. The mines reopened and the soldiers went home. In one of the accompanying photographs, the troops at Elkton posed in the business district.

When it came to public transportation, Elkton was remarkably well endowed. The Florence and Cripple Creek Railroad, The Midland Terminal Line, and the Colorado Springs and Cripple Creek District Railway all built through the community. In all three instances their tracks were on the same level as the town. The Low Line Interurban System built an overhead bridge to allow passage above the Midland Terminal tracks. In addition to the electrified passing track, the streetcar line, and regular road tracks, Elkton also boasted a station house below the Elkton mine and a nearby telegraph office. The station closed in 1919.

While the decline of many mining camps was abrupt, the abandonment of Elkton was gradual. On today's market, the price of gold is still fixed at thirty-five dollars an ounce. Although costs of mining equipment, labor costs, and other factors have gone up, the controlled price of gold has not kept pace. At present, gold mining is no longer profitable. Large quantities of the yellow metal still repose in the Elkton and in the Cresson. But most of the people moved away;

some went around the hill to Victor. Occasionally families still move into the old homes in the town, but most of them stand empty now. There were once twelve towns in the whole Cripple Creek District. Today, only three are still occupied and even their populations are small.

State Highway 67, between Cripple Creek and Victor, is a fine paved road that works its way around Raven Hill. Above the grade, a dirt road leads up the hillside to the sun-browned houses of Elkton. In summer, a herd of cattle grazes here under the watchful bloodshot eye of a noisy and ill-tempered old bull. His big horns and passion for raising clouds of dust make this a less than desirable picnic spot. There are no fences at Elkton. Neverthless, the view to the northwest is great on a clear day. Although the buildings of the mine and the railroad tracks are gone, much of the past remains to remind the visitor of the Elkton that was.*

---

* In this same general area, see also Gillett, Goldfield, Mound City, and Eclipse.

During the 1904 labor wars, troops of the state militia posed at Elkton

Elkton now. Note the same false-front building at the left in both pictures

19.

FAIRPLAY

SHORTLY AFTER THE Pikes Peak gold rush of 1859 had started, many of those who came met disappointment. At one point the "turn backs" actually outnumbered those who were headed for the Cherry Creek diggings. It was soon clear that the late arrivals would need to take second best. As a result, many drifted deeper into the mountains. Good placer gold beds were found on Tarryall Creek, north of present-day Como. Two towns, Tarryall and Hamilton, grew up there. Here, again, the first arrivals grabbed off all the best claims and guarded them jealously. In this case the late arrivals were literally driven out of the camps.

When faced by the need to survive, the émigrés who had been expelled from Tarryall started referring to that camp as "Grab-All," and moved across South Park to start a town of their own. As a slap at their oppressors, they named their location Fair Play Camp, and invited all who had suffered at the hands of those in the older settlements to come here and receive fair treatment. Actually, this location was not so new. Others before them had also found this spot to be a desirable place in which to live. Chief Tierra Blanca of the Utes had camped here regularly, on Sacramento Flats, through the 1840's. Even John C. Frémont (see Alma) once made camp in this vicinity.

On the north bank of the Middle Fork of the South Platte River, A. L. Doge (or Dodge) erected what has generally been credited as the first cabin in the town. Jim Reynolds, who later gained a measure of notoriety as a Confederate renegade leader, quickly established himself as boss of the camp. In 1864, when the town was still in its infancy, an Indian uprising stopped all mail service for three months. Finally, Rev. John L. Dyer (see Dyersville) set an example of bravery by driving the mail coach to Denver. The deadlock was broken and service was restored.

Fairplay also claims the oldest operating courthouse in Colorado, dating from 1874. When a second Indian scare developed in 1879, its stone walls sheltered all of the women and children in town. As things turned out, it was all a hoax. One of the town's most notorious drunks shot his own hat full of holes. As his alcoholic dilemma became more intense, he decided Indians had done it and staggered, wild-eyed and screaming, through the main streets of Fairplay. When someone yells, "fire," people act first and investigate later. The same rules must have applied for Indian scares.

Effective in 1866, Fairplay became the county seat, following the demise of Buckskin Joe. One newspaper, the *Fairplay Flume*, was published as a weekly. Adolph Giraud put a waterwheel into a stream that flowed close to his ranch in order to operate a butter churn, because he hated doing it by hand, and acquired one of Colorado's first water rights through the doctrine of prior use. Later, residents settled around his ranch and anglicized his name to "Garo." A small settlement by that name now occupies the site of his ranch.

Quite a large number of well-known religious leaders were active in early Fairplay. Rev. John L. Dyer moved his building down from Montgomery to establish the first Methodist church in the town. From Santa Fe, the Rev. Joseph Machebeouf, who later became a bishop, arrived and rode the circuit for Catholics in the South Park region. Sheldon Jackson built his beautiful little white Presbyterian church in 1874. It still stands and is now called the Sheldon Jackson Memorial Chapel.

Going from the sublime to the ridiculous, Fairplay also came in for its share of criminal activities. In an earlier day, the notorious Espinosa brothers committed six of their many murders in the area between Alma and Red Hill. When the United States acquired this portion of the Southwest from Mexico, the Espinosas lost some land and swore vengeance on all Anglo-Saxons. Tom Tobin, early-day mountain man and contract hunter at Fort Garland, finally ran them down and beheaded them to prove his claim to the reward.

Fairplay had a full-blown lynching in 1880. A murderer named Hoover was given only a life sentence following a particularly brutal crime. That night, a vigilante group broke down the jail door, got the sheriff out of bed, used the keys to extract Hoover from his cell, locked the sheriff up in his own jail, put a noose around Hoover's neck and dropped him out of a second story window of the courthouse.

When Judge Bowen arrived to hold court again the next morning, there was Hoover dangling above the courthouse door. To make matters worse, another noose was found beside the judge's gavel on his desk inside. Bowen took the hint and left at once for Denver.

A second version of this story also gets bandied about occasionally. In this case, Hoover's neck was broken but he did not die. Some of his friends cut him down and smuggled him out in a hay wagon. A physician in the Kenosha area tended a man with a broken neck who arrived in a load of hay the next evening. Somehow he managed to recover. When he was recaptured, the crowd felt it was "probably unconstitutional" to hang a man twice for the same crime, and let him go. Although the initial story has likely grown more lurid over the years, the second sounds like sheer folklore.

Once, during a jailbreak, the escaping man hired a fiddler to play loudly in order to cover the sound of sawing the bars (Music to Break Jail By). Later, allegedly, the fiddler decided that he knew something about crime and became a candidate for sheriff of Fairplay.

Most of the mining around this end of the park was of

the placer variety. Huge dredges sought and found gold among the coarse gravel of the bars along the South Platte. Many of the better placers were worked by hand. Large numbers of Chinese came into the area and built cabins along the south bank of the Platte, called "Chinaman's Gulch." The "celestials" were charged one dollar per day per man, whether they found any gold or not. Some deep mines existed in the nearby Mosquito and Horseshoe districts. Many of the workers lived at Fairplay. The far-famed silver rush to Leadville after 1878 brought hordes of people through Fairplay. Earlier, in 1872, there was a minor flurry of excitement over some silver discoveries in the South Park neighborhood. When George Crofutt visited Fairplay in the seventies, he recorded a population of 515.

To assure access to and from the outside settlements, a thrice-weekly stagecoach ran between Fairplay and Denver. A total of eighteen hours was required for the trip each way, with an overnight stop. From Denver the road came up Turkey Creek and crossed Crow Hill to the depths of Platte Canyon. For several miles it followed the river. From Webster, it crossed beautiful Kenosha Pass into South Park. Here the trail was an easy one until they got to Red Hill, the last obstacle before Fairplay. From the top of Red Hill, drivers often whipped up their horses for the last couple of miles and made a dramatic dash into Fairplay. Another wagon and staging road crossed the Mosquito Range from just north of Fairplay. This was the Mosquito Pass road to Leadville, one of the most spectacular cliff-hangers in North America. When the 112-mile-long narrow rails of the Denver, South Park, and Pacific Railway reached Fairplay, one could ride all the way in a single day for only $9.90. In general, the railroad followed the canyon of the Platte River. In many places its tracks paralleled the old stagecoach road. Today, U.S. Highway 285 follows this old road over many of the original grades between Denver and Fairplay. In many other places, old cuts and grades from the original railroad route may also be seen paralleling the highway.

Fairplay is one of Colorado's oldest mining centers, a place literally loaded with history. Mercifully, it survived the ghost town epidemic and a fire that destroyed much of its business district in 1873. In fact, the gutted structures had been rebuilt by 1879. In 1930, Prunes, the burro, a local fixture that became a local pet after outliving the mining era, was laid to rest in the town. The monument is unique, one of the few ever erected to an animal. The ashes of "Rupe" Sherwood, last owner of Prunes, were entombed behind the monument.

Two miles away, across the meadow, one may also see an original dredge sitting among its huge piles of boulders; also something of a rarity today. The whole Fairplay area is reached most easily by driving southwest from Denver on U.S. Highway 285, an excellent paved road that offers the traveler or the native a remarkable variety of scenic vistas. Incidentally, Fairplay is still the seat of Park County. In addition, it is a mecca for fishermen and hunters. It survives today as a center for people engaged in hay ranching, cattle raising, and agriculture. At the northern edge of town, South Park City may be seen. This is an authentic restored pioneer Western town, with original buildings and fixtures from Rosita, Alma, Buckskin Joe, Montgomery, and other locations from the long roster of Colorado's yesterdays.*

---

* In this same general area, see also Alma, Buckskin Joe, Puma City, Quartzville, Montgomery, Leavick, and Sacramento.

Fairplay, in South Park, as it appeared in 1879

*When this picture was made in August, 1965, the old stagecoach
road could still be seen in the foreground.*

20.

FALL RIVER

By the fall of 1863 the great silver discovery near Georgetown found a wealth of new technical knowledge about
mining and refining that allowed for a far greater and more
prosperous mineral development. In the excitement connected with these discoveries of the white metal there, at
Saints John and elsewhere in Summit County, the earlier
rush to Fall River has often been overlooked. Most stock
Colorado histories attribute the initial silver finds in the state
to the Georgetown area and use the 1863 date. In actual fact,
silver was found, but not successfully refined, at Fall River
in 1860. In addition, the little town of Fall River survived
for many years after its silver excitement was over.

Quite apart from the error in chronological history, Fall
River is also interesting geographically. Its location was at
the point where Fall River flows into Clear Creek; the only
spot in the United States where a river flows into a creek.
Usually, it's the other way around, with literally thousands of
creeks that flow into rivers. Below, just a few miles, stood
an early placer gold camp called Paynes Bar which eventually
evolved into the modern city of Idaho Springs.

Fall River was just a small hamlet but in 1860 it boasted
an excellent hotel, several assorted stores, and a variety of
residences. In 1860 it also had its own post office. All around
the town the mountainsides were pockmarked with huge
numbers of prospect holes but no shafts were sunk to any
appreciable depths. Some gold was mined here but such
operations were of brief duration.

By mid-1860 most of the gold-panning ventures were proving to be worthless. On July 1, 1860, either William Ritter or a Mr. Weller (the accounts do not agree) wandered over the hill from Central City. Other sources credit the first discovery on Fall River to William White and his brother, although they didn't record their claim until August 30, 1860. Back then very few people bothered with who was first. It wasn't very important to them.

At any rate, instead of gold they found silver, which no one knew how to handle profitably, and these first silver discoveries were brushed off. Despite these problems, a strike is a strike and even the vaguest rumor or faintest of hopes will often send discouraged miners stampeding to new localities. Maybe, they reasoned, silver was the answer. Eight thousand would-be miners had swarmed into Fall River by autumn. There were far more people than there were paying claims.

Staking their claims proved to be only the beginning. These men knew little about silver mining. It proved to be expensive just getting the ore out of the earth and even more costly to mill it by then-known methods. All along the course of Fall River, all the way to its head, a visitor might see discoveries but little profitable mining. The silver excitement turned out to be mostly recording claims. Meanwhile, gold panning continued on a limited scale. In all, over seven thousand claims were filed along the course of Fall River from its source at St. Marys Glacier, some ten miles away, down to the townsite at Clear Creek. At Georgetown, the small leather-bound record books in the office of the county clerk contain hundreds of names of would-be miners from faraway places who chose their silver lodes along the canyon walls above the river.

Since the canyon is rather narrow, Fall River itself was unable to accommodate all of the people who came. Other towns were established farther up. The Upper Fall River Mining District had been founded in July of 1860 to provide for a measure of government among the migrants. Silver City was built near the head or source of Fall River. Almost overnight the place grew up into a town consisting of slightly over one thousand men who slept in tents, under trees, and in some instances on the bare hillside.

Today, a single log cabin on the shore of Silver Lake dates back to these early days. Although it is not far from the original site of Silver City, the nearby town of Alice was built at a later date than the 1860 excitement. Farther down the canyon the Lincoln Mining District was formed. Within it stood Glenard City with a small resident population of working miners.

Fall River itself was really the third settlement of the group. Being by far the largest, it became the actual seat of government for the Lower Fall River Mining District. To serve it and to tie this ramshackle series of settlements together, a stagecoach road came over from Central City to Georgetown. After climbing the steep grades across Yankee Hill, the road followed down the stream to Clear Creek before continuing on up to Georgetown. In fact the life of this road exceeded the life of the Fall River towns it served, and it was used extensively until the railroad was completed in 1877.

By the late autumn of 1860, Fall River had reached its peak. New refining processes would be required before either gold or silver discoveries could add up to much in this location. Smelting was still something new. Soon the silver excitement was forgotten. Gradually the eight thousand prospectors had to seek comfort in a different locality. Some, however, stayed on.

Today, Fall River still flows into Clear Creek but no trace of the early town remains. Some evidence of mining is still visible but it dates from a later time. U.S. Highway 6 became a four-lane throughfare during 1965 and now passes right over the bar where the town stood. The location is barely west of Idaho Springs, on the right side of the high-

Fall River, a very small town at the mouth of Fall River Canyon

The old site of Fall River, west of Idaho Springs

way as you drive toward Loveland and Berthoud passes. Only the sign which points the way to St. Marys Glacier marks the site now. The accompanying pair of pictures show the location from the other side of Clear Creek, looking up Fall River. The background mountains still retain their same contours but just about everything else has changed.

With disuse, the original stagecoach road over Yankee Hill is returning to nature. Tremendous rocks, long rough sections, and steep grades have relegated this once-important thoroughfare to the status of a wild Jeep road. In the overall chronology of Colorado mining developments, Fall River was a little before its own time. Given a later date, it might have made it. Now, however, it is little more than a memory.*

---

* In this same general area, see also North Empire, Gilson Gulch, Freeland, Brownsville, and Silver Plume.

21.

FORKS CREEK

THE EXISTENCE OF Forks Creek came about as a direct result of a feud between the Kansas Pacific and Union Pacific railroads. In March of 1872 an organization was formed to construct a railroad across the mountains to Salt Lake City. Named the Kansas Pacific, this group sought an independent outlet to the coast. As a first goal, they planned to connect Denver with the mining camps and to tap the coal, iron, and precious mineral deposits in Middle and South Parks. Beginning at Denver, the route was to proceed west through Idaho Springs and across the mountains. Another branch would serve Black Hawk and Central City.

R. E. Carr was elected president and John D. Perry became a very busy vice-president. Almost at once, Perry found himself thrust into the role of a commissioner to negotiate with Clear Creek County for the issuance of subscription railroad bonds. When the county commissioners submitted their proposal to the electors, $200,000 in aid was approved.

Meanwhile, the Colorado Central Railroad, backed by the Union Pacific, also hoped to build west from Golden, bypassing Denver and making Golden the greater rail metropolis. This latter proposal was advanced as a foil to the other plan with the hope that the Denver Pacific might be destroyed in the process. For months the news media brimmed with arguments pro and con. Senator Henry M. Teller and W. A. H. Loveland headed up the Colorado Central contingent in opposition to Carr and former Governor Evans who led the Denver interests.

Teller and Loveland regarded the mountain counties as their exclusive property when it came to laying rails. Denver people, they felt, had no right there and should be kept out, even though the Colorado Central had no intention of building at that time.

When General T. E. Sickels, chief engineer of the Union Pacific, arrived on the scene in June of 1872, he brought a plan that would reduce the Colorado Central to some practical order. Also in the offing were additional plans to extend their rail connections to Black Hawk.

Meanwhile, the residents of Clear Creek and Gilpin counties were becoming restive over the many delays that had deprived them of their railroad. Most felt that if the Union Pacific delayed much longer, support should go to anyone who would construct the line. General Sickels put on his best public "airs" and went to work on a grass-roots campaign to curry public favor.

As a result, a new proposition was advanced by the county commissioners. In effect, this amounted to another bond issue of $250,000 which was to be submitted to the voters. If approved, the railroad promised to finish its line from Golden to a point near the North and South forks of Clear Creek by September 1, 1872. Scarcely less significant was their promise to build into Black Hawk by January of 1873 and on to Central City within the next year. Although the Denver interests had originally planned to extend the line on to Nevadaville, the more realistic Colorado Central eliminated this projection from their plans as being too difficult.

Fortune seems to have smiled on the Colorado Central and they succeeded where their opponents had failed. On September 1, 1872, their tracks had reached the site of Forks Creek and the first excursion was run on the line that same day. A total of 13.11 miles had been built up the canyon from Golden. By December 15, Black Hawk had its rail-road at last.

Forks Creek was never actually a town in the sense of being a permanent community of persons. Instead, it consisted of a small cluster of buildings that grew up on a prominence of land where the North and South forks of Clear Creek combine their waters. Forks Creek, sometimes called the Forks of Clear Creek, existed primarily as a fueling station for the Colorado Central. Here also the tracks separated with a wye. The left, or south branch, went to Idaho Springs and Georgetown. The right, or North branch, carried the traveler to Black Hawk where the tracks ended until May 21, 1878. On that date the last rails and spikes were installed near the depot on up the hill at Central City. At the Forks Creek wye, a wooden bridge divided the tracks, routing the locomotives and their strings of cars in either of the two directions.

Here at Forks Creek, the altitude was 6,880 feet and it marked milepost 28.71 on the company's line. When a station was erected there it was designated as number 1346. Its depot was housed in a two-story frame structure measuring 14x24 feet. Inside, one could also find comfortable living quarters for the employees. An iron roof assured protection from the rigors of mountain winters.

Outside, above the rushing waters of the creek, stood an incredible 1,943 square feet of wooden platform. As shown in the accompanying photograph, there was also a two-story section house of frame construction. Curiously, no brick structures were ever put up at Forks Creek. To provide a ready supply of water for the locomotives, a tank of wood construction, with a capacity of 8,930 gallons, was kept filled from Clear Creek. Not far away, an 11x13 coal shed held the vital fuel. To assure a trouble-free passage of trains bound in opposite directions, 577 feet of siding were installed. During those years when the trains still ran up Clear Creek, Forks Creek functioned primarily as a coal and watering station for the wye going either to Black Hawk or to Georgetown.

Many years later, as passenger and mining loads decreased, abandonment was of course the inevitable fate. The last train passed through Forks Creek on May 4, 1941. Work crews were brought in and the tracks were removed in late May and in June of that same year. Forks Creek had been active for an impressive total of sixty-nine years. At several locations along the way, many sections of the original grades are still visible. A fine paved highway now leads from Denver out through Golden and enters Clear Creek Canyon at that point. Over much of its route, the pavement follows the original grade. This is U.S. Highway 6. Where the pavement divides beyond the three tunnels was the site of Forks Creek, ghostly reminder of a colorful period in Colorado's early mountain railroad era.*

---

* In the same general area, see also Russell Gulch, Mountain City, and Perigo.

Collection of Malcolm E. Collier
At Forks Creek, two locomotives headed downstream toward Denver

Collection of Robert L. Brown
Highways 6 and 40 now separate at the site of Forks Creek. Note the background rocks and cliffs. Note also that part of the original abutment of the railroad bridge is now being used as a part of the present highway bridge.

22.

FREELAND

SHORTLY AFTER THE first spring thaw in 1877, good silver ore was found near the head of Trail Creek, just a few miles from Idaho Springs. Generally speaking, the discoveries were made on the silver belt that crosses Clear Creek County. Here, at an elevation of 8,914 feet, where the Freeland Lode crosses Trail Run or Trail Creek, a town was built. In addition to being close to Idaho Springs, the community was only about eight miles from Georgetown, and Lamartine was on the mountainside a couple of miles above Freeland.

An issue of the *Georgetown Miner*, published in September of 1878, reported that there were seventeen houses at Freeland, all of which had been completed within the past twelve months. Many more, it was reported, were nearing completion. That next week another reporter visited the camp and noted that thirty-four homes were occupied. Quite a large number of business houses seem to have flourished at Freeland from its earliest days. J. D. Armstrong operated a general merchandise store. The village meat market was run by John T. Jones. In the corner room of an old stone mill, Edward Jones and Company had a grocery and variety store. The town's single assay office was manned by George Vivian.

After 1879 a public school was conducted by Miss Emma Hull who reported twenty-one pupils in daily attendance. In later years, Bernice D. Poppen, a veteran teacher from Dumont, came up to Freeland and reported that many of her pupils were older than herself. A Mr. Price organized the first church service, prayer meeting, and Sunday school to be held at Freeland. Although they met in whatever quarters were available in the beginning, a later newspaper reported that Price organized a Presbyterian Church at Freeland in March of 1879. Price also doubled as the village blacksmith, operating an iron works in the town. On Sundays he was described by one of his contemporaries as one who "points out the errors of their ways to perishing sinners on Sundays." Without a newspaper of their own, the *Georgetown Miner* was read avidly. Along with their mail from the outside, it was carried up to them from the post office at Dumont. Freeland got its own post office on February 1, 1879. J. D. Armstrong moved the facility into his general store and became the town's first postmaster. He apparently filled the position capably for many years. The post office was later moved to the Kramer General Store. There is also a record of a Mrs. C. Redding who became postmistress at Freeland in December of 1896.

Water for community uses was obtained from Trail Creek by the simple expedient of the old oaken bucket. Family life in the town seems to have been rather well developed even in the early days. One visitor reported that Freeland was a "severely moral town." In another story a statement appeared to the effect that there was "no enticing jingle of beer glasses at Freeland." A roving journalist from the *Georgetown Miner* noted in March of 1879 that there were twenty-nine "legally ordained" families in the town already and that the better half of a thirtieth was already on the way from Kansas. Among the single men who worked in the mines, the same reporter noted that "many of their houses rather suggested of celibacy." His articles then went on to state that there were only "six correspondingly lonesome bachelors in the camp." Since the published census figures for Freeland in 1879 showed two hundred people there, one might wonder at the matrimonial propensities of all those other people not accounted for among those six celibate bachelors and the twenty-nine "legally ordained" marriages. It's probably a good thing that Freeland was a severely moral town.

Politically speaking, the Trail Creek Camp seems to have been fairly typical of most Colorado communities in this period. In 1878 there were only fifty registered voters, most of whom were Republicans. One of the exceptions to this rule was J. K. Mills, a Greenbacker, whose minority ideas were particularly offensive to the Republicans. Mills spent considerable time working with the members of the majority party, trying to help correct the error of their ways. In reality, fifty registered voters was a pretty good average for a town of this size when we realize that as late as 1954, the national election was decided by only 43 percent of the eligible registered voters. Even the Kennedy-Nixon contest enticed only 64.5 percent of those who could have voted.

From a total population standpoint, Freeland was pretty typical. In 1878 there were 175 people prospecting along Trail Run. Figures for the years between 1893 and 1900 showed a consistent four hundred souls. The *Georgetown Miner* remarked that most of them were males. From 1901 to 1905 a head count of only one hundred was recorded. Curiously out of place in the midst of all this was a last paragraph that told how "Freelandites have a decided, profound and chronic weakness for pumpkin pie, serious enough to provoke an appetite in a marble statue." Facetiously, perhaps a massive loss of appetite accounts for those three hundred souls who left between 1900 and 1901.

In addition to silver, some quantities of both gold and copper were also produced at Freeland. The Lone Tree Mine was notable, owned by Buttingham-Jones and Company. The Freeland Mine, above the town, was larger and turned out somewhat greater quantities of ore. It also had its own sawmill, built right there at the mine. John M. Dumont was the proprietor. Ex-Governor, ex-Senator Herbert Lehman of New York once owned stock in the Freeland. Down in the town, the Bullion smelter employed a small work crew

A photograph of Freeland taken in the 1880's

A large dump, roads, and scattered cabins are all that remain of early Freeland

and maintained a busy schedule during the boom years. The *Colorado Business Directory* lists Freeland in its volumes from 1893 through 1905. It declined rapidly in the years that followed.

Although there is more than one way to reach Freeland, only one of them is easy. Drive west on U. S. Highway 6 and 40 out of Idaho Springs. At the first exit past West Chicago Creek, get off the four-lane divided highway and onto the service road that parallels Clear Creek on the south side. Go on past the Stanley Hotel on your left. After passing a group of cabins, take the next good dirt road that goes off to the south or left. This road climbs sharply up the hill for several miles. You will see many abandoned mining properties along the way. When you come to a large field-stone mill foundation on the left side of the road, Freeland is just around the corner. A few houses across the creek to your right are about all that remain of the town. A big dump beyond the houses on the way to Lamartine was probably the Freeland Mine. In the gulch directly behind the field-stone mill foundation, the remains of several more homes can be seen. Once upon a time a street led up this steep hill, bisecting the rows of homes. This was either a suburb or the very earliest beginning of Freeland.*

---

* In this same general area, see also Brownsville, Silver Plume, Fall River, North Empire, and Gilson Gulch.

23.

GILLETT

MANY AMERICAN COMMUNITIES have secured their place in the sun by capitalizing upon some unusual event that transpired there. Gillett registered its claim to fame by boasting that it was the only place in the United States where a genuine, bona fide Mexican bullfight was ever held. Although there are rumors that Dodge City, Kansas, also staged a bullfight in its early days, the Gillett "fiesta" is definitely out of the rumor category. It really happened.

Like Goldfield, Gillett was always a family town from the days of its inception. It all started back in December of 1893 when it was decided to erect a town in the huge, very level meadow known as West Beaver Park. In elevation, the site was barely four thousand feet below the nearby summit of Pikes Peak, best known of the visible landmarks that surrounded the town. On January 19, 1894, the town was formally plotted. When an identity was sought, it was decided to name it for W. K. Gillett, an official of the Midland Terminal Railway. Throughout its life, Gillett was always remembered as being the most remote or outermost of the several towns in the Cripple Creek District.

At its peak the population amounted to only seven hundred people. Nevertheless, it enjoyed good transportation facilities in the form of a fine wagon road that crossed the meadow and dropped in over the edge of the old crater to Cripple Creek. In addition, the Midland Terminal's wide-gauge tracks bisected the town. During the peak years, two daily trains ran to and from Gillett. A wooden station house and a telegraph office were put up almost immediately. For many years the community boasted of the existence of forty-one assay offices, a rather startling total when we consider that only a few mines were located around Gillett. Discovered in 1892, the Lincoln was the top mine. It paid $114 to the ton in its best years. Surprisingly, little outside capital was invested in the mines around the town. Most of the operators owned their own properties.

In the town, a barrel concentration works was in operation. According to a couple of different references, it processed either 50 or 100 tons of ore daily and employed about 100 men. Out of its population of 700, Gillett boasted that it had 91 practicing attorneys, a rather startling ratio of the whole, if true. Very early in its life, the community built and began the operation of a fine water system, fed by waters from the melting snows of Pikes Peak. They also had a good system of fire hydrants. To supply a variety of other community wants, a local electrical plant was organized. It was owned by the Golden Crescent Water and Light Company which, in turn, was owned by Warren, Frank M., and H. E. Woods. At Eclipse, on the other side of the crater, these same men also owned the huge Economic Gold Extraction Company mill.

Many churches seem to have flourished at Gillett. From one source we hear that the first church in the Cripple Creek area was erected here by Reverend T. Volpe. If true, this would be Father Volpe, early-day Catholic priest who first resided at Anaconda. First or not, Volpe did put up a church, doing the manual work with his own hands. It was constructed of a combination of brick and native field stone. Winfield Scott Stratton, who made millions from Cripple Creek mining, once gave Fr. Volpe a large sum of money to assist in this church building project. By contemporary standards, Stratton was a notoriously irreligious man who publicly proclaimed his disdain of preachers throughout most of his later life. In Stratton's estimation, Volpe was a notable exception who did good work and was, therefore, deserving of help.

In August of 1895 this tiny hamlet really broke into the news and found its place in the sun. Going from the sublime to the ridiculous, Gillett had the only available racetrack near Cripple Creek. Charles Tutt and Spencer Penrose, district capitalists, laid out the track and had circular stands erected in the big meadow. The track became the pride of the area and a valuable recreational asset. Here many of the Cripple Creek District people raced their horses and exchanged proceeds from a few side bets. In 1895 some unusual events at this racetrack really hit the headlines.

Arizona Charlie Meadows, an itinerant cowboy, stood nearly seven feet tall without his boots. Joe Wolfe was a gambler and sometimes confidence man. Together, they pooled enough talent to organize and carry off a bullfight. After two Cripple Creek merchants had agreed to back the venture with five thousand dollars, Meadows and Wolfe rented the racetrack for August 24, 25, and 26. Next, they laid plans to get the bulls from Mexico into the country under provisions of the recently relaxed embargo on Mexican cattle. Only a few problems were encountered in securing the services of the necessary assortment of matadors, toreadors, and other varied window dressing necessary to this scheme.

To tie things up in a cozy fashion, Wolfe appointed all of the elected officials of Gillett to the board of directors of the Joe Wolfe Grand National Bullfight Company. Twenty tiers of seats were erected around the 250-square-foot bull pit. Tickets were printed and a gala affair was promised. Then the Humane Society of Colorado Springs got wind of the doings and lodged protests with a variety of state and national agencies. They seem to have been successful in securing the government order that stopped the bulls at the Mexican border.

When the great day arrived, special trains were run to

bring spectators from Denver and Colorado Springs. Most estimates agree that about fifty thousand people came to Gillett for the occasion. To assure that everyone was properly cared for, Wolfe had invited his old friend Soapy Smith to come down from Denver. Widely heralded as the King of the Con Men, Smith had set up five banks or rows of assorted bunco and gambling concessions around the track entrance. No less of a contribution was the saloon which had been hastily installed. From one source we hear that Soapy fleeced so many people before the gates opened that it interfered with the volume of ticket sales. After playing Soapy's games, many lacked the price of admission.

Meanwhile, Joe Wolfe was busily engaged in recruiting substitute bulls to replace the missing animals from south of the border. From a nearby ranch he inveigled the necessary quota of untrained domestic pasture stock. Wolfe became so overwhelmed with his own importance and with the auspicious occasion that he donned a cape and flat-crowned Spanish hat to become José Wolfe, the great impressario.

During the festivities a few unenthusiastic bulls, which didn't want to fight anyway, were killed in a series of pretty sloppy exhibitions. At the beginning of the second day, nearly all of the remaining bulls refused to fight. By this time the S.P.C.A. from Colorado Springs had the bit in their teeth and were demanding that arrests be made and the killing stopped.

Law enforcement officials arrested Wolfe and Meadows and jailed them in Colorado Springs. Later they admitted that the men had been clapped behind bars to protect them from the angry crowd which had finally resented being taken. The only positive result of the entire fiasco occurred when the dead bulls were cut up and given to the poor.

When the fortunes of Cripple Creek began to wane, Gillett was carried along inevitably. By 1900 the population was down to 524 people. By 1911 the racetrack stands had been torn down and the land was plowed up for farming. One

*In its heyday the principal business street of Gillett was
lined with many double-storied buildings.*

*Today's paved highway passes through the old site of Gillett and
cuts obliquely across the former business district.*

of the surest signs of decline was the closing of the chlorination mill. Father Volpe's old church was now used as a hay barn. The interior trappings were removed and now repose in St. Peter's church at Cripple Creek. A fire in 1949 destroyed most of the remaining shell. Today its rocky foundations stand alone, a forlorn symbol in the middle of a vast hayfield.

State Highway 67, a beautiful paved road, leads south from Divide and passes right through what is left of Gillett, just before you reach the crater rim and Cripple Creek. Father Volpe's church is on your right just before the road makes a curve. Beyond it are two buildings and an assortment of smaller farm-type structures. Behind them is a wind sock to guide light planes that occasionally land here in the flat meadow. These are the only reminders of the Gillett that was, once upon a time.*

---

* In this same general area, see also Goldfield, Mound City, Eclipse, and Elkton.

24.

GILSON GULCH

MANY SMALL COLORADO communities with far less to justify
their existence than Gilson Gulch, frequently put on airs,
incorporated themselves, and added the dubious distinction
of "City" to their names. Professional windbags were often
hired to trumpet the local civic virtues, real or imagined,
to a gullible nineteenth-century society. Exorbitant claims
were made for the richness of nearby mineral deposits and
for the zestful climate which produced such longevity that
the town undertaker was forced to move elsewhere. In terms
of a stable population, extent of economic development, and
of legitimate community activities, Gilson could have qual-
ified but never took the trouble to do so.

The Gilson family first settled here in the late 1870's or
early 1880's following the discovery of some very good gold-
bearing lodes. Two conflicting sets of chronology are available to confuse attempts to establish a firm date when the
settlement actually began. A small community soon grew
up in close proximity to the several mines. The inhabitants
were principally Italians with a few families of French and
German extraction. It is doubtful if the total number of
residents at one time ever exceeded 150 to 200 persons.

The Gem Consolidated Mines Company had the best paying properties in the gulch. So rich were their ores that it was
found profitable to drill a tunnel connecting Gilson Gulch
with the Newhouse or Argo Tunnel down below at Idaho
Springs. A large number of other mines also dotted the surrounding hillsides. Among the better known were the Dove's

Nest, Freighter's Friend, Garden, Franklin, Silver Age, Gold Medal, and, high on the hill above the town, the Southern Moon. Large four-horse ore wagons plied their way up and down the narrow trails carrying the rich ores to and from the mines and the smelters far below.

In 1893 the Dumont family arrived to open a boarding-house since no hotel has ever been recorded as having existed in the gulch. The Dumonts also opened a new saloon along the principal street. In addition, brewery wagons constantly plied the Virginia Canyon road from Central City with a barrel of beer on each side for Gilson Gulch.

The town itself, if such it may be called, was built low down in the bottom of the gulch. One grocery store was the only such enterprise in the community. Actually, it functioned more in the nature of a general store. Twice during each week a wagon came up from an Idaho Springs meat market to supply the residents with fresh beef, pork, and poultry. A similar service was rendered by a bakery wagon which came over from Black Hawk. The closest post office was at Idaho Springs and there was no free, home delivery in those days. Most people alternated with their neighbors in order to cut down the number of mail trips that might otherwise be necessary.

In the beginning, children from Gilson Gulch rode or hiked down the steep grades to Idaho Springs. In later years the volume of school children increased, a schoolhouse was con-structed and a teacher was hired to ride up from Idaho Springs each day on horseback.

Since most communities seem to need a local mystery to keep things interesting, Gilson Gulch managed to fill the need with a real baffler. The man's name was Demi, possibly a contraction from Dimitri if local stories were true. Ru-mors were rife throughout the district that Demi was a turncoat member of the Russian royal family who had run away to make a new life for himself elsewhere. Why he chose to live in a mining camp is unknown since he was never known to have engaged in the extraction of precious metals. None of the residents who are still living is able, in fact, to recall any instance when Demi ever worked at anything. There seemed to be enough money at all times. His home was one of the larger structures and stood below the mines in the lower end of the gulch. Facts concerning his early life are very scarce. A large steamer trunk that belonged to Demi still exists in the possession of a former Gilson Gulch resident. Perusal of its contents may yet provide some clues to the enigma.

The present condition of Gilson Gulch is disappointing. A very few buildings, some empty foundations, many yellowing mine dumps and the old roads are all that remain. A comparatively easy route follows Virginia Canyon up out of Idaho Springs and winds its way steeply around the hills on the way to Russell Gulch and Central City. At one point the road divides. It matters little which branch you take since they both rejoin each other a few miles farther up. The right branch is longer but contains easier grades; that is the reason why it was built. The left fork is steeper, more direct, and therefore shorter. This was the original toll road. Beyond the point where these two branches come back together are several blind corners and the road seems to emerge on the crest of a small rise where it forks again. The left branch is still the Virginia Canyon road. Turning right will quickly take you to Gilson Gulch. Park your car at the turnout by the next fork in the road. Below you is Gilson Gulch. The right branch of the road now descends steeply to the townsite. It is usually passable for conventional cars but better have a quick look first. The distance is short. Turning left from the turnout will carry you along a delightful little single-lane road which permits several good vistas of the gulch before it climbs over the hill and eventually enters Russell Gulch from the back side. In autumn this is an extremely pretty ride and as of this writing is still passable for regular cars. Many small trails leave this road from one side or the other and most terminate at old mines in the surrounding valleys. Many of these latter are Jeep roads.

Despite the number of turns, the trip to Gilson Gulch is an easy one and all distances are comparatively short. It can be made effortlessly in a single day from Denver, leaving more than ample time for lunch, exploring, and other pursuits before embarking on a leisurely late afternoon ride home.*

---

* In this same general area, see also Freeland, Brownsville, Silver Plume, Fall River, and North Empire.

In its heyday Gilson Gulch was a busy and prosperous place

The site of Gilson Gulch now shows few signs of its former activity

25.

GOLDFIELD

ALTHOUGH MUCH OF THE Cripple Creek district was already booming in 1894, Goldfield was still a timberline cow pasture. During the next year the town was founded by the owners of the great Portland Mine, James Doyle and J. F. Burns. Doyle and Burns were a couple of inexperienced Irish prospectors from Portland, Maine, who had struck it rich on Battle Mountain above Victor. One of them had been a carpenter while the other was an ex-plumber. In secret, Winfield Scott Stratton had assisted the two men in developing their claims which eventually became two of the greatest producers in the district, the Portland No. 1 and the Portland No. 2.

Barely north and slightly east of Victor, just around the slope of Battle Mountain, Doyle and Burns found a large open meadow that seemed ideal for their purposes. Here their Gold Knob Mining and Townsite Company went to work on the business of starting a town. Jimmy Burns, who actually headed up the Gold Knob Company, put his men to work laying out streets and selling lots here in the valley that lay between Bull Hill on the northwest, Battle Mountain to the west, and Big Bull Mountain on the east.

Contrary to popular opinion, most Western mining towns of this era were surprisingly quiet and decorous places in which to live. Although the West had known such places as Dodge City, Leadville, Tombstone, and Abilene, these were not typical. If their overly-publicized bacchanals had been emblematic, the mortality rate would have precluded any "settling" of the frontier. Even the most lawless settlements calmed down within the first year or so of their existences.

From its beginning, Goldfield acquired the reputation of being a family town. Homes, schools, and churches were far more common here than were saloons and dance halls. In some records, Goldfield was referred to as the "City of Homes." It also had more sidewalks than any other town in the district. Over the years residents have also laid claim to having the oldest, continuously operating Sunday school in the Cripple Creek area. There is a very good chance that it was the highest Sunday school, too, since Goldfield was built at an elevation of 9,903 feet above sea level.

As the town developed, a fine business district grew up along the principal streets. Many of the best mines were only a stone's throw from the settlement. Consequently, many families elected to settle here in order to be closer to the husband's work. By the end of the first year, 2,191 people had already found homes at Goldfield. Not far away, the town of Independence had grown up around the Hull Placer deposit. Within an incredibly brief time the two communities grew toward each other and merged. By 1895 Independence had been taken in or annexed by Goldfield. In the process, the population for 1895 had grown to 3,000. By 1900, there were 3,500 people there and Goldfield had become the third largest town in the district.

Among the nearby mines that contributed to the influx of population were the Findley, the Independence, the Portland No. 1 and No. 2, the Golden Cycle, and the Vindicator. Together they shipped twenty thousand tons of ore per year. The previously mentioned Hull City Placer had furnished the initial impetus that resulted in the founding of the now absorbed town of Independence. To better serve this massive mining complex, all three of the major district railroads extended lines into or through Goldfield. Since the town had been fortuitously located in a huge open meadow, all three of the railroads took advantage of this precious space and built freight yards here. There were also wooden stations and a telegraph office. Ultimately, three fourths of all the ore mined in the Cripple Creek basin was shipped from Goldfield.

Although the labor wars of 1894 and 1903-4 have been mentioned in two other chapters, Goldfield was also affected and in a rather unusual way. It seems that all of the elected city officials were members of the Western Federation of Miners. To put it bluntly, Goldfield was a veritable hotbed of unionism. When Governor Peabody called out the state militia and placed troops in the district to maintain order, it was deemed prudent to station one of the garrisons at Goldfield. Less than a mile away, the Strong Mine had been captured by the strikers in the first clash. Ultimately the operators won their victory, the unions were broken and known members were loaded on flatcars for deportation out of the state. By the close of 1904, nearly half the homes at Goldfield were empty. All unionized city officials were ousted from office by a group of nonunion citizens in 1904 and control of the city was restored to the mineowners. Incidentally, the original city hall still stands. Although badly in need of repair, it is an architectural gem with weathered brown exterior walls. For more than two decades it has been unused. Upstairs one may see the old courtroom and a huge safe still emblazoned with "City of Goldfield" in gold-leaf lettering. Nearby is the ancient firehouse with its original hand-drawn pumper still inside.

With the coming of electricity, the La Bella Power Plant was erected here. For ten years or so it supplied power to a variety of communities including Cripple Creek, Victor, Anaconda, and of course Independence and Goldfield.

Currently Goldfield still has a small resident population. To find it, merely drive around the corner to the northeast from the edge of Victor where State Highway 67 stops. If time permits, the old Florence and Cripple Creek railroad grade is now a fine dirt road and you may enjoy driving over

Goldfield, the family town of the Cripple Creek Mining District

With Pikes Peak on the horizon, a few families still carry on life in lofty Goldfield

it through Phantom Canyon, coming up from Florence. Another choice, and a very scenic one, allows you to drive over the abandoned grades of the Short Line from western Colorado Springs. This is the fabulous Gold Camp Road. Although longer, either of these two latter routes provides a most unforgettable approach to Goldfield.*

---

* In this same general area, see also Mound City, Eclipse, Elkton and Gillett.

26.

JASPER

ALMOST TWO DECADES had passed into history since the original Pikes Peak gold rush when a group of experienced miners from Cornwall, England, chose to seek the yellow metal within the virgin wilderness southwest of present-day Monte Vista, Colorado. Deep in Rio Grande County, where Bitter Creek empties into the Alamosa River, their efforts met with success and the Conejos Mining district was established.

There, in 1880, they started erecting a ramshackle assortment of tents and log cabins on the north side of the Alamosa River. They named their settlement Cornwall, after their former home. Another source tells us that the town was named for John Cornwall, the first postmaster. There is also a difference of opinion concerning the town's chronology. In her superb *Stampede to Timberline,* Muriel Sibell Wolle tells of finding information about Jasper having been established in 1874-75.

Within a few months the town had doubled both its population and its building construction. Early records described the settlement as being 18 miles south and 4 miles west of Del Norte. From another source we find it described as being 10 miles east of Summitville, at an altitude of 9,145 feet above sea level. In reality both directions were correct and would get you there.

To provide for the miners' welfare and to assure themselves a tidy profit, the Marion Gold Mining Company began its operations on April 4, 1880. For many years the Perry and Miser lodes were the two best producers at Cornwall. Ultimately, two separate but adjacent towns grew up at the site. For some reason the second community assumed the name of Jasper and few obstacles could check its growth, although the two locations existed for a time, side by side. In any case, Jasper gradually absorbed Cornwall and its separate identity was no more.

Within an incredibly short time weekly stagecoach and mail service from the outside world had reached the community. When George Crofutt visited the camp it was still named Cornwall and had apparently just acquired its mail service. On that occasion Crofutt remarked, "The mail to Cornwall is being transported on a broncho, straddled by a Fifteenth Amendment." Since this was the Negro Suffrage Amendment, passed in February of 1870, I assume that the rider must have been a colored man. Crofutt also described the town as being on an old wagon road that ran from Fort Garland to Pagosa Springs. He also wrote that it was impossible for wagons to go on for any distance west of the town. Actually, the legal plot for Cornwall was filed with James A. Shields, a county judge, on April 5, 1881, not long before Crofutt arrived in camp.

By 1886, there were two hundred people living and working there. Ten years later, the first post office was established and D. A. Wolfe was appointed to be the first postmaster on December 3, 1896. This account of a first post office and a first postmaster differs from the one given earlier in this chapter. Since both bits of information came from very reliable sources, I decided to include both accounts and let the chips fall where they will. Obviously, the first postmaster could not have been both John Cornwall and D. A. Wolfe.

All sources of information about Jasper seem to be in agreement concerning the beginning of its demise. Instead of being content with local conditions, the operators loaded up a ten-ton shipment of ore to be refined at Denver. An impatient crowd milled about at Jasper awaiting the results of the assay. From then on, things went from bad to worse.

Jasper, on the Alamosa River south of Del Norte, as photographed by George Beam

Many trees now obscure the terrain at what remains of Jasper

Word soon arrived that the smelter had burned down. To this day the results are unknown. In any case, the exodus began and the population of Jasper started to dwindle. Within a few years, the town was on the skids.

Then in 1902 a group of capitalists from Massachusetts appeared on the scene with $100,000 clutched in their hot little hands. Directly they opened up the Sanger Mining and Milling Company, a reduction plant capable of treating 125 tons of ore daily. Located about two and a half miles above the town toward Stunner Pass, the Sanger operation gave Jasper a second lease on life. Fortunately they located a good mine on the hillside directly above their mill. Ore was brought down the incline by wooden chutes.

Eventually the Sanger properties pinched out and Jasper resumed its slumbers until some years ago when many of the old residences were refurbished to become fine mountain cottages for the fortunate people who now return to Jasper each summer.

Like so many of the towns in this book, Jasper is an easy-to-reach location. Drive straight south on Highway 15 out of Monte Vista. After 12 miles the pavement stops. At this point turn right, or west, and follow the graded dirt road that gradually climbs into the hills. After you enter Rio Grande National Forest, a road to Capulin branches left; don't take it. Keep straight ahead past two campgrounds, to Jasper. If in doubt, follow the signs to Platoro Reservoir. This road goes through Jasper long before reaching the reservoir.

It is also possible to drive the somewhat longer route southwest from Del Norte to Summitville and beyond to the forks of an unnumbered road. Keep left at this point and follow the Alamosa River to Jasper, a gem of a town in a truly beautiful, wooded alpine setting.*

---

* In this same general area, see also Platoro and Stunner.

27.

KING CITY

BACK IN 1871, George Lechner discovered some rich semi-bituminous deposits of coal in South Park. Eight years later he sold some of his holdings to the South Park Coal Company. From April of 1879 until the area declined, this company operated the King mines. Among the workers who labored in the pits, Europeans predominated. In the beginning these people were mostly of Italian extraction. Their nostalgia for home resulted in a name for the community that grew up around the mines. They called it Como, for the beautiful lake in northern Italy. The name was retained until the Denver, South Park and Pacific Railway erected a station at the end of their tracks in June of 1879. At that time many of the residents moved over the three miles or so to the new location and took the name with them.

In a historical sense, the first or original site of Como ultimately became King Park or King City. Both names have survived. As a source of the new designation for their momentarily nameless settlement, they chose W. H. King, clerk of the South Park Coal Company. King also kept the general store, and when postal facilities became available, he was made the first postmaster.

In the accompanying photograph we see a typically unimaginative company town. Apparently no effort was made to harmonize with the surrounding ranges of tumbling peaks that encircle one of the most majestic high-altitude parks in all of North America. Within a few years about sixty two- and three-room company houses had been put up. Later, of course, the inevitable saloon also appeared. For those families that had the time and inclination to travel, there were four livery stables that stood ready to supply both wagons and horses. One busy blacksmith shop took care of keeping all of the animals well shod. Since most Europeans have a high regard for craftsmanship, King City soon boasted a fine carpenter shop. From earliest times the coal company had built and operated its own store here. Such facilities became a fixture in most of the company-owned towns during this period.

Although the average population of King City ranged between two hundred and four hundred people, it was an active and proud little place and for years the residents even insisted on having their own school. For the company-owned mines, there was a powder house for storage of all dangerous explosives. They also had a scale house for weighing the coal. To store water, there was a wooden-sided water tank. Near the edge of town, not far from one of the stables, stood a livestock pen. Although there are references to a cemetery, my research leads me to believe that most of the dead were interred at nearby Como.

Since there were no civil rights laws to twit men's consciences, segregation of the races at King City became an accepted pattern of life. Traditionally, the Germans, Italians, Austrians, Hungarians, and Swedes occupied the north side of the town. The southern portion was populated by Americans and persons of British descent. When the Chinese were brought in to work in the mines during 1880, they lived wherever they could find a place. In point of time, their tenure at King City was rather brief. The resentful Italians attacked in force and drove the Chinese out before peace could be restored. Scarcely less significant was the continuance of this segregation in the life of the only church in the town.

Taken as a whole, there were seven coal properties being worked at various times. When one was exhausted, another would be opened. A few, like the King No. 1, succeeded abundantly while others produced less well. All of the King Mines were slope rather than shaft mines. Allison Chandler, my source for much of the material in this chapter, says that the prime year was 1884. Accumulations of explosive gas in the several underground levels contributed to a perpetually dangerous situation. Many Chinese were killed in an explosion at the King No. 1 in 1885. Subsurface fires swept this same mine in 1886 and again in 1889.

Then, on January 10, 1893, came the most awful tragedy in the town's history. An underground explosion in King Mine No. 5 took the lives of something over twenty men; the totals vary. Among themselves, the survivors decided on a mass funeral for seventeen of the men, with subsequent interment across the way at the cemetery adjacent to Como. The rest of the bodies were shipped out for later burial at their own homes elsewhere. From the time of the tragedy until the day of the funeral, bad weather added to the general atmosphere of gloom. A sullen, lowering rack of storm clouds and driving, whirling snow had enveloped South Park. Dense white mists rose like smoke from Tarryall Creek, contributing an eerie quality to the entire saddening sequence of events.

The day of the funeral brought a change. It dawned clear and cold, filled with the icy breath of the great winds that swept down from the tumbled mountaintops and roared through the high pine forests. At the tiny church far below, the minute interior could not hold all of the bodies, let alone the mourners. A single coffin was selected and brought inside to symbolize all of those who had perished in the tragedy. Following the services, the coffins filled two railroad boxcars. Accompanied by sorrowing families, the train moved slowly across the meadow, through Como, and out to the cemetery. Two trenches, each about twenty feet long, had already been dug. Eight coffins were somehow placed in each of the two excavations. Andy Anderson was the seventeenth or odd-numbered body. Since he had been of a different faith, his remains were buried apart from the others.

In a historical sense, King City only lasted for about twenty years. After the coal deposits had been exhausted in all seven of the King Mines, the town was abandoned in the late 1890's. Some short-term leases were taken to rework a number of the properties in the 1930's but, except for these instances, the town has been dead for most of the present century. Gone now are the lawns and beds of flowers that once fringed the neat rows of little white houses. Nothing more than a string of depressions in the earth now marks the former sites of the workers' homes. Only the dumps of the several King Mines show that life once existed here.

From U.S. Highway 285, about halfway between Jefferson and Fairplay, a one-mile-long road leads north to Como. Almost directly across the highway is the start of the Elk Horn Road, a dirt trail that leads off across South Park to the south. Roughly a mile south of U.S. 285 you will come to an intersection. The main or best road keeps to the left. A much less desirable but passable pair of tire tracks turns off to the right and goes down for a half mile into the gulch that once held King City. When you park above the banks of the twisting creek, you are in King City.

All around you, the barren gulch is now deserted by everybody and the curious antelope and other animals have returned to drink from the little stream that once more flows nearly as clear and pure as it did when George Boyd first viewed it.*

---

* In this same general area, see also Boreas, Como, Dyersville, Tarryall, and Hamilton.

King City, the old coal-mining town in South Park

Apart from the mountains and the dump, King City is only a memory

28.

KOKOMO

SWEEPING DOWN from the icy pinnacles of the Ten Mile Range, the cold blasts of a high-altitude blizzard roared across the valley below, engulfing a small party of migrants who were defying the odds in an effort to reach Leadville. On nearby Fremont Pass, a ten-foot snowfall had blanketed the slopes. The biting cold had already taken its toll when one member of the party, a Scotsman, had died. Pausing temporarily, a burial party was dispatched to prepare a grave. While hacking away at the frozen earth, they discovered silver about four feet below the topsoil. "Scotty" was stashed in a convenient snowbank, the claim was named and became the productive Dead Man Mine, and that's one version of how Kokomo got started.

Still another story relates that it was founded by the Recen brothers. They, too, discovered subsoil deposits in December of 1878. One more version still favors the Recen brothers but moves the occasion ahead to early 1879. George Crofutt says the town was incorporated on June 3, 1879. All versions agree that the town's name came from Kokomo, Indiana, hometown of most of the first party that came into the valley. Although the first story is a little too perfect as a story and certainly makes for superb theater, there was, nevertheless, a Dead Man Mine and the time is about right.

Little doubt exists in regard to the role of the Recen brothers in getting things started. However, although I believe this spelling of Recen to be correct, there are also references which report the name as "Racene" and as "Racine."

Almost immediately, a second town grew up beside Kokomo. It assumed the name of Recen. Within an incredibly short time, the two communities grew toward each other and met. Most contemporaries were unsure just where the dividing line was located. One reference noted that Kokomo and Recen were separated by the little rill (stream) that flows from the mountains, running between them and bisecting the meadow at a right angle to the present paved highway. Another source says the two towns were divided only by a street. In any case, the rivalries between them were intense.

In this meadow where the town developed, the elevation is 10,618 feet above sea level. Population statistics from some sources stretch credulity to the breaking point. In a few cases the totals for Recen may have been combined with those of Kokomo. For example, in 1879 Kokomo supposedly had 1,500 people. Yet, in 1880 it is reported as being down to 808. By the end of 1880 it seems to have returned to the 1,500 figure. During its peak year, 1881, a figure of 10,000 has been given.

Mining developments here seem to have started with the previously mentioned subsoil deposits in the meadow where the town grew up. Nearby, George Crofutt reported that there were placer claims along the banks of Ten Mile Creek. In the mountains a wide variety of mines were worked. The aftermath yielded between $80 and $400 to the ton from carbonate of lead. The Crown Point and the Ruby Silver assayed out ore at $1,500 per ton. Other notable properties were the Hoodoo, Grand Union, Gilpin, Wheel of Fortune, Silver Blossom, Michigan, Reconstruction, Queen of the West, Snowbank, Forest Combination, Wilfley, Little Chicago, Eagle Mining Company and the White Quail on Elk Mountain. The Mayflower and Enterprise were on Jack Mountain, and there were also some gold mines on Fletcher Mountain. Two smelters, the White Quail and the Greer, maintained a heavy schedule.

In the combined townships there were several hostelries.

Among them was the Woods Hotel which had two large tents on the principal street and an annex in the form of an additional tent for boarders, pitched on the hillside. Some other hotels were the Pennsylvania House, the Summit House, and the Western Hotel. Early in 1882 a fine two-story Masonic hall was erected. It gave up its home in September of 1965. Furnishings from Kokomo's eighty-five-year-old lodge are now preserved in a special room at the museum in Leadville. Members of the lodge have currently joined with the one at Leadville and the two have formally merged. In its heyday, the Kokomo Lodge boasted that it was the highest in the nation, 10,618 feet above sea level. At the time of the merger with Leadville, there were still 137 members on the books. With Leadville at 10,200 feet, the newly consolidated lodge may still hold the altitude record.

A rather pretentious two-story school, complete with belfry, was also among the town's early achievements. Children frequently attended school on skis or snowshoes. In fairly recent years, a modern school was built to replace the ancient two-story frame structure. At least one church, a bank, four sawmills, and several general stores were also built. Three newspapers seem to have flourished in the early days. Earliest of all was the *Summit County Times*, published in September of 1879. Prices here at this location reflected the remoteness of Kokomo. Flour brought twelve dollars a sack. On the other hand, ham or sugar sold at only twenty cents a pound.

A disastrous winter fire in 1882 nearly cleaned out Ten Mile Avenue, the principal business street. Losses ranged between $300,000 and $500,000. The fire had several results. Actually, the blaze had been in the Kokomo end of the settlement. Recen offered free lots within its town limits to all survivors. Although Kokomo had been known for a short time as Kokomo City, the "City" was dropped from the name after the fire. Also, as a direct result of the conflagration, Kokomo moved its post office to Recen. Although

Looking down Ten Mile Avenue in early Kokomo

A contemporary view of Kokomo in the 1960's

much of Kokomo was later rebuilt, the two towns, nevertheless effected a permanent merger. While the post office retained its legal designation as the Kokomo Post Office, Recen became the legal name for the town. Incorporation papers with these changes were duly filed. Despite this, only one map (from an oil company) currently lists the town of Recen. To all others it is still Kokomo.

In the early days, Leadville served as the chief supply center for most of the satellite mining camps. Teams of horses and packtrains hauled freight over the twenty miles that separated Kokomo from Leadville. Freight was hauled for seven cents per pound. It cost twenty dollars to haul a barrel of vinegar over the road. From Georgetown, the Ten Mile Toll Road Company built a grade across the range to Recen and Kokomo. Stagecoaches operated over the road between 1879 and 1886.

Later, the Denver and Rio Grande extended their rails into the valley. Two railroads, the Denver, South Park and Pacific and the Rio Grande, served the town. At this writing, one of the old depots, which later became a store, is still standing. Fare on the Rio Grande line was $16.50 to ride one way from Denver to Kokomo. An alternate route could be arranged by riding the stagecoach from Denver to Georgetown for $7.00. Passengers might then switch to the Colorado Division of the Union Pacific and ride to Leadville for $10.30 more.

With such a well-developed system of transportation, food was more varied here than elsewhere. Upon his visit to the camp, George Crofutt remarked that the pioneer larder could be varied by the availability of wild game nearby. Deer, elk, bear, mountain lions, grouse, and quail abounded in the Ten Mile Range.

When winter snows covered the valley, the residents of Kokomo kept track of the miners who toiled high on the mountainsides, in an unusual way. Shortly after it got dark each night, at a prearranged hour, all miners placed kero-

With the school as a backdrop, here was a D. & R.G. train waiting at the station in Kokomo.

In April of 1966 only the school remained of the group of buildings shown in the photograph above.

sene lamps in their cabin windows that faced toward the town. Should a lamp fail to appear, people in the valley acted accordingly and a snowshoe rescue mission soon brought aid.

Even now the fate of Kokomo has not been entirely decided. It was formally abandoned in 1965, and the Climax Molybdenum Company purchased the site. Several years ago the settling pond of the Climax Company buried the town of Robinson, just up the valley. Presumably, Kokomo is destined to share the same fate. When last seen, the dump was already close to the edge of the old town. In October of 1965, the Kokomo Post Office closed its doors for the last time. Up until the very end, the town retained a vestige of its municipal government. Mrs. Helen Byron was the last mayor. With so few people in town, every other homeowning family was represented on the six-man town council. All early municipal records of Kokomo have been gathered up and now repose in the office of the Summit County Clerk. Approximately one hundred graves in the Kokomo Cemetery have been moved to higher ground. The Robinson graveyard had to be moved earlier.

To reach Kokomo, drive on U.S. Highway 6 over Loveland Pass to State Highway 91. An alternate route may be taken by driving on U.S. 24 through Leadville to the southern end of State 91. In November of 1966 a new section of highway was completed to replace this older portion that passed close to Kokomo. The new road is located somewhat higher on the mountain but both the old grade and the townsite are visible below you. Access to the original road, still paved, is from the north end, at a point three miles south of the intersection of Highway 6 and State 91. The town was below the old highway and west of it on the north side of Fremont Pass. Kokomo and Recen, once proud names on the roster of historic Colorado mining centers, have lived out their last days.*

---

* In this same general area, see also Oro City.

29.

LEAVICK

THE OLD TOWN OF Leavick was formerly one of Colorado's most picturesque ghost towns. Then, in 1948, operations were temporarily resumed at the Last Chance Mine. The name of the lode proved prophetic for what was to be the fate of the town. Arrangements were made by the mining firm to purchase the right-of-way of the old Denver and South Park rail line. Park County agreed to maintain a graveled road on the old grade from U.S. Highway 285 up to Leavick. Opening this road also opened up the valley to senseless vandalism and curio seekers at a later time. These elements, coupled with some particularly severe winters, have combined to leave the site in ruins.

Possibly the earliest prospecting activity in this valley dates from 1869 when the first traces of silver and lead were discovered. The ore deposits were exploited solely for their precious metals and little interest was manifested in building a town. At that time silver had a market value of fifty-three cents an ounce while lead sold at four cents a pound.

The actual beginnings of Leavick date from 1873 when the Last Chance lode was discovered. Its location was high up on the 12,600-foot saddle ridge between Mount Sherman and Mount Sheridan. Later, the Hilltop Mine was opened up only a short distance away, on the same saddle in the lofty, rich Mosquito Range. Both were silver properties. Eventually, two huge mills were placed at the base of the range in Horseshoe Gulch. Water was readily available from Four Mile Creek for their operations. In the beginning the ore was hauled down to the mills by teams of horses and by mule-drawn ore wagons. As the volume of their production increased, a three-mile-long tram line was installed, with tremendous steel cables, to connect the mills with the mines. Huge black iron buckets moved overhead, dumping tons of rich ore into bins at the mills. The momentum of full buckets coming down pulled the empty buckets back up the tram for another load.

The cluster of cabins and other structures that grew up around the mills was named for Felix Leavick, an early prospector in the district. The mills and mines gave the town its lifeblood. At the peak of its boom, Leavick housed slightly more than one thousand people who came to wrest a fortune from this rich, rocky, timberline basin in the shadow of Horseshoe Mountain, a glacial cirque that has long been a landmark at the western head of the valley. The town stood at an elevation of 11,294 feet, nestled in the bottom of a high gulch beneath the towering 14,000-foot peaks of the Mosquito Range. Although Leavick was actually closer to Leadville, a scant seven miles across the Mosquitos, the fifteen-mile approach from Fairplay was far easier. An approach from the Leadville side would make a wonderfully scenic ride but cutting such a road would be a dangerous and complex proposition.

One early and rather overoptimistic account said that Leavick had just one street which extended all the way up from Fairplay to the top of Horseshoe Mountain. Although such gross exaggerations were common among nineteenth century tub-thumpers for early mining towns, local people accepted these lies with tongue in cheek as necessary for attracting outside capitalists or to impress Eastern tourists.

During its boom Leavick was a busy and a happy place. There were two saloons, a community-sponsored baseball team, and a brothel on the edge of town. A dentist and a barber found community need sufficient to justify their full-time attention in the community. Further prosperity seemed assured when the Denver and South Park built a narrow-gauge branch line up Four Mile Creek through Horseshoe and Mudsill to the Last Chance Mill. Ores and concentrates were hauled out in quantity during good times and, in the 1920's, this same line took out zinc.

In terms of up-to-date communications, the town lagged behind. No telegraph office existed in the camp and no telephone line connected the community with the outside world. In order to find out what was going on, the mill superintendent drove down to Fairplay each day for his market letter, which came by telegraph, and brought back the latest news. I have never found any record of a newspaper being published at Leavick. Under such conditions gossip probably flourished to a high degree.

As one entered the town along its principal street, the first building was the Baker boardinghouse where many of the unmarried teamsters and miners "batched." Farther along up the hill stood the school. In winter the children climbed up the hill on web snowshoes to attend classes. Back down the street on the opposite side were some private residences with barns which were used only occasionally. On the upper side of the street stood the cookhouse. Behind it were two long, low barns which house the fine big teams used to haul supplies up to the mines and to bring the ore back down. One general store and the post office stood at the far end of the settlement. Farther down the valley, about three miles below Leavick, the older town of Horseshoe was gradually abandoned with the miners moving up the creek to be absorbed into the larger population.

July 4 was always a great occasion. The men came down from the mines to participate in a big camp picnic. Huge bales of hay were dragged in and spread all over the floor of the old hotel until it was quite smooth. Close to one hundred pairs of feet spent the evening dancing quadrilles, waltzes, and polkas.

With the repeal of the Sherman Silver Purchase Act in

1893 history repeated itself once more at Leavick. When word came by telegraph that the price of silver had fallen, a spectacular exodus that has few parallels began. One source says that the town was emptied of people in a single day and a night. Improbable as this may seem, there are many accounts which try to substantiate it. One story says that when word of the market crash reached the camp, miners were finishing their noon meal. Without waiting to clean up, the men just left the table, grabbed a few belongings, and departed for the gold camps. Years later, when Leavick was "rediscovered," the dirty dishes were still on the tables just as they had been left when the unwelcome news came.

In another account the superintendent reached the workings of the Hilltop Mine with his telegram, which read, "Blow your whistle and pack your diggers. We're through!" Apparently he did just that, but some limited operations were nevertheless pursued until the autumn of 1899, at which time all operation shut down and the town has never made a successful comeback. The attempt to reopen Leavick in 1920 was not successful and the last mill closed down again in 1923, never to turn a wheel again. This repeal of the Sherman Act was the same debacle that ruined Horace A. W. Tabor and others in Leadville and, in fact, sounded the death knell of the pure silver camps throughout the American West.

Leavick remained virtually isolated and almost untouched in its lonely valley, unnoticed until after World War II. Reaching Leavick today is simple. Drive south out of Fairplay on Highway 285 for about one mile. At this point a dirt road turns west beside a small white sign that says "Horseshoe." Follow this well-graded dirt road for about ten miles, through the empty meadow that once held the town of Horseshoe. From this point another two miles will carry you past the crumbling remains of Mudsill. One more mile and you are at your destination.

A few old snow-crushed buildings can still be seen. The

In this early photograph of Leavick the two mills are at the right and the town is at the left.

Leavick as it looks today, photographed from the same angle

huge old tram house of the Hilltop operation is on a knoll above the road to your right. As of this writing the Last Chance Mill was still standing by the edge of the stream. Beyond it are the crumbling foundations of the Hilltop Mill. Above the road, leading up the mountainside, are a few of the tramway towers while piles of decaying timbers mark the sites of the others. A scar that was once the main street still has a few rock foundations on both sides. Now the last of the still-standing small buildings have been transported down to Fairplay where they currently repose as museum pieces and Leavick has been left in shreds.*

---

* In the same general area, see also Alma, Buckskin Joe, Fairplay, Puma City, Quartzville, Montgomery, and Sacramento.

30.

LULU CITY

NEARLY EVERY COMMUNITY has some unusual historical claim to fame if one digs deeply enough in search of it. Lulu City was no exception. It was founded on a hoax, perpetrated to make people believe there was placer gold in the sands of the upper reaches of the Colorado River. At that time the river was known as the Grand and several locations still belie its former identity. Such places as Grand Mesa, Granby, Grand Junction, Grand County, and Grand Lake, among others, are keys to its earlier name.

Lulu City was founded during 1879 near the headwaters of the river's north fork, deep in the Never Summer Range. Fortunately for all concerned, both gold and silver were found nearby in limited quantities. In the spring of 1880, it was rumored that the surface outcroppings "surpassed anything known in mining history" a completely ridiculous claim. The actual fissures were quartz lodes, found lying between the walls of granite, and containing more gold than silver. The elevation here was 9,400 feet above sea level.

During the brief flurry that followed, sometimes called a mining boom, several towns sprang to life in the area. In addition to Lulu City there were three others, called Dutchtown, a mile away, Gaskill, to the south, and Teller City. Near the towns, several mines were opened up. Some were good and others left something to be desired. Their names displayed the usual touch of adventure and nostalgia so frequently encountered among lonely men so far from home. Some of the names were fanciful ones like Southern Cross,

Wolverine, Tiger, Rustic and Friday Nite. From the start, they were beset with troubles, principally transportation. It was just too far to the railroads and the smelters. Shipping costs quickly ate up the profits and the last of the mines closed in the nineties.

When discussing this town, someone invariably wants to know, "Who was Lulu?" With such a name she should have been a dance-hall girl and that's how folklore gets started; but she wasn't. Lulu was the favorite daughter of Benjamin Franklin Burnett (or Barnett); the accounts vary. In the finest Victorian tradition she was described as being beautiful and popular in the community, so Daddy, who was the founder of the town, named it for her. Sandwiched away in an old document at the State Historical Society of Colorado is a notation that Lulu Burnett was a "raven-haired belle." She must have been very beautiful and very popular because the principal street soon became Lulu Avenue and the chief crossing of the range to the north became Lulu Pass. As time passed, she must have faded, though, because it's called Thunder Pass now. In researching information about mining camps, one is frequently struck by the sameness of the descriptions reserved for the feminine contingent. All are described as "beautiful, popular," etc. Didn't any plain girls ever settle in a mining camp? The term "plain girl" is a euphemism employed by older people to designate otherwise nice, wholesome girls who, being sound of wind, limb, and character, are somewhat deficient in pulchritude. In the predominantly male environment of a frontier town in the days of chivalry, all women looked beautiful. Even Calamity Jane was so described in one lonely narrative. The men got there first and opened the country. The women, as usual, took their time.

Meanwhile back at Lulu City, an ambitious town plot had been laid out with about one hundred blocks, divided up by nineteen streets and about four avenues. At first the anxious men lived in tents, but gradually the more substantial log cabins predominated. By 1881 there were about five hundred people here although one source kites population statistics to a highly unlikely one thousand. Before long, the customary array of stores and saloons had found their places on Lulu Avenue. Sandwiched in among them were one assay office, several restaurants, a land office and the inevitable hotel. No church ever got a foothold at Lulu City. In the June 5, 1882, issue of the *Rocky Mountain News* a report about Lulu City was carried. It said that thirteen business buildings had been put up in the previous month alone. Three lumber mills, the Hertel, the Tabor, and the Boyd and Harrington, all turned out green lumber for the booming town. To supply the miners' other wants, the Godsman and Company General Merchandise Store was opened. At times it seems to have doubled as a hotel. Other businesses included the William Dugnay Drug Store, the Holly Saloon, the Denver Saloon, the Howard Mountain and Galena Mining Company.

Above the bustling community, impatient prospectors staked their claims on the rocky hillsides, looking for the elusive deposits that would pour tons of gold into their laps. The dark blue-green forest world of leaf and needle gave way as the hills and gulches swarmed with men, burros, and machinery. By May of 1882, a crude road from Georgetown had been opened to a point only six miles from Lulu City. Another road came in over the pass from Fort Collins and was reported to be free of snow by June. Three times each week stagecoaches lumbered up from Fort Collins with more people for the growing community. Along the way, this same line also made stops at Teller City and Grand Lake. During 1884, a new mine, the Rabbit Ear, was discovered. Active lumbering filled an economic void for a while.

Within the short life span of Lulu City, the miners regrettably found very little gold and those silver deposits that were located proved to be of a low grade. Some sources place the beginning of decline late in 1884, while others prefer the following year. Without a mill or refinery at the site, costs of shipping the ore out of the district to Denver, 113 miles away, were staggering. With such a ready supply of water, it seems incredible that none of these enterprising souls saw fit to put up a mill. It was just too far from either railroads or the smelters at that time.

A few of the mines were worked into the 1890's but most of the people had pulled out long before that. With little idea of permanence, the families moved out, heeding the call of more promising strikes elsewhere. Behind them they left rows of stoutly chinked cabins, strung out along the river. At the edge of town a wagon petrifies, waiting for the last resident to depart. Most accounts speculate upon the speedy evacuation of Lulu City. Apparently the people were so anxious to get out that they left most of their accumulated belongings behind. Dishes remained on tables, clothing was not removed from closets, and one highly unlikely story tells us that dinners were left cooking on the stoves. By January of 1886 even the post office had been discontinued.

Instructions for going to Lulu City are a bit different than those for any other location in this book since the site is now within the boundaries of Rocky Mountain National Park. Without a doubt the simplest way to find it involves going into the park at the Grand Lake entrance. From that point drive north along the north fork of the Colorado River past Timber Creek toward Milner Pass. Just before you get to the switchbacks that climb the pass, watch for a small sign about Lulu City on your left. Follow the short dirt road beside the sign to a picnic ground where you can leave your car. From here on you must walk or rent a horse.

A fine trail begins here and goes generally up the valley, sometimes following the river. Since the National Park Service uses two sets of figures, the trail is either 2.6 or 3 miles long. The difference is of little significance, however, since it is one of the very easiest of walks as mountain trails go. Total distance will be about six easy miles for the round

*Lulu City flourished briefly in the handsome valley near the
headwaters of the Colorado River.*

*Lulu City is practically gone now, and the area is a part of
the Rocky Mountain National Park.*

trip. In many places the trail follows the old grade which was originally used to reach Thunder Pass. In some instances the Park Service has cut fine new approaches to avoid swamps and assure a dry and easy walk. Almost no steep sections will be encountered and even the novice should make this one with ease and relish. Pretty mountain scenery and occasional glimpses of wildlife offer pleasant diversions along the way. There's even a sanitary facility just off the trail near Shipler's cabins.

As you will doubtless gather from the accompanying photographs, Lulu City is apt to be something of a disappointment to the purist in search of prime ghost towns. Although the remains of many cabins still dot the beautiful meadow, nothing approaching the one-hundred-block town plot was ever built and there are no whole buildings still intact.

Personally, I'm fond of Lulu City not only because of its unusual history but because I also like pretty mountains, abundant trees, and restful green valleys. A short hike with pleasant companions is also much to my liking. Potentially, this trail offers all of these. If you take this walk, I hope you will also take the time to enjoy nature in this handsome Rocky Mountain setting.

31.

MARBLE

IT WAS A RELENTLESS search for silver ores that brought the
first group of white men into the beautiful Crystal River
Valley. After pushing in across Scofield Pass, the small party
made its way down Rock Creek, now called the Crystal River.
At the point where Yule Creek flows in from the southwest,
they made a permanent camp and began to put up their shelters. Exact dates are difficult to prove in this case and most
people take the easy way out by placing the crossing in the
late 1870's. Their settlement was first called Yule Creek,
then Clarence, and finally Marble City.

Some silver was found, along with a lesser amount of
gold and lots of lead. Most of the mines were on Whitehouse
and Treasure mountains. Among the better producers
were the Lead King Mine and the Black Queen Mine which
was found in 1886. By 1890, the Hoffman Brothers Smelter
was working and in 1897 there was a second refinery in the
valley. From one other source we find dates of 1879-1900
for the Hoffman plant. Anyway, there was smelting being
done, even though the mines were not very good.

Despite admittedy slim mineral leads, the aforementioned
town of Clarence seems to have been located in 1880. John
Mobley and W. F. Mason, acting on behalf of the Clarence
Townsite Company, seem to have been the chief instigators.
Within a relatively short time, another town grew up beside
it, calling itself Marble City. William Woods and W. D.
Parry founded the latter town in the winter of 1882-83. Al-

most at once the two towns grew together and became one. Clarence ceased to exist as a separate entity and Marble City became just plain Marble.

With a nucleus of population already settled in the bottom of the canyon, it is indeed fortunate that a better economic base was found. The finest grade of quarrying marble in the world, a nearly solid mountain of it, was found at a point less than two miles from the town. In this, as in so many other discoveries, confusion exists about who got there first. As a result there are references which credit the find to George Yule in 1874, before the valley was even peopled by mineral seekers. Nevertheless, William Wood and W. D. Parry are also credited as first locators of the deposit in 1882. In any case, the site was Whitehouse Mountain. First among the several who eventually opened quarries on the slopes were the Kelly brothers in 1890. Two years later, J. C. Osgood opened up a second quarry nearby. Curiously, the White Quarry and the White Marble Company on nearby Treasure Mountain, were owned and operated by the Mormon Church.

Best known of all the companies was the Colorado Yule Marble Company which arrived on the scene a bit late and went into operation after 1900. Down in the town, they set up the world's largest marble finishing plant. It measured 1,700 feet in length by 150 feet wide. To assure a consistently high quality of work, expert stonecutters were imported from Italy. In a nearby mill the blocks were cut before being sent to the finishing plant for final shaping and fitting.

In the early days marble blocks were loaded on packtrains of forty burros for transportation to the outside world. During the winter of 1895-96, horse-drawn sleighs carried the huge blocks over the same route. As the quarried chunks increased in size, heavy-duty freight wagons came into general use. A wagon road was built up Yule Creek to the quarries in 1905. From Carbondale, the Denver and Rio Grande Railway began hauling the ponderous marble cubes to their varied destinations. To cut costs and improve service, the Colorado Yule Marble Company built the Crystal River and San Juan Railroad from Placita to Marble in 1906-7. It continued to run until it was torn out in 1942, during World War II.

In the town, population figures fluctuated according to the prosperity or decline of the marble business. Here as elsewhere, the head counts are open to doubt. In general the number varied between one and two thousand souls during the peak years of the early twentieth century. Most of the streets in town, and a majority of the houses, were illuminated by electricity. Good churches, an elementary and a high school, and a motion picture theater added diversion and enlightenment to life in Marble. There were also five general stores, two hotels, a drugstore, a dry-goods establishment, two pool halls, a Masonic hall, two barbershops, and six very busy saloons.

Civic improvements arrived in the form of a wagon road up the valley from Carbondale in 1907. There was also a city water system. A circular bandstand of the usual proportions was put up and Sunday afternoon band concerts were a popular pastime in Marble. Suspended on a high tower, a fire bell was installed to warn the town in emergencies. It proved most valuable in 1926 when a disastrous blaze nearly wiped out the town.

Two newspapers flourished during the town's life. One of these was known as the *Marble Booster*. The other was the *Marble City Times*, published in the decade from 1892 until 1902. The *Times* once had a crusading woman editor who attacked a lack of social sensitivity by the Colorado Yule Marble Company. Since this stand threatened the jobs of many of her readers in a prosperous time, her efforts were unpopular.

Over the years, the output of Colorado's quarries met with a remarkable degree of public and official acceptance. Quite an impressive array of public structures utilized Yule marble in their construction. A total of $1,070,000 worth of marble became the Lincoln Memorial, a large number of civic buildings in San Francisco and elsewhere used marble wholly or in part. In Denver, the Customs House, the Colorado National Bank, and the Colorado State Museum were erected from the Treasure Mountain quarries. By far the best known of all was the one-hundred-ton block that became the Tomb of the Unknown Soldier at Arlington National Cemetery near our nation's capital.

Thus far, this single block holds the record for being the largest chunk of monument quality marble that has ever been removed from a quarry anywhere. At the mill it was scaled down from its original weight to fifty-five tons. Old photographs show the huge unfinished piece loaded on a railroad flatcar for removal. At the quarry, slightly more than a year of work was required to remove it from the mountain. Final processing and polishing were done by the Vermont Marble Company at their New England plant before sending it to Washington.

Although the demise of Marble is directly attributable to a combination of high shipping costs coupled with increased use of marble substitutes and veneers, the decline was certainly hastened by the snowslide of 1912 and the catastrophic mud avalanche that nearly buried the town in August of 1941. Some people blame the whole thing on overgrazing by sheep on the alpine slopes above the town. One resident of the valley showed me a photograph of the lush mountaintop rangeland in the early days. Next, he displayed a second picture showing an ugly, barren view of the same region, now nearly devoid of any vegetation, after sheep had grazed there.

In any case there was a cloudburst near the head of Carbon Creek that was not absorbed in the normal manner. Without adequate cover crops the whole mess just slithered off and took the path of least resistance—downward. As the rushing water coursed down the valley of Carbon Creek, it picked up tons of the rain-soaked coal shale. By the time it reached Marble, it had assumed the form of a mass of heavy gray mud. Several blocks of the Main Street business district along the creek were carried away and many private residences were buried. Carbon Creek cut a new channel across Main Street and the bridge that had crossed it was reduced to tinder. The fire warning bell and the community bandstand were inundated. In one house a grand piano was buried. Once again, as it happened at Brownsville, there were those people who recall hearing a tinkling melody as the silt-packed mess pressed down on the keyboard. Can't you just imagine people, in the midst of a tragedy, with nothing better to do than stand about, listening avidly to the accidental musical propensities of a mud slide covering a piano? It is extremely doubtful that any tone as delicate as piano notes could have been heard over the din.

The river cut a block-wide swath, north to south, across the town. Street after street was filled with mud and debris. In addition to damaging the town, the deep mud and silt destroyed the mill. The quarry closed shortly after the flood and never reopened. Actually, it might have folded anyway since the Colorado Yule Marble Company had gone into receivership back in July of 1916. It was out of operation until April of 1922. When work was resumed, things went along spasmodically until 1941. Its Crystal River and San Juan Railroad was taken out in 1942. Another flood dropped more mud onto the town in 1945, and several minor slides have come down in the intervening years.

Several years ago, my family and I had driven across the Scofield Pass Jeep Road into the valley. We spent the night at Marble and had planned to go back out by the same route. During the night it rained and the mud came down across the road between Marble and Crystal City. Two vehicles were buried until bulldozers cleared out the ooze some days later. Needless to say, we revised our plans and left the valley by another route.

In Marble today, the remaining structures shelter a few families during the summer months. A few years ago, Mrs.

Ruby Isler, of Carbondale, wintered up there. Lately, several plans have been considered to find contemporary uses for the still-ample supplies of marble in the valley. Only time can tell what the future holds.

Marble is a very easy place to visit as things stand at present. A new road is now under construction over McClure Pass from Paonia. In addition, State Highway 133 is currently paved from Carbondale to a point some distance beyond Redstone. This highway follows the Crystal River south to Marble. For the more adventuresome there's always the 27 percent grade on the road over Scofield Pass from Crested Butte and Gothic to Marble. Much of the town remains and there are Jeeps available to take you up Yule Creek to the quarries. Limited accommodations are available in the town and there is a beautiful campground west of the highway on the river just north of the town. In a very real sense of the word, it is appropriate to say that Marble wrote its own epitaph with the great quantity of statuary marble now standing in monuments and public buildings all over the United States.*

---

* In this same general area, see also Scofield City, Crested Butte, and Crystal City.

In this early photograph of Marble the extensive business district is clearly visible in the valley below the cliffs.

The full extent of the mud slide that buried the commercial portion of Marble is apparent in this contemporary picture, taken from the same angle.

32.

MONTGOMERY

MORE THAN A CENTURY AGO, gold seekers from the Cherry Creek diggings overflowed into South Park to seek the elusive yellow metal. In the process they established some of the very earliest mining camps in Colorado. One of these was Montgomery. When the ice chunks had stopped floating down from the headwaters of the Middle Fork of the South Platte River and summer breezes warmed the alpine meadows of South Park, gold was discovered here in 1859. In a historical sense, this was nothing particularly new. When Lieutenant Zebulon Montgomery Pike was here in 1806, he met a trapper named James Purcell at Santa Fe who told him about having found gold near the headwaters of the South Platte. But those were relatively prosperous times and there was no economic depression to goad men across far-distant horizons in search of a proverbial pot of gold beneath the terminus of some vague and elusive rainbow.

All things considered, it is rather surprising that a period of two years would elapse between the initial discovery and the founding of a settlement. Nevertheless, an early issue of the *Rocky Mountain News* tells us that the Montgomery district was laid out, defined, and established on August 22, 1861, at the point where the Platte River emerges into its valley from the mountainous western fringe of South Park. Sometime during September of that year, the first log-walled cabin was put up. Allegedly, this first structure became the original post office and general store at a later date.

When the town was laid out, there were three principal

streets. By 1862 there were already more than seventy cabins occupied, and others were in the process of construction. When the first water-powered sawmill appeared, business was booming and demands were great. In the final stages, a grand total of five sawmills was running in the town. A total of three hotels was built. One of these was a 50x100-foot structure with a large second story that sometimes doubled as a public meeting hall until the new theater was completed. By the time the showhouse was ready in 1862, it was the largest in the region. Carroll's Minstrels, a popular touring variety show of the times, played alternately at Buckskin Joe and at the Montgomery Theatre. When there were no shows in town, the huge structure doubled as a dance hall and could also be rented for parties. Of course, Montgomery had its quota of saloons, and there were several general stores there as well.

When William N. Byers sent another reporter from his *Rocky Mountain News* to the town, the published story listed an enterprising physician, Dr. Bailey, who also owned the drugstore and a shoe store at Montgomery. At that same time a man named Alex Ray was running a bakery and a restaurant. By July of 1862 the town was still growing and there were now 150 cabins there plus a new stable to care for the town's livestock. When the townspeople wanted to show their high regard for President Lincoln, they named the great peak that rose behind their town in his honor. At that time it was thought that the new Mount Lincoln was the highest peak in Colorado Territory. As a token of their gratitude to the President for having granted territorial status to Colorado, the men at Montgomery also sent a bar of solid gold ore from their mines to Mr. Lincoln.

To acknowledge the honor, President Lincoln sent Schuyler Colfax, a member of his cabinet and a leading Republican politician of that era, to Colorado. Colfax came to Montgomery, fell in love with the area, and frequently spent vacation time there in the years that followed. There is even an account that relates how Colfax brought his bride-to-be out to Montgomery and proposed to her on the crest of Mount Lincoln. Several puns were made about this elevated occasion but they would not be worth repeating by today's standards. For the record, Colfax was definitely known to have climbed Mount Lincoln.

In later years, both Montgomery and Mr. Colfax fell on evil times. In the case of Montgomery the gold played out later in the 1860's and the town lay dormant for about a decade. Many people became discouraged and moved over the hill to Buckskin Joe. In some instances they even took their cabins with them.

Mr. Colfax became Vice-President of the United States during the first administration of President Ulysses Simpson Grant, 1869-73. Most standard American history texts dwell at some length upon the scandals of these years. Schuyler Colfax was one of those caught with his fingers in the till, having accepted a bribe in the odious Credit Mobilier scandal of 1872. Although it was in a period of decline when Colorado achieved the status of statehood in 1876, the name of Montgomery was considered by the legislature along with Denver and some other cities as a possible state capital. At this time Montgomery was bigger than either Fairplay or Buckskin Joe.

Originally, the mines around Montgomery were included as a part of the Snow-blind Mining District. Then, in the fall of 1861, the name was changed to the Montgomery Mining District. Two years later, the residents of the Montgomery, Jackson, and Independent Districts held a meeting on June 20 and voted to consolidate all three into one. This new aggregation was to be called the Consolidated Montgomery Mining District, sometimes incorrectly referred to as the Montgomery Consolidated Mining District.

Meanwhile, back at the town, the old dumps were reworked often as people hoped for a new boom with the better methods that had become available for refining the ores. From the mountain stronghold far above the town, there suddenly came word of great silver discoveries on the slopes of Mount Lincoln and Mount Bross in 1881. Here, at an altitude of 10,800 feet, Montgomery embarked upon a second boom, becoming a residence center for those who worked in the nearby mines. Outstanding among the several mineral properties was the Robber's Roost which was so vertically situated that it could be reached only by way of a ladder which had something over two hundred rungs. Three other mines were important in the town's life span. They were the Magnolia, Pendleton, and the Montgomery. Two arrastras, crude ore-crushing devices, were at work in the surrounding gulches. In the town, along the river, four steam-powered and two water-propelled quartz mills were in operation from the earlier period.

On the transportation front, wagon trains provided the earliest access to and from the outside world. In the early days all mail came to Montgomery by way of a weekly delivery from the Overland Express Company. Later on there was a daily express line in operation between Montgomery and Buckskin Joe. This afforded a connection with the semiweekly service being operated in Buckskin Joe by the Green and Duncan Express Line. Beginning in July of 1862, W. C. McClellan and Ab Williamson started a four-horse run with Concord coaches. From Denver the line crossed Kenosha Pass to South Park and had stops in both Montgomery and Buckskin Joe. Without a doubt this was the most ambitious undertaking thus far. In addition to passengers, express shipments, mail and commercial parcels were also carried.

Following the repeal of the Sherman Act in 1893, Montgomery's silver boom collapsed, and prophets of doom began carrying on like medieval chroniclers in a plague year. Beyond this, there was a slight revival in 1898. Even with newer refining methods, everything they attempted failed. It was soon clear that Montgomery was finished.

Several years ago, the city of Colorado Springs purchased the old site of Montgomery, cleared out the empty cabins and debris, and built a new reservoir to assure the future of their supply of fresh water. Before it was filled, the graves in the old Montgomery cemetery were disinterred and the remains moved elsewhere.

Colorado State Highway 9 runs north and slightly west from U.S. Highway 285 at Fairplay. Just north of Alma, near the southern foot of Hoosier Pass, a dirt road turns left or west and follows up the valley of the Middle Fork of the South Platte River. When you arrive at the reservoir, there can be little doubt about having reached your destination. Here, beneath the clear, sparkling surface, is the watery grave of old Montgomery.

Montgomery, as photographed by George Wakely in the early 1860's

The watery grave of Montgomery, with Mount Lincoln rising behind the site

33.

MOUND CITY

AFTER MANY YEARS of frustration, Bob Womack found the El Paso Lode inside the extinct volcanic crater that is now called the Cripple Creek Basin. The year was 1890. This single strike gave impetus to the entire Cripple Creek boom and hundreds of other mines were soon established. In the process twenty-eight new millionaires made their marks. Something in excess of $430,000,000 in gold has been produced over the years. To provide living space, twenty-two "towns" were started. Many of these were merged later with some of the bigger ones and lost their identity. Mound City was one of these.

The earliest beginnings of Mound City date back to 1891 when the ramshackle assortment of log cabins and frame structures, seen in the accompanying photograph, started being built. In the valley just northwest of Rosebud Hill, the elevation measures about 9,360 feet above sea level. Actually, this location is the lower end of Squaw Gulch, named for the disinterred remains of a female aborigine that had been "rediscovered" while a mining claim was being excavated. In this single gulch, four towns grew up. These were Anaconda, Barry, Squaw Gulch, and Mound City.

By the middle of 1893 there were five hundred people there. During 1894 the community was officially platted. By the late 1890's, one source tells us that the population had reached two thousand, a rather high estimate. By 1900, there were still one thousand people there. In the process of becoming a thriving municipality, three grocery stores opened

up to supply the nutritional essentials of life to the people
who lived there. One of these was also a general store. Two
meat markets, largely supplied from wholesalers in Cripple
Creek, also thrived at Mound City. Inevitably, in a town
of this type, two saloons appeared and did a land-office business. To care for the needs of newcomers and transients,
there was one hotel, believed to have been the large false-
fronted structure in the photograph. Since many riding
horses and draft animals were used to perform a multiplicity
of functions, the one blacksmith in town was kept busy.
One barbershop and one clothing store were also in business
at Mound City.

Sitting on the side of nearby Beacon Hill, the El Paso Mine
helped the town by providing jobs for many of the residents.
By 1951, when it finally closed down, the El Paso had produced $10,800,000 in gold. Its main shaft was 1,300 feet
deep. In some records, this mine has been referred to as the
Beacon Hill. In any event, it should not be confused with
the other El Paso Mine, discovered by Bob Womack, which
was later renamed the Gold King. Although Mound City,
unlike Victor, for example, was never noted for its profu-
sion of mines, it did achieve a measure of fleeting fame for
its two excellent mills. The first of these was the huge Brodie
Cyanide Mill, the first of its type in the entire Cripple Creek
district. Although it continued to operate until 1900, it
could not compete successfully with some of the newer
processes that were introduced in the district just prior to
the turn of the century. When the Brodie closed down, it
contributed one more reason for the decline of Mound City.

The second installation was a French stamp mill called the
Rosebud. It, too, was set up and in operation somewhat earlier
than most of the Cripple Creek mills. In 1893 Winfield Scott
Stratton (see Winfield) tried to run some of the telluride
ores from his Washington Mine on Battle Mountain through
the Rosebud. Since these ores were not of the oxidized telluride variety, technicians at the Rosebud found that they

would not separate easily by the process available to them at that time. Stratton soon abandoned the experiment since high transportation costs were absorbing his profits.

Judge Melville B. Gerry, the jurist who is best known to history for a speech he never made, occupied the bench at the court in Mound City. Gerry, a profound and serious man, became a victim of history as a result of having sentenced Alfred Packer, the man-eater, in 1883. Although his actual pronouncement was a thoughtful and sober one, few people today know about it. Instead, history has preferred to record the profane and ludicrous version that was ululated through the streets of Lake City by Larry Dolan, a bibulous Irish saloonkeeper of the town. In the Doland version, the jurist not only opened up the question of Packer's alleged canine ancestry, but also dragged in partisan politics as well. While Judge Gerry protested this slur on his integrity almost to his dying day, he nevertheless became a creature of history and was never able to shake the spurious skeleton out of the closet. Even today, the Dolan version is quite widely believed.

For those people who sought recreation close to home, there was an organization called the Squaw Gulch Amusement Club which once boasted four hundred members, drawn from Anaconda, Barry, and Mound City. George Carr, proprietor of the original Broken Box Ranch, was its president. For a time, Bob Womack was entrusted with the duties of sergeant at arms. His duties were to exclude undesirables, particularly those female devotees of the "seamier professions." In his magnificent book, *Money Mountain*, Marshall Sprague records that this decision often resulted in a source of consternation to the membership since poor naïve old Bob regarded all women as inherently virtuous. When a club member inferred that a "soiled dove" had somehow slipped in, Bob often took this as a slur on the lady's reputation and was prepared to do battle in defense of the honor of even the most notorious women in the district.

This early photograph shows the short-lived community of Mound City

Here is the site of Mound City in 1966

About 1905 the decline began to set in as people started to move elsewhere: to Goldfield, Victor, or Cripple Creek. By the end of that year, Mound City, Squaw Gulch, and Barry were absorbed by Anaconda and ceased to exist as separate civic entities.

There are very few rewards awaiting the person who wants to see the remains of Mound City today. Practically all signs of former habitation have disappeared with only an occasional scar here and there as nature is in the process of reclaiming the site. State Highway 67 runs southeast from Cripple Creek to Victor. When you round the corner and first see Squaw Gulch below you, start looking for the dim trail where the paved highway crosses the gulch ahead of you. It drops down the spine of the Squaw Gulch and enters the trees. Above you, at the opposite side of the valley, the huge dump and unmistakable log cribbing of the Mary McKinney Mine may be seen. Just below the highway was the site of Anaconda, where only the cornerstone of the jail now remains from what was once a huge town. Our dim trail, in general, follows the original main street of Anaconda. Go on down the hill, following the trail, watching the background mountains as you go. When you reach a point where they correspond to the accompanying photograph, you are in Mound City. All of Squaw Gulch has now been deserted by any forms of human habitation.*

---

* In this same general area, see also Eclipse, Elkton, Gillett, and Goldfield.

34.

MOUNTAIN CITY

FEW AMONG THE multiplicity of Colorado mining camps may boast of the priority in chronological time that can be attributed to Mountain City. No other town can claim the historical preeminence of Mountain City in terms of the mining period and the subsequent settlement of this state. Here, in 1859, John Gregory, of Georgia, made the very first discovery of lode gold, resulting in a vast acceleration of the Pikes Peak gold rush. Mountain City became the first established settlement in the Central City group.

Since the town grew up as a result of finding the Gregory Lode, our story should logically begin with information about the discoverer. John H. Gregory had left his native Georgia in 1858 to work as a government mule driver at Fort Laramie. His real intention was to join up with the prospectors moving to the Fraser River strikes from California. Gregory wintered at the Wyoming post where he was employed not as a driver but as a common laborer.

During that long winter, persistent rumors were heard about gold discoveries along the South Platte. Gregory immediately changed his plans, left the job, and moved south on a general prospecting tour. Within the next few months he had checked most of the favorable mining localities between the Cache la Poudre River and Pikes Peak. On various treks he traced many local streams back up to their sources. Eventually, by a process of elimination, he arrived at the Vasquez Fork of the South Platte River, better known today as Clear Creek.

Alone, Gregory followed the creek, prospecting along the way. Wherever the stream forked, he followed the branch which seemed to show the greatest promise. Using this system, he worked his way up the canyon, being very probably the first white man to invade its solitude. Roughly fourteen miles above Golden Gate City, he reached the division in the stream where today's highways separate to go to Idaho Springs or Central City. Gregory chose to follow the north branch for about seven miles to the gulch that now bears his name.

At this point he left the creek to explore the side canyon along a smaller creek bed. At the point where the little ravine immediately southeast of the Gregory Lode comes in, he prospected once more. Finding it to be the richest of those he had examined, he turned aside into it. As he approached its head, the color grew less and finally faded away entirely. At this point Gregory felt certain that he had struck gold. Before he could explore the lead, however, a heavy spring snow blew in across the mountains. Gregory barely escaped freezing to death. When the weather cleared, he left the discovery and returned to the valley for provisions.

At Golden, Gregory met David K. Wall, a veteran miner with previous experience in California. After hearing the story, Wall supplied him with provisions for a second expedition. Wall is often credited with being the originator of garden farming in this region. Early in the spring of 1859 he had planted two acres of bottomland near what is now the Golden railroad depot. From this venture he realized a tidy profit of about two thousand dollars by selling fresh produce to the miners.

Now amply fortified for his journey, Gregory persuaded Wilkes Defrees, formerly of South Bend, Indiana, and William Ziegler, from Missouri, to accompany him. On the sixth of May, 1859, they arrived in Gregory Gulch. Despite the fact that ice and snow still covered the ground, they began digging. Gregory climbed the hill to about the point where the wash would naturally come down. Here he paused to scratch away the grass and leaves and to fill his gold pan with dirt. When he panned it down his wildest dreams were realized. About four dollars' worth of gold lay at the bottom of the pan, which he dropped immediately.

According to Ovando J. Hollister, Gregory then "summoned all of the Gods of the Egyptians, Indians, Greeks, Hebrews and Christians, to witness his surprising discovery." In the vernacular of the twentieth century, what he said would probably be described with somewhat less delicacy. That night, by his own admission, he never closed his eyes. Defrees fell asleep about three o'clock while Gregory was still talking to himself. History does not record whether he answered his own questions or not. When Defrees awoke shortly after daybreak, Gregory's tongue was still hung in the middle and running at both ends. Between them, they washed out about forty pans of dirt and secured forty dollars before returning to the valley to bring up their friends.

At this point Gregory was already leaving behind the drudgery of common labor for his visions of a princely fortune. "Now my wife can be a lady," he mumbled over and over. The nature of the gold they found convinced Gregory that it must have originated farther up the slope. Abandoning the gulch, they passed along the little ravine that intersects it from the southeast. Upon examining the ground he told Defrees, "dig there because it looks well." Under the surface they found fragments of blossom rock or surface quartz which had been dislodged from the lode by erosion.

At one point where the dirt appeared to be very promising, Defrees filled the pan and Gregory took it down the ravine to wash it. The result was quite astounding. This single pan yielded nearly an ounce of gold. By right of discovery, John Gregory took two claims on the spot. In actual fact the find had been made on the tenth of May but orderly work could not begin until sluices had been completed on the sixteenth. Three days later the erstwhile editor and founder of the *Rocky Mountain News,* William N. Byers, had arrived to see for himself.

Having introduced himself, Byers told Gregory that he had just come over the hill from the Jackson Diggings and wanted some facts concerning what had been happening on this side of the hill. Poor Gregory was a victim of history, still unable to comprehend what had happened to him and how it would change his life. He sat on a log with his head held between his hands. Occasionally he broke forth with incoherent mutterings somehow related to the facts about his previous life.

Byers noted that Gregory had scooped out a place from the hillside for a lodging. Over it he had put up a root and brush roof. The editor noted that he seemed completely dazed by his good fortune and he speculated that Gregory's mind "may have been unsettled while occupied with his dreams of the future." Repeatedly, he spoke of his wife and children back in Georgia, and of the changed destiny awaiting them. More than once, with a distant stare, Gregory speculated, "My wife will be a lady and my children will be educated."

At first he paid little attention to Byers but gradually he softened up and talked. As the two men warmed to each other, the prospector gave the newsman a full account of his progress which has fortunately been preserved for posterity. Reaching out to a nearby bush where his frying pan was turned upside down, he raised it and revealed three large masses of solid gold. Gregory had gathered the samples from his sluices and crudely retorted them in a campfire. Within the space of just three days he had taken out the entire collection now hidden under his pan; valued at roughly a thousand dollars with no confiscatory taxes.

For more than a week, John Gregory had stopped all work to guard his treasure against the possibility of robbery. Scarcely less significant was the fact that his extreme case of anxiety ruled out sleep in any quantity. When editor

Byers visited the gulch, only seventeen other men were there. From then on, as word leaked out, new people came in. By the end of the week 150 men, mostly from Jackson's Bar, had come over the hill to try their luck. An impatient crowd also came pouring up Clear Creek Canyon from Auraria-Denver. From that time on, the influx of people grew almost daily. Some prospectors succeeded abundantly while others complained of "miners' luck."

On June 24 Byers proved to be a true friend in time of need. Taking compassion on Gregory, he loaded a fast team with the treasure, which by this time had grown in value to four thousand dollars, and drove it to Omaha. Fearing robbery, he and a driver traveled day and night, purchasing fresh horses along the route. Fortunately for all concerned, they reached their destination in just twelve days. In this as in so many other similar cases, things got out of hand. Byers still had an office in Omaha. When he exhibited the gold there, it nearly created a panic.

Large crowds gathered to see it. Some, remembering the earlier disappointment occasioned by rumors that had dogged the meager Green Russell discovery, openly declared it a hoax since there was believed to be no gold in the Pikes Peak region. When faced by the need to justify his journey, the editor addressed a public meeting and related the story of the various discoveries that had been made thus far, expressing his own personal confidence in the richness of the country.

In June, Horace Greeley, scrupulously honest owner of the *New York Tribune,* came to Gregory Gulch, also to see for himself. Like a lamb being led to the slaughter, Greeley fell for one of the oldest tricks in the book. Under cover of darkness, the miners loaded a shotgun with gold dust and peppered a dry hole until it literally glittered. Next morning Greeley was given a pan and invited to "see for yourself." What followed hardly deserves comment. The results were as foreordained as a Saturday night wrestling match. Greeley was amazed! His Gilpin County experiences doubtless dictated some part of his later, most famous utterance in which he urged the younger generation to, "Go West, young man, go West, and grow up with the country." That night in Gregory Gulch he made a less well remembered speech at Mountain City while pitch-saturated torches blazed and dynamite explosions rocked the smoky atmosphere. His oration was typical of the man who would later run for President of the United States. In it he extolled the American way of life, castigated the local prostitutes and demon rum, and urged the miners to follow a virtuous life. No shred of evidence exists in the history of Gilpin County to indicate that any of his advice was taken seriously but he was cheered lustily.

Eventually, John Gregory sold his claims for about $21,000 and went to work prospecting for others at a rate of $200 per day, doubtless the finest salary being earned by any person in the United States during that period. In the course of his work, Gregory struck another lode, an extension of his original, on the southeast slope of the gulch. Appropriately, it was named Gregory II. Most of Gregory's clients soon discovered that gold mining was a business which required time, a lot of money, experience, energy, and patience.

Thus, in an incredibly short period, about five thousand people had migrated into the ravine. According to some contemporary sources, hundreds of others arrived in the territory each day while Horace Greeley passed tens of thousands on his way homeward.

Ultimately, cities and towns grew up out of the ramshackle clusters of log and brush shantytowns that adhered tenaciously to the steep sides of Gregory Gulch. Street over street, the camps climbed one above the other up the steep mountainsides behind Clear Creek. Later observers said it was impossible to tell where one town ended and the next began. At the foot of the hill was Black Hawk, with its multiplicity of mills and refineries. Next came Mountain

City, which, of course, grew up around the Gregory discovery. Above it was Central City while still farther up each of two adjacent valleys one might visit Russell Gulch and Nevadaville. Thus in an incredibly short time, the Richest Square Mile on Earth and its environs had a premature taste of the twentieth century population explosion.

Mountain City was laid out by Richard Sopris in the middle of the gulch, almost exactly halfway between Central City and Black Hawk. Like the rungs of a ladder, three streets were cut into the side canyon leading south of Gregory Gulch. Two of these were filled with private residences while the third, Gregory Street, became the false-fronted business district. By the early summer of 1859, Mountain City already had a tent hotel and a log theater in addition to the usual assortment of log cabins, tents, and brush shacks. On July 4, Jerome C. Smiley described the settlement as "A product of the discovery of gold, containing over two hundred dwellings where six weeks before there were none." By August it boasted having had the first show in the mountains at the log theater. Its title was "Cross of Gold."

A number of other notable "firsts" have also been attributed to Mountain City. By August it had the first two newspapers in the mountains, called the *Rocky Mountain Gold Reporter* and the *Mountain City Herald*. Publication was suspended late in October. The first mountain saloon, a dubious distinction, dispensed firewater from unwashed tin cups. The first Masonic hall in Colorado seems to have been there, and the residents boasted the very first church service was held there on June 12, 1859.

In the fascinating diary of Joseph Persons, Jr., thus far unpublished, he wrote the following observation:

Sunday, June 19, 1859.
There is preaching every sabbath at Mountain City. It is a very peaceable place for so many men. There is in the mountains now about seven thousand men and one woman. Her name is Charly. She dresses in black

pants hickory shirt, vest, and moccasins. Her pants project well behind. Her vest does not want any batting either.

Quite apart from the disparity in spelling, the individual referred to in the foregoing diary excerpt was Mountain Charley, one of the rarest characters to enter Colorado during the initial gold rush. Her name was actually Charlotte and her home had been in Iowa. There she married a man who not only turned out to be a professional gambler but one who soon deserted his new bride for another woman. Directly the pair set out for Colorado in 1859 to help keep the miners' pockets from becoming overloaded.

Charlotte, to assure her own protection, donned male garb and became Charley, joining the Westward rush. According to what she told George West, of Golden, Charley found her husband and his paramour at Mountain City and had her revenge. Later she enlisted with an Iowa regiment during the Civil War and kept her secret from being detected for two years. Disguised [?] as a woman, Charley penetrated Confederate lines as a spy while assigned as a male orderly under Union General Curtis. She later reverted to Charlotte, married again, and raised a family far from Mountain City.

One of the difficulties associated with historical research comes in the area of population statistics. Thus far I have repeated two population estimates in this chapter. A third source, Hall's *History of Colorado*, tells us that there were only one thousand people at Mountain City in the winter of 1859. Without trained census takers and with the highly migratory nature of life in the mining camps, far too many inaccurate, uneducated guesses have been recorded as facts.

Only a small minority of the people who entered the Gregory District could secure a permanent foothold. To make the distribution fair, each lode was subdivided into locations of one hundred feet in length along the vein by fifty feet in width. John Gregory himself finally left for his home in Georgia, carrying about $25,000 in gold, earned during this single season of hard labor.

One of the initial movements for statehood was started at Mountain City in Daniel Doyle's Hall, a saloon which dispensed five-cent whiskey for twenty-five cents a cup. Being somewhat influenced by their environment and after having worshipped copiously at the shrine of the grain, two miners spoke up in denunciation of the government for its indifference to the petitions that had been sent. As the bibulous evening wore on, the men repudiated all allegiance to the laws of Kansas and declared that they would never submit willingly to being included in that jurisdiction. Nothing much came of the meeting and it was nearly forgotten in the excitement that followed involving the gold discovery at California Gulch in April. A virtual stampede of the disappointed ones left Mountain City for the latest Eldorado.

During the Civil War, the speculative boom nearly collapsed. One source tells us that the miners here were saved only by a rapid advance in the price of gold. During this time it mounted to the highest figure known in the nation up to that time. Next came a sudden and almost frantic demand for gold mines and mining stocks. Regardless of actual value, speculators wanted them. Since the hills around Mountain City were literally seamed with fissures, the supply became fully equal to the demand and the excitement was fever-pitched for a while. In fact, many of the titles were wholly or partially fraudulent. In not a few other cases the purchasers were unable to find their property. Nevertheless, the craze extended throughout the winter and into the following April when Lee surrendered to Grant. With the end of the war the bottom fell out of the gold price boom.

As a separate entity, Mountain City had only a few years of life before it was annexed, in 1880, to become the easternmost section of Central City. Curiously, during their years as independent communities, no formal line was ever drawn as a boundary between the two villages.

If you decide to see Mountain City, follow State Highway 119 to Black Hawk. In the middle of town, turn east on the paved road up the hill toward Central City. Roughly halfway up the hill you will see a bronze marker on the left side of the highway. You are now in Mountain City. As you face the marker, you are looking up the gulch, above the road, that once held most of the town. All three of the buildings to your right show in old photographs of the town. Many other buildings, now gone, were built in the main gulch all around the point where you will be standing. Facing the marker again, John Gregory's mine was the big slag pile on your right.

In the course of historical events in the American West, Mountain City will always occupy an extremely important position, for here they found the first lode gold in what is now Colorado. Here was the great discovery that dignified and justified and gave substance to the Pikes Peak gold rush.*

---

* In the same general area, see also Russell Gulch, Perigo, and Forks Creek.

Courtesy Library, State Historical Society of Colorado
Stretching up the hillside, above Gregory Gulch, was Mountain City. Note the Colorado Central train above the town, in the upper right-hand corner of the picture.

Collection of Robert L. Brown
Mountain City in the winter of 1966. Note the Gregory Lode slash cut into the hillside to the right of center in both pictures.

35.

NORTH EMPIRE

WHEN GOOD GOLD DEPOSITS were unearthed in the nearby
creek beds and canyons, Empire City came into being and
went on to enjoy a long life as well as the distinction of having been one of Colorado's earliest gold camps. Slightly more
than a mile away, on the North Fork of Empire Creek, a
second group of discoveries was made. Here Henry DeWitt
Clinton Cowles and Edgar Freeman found wire gold deposits
imbedded in the rocks of both Eureka and Independence
mountains. Rich gold placers were also found on Silver
Mountain, and people began to settle there as early as 1860.
Actually, the main ore body was located farther up the gulch.

To connect Empire City with these new discoveries, "the
longest main street in the county" was built along the hillside grades above North Empire Creek. Quite naturally the
settlement that grew up on the mountainside above Empire
City came to be known as North Empire. Unofficially it was
occasionally referred to as Upper Empire, but the name never
really caught on enough to cause any serious confusion. Built
at an elevation of about nine thousand feet, North Empire
enjoyed a boom that lasted through the 1860's and seventies.
In the beginning a plentiful number of wild game animals
provided a welcome relief from the usual monotony of the
typical miner's larder.

Quite a number of mines were soon in operation and were
providing for the prosperity of North Empire. Among them
were the Ben Franklin, Gold Dirt, Empire, and the huge
Gold Fissure Mine which was made up of five claims. Its

owners had already sunk a two-hundred-foot shaft on the property. Just a short distance above the town stood the Atlantic Mine. Up the valley another mile or so, many North Empire men were employed on the rich Conqueror property, owned by Colonel John Dumont. Superintendent Clark Disbrow closed the operation down for a time after the fire of 1869. In the seventies the Conqueror management hired carpenters to construct a huge two-story white board-inghouse which still stands at the site. In later years, the miners "lived in" and the commuting problem from North Empire was solved.

For many years the Benton Mine produced gold ore that assayed at sixteen dollars to the ton. They also put up a company-owned barracks for the employees and called it the Blue Boarding House. Like the Conqueror structure, it still stands. The Benton property was managed by Fred Bishop. Little more than the shaft house of the once productive Tenth Legion Mine still remains. In addition to wealth from the deep mines, the Negus Placer produced fifty thousand dollars in 1878-79.

During the visit by George Crofutt to North Empire, he recorded the presence of "several" mills. There were at least two. One of these was the Hartford Mill. The other that we are sure of was the Peck Mill, an ambitious structure with twelve stamps.

As the mines continued to spew forth a very respectable torrent of gold, better transportation facilities were con-templated. Suddenly the Great Empire Cable Railroad Com-pany appeared on the scene and announced plans to con-struct a cable railroad up the hill from Empire to North Em-pire. Heading up this company as its president was a Dr. Van De Voort. Within a few years the tracks of the Colo-rado Southern Railroad had been extended into Empire. In 1898 it was bought out by the Colorado Central Railroad. Neither line made any attempt to extend its tracks on up the hill to North Empire but there were always coaches, teams, and saddle horses for rent at Empire.

Obviously the trip back down that long hill was much easier than the trip up. During the long chilly winters, coasting parties were formed to slide down the steep grade on sleds with oxbow runners. On Saturday nights, those miners who imbibed too freely at the saloons in Empire, often found it more than a little difficult to negotiate the sharp grades between the lower town and their homes in North Empire.

Several passes were built, and these contributed in a variety of ways to the lives of both Empire and North Empire. First of all, there was Empire or Union Pass, a short road that switchbacked for two miles over the low mountain range to Georgetown. By 1861, the thirty-mile road over Berthoud Pass, from Empire to Frazer, had been completed. Beyond Georgetown, Argentine Pass crossed the range at a point somewhat above thirteen thousand feet and descended into the valley of Peru Creek. Also from a point west of Georgetown, Loveland Pass was completed and in use by the late 1870's.

When a mining slump set in during the 1880's, North Empire came close to being depopulated. Although it never achieved another boom such as it had enjoyed in the previous two decades, some men stayed on and worked the old properties on an uncertain schedule. This pattern continued until World War II.

Currently, you will find the drive up to North Empire to be an easy and pleasant one. If you are approaching the site from the Denver area or from points to the east, get onto the combined U.S. Highways 6 and 40 west of Idaho Springs. Still going west, these routes divide in a few miles. Turn right at the forks and stay on U.S. 40 for one mile, going toward Berthoud Pass. As you enter Empire, watch for the main intersection in the center of the town.

Here a dirt road crosses the pavement. A left turn will take you up onto the top of what remains of Union Pass.

*North Empire, high on a mountainside above present Empire,
was photographed by George Wakely in the 1860's*

With vacant streets, North Empire is now an empty wooded shell of its former self

A right turn will lead you up the hill to North Empire in about a mile. At one point where the road makes a switchback, a huge mine dump can be seen on the left or west side of the canyon. A few cabins lie above and below the road, at a point several yards behind you. Stop and park here on the curve. Walk out on the foot trail along the crest of the big dump. From the end, look back across the valley at the road you used to get up here. You are now facing what remains of North Empire. This is the point from which both of the accompanying photographs were made. Although some structures remain at the site, the town is a mere shadow of its former self. The Conqueror boardinghouse is reached by continuing on up the hill on the same road above North Empire. When last seen, this road was passable as far as the Conqueror. In autumn, this is an especially pretty valley and is well worth the trip.*

---

* In this same general area, see also Gilson Gulch, Freeland, Brownsville, Silver Plume, and Fall River.

36.

ORO CITY

BEFORE 1859, the wide, open valley watered by the upper Arkansas River had not been occupied by white men. For centuries prior to the discovery of precious metals, Indians had used it as a desirable mountain hunting ground and as a secure hiding place for large hunting bands. Apart from this bit of early history, the development of Lake County has been marked by two rather striking periods.

First, there was an enormous influx of a miscellaneous population and the incidental outpouring of gold between 1859 and 1868. Second, there was the disclosure of immense deposits of carbonate of lead in 1874. The second period has been permanent and has resulted in the foundation of Leadville while the first was of brief duration and brought about the beginning of two communities, each known as Oro City.

Except for the Boulder district around Gold Hill, Russell Gulch, and the Gregory diggings, no remarkable gold deposits had been found in the territory. The golden yields of California Gulch proved to be one of the first incentives resulting in attraction of the multitudes of people who came during 1860. On April 25, 1859, there was much excitement resulting from a discovery made by S. Slater and Company. Rich placer gold deposits had been found in the gulch about twenty miles above Kelly's Bar. When the word spread, it caused the usual stampede from the older mining districts to the newer one.

To date, there are two versions which attempt to explain how the gulch got its name. The first tells us that it was due to the immediate influx of a large number of Californians, hence the region took on the name of California Gulch. Another story quotes Abe Lee, an early prospector in the district who, incidentally, was from California. Allegedly, he scooped up a pan of gravel and began washing it. When he saw the quantity of gold dust at the bottom, the startled Lee exclaimed, "Boys, I've got all California in this pan." The site of the original Abe Lee discovery was just below the first Oro City, at about the point where the Rock Mine juts out into the gulch. In any case, the region soon became known as California Gulch.

Some preliminary work was done while the snow was still very deep, indicating that a rich placer probably existed there beneath the thick white cover. In length, the gulch climbs upward for about ten miles. At that time the terrain was filled with clay and decomposed quartz which was high in gold content. In many ways it resembled the decompositions found at the surface of the Gregory Lode and was well adapted to washing by the same methods employed at Mountain City. At the height of the runoff, the available water was about enough to supply five or six lines of sluices. When the extensive nature of these deposits became known, huge numbers of prospectors went over the range from the eastern slope to form a settlement there in the gulch. Panning or sluicing brought enormous returns. Frequently, a man could fill an oyster can with nuggets in a single day of work. Gold, at that time, was worth eighteen dollars an ounce. Beyond this, the placers were among the richest ever opened in the Rocky Mountains, producing great quantities of precious metals.

Oro City has been referred to by a rather wide variety of names. Among them were Sacramento, California Gulch, Sacramento City, Sacramento Flats, Slabtown, and Boughtown. In the early days there were a great many tents at Oro City. One source tells us that tents and wagons extended down the road all the way to Malta. The mining portion of

Here, in the early 1860's, was the first and original Oro City.
The site was barely within the limits of present Leadville.

In May of 1966, lower California Gulch contained this dump. Background buildings are
part of the southern portion of Leadville. The picture was made from a point
among the ruts of of the original trail above the present road.

the gulch was about six miles long. In addition to wagons and tents, people also slept on the ground, in outhouses, under packing boxes, or, in fact, anywhere that gave the promise of shelter from the bone-chilling cold.

Wagon roads and tracks extended up both sides of the mountains. Several of these ruts became tributary streets. In many cases wheels were blocked, cargoes packed up, and people lived right in the beds of their wagons.

Gamblers and prostitutes were also there in force, operating in their own tents and wagons. Most gamblers also had their tables stretched out along the trails to the mines, to spare the prospectors those long walks. Three-card monte took in the most money. Some of the larger wagons were used as hotels, after food and dishes had been stacked on the ground between the wheels.

Some other families began by sleeping in their wagons until they could get a quantity of rough slab boards to make tables. This accomplished, they might then take in boarders and serve meals. Among these people were Augusta and Horace A. W. Tabor. Three months were required for the Tabor party to travel from Denver to Oro City. Their route crossed Ute Pass to South Park, then over Trout Creek Pass to the Arkansas River. After surviving a treacherous ford, they followed the Arkansas Valley up to their destination. Several histories have recorded how Augusta took in boarders while Horace received some primary lessons in the highly inexact science of mining. Also busily learning how to acquire gold were quite a number of those hard-bitten old crones who termed themselves "dance hall girls." At one time, Augusta Tabor was described as the only "family type woman" in the gulch. The women's great fortune was delayed until 1879 when the Leadville blanket veins opened up their hidden treasures of silver.

By July of 1860 there were many log and frame buildings, and one source tells us that there were eight thousand people here. Large quantities of gold were being taken out, and many of the claims paid well. No law had been established as yet. Once a circus tent was put up and sleeping space was sold at one dollar per body. Many nights the owners took in one thousand dollars. The streets looked as if most people had built their own cabins without regard to survey. As a result, nearly all streets were very crooked. Wolf Londoner, a pioneer merchant of Oro City, estimated that there were ten thousand people there in 1861.

Along the spine of the gulch was the long, continuous main street which could be followed for the entire distance. Thick with mud from constant reuse, the stream ran down the middle. Most of the business structures were eventually located at one point. Along the north bank, where the hills flatten out beside contemporary Leadville, was the site of this first Oro City. Its chief disadvantage was the previously mentioned water situation. It had been used over and over again, until by the time it reached Oro City and the claims at the lower end of the gulch, it was almost liquid mud.

Father Joseph P. Machebeouf, earliest of the Catholic circuit riders, was the first to hold a religious service in the gulch. The time was early in the summer of 1860. Tom Starr's blacksmith shop was commandeered for the occasion, using an anvil for the altar. Father Machebeouf, best known of the early Colorado Catholic priests, records that he often slept under the stars and sometimes in the snow on his trips from Denver to California Gulch. He once contracted mountain fever in the gulch and was unable to say mass for two months. Both Rev. William Howbert and Rev. John L. Dyer, pioneer Methodist circuit riders, included California Gulch in their territories.

While in session during 1861, the territorial legislature formally organized Lake County and defined its boundaries. Ironically, after 1861, each summer saw fewer and fewer miners returning after spending the winter on the lower plains.

Generally speaking, the mines in the gulch were very productive for about three years. By that time the cream of the harvest had been taken by the original locators and their workers. One shortcoming of these placers was the climate, which prevented them from being worked for more than a short season. Due to the altitude, most mining years were made up of about eight months of winter and four months in the late summer and early fall when life was more pleasant. Despite this, considerable amounts of gold were still secured along the gulch during each successive season until 1870. At that time it was found advisable to enlarge the water supply, necessitating the construction of a canal some twelve miles in length. It extended from the source of the principal stream to the placers.

Three miles farther up the Gulch, Charles Mullen discovered the Printer Boy Lode in 1868. Although it was operated only by the imperfect methods of that period, it still gave some extraordinary returns. Large bodies of soft and porous decomposed quartz were also found in 1868. These carried large masses of free gold in the form of nuggets. Frequently the miners encountered bunches of fantastically formed and matted wires with beautiful crystallization. Many large glass jars were filled with these remarkable specimens and they were exhibited at banks in Denver, Philadelphia, and New York. Mr. J. Marshall Paul, of Philadelphia, owner and manager of the property, realized handsome returns from his rude workings while the rich deposits held out. Although a lot of prospecting was done to develop other mines like it, none of them succeeded.

Life in the upper valley went along peaceably for some years with only an occasional conflict between the settlers and roving bands of stock thieves who preyed upon the flocks and herds. When pursued, the miscreants took refuge in the mountains. There were few formal attempts at law enforcement in the upper gulch during these early years.

Most inhabitants of the earlier Oro City simply moved up

the stream and became residents of the newer town. At this point, just below the Printer Boy, the second Oro City grew up. It was here that the Tabors had a general store. For some years Augusta also operated a restaurant and bakery. Her well-cooked meals and famous pies attracted a wide following. Being popular, Mrs. Tabor was made postmistress for the gulch. A third facet of the Tabor enterprises involved running an express service from Oro City to Denver. Two weeks were required to make the round trip until roads were improved. From then on the time was cut to eight days. Frequently their messengers were robbed.

By the end of 1868, large-scale mining at Oro City was about over. Most stock Colorado histories record the complaints of miners who were unable to cope with the heavy black sands that clogged their sluice boxes, making extraction of the gold difficult. Nevertheless, a twenty-eight ounce gold nugget was found here in 1868. Later, more knowledgeable miners recognized this black sand as carbonate of lead, which was extremely rich in silver. Carbonate kings who grew rich there also founded the city of Leadville, easily one of the West's greatest mining camps, and certainly one of the wildest.

The boom at the new location lasted only two and a half years although there was an Oro City well into the twentieth century. One of the last acts of those remaining in the camp was to pull down the old log gambling house and saloon, to recover from its dirt floor over two thousand dollars in gold dust that had been dropped by drunken patrons.

Both towns are gone now except for a few signs which show some of the locations at the second settlement. Currently, the last remnants of Oro City are the bits and scraps of rusted mining machinery which dot the high meadow, all that managed to survive after the scrap drives of World War II.

To see the site today, drive out of Leadville on East Fourth Street to Toledo Street. Turn east and follow the dirt road into California Gulch. The site of the second Oro City, near the Printer Boy Mine, is marked. Most traces of the first Oro City had disappeared by the turn of the present century. I am told that there were some shacks there until that time but these have long since disappeared. The regular road leads around the upper Printer Boy workings and over into Iowa Gulch. Oro City was the site of one of our very earliest attempts at settlement in the high Colorado Rockies.*

---

* In this same general area, see also Kokomo.

*William H. Jackson, famed pioneer lensman, made this early photograph
of the second Oro City, high up in California Gulch.*

*All traces of Oro City are gone now, although signs now indicate
the former locations of a few important buildings.*

37.

OURAY

ON THE SLOPES of the high peaks that surround the natural amphitheater where Ouray is now located, prospectors came in search of silver ores as early as 1874. At that time Ute Indians were still in legal possession of the territory. Felix Brunot, who later appeared with his Washington-imposed covenants to hoodwink the aborigines out of their inheritance, was an as yet unforeseen eventuality. In the meantime, those who sought the white metal were either unaware of or completely indifferent to the rights that had been guaranteed to the Utes. Most who came sought to establish claims along the headwaters of the Uncompahgre River or on the slopes that rise above Poughkeepsie Gulch.

As an appropriate name for the community that grew up in the natural basin along the river, the men chose Uncompahgre City. When Chief Ouray and his wife Chipeta arrived unexpectedly in camp one day, the residents were both impressed and fearful for their scalps. The only exception in town was a freighter who had already electrified one band of Indians by removing and replacing his toupee before their astonished eyes. Allegedly, the warriors lost little time in departing, "in several directions at once." Ouray was always a "model" Indian, who had long ago accepted the inevitability of white supremacy. His remarks to the settlers who attended a mass meeting at Uncompahgre City were designed to allay their fears and put their wildest apprehensions at rest. Eventually the settlement was renamed in honor of this most remarkable man.

The setting chosen for Ouray is one of the most beautiful in Colorado, situated at the bottom of a mountain-ringed bowl. To the south, snow-crested Mount Abrams rises sheer from a tumbled mass of surrounding peaks, to form a most majestic backdrop for the town. In size, Ouray measures about a quarter of a mile in width by just over a mile in length. Most records credit its founding to A. W. Begole and Jack Eckles who arrived during the summer of 1875. Both men had entered the San Juan country by crossing lofty Stony Pass. From Cunningham Gulch and Baker City, they had followed Red Mountain Creek over the range to the north before descending into the canyon of the Uncompahgre River. By 1876, the fledgling settlement had been duly incorporated. Before the end of that year, J. D. Crane had freighted in enough goods to open the first store at Ouray.

Due to its fortuitous location, growth was rapid. The *San Juan Sentinel,* Ouray's pioneer newspaper, was first published in 1877. Other imitators lost no time in following up its success. That same year also saw the introduction of the rival *Ouray Times,* which in later years became the *Plaindealer.* In successive years, the *Miner,* the *Pilot,* and the *Argus* all thrived and expired from the newspaper scene at Ouray.

Probably the most singularly colorful newspaper ever to be published in Colorado was the often libelous and always irreverant *Solid Muldoon,* brainchild of the incredibly talented David Frakes Day. Between 1879 and 1892, Ouray alternately seethed in anger and rocked with laughter at the unique opinions and news interpretations penned by the unpredictable Day. Highly placed political factotums who had become too pompous were the most frequent targets of his barbed jibes. His scandalous reporting became so popular that the *Muldoon* was published as a daily after 1882. Most readers were motivated either by morbid curiosity or by fear of what they might find in the *Muldoon.* Under circumstances that are still somewhat vague, Day was "induced" to move his scurrilous sheet to Durango in 1892.

Quite an impressive array of very fine mining properties were developed in the immediate vicinity of Ouray. One of the earliest was the Trout and Fisherman Lode, found by two sportsmen named Logan Whitlock and A. J. Staley, who were just looking for good fishing holes. During the summer of 1875, the Grand View Claim was registered. The Belle of Ouray became a factor in the local economy during 1881. Other good producers were the Clipper and Cedar lodes. Many of the best producers were located high up on the slopes of Mount Sneffels. As early as 1875, with no prior knowledge that a town had been started in the valley far below them, Andy Richardson and William Quinn were busily engaged with prospecting in the Sneffels vicinity. Later, in 1895, as an agent for Tom Walsh, Richardson found the immensely rich Camp Bird gold vein high up in the Imogene Basin (see Camp Bird). Imogene, by the way, was the name of Richardson's wife. Walsh was already a millionaire by 1902. For a time, he and his family made their home in Ouray.

Somewhat earlier, but only a few miles away, the remote Virginius was found in 1877 by William Freeland. Barely a stone's throw away was the Humboldt. Both of these were later merged under a single management. Their location, barely below the treacherous St. Sophia's Ridge, resulted in many summer accidents and all too frequent deaths from snowslides in winter.

Within a few years Ouray became the county seat and the Star Saloon was hastily renovated to serve as the first courthouse. The Fourth of July celebration was always a favorite time at Ouray. In the streets, foot races were run, contests of skill were promoted, quite large sums of money changed hands on the several horse races, huge floats were paraded in the streets, and some celebrants nearly "floated" out of town on their own.

In the early days, the Ashenfelter Packing Company carried most of the equipment and supplies to the surrounding mines and, on the return trip, brought the raw silver down to the smelters at Ouray. Later, as trails were widened, mule drivers rammed their unwieldy steel-tired wagons up and down the steep roads. From the south, the incredible Otto Mears hacked out his cliff-hanging, twenty-six-mile Million Dollar Highway from Silverton up over Red Mountain Pass to Ouray. At Bear Creek Falls he built a toll gate where fees were collected in return for the use of his road. Mears' original grade measured 21 percent and was built at a lower point down in the canyon. Today's Million Dollar Highway is cut higher up on the cliff sides and measures only a 6 percent grade.

Utilizing many of the same grades, Mears began construction of his narrow-gauge Silverton Railroad, the far-famed Rainbow Route. Beginning once more at Silverton in June of 1887, the narrow irons had reached Red Mountain by the fall of 1888. At Ironton, on the north side of the range, construction came to a grinding halt when it was found that the canyon walls were too narrow, steep, and twisting for further railroad construction. With only a few miles to go, Mears had to abandon Ouray as his coveted objective. For a time, rumors were rife that he intended to build a cog railway from Ouray up to Ironton. Like most rumors, this one was groundless.

But Otto Mears was not a man to be easily beaten. If a railroad to Ouray was his objective, then some way would be found to get there. Thus, in an incredibly short time he had started building his Rio Grande Southern around to the south of the range by way of Durango, then north over Lizard Head Pass to Ophir, and through Ridgway to Ouray, Mears was happy and, at last, Ouray had a railroad.

Since Ouray survived the silver crash, it never became a ghost town. Today's visitor will find dozens of interesting things to do and all sorts of wonderful things to see. For many years our family has enjoyed spending a few weeks at Ouray each summer. To reach Ouray, simply follow the fine, paved grades of U.S. Highway No. 550 south from Montrose or north from Durango. Although the elk and mountain sheep of former years no longer graze in the streets, it's still a great place to visit and a wonderful spot where one may "unwind" and forget some of the frustrations of the world outside.*

---

* In this same general area, see also Silverton, Camp Bird, and Dallas City.

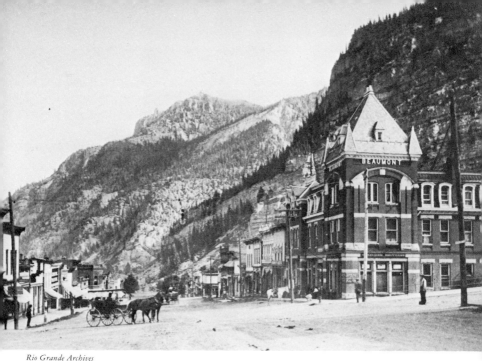

Looking north from Fifth Avenue in Ouray shortly after the turn of the century

Several original buildings stand along the business street of picturesque Ouray

38.

PANDORA

AFTER TRAVELING ACROSS the Uncompahgre Plateau and into the San Miguel Valley, early prospectors made a series of mineral discoveries that blazed the way for thousands of pioneers. Following its discovery in 1875, the Pandora Mine played a major role in the mineral development of San Miguel County. Since names are not always a true indication of origins and purposes, the exact derivation of Pandora remains nebulous. In Portuguese and Spanish, Pandora is the name applied to a three-stringed musical instrument. Somewhat more commonly, the word is found in Greek mythology, meaning "hope in the box," from the famed story of Pandora's Box.

Although the early town of Columbia, later called Telluride, already existed at a point only two miles away, a second town was founded near the head of the valley, at the bottom of the natural cup formed by the surrounding gray granite mountains. Initially it was called Newport when it was first started by a small group of hopeful prospectors in 1876. Since some of the men had come west from Newport, Kentucky, the origin of this first name is quite obvious. Postal authorities soon discovered that Colorado already had another Newport and some unfortunate confusion was perpetrated. By request, the name was changed in August of 1881. Pandora has been its designation ever since.

There were listings for Pandora in the Colorado State Business Directory for all of the years between 1882 and 1903. In the early years, until their own post office was established, all mail came in from Telluride. Many good buildings were put up, the homes were well kept with green lawns, and fenced yards were the rule rather than the exception. For many years, Dave Wood distributed nearly all of the coal and wood to the homes at Pandora. Due to the almost vertical cliffs that virtually surround the town on three sides, snowslides were a constant peril on warm spring days. One slide came roaring down in April of 1884 and wrecked the Pandora Sampling Works. In 1902, a tremendous bank of snow broke loose and sent the "white death" surging down toward the town. In some near-miraculous way it was deflected, and came to a stop barely short of Pandora.

Fires also took a fearful toll. On May 19, 1903, a patron of one of the stores threw his cigar stub into a woodbox. By 1:00 A.M. the next morning flames were raging through several structures. A grocery store was destroyed and the stock of E. J. Hawkesworth suffered $1,500 worth of damage.

The population of Pandora has never been large. In 1884 there were about two hundred people there. Between 1885 and 1892 this figure dropped to around twenty-five. Then, in 1902 and 1903, it was back up to one hundred.

In addition to the Pandora Mine itself, several other valuable and well known mineral properties figured prominently in the story of life at Pandora. J. H. Ernest Waters, a professional mining engineer who had been retained by the Imperial Government of China, also acted as an agent in several mining deals for English and Scottish banking houses at Shanghai. Instead of seeking out and developing new locations of their own, Waters' capitalist backers urged him to secure controlling interests in some of the better-known properties around Telluride. With this in mind, he approached the Pandora and Oriental Mining Company in 1888 and purchased the Pandora Mill. Shortly after the transaction had been completed, Waters ordered new equipment and made several changes to facilitate treatment of those ores from the company holdings in the Marshall Basin. At that time, this financial combine either owned or controlled the Mendota, Sheridan, and the combined Smuggler-Union mines.

For many years Pandora was practically a company town. From the great mines on the peaks above, a rather expensive 6,700-foot-long aerial tram was built from the site of the Smuggler-Union down to the flotation mill at Pandora. When it operated at peak efficiency, between three and four hundred tons of ore were moved down to Pandora each day. Powered by electricity, this engineering marvel carried supplies on the return trip back up to the mine in the otherwise empty buckets. Only thirty years ago, visitors could still ride the tram on the twenty-minute trip each way between Pandora and the Smuggler-Union. One condition prevailed, however. The rider must waive all liability in the event of an accident.

During the boom years, Otto Mear's Rio Grande Southern Railroad ran a wye or spur line from Telluride out to Pandora to facilitate the shipment of ores and supplies. For many years the Smuggler-Union maintained managers' quarters at Pandora. During the evening of November 19, 1902, one of their resident managers, Arthur Collins, was sitting by the window in the living room. Viewed in retrospect, this was an unfortunate and careless act on Collins' part. In the course of a particularly bitter labor dispute, acts of personal violence had become common. In any case, a shot came through the window, killing Collins where he sat. Although few people entertained serious doubts about its instigation, the act was never successfully pinned on the Western Federation of Miners.

Following the murder, Colonel Livermore placed Bulkeley Wells in charge as the new manager for the Smuggler-Union. Wells was not only a colorful character in his own right but was also a much-overlooked and rather important person in the affairs of San Miguel County at the turn of the century.

His varied career has been well detailed by Wilson Rockwell in his fine book, *Uncompahgre Country*.

While the company headquarters was at Boston during this period, Wells nevertheless spent considerable time in Colorado. On his frequent visits he always stayed at the same house in which Collins had been murdered. During the 1903 strike, Colorado's governor had sent in the state militia in an effort to restore order. Bulkeley Wells was sworn in as a captain of the militia and a state of martial law was declared. Later, of course, the strike was settled after some unionists had been deported from the district.

Years later, on another of his visits to Pandora, Wells retired for the night on March 28, 1908, choosing to sleep on the second-floor porch of the company-owned residence. During the early morning hours, a time bomb exploded beneath his bed. The blast nearly destroyed one side of the house. Wells was propelled, mattress and all, out into the yard. Miraculously, he managed to ride the mattress down, staying on the top of it and thereby avoiding serious injury.

Next morning, a company employee visited the site after the *Denver Post* had phoned him a report of the incident. In a recent interview he told me about entering the house and what he found there. Wells, it seems, always slept with a loaded revolver beside his bed, a fact that should shed some light on his feelings about the personal safety of Bulkeley Wells at Pandora. Next morning, the gun was observed imbedded, barrel first, handle extending downward, from the porch ceiling. Below the place where the bed had been, a huge hole in the floor made it possible for one to look directly down onto the top of the dining table in the room below.

Today, milling still goes on at Pandora, and a few of the homes are occupied. Actually, Pandora is a most accessible town. Its altitude is only 8,995 feet above sea level and a fine road, State Highway 145, will carry you the two miles southeast from Telluride. From the edge of town, interesting footpaths traverse the cliffs above. One of these goes to the beautiful 365-foot-high Bridal Veil Falls and a breathtaking view of Pandora and the magnificent valley below you.*

* In this same general area, see also Tomboy, Vanadium, and Telluride.

With many of its neat little cottages, here was Pandora-Newport in its infancy

*A wide variety of mining activities has done much to alter
the present appearance of Pandora.*

39.

PERIGO

A. C. Gambell had left his home in Ohio to participate in the westward trek of nineteenth-century gold seekers. Prior to his arrival in Colorado, he had mined actively in California. When his luck took a turn for the worse, he joined the throngs of "go-backs" who turned their faces eastward once more. May of 1859 found him among the fresh arrivals at Golden Gate City (present Golden) where he proceeded to organize other miners for a concentrated mineral-seeking expedition. The first of the Pikes Peak boom towns mushroomed into existence in 1859 and in the early sixties as hordes of prospectors like these explored the hills in ever-expanding waves. Placer gold was the object of their search.

Following a few false starts, the Gambell party loaded supplies on their string of pack mules and started prospecting up South Boulder Canyon. In this, as in so many similar instances, the party became enveloped in a spring blizzard. In the face of the blinding snowstorm, their mules were turned loose to fend for themselves, while the men hoisted the packs onto their own shoulders. When the storm abated, they found their way into a high broad mountain meadow, watered by a stream that was tributary to South Boulder Creek. Here they made a primitive camp and threw up an array of hastily devised brush and log shelters.

Since both frost and deep snows often remain rather late at this elevation, Gambell and his men gathered dry wood for fires to thaw the ground. On June 6, 1859, promising deposits of placer gold were found adjacent to the stream bed.

When their quantities of food supplies were nearly depleted, Gambell and a few of the other men set out for Denver to buy hardware and to lay in a new supply of grub. Unfortunately, since hard money was in short supply at that time, the men took out about ninety dollars' worth of their gold dust to pay for the purchases.

In an environment already gone mad with the gold fever, the appearance of such a quantity of dust set off a near riot. Gambell should have known that such a quantity of gold would give him away like a shirt full of fleas. When Gambell and his men responded to questions with understandably vague answers about the source of their riches, antagonisms developed. Under cover of darkness, they slipped out of Denver and made their camp near Golden. When the rays of the morning sun roused them from their slumbers, an angry crowd of Denverites, who had followed along, surrounded them. Too sleepy to defend themselves, Gambell and his crew became prisoners of the impatient mob. The chances for help at this point became as scarce as hiccoughs at a prayer meeting. One thing led to another until the hapless Gambell was forced to tell where he had found the gold. Once the cat was out of the bag, the prisoners were rewarded with a fine breakfast and were released by their captors. Shaken but somewhat wiser for their experience, they returned to what was soon to be known as Gambell Gulch.

Among the variety of incoming migrants was a huge giant of a man named John M. Dumont who had come from Nebraska on a very exhausted mule. Accompanying him was a partner named Perigo. Not content to merely work the placer beds, Dumont and Perigo began searching for the hidden veins from which the placer gold must have washed down. Between them, they uncovered both the Gold Dirt and the Perigo lodes, on opposite sides of the gulch. The Gold Dirt produced somewhere between $30,000 and $2,000,000, depending on which sources one prefers to believe. John Q. A. Rollins once sold a thirty-three foot long claim on the Gold Dirt vein for $250,000.

Up from Black Hawk came W. L. Douglas who also staked out a claim on the same Gold Dirt vein. The profits extracted exceeded his wildest dreams. Douglas amassed a sizable fortune from a combination of hard work and incredible luck. When he sold out and left the district, he carried a roll of bills that enabled him to establish himself as a leading tycoon in the shoe business. In the years that followed, good fortune smiled and the W. L. Douglas Shoe Company of Brockton, Massachusetts, made its namesake both rich and famous. Above town, the Golden Flint Mining Company sank a deep shaft into the earth. Nearby, the Ophir, Savage, Golden Sun, Crown Point, Free Gold, and Virginia, poured out a golden torrent for several years.

As increasing numbers of people entered the gulch and their efforts to devise shelter resulted in the founding of a town big enough to house about five hundred people. At first it was called Gold Dirt, after the rich lode. Its best days were between 1862 and 1864. Nearly all of the buildings were of the conventional log construction. Quite an impressive array of one- and two-room cabins were built. Some housed saloons and stores along what was to become the business street. Later on, there was a mining revival in the 1870's and eighties. When their efforts met with success, they changed the name of the earlier town from Gold Dirt to Perigo.

During this period of renewed activity, more new buildings were put up all along the spine of old Gambell Gulch. Beyond this, some confusion has grown up around the intricate process of town naming. Quite apart from the usually accepted story about how Gold Dirt later became Perigo, another story also exists. This one insists that Gold Dirt and Perigo were actually two completely separate towns which grew up in the same gulch, but which were located about a mile apart. To further complicate things, there is in fact another little town just a mile below Perigo. Judging by the log construction, it is obviously very old. One other reference was found that described several small settlements,

In this early photograph of Perigo we see the settlement with its clusters of small log cabins.

Except for the background and the curves in the road, Perigo, today, bears little resemblance to its former self.

strung out for nearly the entire length of the gulch. In any case, the whole thing was known as the Independent Mining District.

In the early days, several arrastras are known to have been in operation here. Later, three different stamp mills were built. The largest and most successful of these was subsequently taken over by Peter McFarlane and Company of Central City, in partnership with Hendrie and Bolthoff of Denver. With a measure of prosperity achieved, Perigo acquired a post office. As time passed and life here assumed its own distinctive characteristics, Perigo became known as a particularly sociable sort of place. An exclusive Perigo Social Club grew up and flourished for many years. Frequent community dances were held to help the residents pass the time. Even legitimate theater was attempted, and serious efforts were made to attract road shows from Denver and Central City.

As time passed, the mines played out, and when the golden sands were exhausted, the miners moved on, leaving little behind to mark their brief stay. A. C. Gambell moved over the hills to mine at Nevadaville. Still later, he tried his luck once more in Middle Park. Concluding a very long and full life, he died in Denver on September 10, 1908. Today, his name has been victimized by contemporary misspelling and the site of his discovery is now known as Gamble Gulch.

To see this area, drive south of Rollinsville on Colorado State Highway 119 toward Black Hawk. Just under a mile outside the town, the road bends around a hill and Rollinsville is out of sight. From this point, take the first dirt road on your right and head up the gulch. At the only fork, keep to your left. The distance from the pavement to Perigo is almost exactly three miles of very passable dirt road. Most of Perigo is gone now. It was never a very large town, but its priority in time and its brief life have combined to furnish us with a true ghost town.*

---

* In the same general area, see also Russell Gulch, Mountain City, and Forks Creek.

40.

PITKIN

LATE IN JANUARY, 1879, a small band of prospectors carefully picked their way up into the heavily wooded and snow-filled valley of Quartz Creek, a branch of Tomichi Creek. There were already a number of locations where rich mineral float had been obtained along the banks of this same stream. Further prospecting convinced the party that they were in an area which might potentially rival and possibly even surpass the rich Leadville district. At a point roughly twenty-seven miles northeast of Gunnison, on the north bank of Quartz Creek, they made their camp. For several weeks they prospected. At last they decided that this location was, in fact, going to be a good one, and a crude building was started in the dead of winter. On George Washington's birthday, February 22, 1879, they located their town. Roughly thirty men stayed in camp that first winter. In addition to their tents, a few cabins with dirt roofs were put up. There was also a tent hotel which charged fifty cents per body per night. For a name, they chose Quartzville, although some in the party preferred just plain Quartz or Quartz Camp.

By April, with heavy snows all around and not much else to do, the men grew tired of the original name. Frank Curtiss, a miner, was a close friend of Frederick W. Pitkin, popular governor of Colorado. After some discussion, they decided to call their town Pitkin in honor of the chief executive of the state. A. J. Sparks surveyed the townsite but neglected to file his plot at Gunnison until July 16, 1879.

As Pitkin, the town was formally incorporated in April of 1880. By May of that year there were fifteen hotels and boardinghouses. Best known among them were the Pitkin Hotel and the European House. Soon a post office was established and, to no one's surprise, Frank Curtiss became the first postmaster, proving once again that it's not so much what you know as who you know. Prior to this, all mail had been carried in on horseback from Alpine.

As the town grew, the business district started to fill up. There were the usual stores and saloons, a bank, a sampling works to test the quality of new ore discoveries, two schools, and several churches. The first formal sermon was preached in the town on June 6, 1880. On the surface, this would seem to be a rather imposing array of enterprises for a new town, but you can't win them all. When a reporter for the *Ouray Times* was in town, one disgruntled resident complained as follows: "There are only three women, seven children, one hundred and eighty dogs, one cat, two burros, and three fiddlers in Pitkin. What we need is a newspaper and a saw mill." On July 23, the paper published this account in full.

Before the year was up, Pitkin had acquired both of its "needs." A weekly newspaper, the *Pitkin Independent*, was a reality beginning on July 1, 1880. Frank Sheafor was the founder, owner, publisher, and chief reporter. Well before the first snow fell there were also five sawmills running in the town. About seventy-five new prospectors per day had come in during the summer of 1880 to seek their fortunes. In this early phase, Pitkin was a rather rough and tumble place. Work crews from the Alpine Tunnel descended onto the town every weekend and kept the saloons and dance halls humming. When these toughs were in town, the respectable citizens locked their doors and went to bed.

Although there was an abundant supply of wild game, local cooks demanded, and got, more variety. All foods and most other supplies were freighted up from Alamosa until the railroad was finished. Hay sold at $100 a ton and flour cost 80¢ per pound. Ham and beefsteak were more reasonable at 18¢ and 20¢ per pound respectively. Eggs sold for 40¢ a dozen. Later there was daily stagecoach service from Gunnison. After the Alpine Tunnel was completed, the first train steamed down into the newly erected station on July 12, 1882. In fact, Pitkin became the first permanent settlement on the Denver, South Park and Pacific Railway on the western slope of the main range. From a distance standpoint, Pitkin is twelve miles below the Alpine Tunnel, twenty-five miles northeast of Gunnison, and about forty-two miles from Buena Vista, as the crow flies.

When Frank Fossett visited the town in 1880, he was quite well impressed. He described it as a "lively and populous mining town with many civilized institutions." The population of Pitkin was fairly stable. It had 1,050 people in 1880, about 1,500 in 1881, and could still boast of 1,881 souls in 1893.

Mining claims were almost as numerous as the people. An accidental discovery in 1878 revealed the presence of wire silver and started the Fairview, Pitkin's first mine. It continued to ship increasing quantities of good ore to market until 1893. When mining interest declined in Gunnison County, Pitkin suffered along with the rest of its contemporaries. Prestige was restored a few years later when the deposits were better understood and subsequently were worked by more experienced miners. Among the more prominent mines were the Red Jacket, the Silver Islet (or Eyelet), which produced 744-ounce silver bricks, and the Sacramento which was worked almost continuously after 1890. It was made up of twenty-three claims on the same gold belt and was located about three miles northwest of Pitkin.

Most of the mines around Pitkin produced both gold and silver. In general, they produced ores that assayed out at from $60 to $20,000 to the ton, a rather wide range in values. For many years the roster of mines around Pitkin was an extensive one. It carried names like the Iron Cap,

Little Per Cent, Sultana, Silent Friend, Chloride King, Terrible, Nest Egg, Sulton, Wampum, Tycoon, Little Nellie, and Silver Age. Some among them were fine producers. Each new discovery was heralded as a great bonanza and sent hordes of people into deep shafts to chip away the mountainsides, a pound at a time. A few succeeded abundantly and accumulated generous fortunes over the years.

For the most part mining was suspended after 1893. Here, as elsewhere, the reason was Grover Cleveland's interest in tariff reform and in preserving the credit of the government. On August 7, 1893, he called the Congress into extra session and asked for an immediate repeal of the Sherman Silver Purchase Act. In late October, after extended wrangling in the Senate, he got his wish. Gold production around Pitkin continued sporadically but silver mining went into an eclipse. A new city hall was built in 1901, and the first telephones in town were installed in 1904.

So, gradually, other activities than mining began to dominate the local economy. Two years previously, in 1891, a State Fish Hatchery was built just below Pitkin. Still in operation, it now produces about 91,000 tons of trout annually. Here, where the altitude is 9,220 feet, fine timber stands grow. In the 1890's a lumbering industry was started. Presently, sawmills account for much of the town's prosperity. Many families left as a result of the depression of 1925. At that time the only industry in town was cutting timber for railroad ties.

Pitkin is a beautiful mountain spot. To see it, drive to Parlin on U.S. Highway 50, west of Monarch Pass. Turn northwest at this point and go nine miles to Ohio City. From there, go on for seven more miles to Pitkin. Just north of the town there is a beautiful campground. Nearby is the new road to the west side of the Alpine Tunnel. Fishing is usually good in the nearby streams and there are many attractions in the Quartz Creek Valley to make your stay enjoyable.*

---

* In the same general area, see also Alpine.

An early picture of Pitkin, looking toward the northeast

Pitkin, today, is a busy logging camp

41.

PLATORO

UNLIKE THE OBSCURE NAMES of its immediate neighbors, Stunner and Jasper, we know the origins of the name of Platoro. Quite simply, it was contracted from two Spanish words, *plata* for silver and *oro* for gold. Fortunately, limited quantities of both metals were found here. To pinpoint its location on a map, look at southern Colorado, in the central part. Platoro is twenty-two miles north and about fifteen miles west of Conejos. Here, in the high meadow which was chosen as a townsite, the elevation is 9,700 feet.

Although some earlier prospecting was done in the neighborhood, most accounts agree on 1882 as the actual year in which Platoro began to be built. During that year some claims were worked on the eastern slope of Conejos peak. Hall's *History of Colorado* specifically mentions the Peoria and Eurydice lodes and says that they were southwest of town. Whether both of my sources were referring to the same mineralization or not is unclear. From another quarter comes mention of the Parole and the Mammoth mines and their contributions to the wealth of Platoro. Also prominently mentioned were the Anchor, Merrimac, Chief, Mammoth, Puzzler, and the inevitable Last Chance mines. Spanning a somewhat more extended time schedule than that occupied by most of its neighbors, Platoro seems to have been a relatively stable district with new gold and silver claims recorded as late as 1901 and 1902.

Population statistics fluctuated typically through the eighties, with 1888 and 1889 listed as the peak years. After that things seem to have settled down somewhat since the population was reported at three hundred people in both 1890 and again in 1895. Transportation, or the lack of it, played a dominant role in the history of Platoro. Good roads were the greatest need from the start. During 1888 a wagon road was built toward the southwest from Del Norte. Late that year it reached Summitville and crested the range. Following an already established trail, it descended the southern slopes and followed the Conejos River into Platoro.

Being built in the wide meadow cut by the Conejos River presented both advantages and problems. The advantages are too common and too obvious to be worthy of mention. One of the problems is obvious from the accompanying pictures. During those years when heavy snowpacks built up on the peaks above the town, warm spring days sometimes brought a flood rushing down into the town, overflowing the banks of the river. Three separate floods have inundated Platoro during its recorded history. When the town was barely two years old the Conejos spilled over its banks for the first time. Old records say that the flood of 1884 reached a "record high" but fail to give any statistics. When history repeated itself on June 10, 1905, the *Del Norte Prospector* carried an item calling Platoro's water level the "highest in twenty years." Again, no depth figures were supplied. On October 5 and 6, 1911, Platoro got its feet and foundations wet for the third and final time. A recently constructed reservoir nearby seems to have decreased the chances of a recurrence in the immediate future.

Further relief on the transportation front seemed in sight when the Platoro Toll Road Company filed their articles of incorporation on July 14, 1890. Almost at once they began to construct a road from McDonald's Ranch, on the Alamosa River, over the mountains to Platoro. Immediate work not only improved the mineral prospects but assured winter access to the district beginning during 1891. Before it was completed, this formidable undertaking ran up a bill of eighteen thousand dollars. Even today the grades are still there and are known locally as the Silver Lakes Road.

Over the long haul, most of the factors that had contributed to the demise of nearby Stunner helped to spell out the final act at Platoro. Although many of the "mines were still doing relatively well, Platoro was just too isolated for full development under these circumstances and at this time in history. At another time the story might have been different.

In its contemporary existence, Platoro is a sleepy little resort village where vacationers and sportsmen come to get away from it all, to pursue the wily trout or just to relax. A ranger station and good accommodations are available in the town.

Platoro may be visited by driving west on Highway 17 from Conejos and then north along the Conejos River to the town. It is also accessible by the road that goes southwest from Del Norte through Summitville and over Stunner Pass. From atop the pass, Platoro is clearly visible in the high meadow below you. My favorite route follows the same instructions given in the chapters about Jasper and Stunner. Briefly, follow Highway 15 south of Monte Vista for twelve miles. Here the pavement stops. From this point a graded road leads directly west. All along the way, frequently spaced signs direct you to the Platoro Reservoir. The town is beside it, surrounded by pretty mountains, and nestled in a quiet, restful, historically rich environment.*

---

* In this same general area, see also Stunner and Jasper.

Looking along the main street of Platoro, with Stunner Pass in the background

A few original structures still line the old road through Platoro

42.

PUMA CITY

IN 1896 A VETERAN GOLD SEEKER, known to history only as
Rocky Mountain Jim, had been prospecting in the Tarryall
country. Jim was an experienced miner who had cut his eyeteeth on the Cripple Creek excitement. On this occasion he
made camp on an outcropping of porphyritic quartz that
had attracted his attention. At the time he had failed to stake
a formal claim. Four days later, he thought better of his
actions, gathered up his two partners, and returned to the
site. His associates were Sam Swingley and W. H. Preston,
the clerk and treasurer, respectively, of the city of Victor.
This edition of Rocky Mountain Jim should not be confused
with the original Rocky Mountain Jim, James Nugent, who
was murdered near Estes Park in 1874.

On this second trip the proper claims were filed around
the outcroppings in the midst of a large, open meadow at
an elevation of 8,500 feet. Soon the word was out and the
ensuing rush resulted in the founding of Puma City. Within a few weeks C. W. Gilman had laid out the plat for a
town covering approximately forty acres of placer ground.
By the time winter snow fell, there were about fifty houses,
log cabins, and tents. Roughly twenty-six of these were
spread out along both sides of Simmons Avenue, the principal
business street.

One newspaper, the *Puma Ledger,* told the outside world
about life in the new camp. Two sawmills were kept busy
turning out rough planks and finished lumber for the growing construction demands at the town. Five saloons also en-

joyed a flourishing business. Several restaurants took care of the hopes of a migrant population for a more substantial fare. Among the stores one could find a general merchandise, a hardware store, and a meat market. Lodging houses did a good business and there was also a dance hall which was never in want of customers.

Three hotels kept their doors open during the boom. One of these was a large structure with many rooms that had been torn down and moved from Cripple Creek. At its previous location this building had been known as Casey's Flats, a bordello in the red-light district on notorious Myers Avenue.

By 1896 the Tarryall post office had been established to better serve the three hundred people who had settled there. When 1897 rolled around, this number had grown to one thousand. Most accounts agree that Puma City had reached the peak of its boom. An estimated fifty newcomers poured into the camp daily during that year. Lots of others must have pulled out during this same period—otherwise the population would have soared astronomically.

A daily stagecoach brought in both passengers and mail from Lake George, thirteen miles to the south. The same line also ran on to Florissant and Cripple Creek. From the latter point, the distance was forty miles and the time required to ride from there to Puma City was eight hours. The nearest railroad connection was at Lake George where the Colorado Midland could be boarded for the ride to either Colorado Springs or Cripple Creek.

Because the climate was relatively mild here, people remained at the site all year and the mines stayed open through the winter. Among them were the Boomer, which had a shaft only forty feet deep. Nevertheless, it was shipping ore that assayed between $85 and $100 to the ton in gold, silver, and lead. The Comstock produced less valuable ores that were worth only $10 to $18 in gold. J. V. Malone, who may have been the Puma City Rocky Mountain Jim according to one source, located the June Mine on June 1,

1895. It actually adjoined the Puma City townsite. The Tarryall Prince had a naturally formed round chimney of ore, a geological rarity.

On Scheppe Hill, the No Name Mine was owned by A. K. Bay, of Denver. It had a one-hundred-foot-deep shaft with a ninety-five-foot crosscut. Their assays ran $25 to $58 in gold. Nearby, the Louisa group had only a fifty-foot shaft and was not nearly as rich as its neighbor. A Chicago syndicate owned the Hammond group of mines and their 2,200-foot-long Big 6 Tunnel. Another tunnel, the Bonnie H, was only 110 feet long. It was owned by Mr. H. Webb, of Milwaukee. Ore shipments from the Sunday Mine assayed $47 at the Grant Smelter in Denver.

The Colonel Sellers Lode was worked by the firm of Walsh and Scott, under bond for $11,000. Edward Parker, of Colorado Springs, owned a property called the Hard to Beat. From Omaha, C. M. Hunt came west and operated the Redskin Mining Company. In addition there were the Climax, Tenderfoot, Allie S, Electric, Plymouth, and Barnaby. Quite apart from the extraction of the more precious metals, many of these mines also shipped copper ores which were worth an average of thirty dollars a ton. Between fifteen and twenty properties were shipping ore on a year-around basis. Using this number, the newspaper pleaded for a mill in 1898.

The decline of Puma City is attributable to nothing more sophisticated than a wholesale collapse of the mining boom. One account says the whole show came dangerously close to a hoax anyway and that the mining estimates were rather inflated. When the true facts became known, the whole thing just collapsed like a house of cards. In any event, its life span was a very short one.

In the present century, old Puma City has taken the name of its post office and is now officially called Tarryall. It is reached by a good dirt road that runs northwest from Lake George on U.S. 24. The dirt road passes through Tarryall, cuts up through South Park and ends at Jefferson on U.S.

Photo by U. S. Geological Survey
This early picture of Puma City shows some of the typical Western architecture

Collection of Robert L. Brown
*Puma City is now called Tarryall. The old city is adjacent
to the contemporary community.*

285. Access is equally good from the north or Jefferson end of the road. The original Puma City was barely west of the present town of Tarryall, in the open meadow toward the mountains. Only a few traces of it remain.*

---

* In this same general area, see also Alma, Buckskin Joe, Fairplay, Quartzville, Montgomery, Leavick, and Sacramento.

43.

QUARTZVILLE

IN POINT OF TIME, Quartzville dates from the very earliest phases of Colorado's mining period. For three years disappointed miners from Denver, Gregory Gulch, the Blue River district, and California Gulch had been combing the promising terrain of South Park. As a result, towns such as Montgomery, Tarryall, Hamilton, and Buckskin Joe had grown up around a variety of rich gold deposits. Almost inevitably, other strikes would be made. Before the mining period ended, a grand total of something over twenty-five gold and silver camps came into existence in and around South Park.

In the process of prospecting among the towering peaks of the Mosquito Range at the western extremity of the park, promising quartz lodes were unearthed on the high, subalpine slopes of 14,163-foot-high Mount Bross. There, on the eastern face, a sheltered, cuplike depression was found just below timberline. In this bowl or sunken meadow, the miners hastily erected a collection of log dwellings. One early account tells us that there were fifty cabins in 1861, plus an assortment of tents.

Shortly after the initial discovery had been made, the miners came together in a common meeting and formed the Independent Mining District. For most of the remainder of that year, the population of Quartzville hovered between sixty and one hundred men. In his book *The Snow-Shoe Itinerant* the Rev. John L. Dyer recalled a trip up Mount Bross to the 11,300-foot elevation where Quartzville was cinched down tight to the mountainside. There, in August of 1861, Father Dyer preached his doctrine of salvation to about thirty attentive listeners. His sermon was calculated to keep them from the alluring and, under the bone-chilling circumstances prevalent at this high altitude, utterly desirable flames of Hades. Dyer said that he "felt that the Lord was with us indeed." Following the service, he walked back sixteen miles and held two other services at unspecified locations. Incidentally, at that time Rev. Dyer referred to Mount Bross as Quartz Hill.

Later that year there was a decline in local mining fortunes, but there was also a revival before the end of 1861. At that time silver was discovered in the Moose Mine, high above the town, and Quartzville entered a second phase of life as a silver camp. As an interesting sidelight, the entrance to the main tunnel of the Moose was situated at an elevation of nearly fourteen thousand feet above sea level. The Moose was also the only property on the peak that was worked during the winters of 1871 and 1872. Over the years, the combined Moose and Russia mines turned out ores worth something over three million dollars.

Other mines that contributed to the economy of Quartzville included the Putman Lode, which had actually been the first discovery, the Hail group which were located in 1871, and the Democrat, which was a gold producer. Inevitably, many claims changed hands over the years. In most instances the prices of claims in the Independent Mining District ranged between one and two thousand dollars.

Shortly after the camp was founded, some placer mining was attempted but in general it was not a successful proposition. At one point there were also a few arrastras in operation but these, too, were abandoned. Some of the silver ores were of a type that was difficult to treat locally. In this, as in so many such cases, the ores were shipped overseas to Swansea, Wales, for refinement. Much ore from the Montezuma–Saints John area of Summit County was also sent to Swansea. More cabins were built during the early 1870's and by the

Here are some of the ten or fifteen remaining structures at Quartzville

Here is Quartzville, under a mantle of fresh snow

summer of 1872, over two hundred people were living there. Once more the fortunes of the town began to fade in 1878 or 1879, and the town was abandoned once again. But Quartzville steadfastly refused to die. A third revival was effected in 1884 when the Quartzville Tunnel had been excavated. For the pioneers who returned, life went on as usual for some years but the peak had been passed. Some traffic, principally ore and supply wagons, moved up and down the old wagon road from Dudley. In winter, jack teams hauled supplies up the mountain and packed the unrefined ores down to the mills around Alma and Fairplay. Finally, the repeal of the Sherman Silver Purchase Act in 1893 succeeded in emptying Quartzville for the last time.

From the empty site of Dudley, just northwest of Alma, the old original wagon road leads off to the left from State Highway No. 9 as you drive north. Dudley, was just beyond the point where the highway crosses the Platte River. From the Placer Valley settlement that now follows the river up to the site of Montgomery and the Colorado Springs Reservoir, a new road leads off across the stream and goes directly up the mountain to Quartzville. Both of these are four-wheel-drive roads and should not be attempted before July in most cases. At Quartzville today, the tumbled-down remains of several cabins may still be seen, nestled in one of the wildest and most beautiful of high-altitude mountain settings, a truly remote and nearly forgotten relic of the period when gold and silver held the promise of Colorado's future.*

---

* In this same general area, see also Alma, Buckskin Joe, Fairplay, Puma City, Montgomery, Leavick, and Sacramento.

44.

RUBY

For the pioneer postmasters of Colorado, life must have been confusing indeed. In several instances the same names were chosen for different and often widely separated communities. For many years Ruby was one of these. Although the town of Ruby in Gunnison County was often called Ruby-Irwin, some confusion has resulted over the years. All of the material in this chapter will deal with the town of Ruby near Aspen, in Pitkin County but close to the edge of Chaffee County.

Quite apart from some published information which places the town's chronology in the 1890's, the area's beginnings should be moved back to about a decade earlier. In the course of seeking out good mineral prospects, unemployed argonauts from Independence (not the Independence by Cripple Creek, but the one on Independence Pass) explored the possibilities of a variety of streams tributary to the Roaring Fork River. After negotiating a crossing of nearby Green Mountain, they prospected up Lincoln Gulch, following the stream back into the high country.

In the spring of 1880 they found several veins of good ruby silver ore at a point about ten miles south of Independence. This distance should be regarded with an "as the crow flies" computation since by road or trail the actual distance one must travel to get there was and is considerably greater. In reality, the two towns are just over the mountain from each other.

Inevitably, when the news spread, a small rush came rolling

up the creek bed. Most of the early mines were holed in at the head of the gulch, barely below timberline. And wherever there was a mine, a settlement sprang up. The largest and most prominent of these early attempts at colonization was known as Hurst's Camp. Among the early claims were the Scottish Chief, Lone Bay, Jennie Larson (or Larsen), Windsor, North Star, and Tenderfoot.

Before the first snows fell, the miners got together and decided to set up a mining district. Its name was chosen from the nearby creek and the Lincoln Mining District came into existence. Although most of the organizers seem to have come from Hurst's Camp, the name of South Independence appears to have been in rather general use at about this time.

Changing the name of one's town to fill the idle hours was a highly favored form of pioneer recreation. Nearby Independence went through a grand total of five completely different names before it finally settled down. Seemingly the only deterrent to this continuing practice was exhaustion of the mineral deposits and abandonment of the towns.

From the beginnings, perceptive persons should have been able to predict causes for the town's eventual demise. Actually, poor roads and high transportation costs killed the town. Most of the mines were relatively good producers, capable of returning a fair share for a day's work. In the beginning most of the unrefined ores were transported out by burro packtrains to Leadville. No refineries were erected at South Independence in this earlier period.

Their trail led out over Red Mountain (another multiple namesake), through Taylor Park to Everett, and ultimately to Leadville. For many years this long haul cut deeply into profits. Thus, in the course of time, mining operations at Ruby tended to grow less and less attractive to risk capital. When a new trail was built to the site in 1900, it improved matters somewhat but in general it was described as "too little, too late."

Quite apart from the difficulties imposed by the natural

or geographical environment, the town's name now underwent its third and final change. From then on, Ruby became
its official designation, derived from its close proximity to
Red Mountain or to the presence of ruby silver, the accounts
vary. In another source it was stated that the name Ruby
was assumed in 1900 when the Ruby Mines and Development
Company (or Corporation) began operating in the valley.
Physically, the town was composed of a single, rather steep,
principal street which stretched up the mountainside for
approximately a mile. Along both its sides, log structures
of various sizes and shapes, lined the solitary thoroughfare.

Apart from stores and a few other commercial houses,
log-sided cabins that were homes for the miners were about
the only structures in the town. Down near the trail one
may still see the old stable and a moderately good-sized
boardinghouse that usually sheltered about forty or fifty
unmarried miners. No particularly notorious saloons or
gambling dens are described in the old records. There were
never any churches at Ruby either. An occasional circuit
rider sometimes found time to conduct services in private
homes, however.

In 1900 the Ruby Mining and Development Company put
up a fifty-ton concentrator which was equipped with a
crusher and shaker tables. Scarcely less significant was the
long tunnel they drilled deep under Red Mountain. To better supply the miners' wants, a better wagon road was built
up from the original Roaring Fork road in 1906. Taken as
a whole, the activities of the company showed signs of prolonging the life of Ruby. With the transportation problem
temporarily whipped, large quantities of the ore were hauled
out to Aspen for shipment.

For more than six years the future seemed assured. New
people migrated to Ruby to try their luck in the mines.
Wherever the miners went, shopkeepers, lawyers, and all the
other multitudinous elements that combine to bring that pe-
culiar state of affairs we call civilization, followed along and

the future appeared promising. With a grubstake, shovel, pick and washing pan strapped to a mule's back, the prospectors came up the new trail. Few obstacles could have checked their enthusiasm. A few succeeded abundantly, but taken as a whole the new activity merely forestalled the inevitable decline for a few more years.

Like so many fine projects, Ruby's tiny boom amounted to little. The impatient crowd of prospectors, traders, miners, and gamblers were doomed to disappointment. By the close of 1912 the handwriting was on the wall. Although the new road was an improvement, it wasn't enough. The long hauls soon ate up the meager profits that were left after meeting increased milling costs.

When the Barnes brothers, last of the operators at Ruby, gave it up in the face of minimal profits, the exodus began. Over the years several individuals leased the properties and tried to buck the tide. But in general most traffic now led back down the hill.

At this writing Ruby is a completely dead town, far advanced toward the process of complete decay. Although several scattered buildings may still be seen at the site, all of them show the marks of decades of neglect.

From the Twin Lakes Reservoir near U.S. Highway 24, north of Buena Vista, State Highway 82 starts its journey northwest over Independence Pass toward Glenwood Springs. Well down the western side toward Aspen, one may enjoy a choice of several attractive campgrounds. Among these is the Lincoln Gulch campground, situated on the south side of the road.

This site is the key to finding Ruby. As you enter this facility, a fork in the road offers you a choice of turning left to the campsites or turning right on an unmarked road that crosses a small bridge. The latter road will carry you to Ruby. Although several roads intersect along the way, stay on the one that is marked to Grizzly Reservoir. Where intersections are not marked, stay on the well-worn trail. When you

The old town of Ruby had a mile-long street leading up this hill and among the trees

Photo by Dick Lindvall
Being able to observe Colorado bighorn sheep in their natural habitat is one of the fringe benefits that accrues from exploring the back country.

reach the reservoir, drive to the far end where a trail starts up the hill to your left.

Athough a battered sign was standing at this corner during our last visit in 1964, I have heard that it is now gone. It used to show the mileage to Ruby. From this point on, proceed with caution, particularly if there has been any rain in the preceding week or two.

Within the past few years I have heard several times of people who drove their cars to Ruby. We took our Jeep and were glad that we had not chosen to expose our conventional car to this particular road. Many soft spots, sharp dips, and considerable water may be found along the way. Just remember that the greatest problem to the pioneers was that of maintaining a decent road to Ruby and that the same elements still combine to keep this trail primitive.

While you may certainly expect to drive to Grizzly Reservoir without incident, my advice is caution if you choose to drive on up the trail to Ruby. Better yet, why not park and enjoy a beautiful hike up the trail to a most picturesque old ghost town?

45.

RUSSELL GULCH

In most instances the westward migration that settled the trans-Mississippi country proceeded along in a fairly orderly progression. Then came the discovery of gold in California, and the whole tier of what would become the Rocky Mountain states was literally jumped over in the process of getting to Sutter's Mill as quickly as possible. Those Western states ranging from Nevada eastward to the Great Plains were settled in a virtual backwash of disappointed argonauts who had failed in California. Colorado, peopled a full decade after the California rush, was one of these states, and William Greenberry Russell was one of the unsuccessful gold seekers who gave it up and returned homeward, as fate would have it, by way of Colorado.

Green Russell was a native of Auraria in Lumpkin County, Georgia. He considered himself a professional prospector as a result of his having taken part in the 1827 gold rush in northwestern Georgia. Here a pattern was set that would be followed innumerable times during the settlement of the American West. The gold discoveries were on Cherokee Indian land and Russell was part Cherokee. His wife was a full-blooded member of the tribe. When the presence of gold was positively established, "Indian troubles" inevitably developed and the tribes were excluded from Georgia in 1830.

Following some abortive attempts to regain their land in Lumpkin County, Russell and his brother got out and started for Sutter's Mill with the hundreds of other Forty-niners. Enough gold was found to finance another return to Georgia and one more unsuccessful attempt to regain the family estate. By the 1857 financial panic, the Russell family was again impoverished.

Being financially embarrassed and having no place to go, Russell thought back again to his journeys through the Platte River Basin. His prospecting propensities caused him to suspect the existence of gold here. With his brothers he set out in 1858 for the Rocky Mountains. As the men moved westward, others joined them. By the time they had reached the Platte, there were about fifty in the party, mostly Cherokee Indians. To further their search, the men split up and worked both banks of the river. Both Cherry and Ralston creeks were also worked. No thought was given to deep or lode gold at this time. Their efforts were directed toward the recovery of placer gold or "dust."

When a war party of Plains Indians came by, the Georgians scattered to avoid a fight. Some loose gold was found on Dry Creek at a point about ten miles from their camp, prompting the men to work the Platte up to its source in South Park. Meanwhile, with cold weather approaching, Russell started north toward Fort Laramie to purchase supplies for the winter. Upon his return he discovered that a second party had arrived, from Lawrence, Kansas, and had appropriated his campsite. Hastily the Kansans threw together a handful of log cabins and called their settlement Montana City. Russell put up a cabin to shelter the members of his party who planned to spend the winter here while he returned to Georgia to recruit more help. He soon became aware of a growing interest in himself wherever he went. As so often happens, an unfounded rumor was spreading eastward ahead of Russell, describing eloquently how he had found gold. Being an honest man, he tried to squelch these stories of the "Russell Bonanza," only to find that people suspected his motives and figured he wanted to keep it all for himself.

In a shameless conspiracy to turn a tidy profit in the midst of a depression, Midwestern newspapers and businessmen embellished upon the story until Russell was powerless to stop them. The gold rush to Pikes Peak was on, and Green Russell became a hapless victim of history. Before he could return from Georgia, the residents of Montana City moved up to the junction of Cherry Creek and the South Platte River to start another town which they called St. Charles. Across Cherry Creek, a second settlement called Auraria came to life. St. Charles became Denver City and eventually absorbed Auraria, Montana City, and a third community off to the west called Highlands. The whole thing consisted of an amazing collection of tents, sod houses, log cabins, tepees, and mud.

By the summer of 1859, John Gregory and George Jackson had made gold discoveries in the mountains west of Denver, miraculously justifying the Pikes Peak gold rush. Green Russell suspected that the placer gold he had found in Dry Creek had washed down from the hills. At once he started into the mountains to seek the original lode. Instead of seeking his fortune at one of the established diggings, Russell made his way up Clear Creek Canyon, past the Gregory diggings, to a point three or four miles higher up the gulch. Apparently Gregory and Russell had experienced some misunderstanding back in their native Georgia. When they subsequently met in the gulch, they passed each other without a word.

Along the base of what is now known as Russell Gulch, Green Russell hit it again with the discovery of free gold. Word of his find leaked out, causing another stampede into the hills. As a settlement began to grow beside his discovery, the stream bisecting the townsite was worked for both dust and nuggets. Both sluices and waterwheels were used. Before the winter of 1859-60 moved in, a set of covenants for the Russell Mining District were drawn up. In several ways these were rather remarkable documents. For one thing, women were given equal rights with men. Another provision allowed claims to be held by anyone, except children who were under ten years of age.

By September, about eight hundred people had settled at Russell Gulch. Census figures for 1860 show 2,500 residents there. The town was built of log cabins, with a few frame homes of dressed lumber here and there in the large open meadow to the south of Quartz Hill. Soon there was a school, and fourteen pupils were in regular attendance in 1860. Eventually a brick schoolhouse was built. There was also a brick Federal hall in the town, plus the usual assortment of assay offices, general stores, and other business firms. The *Rocky Mountain News* reported on November 14, 1860, that Sunday services were being held at Russell Gulch. The article went on to state that a Dr. Rankin had preached to a crowded congregation; crowded since the house in which services were held was small, not because of the numbers present. Later, a frame-construction Methodist church was built on the hillside above the gulch.

During 1859 the miners took out about $20,000 in placer gold. By the next summer this sum was up to an average of $35,000 per week. After three or four years of work, the placers were abandoned. Moderately successful deep mining occupied the residents during the next twenty years. By 1881, the population was down to four hundred. Russell himself had left town back in 1862 for an enlistment in the Confederate Army. After the war he came back to Colorado and was a familiar figure until about 1875. At that time he left to accompany his wife and the other Cherokees to the reservation in Oklahoma.

Although Russell Gulch has declined in the twentieth century, it is not a deserted ghost town since there are still a few families living there. Also, a uranium boom in the 1920's attracted a population of about one hundred people. During the last depression, local bootleggers sought to circumvent the prohibition law by hiding their bootleg whiskey in the mine shafts. On one occasion the underworld

Russell Gulch was once a busy and prosperous place

To match these pictures, start with the outline of the hills against the sky

members themselves hid out down in the tunnels until the heat was off.

To see Russell Gulch today, drive up through Central City to the Triangle Parking Lot. From here several roads fan out. The extreme left one going up the hill past old wooden sidewalks leads to the Virginia Canyon Road which passes right through Russell Gulch on the way to Idaho Springs. From the other end, start at Idaho Springs and follow Virginia Canyon in reverse.

Russell Gulch was a particularly important pioneer settlement in early Colorado. It was important not only because it was one of the very earliest mining settlements, but also because it bears the name of one of Colorado's most distinguished pioneers.*

---

* In the same general area, see also Mountain City, Perigo, and Forks Creek.

46.

SACRAMENTO

CHRONOLOGICALLY, Sacramento dates from the discovery of silver ores and the location of six claims on October 22, 1878. Their names were Sacramento, October, Lark, Anniboby, Ada, and Watacka. The lucky prospectors were Charles W. Dwelle, a former manager of the Water Company of Denver; W. M. Tobie; D. B. Mullen; Napoleon P. La Duc; and C. J. Birdzell. On November 12, an adjoining claim, the Jessie, was located by A. J. Wells and Peter Hanson. Of this group, only Dwelle retained a long association with Sacramento.

Just across the range, very close as the crow flies, were the great silver mines surrounding the Leadville area. It seemed logical to mining men that the Leadville formation of blue limestone probably extended across to the South Park side of the range. Both Sacramento and Horseshoe gulches are capped with blue limestone. The well-known London Fault is only about four thousand feet west of the spot where the Sacramento Mine was located by careful and systematic explorations on the exposed parts of this blue limestone. The mine was capitalized at one hundred thousand dollars, with principal offices at Sacramento in Park County.

The Sacramento was duly incorporated and La Duc signed his articles with an "X." In January of 1879, stocks in the company were divided five ways. By far the greatest proportion of the original twenty cabins was built during this first year. All were of log construction but some sported an upper story and at least one had multiple gables on its roof.

Back in the trees one may still see a tremendous structure with a double roof, one above the other with air space in between. Perhaps the first one leaked.

In 1879, D. B. Mullen, by now the vice-president of the Sacramento Mining Company, carried a lump of sulphurets the size of his fist into Fairplay. Such an unorthodox and theatrical display threw the local people into a frenzy of excitement. He boasted at that time the ore body was four feet thick and very extensive. The sample assayed at $1.40 a pound in silver. Before 1879 had ended, a large two-story boardinghouse, a 26' x 30' office building, and a few new cabins had been erected at the site.

During 1880 a number of profitable new drifts were opened up and capitalists from Nevada, California, the Lake Superior region and elsewhere, bought into the Sacramento. A Congressman from Michigan and a son of Governor John Evans of Colorado also invested. As prosperity continued, a New York office was opened at 62 Broadway. During the month of July stocks in the Sacramento were on sale at the Hathaway Bank in Fairplay at five dollars a share.

The bonanza period of greatest production seems to have ended in 1881 but work continued into 1882. The ore had been of very high grade but was frequently spotty. Most of the production had come from a single stope at the west end of the mine. Once this main deposit was exhausted, no real ore was found thereafter. This, rather than low-grade ore, caused the decline of Sacramento. Gross profits from the Sacramento have been pegged at $175,000, including 1882. After that year several lessees worked the property from time to time but production was small.

Whether or not you can drive to Sacramento depends in large part upon the condition of the old trails at any given time. Start south from Fairplay and drive about a mile on the paved road. When you reach the top of the first hill, turn right (west) on the good dirt road that follows the old railroad grade. This is known locally as the Horseshoe Road or

Fourmile Creek Road, since it followed the creek and led up through the now empty meadow where a town called Horseshoe once existed. At this writing, a black and white metal sign with the name "Horseshoe" is tacked on a fence post at the point where the road leaves Highway 285. There is also a section of old rail ties in the vicinity of Horseshoe.

The road is always passable to Horseshoe. At this point a narrow trail takes off to the right and follows the original grade of the stagecoach road from Fairplay. Stay on the main road, disregard the two dim trails leading off to the left, until you have driven to the fork where the road again divides with the right branch seeming to enter a high, open meadow. Forking sharply to the left, the other branch stays in the timber and climbs gradually upward toward Sacramento. When last seen, a Forest Service sign marked this intersection with the distance back to Horseshoe. The wooded road up through the timber gets rough in spots and emerges into two or three meadows where huge gray stumps show evidence of extensive lumbering operations.

The miles seem long here since this road hasn't seen maintenance crews since the turn of the century and your progress will be slow. If it's any comfort, station wagons have successfully negotiated this road. Some of the newer cars with long rear overhangs and tiny wheels may have trouble now, however. The only rule of thumb here, or on any comparable road, is to know how much your car will clear since this terrain can hardly be called flat.

A few miles farther and you will emerge into another clearing where a stream bed, shallow or dry in summer, can be seen to your right. This is Spring Valley. Across it, to the north, near the trees, is an old cabin. From the cabin you can see a dim trail up through the trees. This leads without detour to Sacramento and the distance is less than a half mile. Cars have crossed the previously mentioned meadow at its lower or east end. Once across the stream, it's easy to drive north for fifty yards or so to the cabin. Cars have made it all the way up to Sacramento but a short hike might be safer from this point. If you drive, the road is not steep but there is an eroded crosscut near the point of a climbing turn which should be driven at an opposite angle. The road leads generally north and then west to the town which sits at an elevation of about 11,250 feet.

There are several cabins at Sacramento, scattered among the trees and along streets that have long since disappeared. On the downhill side of the town is another group of cabins, not visible from the main cluster of buildings. Continuing up the trail for a short distance, the Sacramento Mine is just off to the left. From the top of its dump one may enjoy a fine panorama including Fairplay and the extensive dredging operations in South Park.

Since Sacramento never progressed beyond the log-cabin stage, all of its structures are of that type. Due to the density of evergreen growth here, pictures including more than two or three buildings are difficult to take. A wide-angle lens helps. If time permits, the lower road from the last meadow below Sacramento may be followed by Jeep for several more miles until it disappears on top of the tundra. From this point the tops of several mountains are accessible, rendering a fine view of Mount Sherman and Mount Sheridan. The ghost town of Leavick is nestled in the valley far down below. At the present time, however, there is no road down the other side and it is necessary to return by the same way you came up.

One source, published not long ago, showed Sacramento as being located on Sacramento Creek, high up in Sacramento Gulch. This is logical enough but is untrue. Its actual location is one more range to the south.

The ride from Fairplay to Sacramento is not a long one and none of the distances is great. The scenery is fine and well worth your efforts.[*]

---

[*] In the same general area, see also Alma, Buckskin Joe, Fairplay, Puma City, Quartzville, Montgomery, and Leavick.

A rock retaining wall held these two houses up above the main road

These crumbled buildings are typical of the remains of Sacramento

47.

SALINA

IN POINT OF TIME, the first discovery of precious metals in Gold Run Gulch dates back to 1859 but it failed to produce a settlement. Although Gold Hill, two miles north, got started in this same year, no population overflow to speak of spilled down into the winding canyon. Another flurry of excitement resulted from a placer discovery in 1872, but once again people preferred to live elsewhere and commute up or down the gorge from other settlements.

The task of colonization devolved upon O. P. Hamilton and a party of six men from Salina, Kansas. Shortly after noon on April 27, 1874, they pitched their tents in Gold Run Gorge, below some old placer diggings. Apart from Gold Hill, the nearest settlement was Boulder, some ten miles to the southeast. Enough good tellurium ore was found to warrant their further attention. From then on things started looking up. Some among the party grew nostalgic and began referring to their cluster of tents as Camp Salina. Quite apart from their hometown as the source of the name, the word Salina is also a Spanish one meaning "salt mine," or "salt pit." Later, of course, the "camp" was dropped and the name Salina has persisted since that time.

Here, as elsewhere, the mines built the town. About thirty families showed up and prepared to settle here during the first year. By 1875 the population had reached one hundred. A telegraph line was extended from Boulder that same year. Cordial greetings from Boulder to Salina constituted the first message to be carried over the "Singing wires." The date was

January 15, 1875. By the end of the year Salina had eight thousand dollars' worth of new construction in place or going up along the crooked street that followed the twisting contours of Gold Run. In the beginning all mail was picked up at Boulder. Later, a post office was established at Salina. G. F. Mayer was the postmaster.

At first there was only one general store in the gulch. Later, as the town grew, so did the business district. In addition to the usual saloons, Salina also had its own assay office and soon there was a full-time blacksmith shop. Both William Hunt and H. C. Sartore opened up general merchandise stores. For the ladies, B. A. Bigger established Salina's first and only dry-goods store. Transients could find lodgings in the Salina House Hotel. Three boardinghouses sheltered and fed the bachelor contingent. One early newspaper account noted that there were many bachelors in town, a common condition in most mining camps. A town well was dug to provide water for most household purposes.

Unlike many of its contemporaries, Salina had a church of its own. In addition, a fine frame school building, which still stands and is shown in the accompanying photographs, held classes during a six-month term every year. When George Crofutt visited the town he mentioned that there were three mills in operation. Mr. Crofutt also spoke disparagingly of Salina's "high priced toll gate."

Without rich mines, the town could not have justified its existence. There were several good properties in the surrounding hills and gulches. The Melvina was probably the best of the lot. It was found almost on the top of Salina Mountain. Below the town, nearby in the creek bed, the Black Swan also turned out good ores. Many of the claims reflected a wistful yearning for home. Among these were the Kansas and the Salina mines. In addition there were the Leona, Baron, Ohio, Melonia, Emancipation, Ingram, Richmond, Victoria, Antioch, Tambourine, Great Eastern, Bessie Turner, and Mayflower properties.

Up until 1881 many people spent their time just washing gold from the creek. At first, most of the ores were hauled over the hills to the smelter in Black Hawk. Large numbers of oxen, horses, and mules were kept to pull the heavy ore wagons. When faced by the need to save transportation costs, the Ohio and Colorado Reduction and Mining Company installed a chlorination mill at the town late in 1875. This brought sufficient prosperity to justify another chlorination mill, owned by Mayer, Penn and Company. Salina boomed on tellurium ores from 1874 through 1876 but mining continued on a lesser scale for many more years.

A daily stagecoach service was operated out of Boulder, up the canyon through Salina, to Sunshine, just a mile over the hill. The line then went on and terminated at Gold Hill. Between 1881 and 1886 passengers could make connections to ride the little narrow-gauge trains over the Greeley, Salt Lake, and Pacific, later known as the "Switzerland Trail," to a variety of other Boulder County mining towns. Between 1881 and 1886 the line was operated by the Union Pacific until a flood washed out the tracks and necessitated abandonment. With the revival of mining, the right-of-way was acquired by the Denver, Boulder and Western. This, in turn, was later reorganized as the Colorado and Northwestern until its abandonment in 1919.

From the standpoint of population, Salina was never large. An impatient crowd of roughly one hundred people had crowded into the gulch by the end of 1877. Beginning with a few tents and four cabins, the town soon expanded to include twenty houses before the first year had ended. At the beginning of 1879, there were three hundred souls there and several more homes had been built along the hillsides. Shortly afterwards, people began to leave; but Salina still had about two hundred residents in 1883. By 1888 the records showed only 150 still holding out.

Then things started looking up a bit with 175 people there in 1897. Another gain was registered as mining interest was

*J. B. Sturtevant, early photographer of Boulder County,
took this fine old photograph of Salina.*

*By September of 1965, a growth of trees had done much to obscure
the view of Salina from this angle.*

renewed enough to attract still more people so that an all-time high of 350 was reached by 1899. Then there was another slump, but seventy-five people were still holding on once more in 1920. Even today, there is still a small resident population that swells slightly in summer and declines between September and June. Many houses, some original, still stand at the site, along with the fine little schoolhouse which is no longer used.

To see this pretty little mountain community, you should drive west out of Boulder on State Highway 119. Shortly after you enter Boulder Canyon, an unpaved road turns right and there is a sign about directions to Gold Hill. When the pavement stops, a well-graded dirt road goes on to Salina. If in doubt, follow the signs to Gold Hill; Salina is at the bottom of the hill just before you start up to Summerville and Gold Hill. If the little church happens to be open, take the time to set your emergency brake on the steep hill and go inside for a look at its minute interior and beautiful antique organ.

In a historical sense and in point of time, Salina has been fortunate enough to avoid the fate of becoming a ghost town. With the booming economy of Boulder County, the chances seem to be good that Salina will continue to be a live town with a promising future.*

---

* In this same general area, see also Tungsten, Camp Frances, and Eldora.

48.

SCOFIELD CITY

As THE WARMING RAYS of the rising sun crept slowly over the lofty ridges of the Elk Mountains, Joseph Evans crawled reluctantly out of his warm blanket roll to face the early morning chill that pervaded his high valley campsite. Although it was August, a thin frost that had formed in the night melted rapidly from the firewood as he slowly prepared his monotonous morning repast. Cautiously he scanned the immediate surroundings for hostile Utes. This was 1879, and Evans was an unwelcome trespasser deep within a hostile territory. Before the sun could retire that night, he would stake out an illegal townsite on the crest of one of the high ridges of the Elk Range.

Evans had been retained by S. H. Baker, Daniel Haines, B. F. Scofield, H. G. Ferris, William Aggee, E. D. Baker, G. Edwards, and A. H. Slossen to survey and plot a townsite on Rock Creek between Crystal City and the Elko Basin. Quite commonly a new location took the name of one of its early pioneers and somehow it was decided that the name of B. F. Scofield belonged on the handsome alpine park that Evans had selected, and on the fledging community as well. Before long a wagon road bisected the terrain and its nearby crest became Scofield Pass.

Some silver had been found on Rock Creek as early as 1872 but fear of Ute reprisals and an economic panic after 1873 served to retard permanent settlement until Evans selected the site near Galena and Crystal mountains. Although initially isolated, the Scofield group soon had company. Some eight miles to the southeast, another band of trespassers was founding Gothic. By 1879, Chief Ouray was busy quieting the Utes, making exploration somewhat safer but nevertheless technically illegal. To avoid possible confusion, Rock Creek is designated on contemporary maps as the Crystal River.

Almost overnight a ramshackle array of fifty to sixty foundationless log cabins sprang up near the edge of the meadow, exactly the right architectural environment for the birthplace of aspiring presidential candidates. Only one President, however, was ever associated with Scofield and he wasn't born here. Several sources have been at great pains to describe the more humorous aspects of a visit to Scofield by President Ulysses S. Grant. These accounts contain some discrepencies that ought to be cleared up. The date of his visit seems to have been 1880. This date seems correct since Grant's visit to nearby Gothic and Ruby-Irwin are also recorded in 1880. He rode into camp on a white mule, accompanied by ex-Governor John L. Routt, last territorial governor and first chief executive of the new state of Colorado. During his stay, E. E. Riland dug deep in his valise and concocted some home brew. This was done after the failure of some elements in the camp who had tried to sell Grant shares in a mine, and after they had failed, to "lose" some shares to him in a poker game. Now they hoped to get him drunk and give the claims to him so that they could boast of the President owning a mine at Scofield.

Prior to his departure, Grant's hosts showed him the Devil's Punch Bowl, a sheer cliff with a waterfall which drops into a deep hole of the Crystal River. For his benefit they identified it as S.O.B. Canyon or Gulch, the accounts do not agree. Needless to say, the initials were not employed, the full name was flamboyantly used. Grant roared his approval and shouted the name appreciatively across the canyon several times. At this point things get confusing. From one source we learn that Grant suggested renaming the spot Schultz

Canyon since he was running for reelection and this was
the name of his opponent. It makes a good story but Grant
was already out of the White House in 1880. His years as
President were between 1869 and 1877. Furthermore, he
never ran against anyone named Schultz. His opponent in
1868 was Horatio Seymour and in 1872 he defeated Horace
Greeley.

Grant may have said or meant Carl Schurz, who once led
an unsuccessful splinter rebellion within Grant's own Republican party with the slogan, "Anything to Beat Grant!"
If any basis for the S.O.B. story exists at all, this may be its
source. It is entirely possible that the old warrior had become confused, or muddled, imagining that he was back in
the political arena. If so, certain conclusions seem in order
with reference to the potency of the Riland brewing recipe.
Fortunately for Scofield, the General was not regressed to
the Civil War. Folklore and history make a dangerous, but
often amusing, combination.

Somewhere between two hundred and three hundred miners came to seek their fortunes at Scofield, quite apart from
the fallacious source that would have us believe two thousand
souls resided there. Counting transients might have swelled
the figure but not to such an extent. During the peak year
of 1882, we find records of the usual assortment of commercial enterprises that were indigenous to most Western
mining camps. They had a post office, a hotel run by a woman from Illinois, one restaurant with problems when they
tried to boil water at this nearly ten-thousand-foot elevation, a general store, carpenter shop, a barbershop, one blacksmith shop, and several saloons. Perhaps one of these was
operated by Riland the bootlegger. Daily mail service was
afforded by the stagecoach from Crested Butte which came
pounding up the stony right-of-way. To provide better
service, a stagecoach station was included at Scofield.

Taken as a whole, Scofield was one of the best developed
camps in the district. From Quincy, Illinois, came a group

of people with plans to install a forty-ton smelter at the park in 1880. Whether or not this was the same mill that was erected in 1881 cannot be resolved at this time. In all the surrounding gulches, men were busy digging for rich ores. Unfortunately, most of it was low grade. Although some good galena was found, the inaccessible location, coupled with high transportation costs, soon drained off the profits.

By 1885 the peak had passed and the post office had closed. All things considered, Scofield enjoyed between twelve and fourteen years of life before the real decline began in 1892. Some of the people moved on down the valley to start Crystal City at one of the prettiest spots in the West. Others left for newer boom towns elsewhere in the state.

Another contributing factor in the Scofield exodus was the almost annual presence of eight to fifteen feet of snow, lasting eight months of the year. Two-hundred-foot-deep slides were recorded more than once, and a forty-foot-deep drift once buried the town. The snowfall was particularly severe during the winter of 1896-97. Although the town was already deserted, a few miners had remained in the park to rework some of the outlying properties. Snowshoes were the order of the day for these men during almost the entire winter.

Scofield Park today is a wonderful spot. Our daughter received her first driving lesson there and can boast of learning to drive on top of a mountain pass. Our son found it the best of all possible places in which to fly his model airplane with no obstructions. The town is gone, except for a few rubble piles, and the area is flat, open, and green.

Only one route to Scofield is completely satisfactory. Drive north from Gunnison through Almont to Crested Butte. At the south edge of the latter town, turn right and stay on the main dirt road through Gothic and up the steep hill past Emerald Lake. You are now on the Scofield Pass road. From this point on, observe caution. While some cars and many

Scofield, high above the Crystal River Canyon in Gunnison County

Only a few scattered foundations now remain to mark the site of old Scofield

pickups have driven all the way to Scofield, it depends a lot on road conditions of the moment. A walk from Emerald Lake is not out of the question. After crossing the pass, the town was in the next open meadow, just a short distance away.

Conventional cars sometimes go down from here to the Crystal Valley but none come back up. A 25 percent grade on slide rock precludes this being anything but a Jeep road. Hot brakes are no rarity at the bottom and few people go back for seconds. With a Jeep, this trip is simple for even the beginning driver. Under any circumstances, barring bad weather, this will be a rewarding trip, one that will long be remembered and discussed during the long, cold winters that lie ahead.*

---

* In this same general area, see also Crested Butte, Crystal City, and Marble.

49.

SILVER CLIFF

FOR MANY YEARS after 1877, the carbonate craze extended all over the mountains, excited by the finds at Leadville, in Chaffee, Lake, Gunnison, and Summit counties. Most prospectors were searching for carbonates, and if what they found bore any resemblance to the ores at Leadville, it was at once proclaimed as a wonderful discovery.

To a decisive degree, silver mining dominated the second and third decades of mining in Colorado. The circumstances that resulted in the discovery and naming of Silver Cliff came about when R. J. Edwards, a transplanted prospector from Racine, Wisconsin, led two friends on a trip near the eastern foot of the Sangre de Cristo Mountains. Robert Powell and George Hofford, along with Edwards, had prospected and leased a number of mines around Rosita. All three men were living in Rosita at the time. Hofford had crossed the plains with the multitude during the original Pikes Peak gold rush of 1859, pushing a wheelbarrow that contained his blanket and provisions.

Three separate dates have been given for the discovery that they made. These are July of 1877, August of 1877, and June 29, 1878. A low, black-faced cliff, roughly thirty feet high, stood alone on the prairie near an old trail that crossed the Wet Mountain Valley from Oak Creek Canyon to Grape Creek. Such a conspicuous prominence could hardly have avoided attracting the attention of prospectors. On this occasion Edwards and his friends rediscovered it and broke off some of the black substance which they carried home to

Rosita for assaying. One sample showed 24¾ ounces of horn silver to the ton. This was a new metal to Edwards. Another sample turned out to have twenty ounces of gold to the ton. Although the gold figure was discovered to be in error, the word got out and there was a rush that nearly depleted both Rosita and Querida. When no other gold was found, the prospectors returned home.

Meanwhile, Edwards, Powell, and Hofford kept their silver discovery a secret. Hofford owned a team which they outfitted for a prolonged journey. While camped at the base of the cliff, they located the source of the horn silver and staked out their claim. At the beginning of the next summer Edwards returned and began to develop two locations. These became the Silver Cliff and the Racine Boy mines. One source states that both locations were found on June 20, 1878. Over the years, both mines were developed to a high degree. Some of the samples taken out during the second year showed 740 ounces to the ton in silver. When word leaked out, there was another rush, sending a stream of humanity into the Wet Mountain Valley, and a large town was hastily built near the base of the rich cliff.

Silver Cliff burst forth upon the Colorado scene soon after Leadville. It was pleasantly situated on the flats between Grape Creek and Round Mountain, at an elevation of 7,920 feet. Most people were confident that it would become a large and permanent city. The first house was built by two men named McIlhenny and Wilson in September of 1878. It was a small frame building that contained a general store and the first primitive post office. There were five thousand people there in 1880 and ten thousand at the peak of the boom a few years later. Ten miles of streets were built and maintained by a chain gang from the local jail. Evergreens and flowers were planted around the homes. W. H. Holmes laid out the townsite on 320 acres and patented it with the authorities on December 8, 1879. Following an election held the next February, the first set of town officers took over.

As the population grew, a water works was constructed, complete with twenty-nine fire hydrants by 1880. In the early days, water from the nearby springs were hawked through the streets at forty cents a barrel.

At first there were no churches. When families started to arrive, all that changed. The Episcopalians put up the first house of worship, followed closely by the Baptists, Seventh-Day Adventists, Presbyterians, Catholics and Methodists. After the churches, schools were soon built and then the other usual businesses followed. The county was divided into twenty school districts and there were some 1,400 children of school age. H. A. McIntyre purchased the interior fixtures of the old Boyd and Stewart Bank at Rosita and then opened a bank of his own at Silver Cliff. Two men named Reynolds and DeWalt bought him out and reopened under the name of the Merchants and Miners Bank. Later, a second bank was opened to handle the growing number of accounts. The Western and Cliff House hotels were soon followed by eight other hostelries, all eager to house those who had migrated to the Wet Mountain Valley.

By 1881, Silver Cliff had become the third largest city in Colorado. There were twenty grocery stores and ten dry-goods establishments in operation. Three sawmills were busy almost constantly, trying to keep up with growing demands for lumber. Cheap Charlie's Clothing Store and seven other similar outlets provided wearing apparel for the residents of the new city. There were seven meat markets, six barbershops, and for the ladies, five hairdressers.

At one time or another, seven newspapers have flourished at Silver Cliff. W. L. Stevens began by publishing the *Silver Cliff Miner* in 1878. Next came the *Silver Cliff Weekly Prospector* on May 5, 1879. Just a month later it dropped one word from the title and came out as a daily. The *Republican* first went to press on April 1, 1880, followed by the *Mining Gazette* in November of that same year. Two years later, Will C. Ferril established the *Daily Herald*. Incidentally, Mr. Ferril was the father of Colorado's distinguished poet-author-publisher, Thomas Hornsby Ferril. Finally, in the 1890's, the *Wet Mountain Tribune* and the *Silver Cliff Rustler* appeared. Shortly after the town was started, an active night life began to develop. For many years there were five theaters in town. Most notable of the group was the Gem Novelty Theatre. In addition to an unspecified number of dance halls, there were also twenty-five very busy saloons. One of these is known to have cleared two thousand dollars in a single ten-week period. They were so busy that the bar glasses were washed only once each day, whether they needed it or not. The well-known antiseptic qualities of alcohol probably saved the day and the customers as well. To assure a steady flow of customers for the rowdy part of town a parade was sometimes held at 6:00 P.M. Leading off in the finest "Pied Piper" tradition was a brass band. Next came marchers, sometimes slightly tipsy, carrying advertising placards and banners for the several sponsoring establishments. Finally, the big treat appeared. Horse-drawn buckboards, filled with the more presentable "dance hall girls," clattered down the street. Invitations were tendered, knowing winks exchanged, and another night was under way.

At the beginning there had been just a few mines on the cliff. With the passage of time, several more appeared. Speculation ran riot, mines were staked, bonded, and sold on the flimsiest evidence, often without development. Among the new mines that had appeared by the mid-1880's were the Island City, Lady Franklin, Plata Verda, Alta Verda, Crescent, Vanderbilt, Songbird, St. Mary's, Terrible, Rambler and Milkmaid. Several sampling works, four stamp mills and two smelters ran on a busy schedule. Most of these mines were rich in horn silver and were worked at the grass-roots level. On the other hand, the Racine Boy was a deep mine. Also in this latter category were the Bull and Domingo properties, in such close proximity to each other that, inevitably, lawsuits followed. In the courts, decisions went to both parties in a long series of trials. Attorneys for the Bull once pursued the harried judge while he was out fishing. With the help of copious libations from one of those twenty-five saloons, they got an order ousting the Domingo owners from their own property. Instead of fleeing, the Domingo group girded themselves for battle.

That night, following a brisk flurry, Bull men captured the surface buildings and boarded up the mouth of the tunnel while twenty-five Domingo miners were still at work far below. To add insult to injury, the Bull men hurled burning wads of waste, soaked with ammonia, sulphur, and arsenic, down into the hole. Fear of permanent respiratory damage or worse drove the men to the surface. Finally, both sides agreed to sell out to an eastern syndicate and the mines were merged to become the Bull-Domingo. Armed guards were placed on the property to keep out nocturnal highgraders and claim jumpers.

Like so many booming towns, Silver Cliff wanted to become the county seat. Custer County had two bitter controversies over this question. Rosita, which had the coveted designation, contested the upstart claims of Silver Cliff. The first election was held in 1882 and Silver Cliff amassed a majority of the votes cast. Some of the records and a few county officials moved across the valley. Quite apart from the results of the balloting, Rosita now began to advance the claim that a majority of two thirds of the votes was required to move a county seat. When the dispute was carried up the line, the State Supreme Court decided in favor of Rosita.

By 1886, Silver Cliff was ready for round two. This time nearby Westcliffe, one and one half miles away, came in as an ally and the necessary majority was racked up. Still licking its wounds, Rosita refused to give up the records until a Vigilante group was formed to forcibly wrest the coveted documents and records from a reluctant Rosita. To assure future peace, a new courthouse was built halfway between Westcliffe and Silver Cliff.

By May of 1881 the Denver and Rio Grande Railway had completed its Grape Creek extension line into Westcliffe from Canon City. No effort was made to extend the line on to Silver Cliff. There was plenty of trouble just maintaining the line that they had. A stagecoach line maintained connections between the two towns. With improved transportation facilities, Silver Cliff suddenly became a mecca for British remittance men. Thus in an incredibly short time English country houses began to sprout all over the place. Almost at once the valley resounded to the ridiculous tooting of hunting trumpets and the coyote and gopher populations were sent scuttling away to avoid the newest common enemy.

Although the railroad stimulated much local interest, the tracks were a source of vast expense to the company. Freak washouts from Grape Creek disrupted traffic and necessitated costly repairs. One storm, on August 18, 1889, entirely destroyed about five miles of the roadbed. The company became discouraged and abandoned the line altogether. By 1890 the rails had been torn out. Although the withdrawal of the railroad greatly retarded the prosperity of the area, it inevitably benefited local farmers and stockmen. While the railroad was in operation, they had purchased their hay, oats and corn from Denver, paying extra to have these commodities shipped in. Now they raised their own crops at home on their own farms.

Silver Cliff had a fire in 1880 and another in 1882. A volunteer fire department, such as most towns had, functioned efficiently. After the 1882 blaze, a new two-story fire house was built. That same year, Silver Cliff played host to the State Fireman's Tournament.

With the passing of the mining boom, the settlers began to rely on other sources of income. Some people feel that mining declined sharply after 1882. Certainly the silver crash of 1893 finished the job. In the intervening years, many

Courtesy Denver Public Library, Western History Collection
This was Silver Cliff in the 1890's. The background mountains are the Sangre de Cristos

Collection of Robert L. Brown
Here is Silver Cliff in 1966

residents moved to the new town of Westcliffe to avoid high taxes. Some cut down trees, trimmed them into logs, and rolled their houses over to the more favored location of the moment.

Westcliffe had been established in 1885 and owed its beginning to the railroad. The two towns of Silver Cliff and Westcliffe were very close to each other and were often regarded as being one. In most instances they worked together for their mutual interests. At the turn of the century there were still over five hundred people there. Small resident populations are still found at both places and there is even a fine little weekly newspaper.

From U.S. Highway 50, west of Canon City, State Highway 69 drops south through Hillside to Westcliffe and Silver Cliff. A somewhat longer, more involved but much prettier route can be followed in from State Highway 115 running south out of Colorado Springs to Florence. From there, State Highway 67 runs through Wetmore and Querida. Then follow State Highway 96 to Silver Cliff, a delightful little hamlet that still retains much of the original flavor that made it one of the truly great mining camps of Colorado's colorful past.*

---

* In this same general area, see also Custer City.

50.

SILVER PLUME

FOUNDED IN 1870, Silver Plume is about the only town in Clear Creek County where the origin of the name is definitely known. Commodore Stephen Decatur, shirttail relative of the great hero of the War of 1812, bestowed the name. Each passing year seems to bring additional hindsight versions of what he had in mind. Although amusing, these stories are far too numerous for repetition here. Allegedly, the date of Decatur's act was July 28, 1870. "The Plume" is located about two miles above Georgetown, and a thousand feet higher, at the base of Sherman and Republican mountains. Denver is fifty-four miles away and nearly a mile lower.

It was a silver and lead discovery by Owen Feenan in 1868 that started things moving in the valley and eventually resulted in the building of a town. Feenan called his discovery the Pelican and kept the event pretty much to himself. When a serious illness made his death seem imminent, Owen confided his secret to a couple of friends. With such friends, he needed no enemies. Within a few days, the two men had stealthily opened the vein. When poor, trusting Owen miraculously recovered in 1871, he found that the tables had been turned and that he had been squeezed out of the partnership at what had formerly been his own mine.

In the course of their history, the mines here produced copper and gold in addition to silver and lead. With very few exceptions, the mines were close to the town. Narrow zigzag trails were cut out on the mountainsides above the settlement to enable the jack trains to carry ore down to Silver Plume. Among the better properties were the Pelican, Dives, Dundenburg, Baxter, Dunkirk, Terrible, and Consolidated-Payrock. Many of these were in clear view of the town. Within a comparatively short time the Pelican and the Dives properties had combined. From the beginning, the shafts of the companies had been close together. Each mine had been working only a short distance from the other on the very same eight-foot silver vein. Inevitably, each felt that the other had been stealing and some very spirited battles were fought below ground from time to time. Most of Clear Creek County took sides as lawsuits and countersuits were filed by the contesting parties. The poor beleaguered judge, who wished he could be elsewhere, actually kept a pistol on the bench.

Suddenly the pot boiled over when Jack Bishop, a hired mercenary on the Dives payroll, followed a Pelican official into Silver Plume and murdered him in a stable. Another version says it was done on a public street. A newspaper report gives the name of the dead man as J. H. McMurdy although Hall's *History of Colorado* says it was Jacob Snider. Since Bishop would not have been allowed to remain at large to do interesting things and since other items in both stories correlate, there is no doubt that both accounts were describing the same event. In any case the issue was solved when the aforementioned merger took place. W. A. Hammil, of Georgetown, purchased both mines and the Pelican-Dives became the best known, and one of the most valuable properties in the district. Hammil eventually sold out for five million dollars.

Despite the fact that it had been founded a full decade earlier, the first settlers were rather remiss in their duties and the town was not formally incorporated until September 24, 1880. Life in Silver Plume followed about the same patterns as those of its contemporary mining camps. Colonel Charles Baldwin and Jane Huff erected the first buildings

in town. Two churches, a Catholic and a Methodist, appeared
eventually and are still standing, although the Catholic structure is no longer used. Since the village expanded rather rapidly, little time was lost in building a school, which burned
in 1893, and in establishing the inevitable post office. In an
incredibly short time the business district had expanded to
include a grocery store, a meat market, several general stores,
many stables, a drugstore and a dry-goods store.

On the second floor of one of the larger structures, Silver
Plume's first theater was established. Seating for three hundred patrons was provided. Covering the stage was a hand-
painted drop curtain which sported a view of the Bay of
Naples and Mount Vesuvius. Most of the traveling shows
of the day, from musicals to Shakespeare, played at the Opera
House in Silver Plume. In addition, local talent groups produced minstrel shows and occasional serious dramatic efforts
which are replayed today as melodramas. To fill a social void,
the Silver Plume Social Dancing Club was organized by a
group of young townsmen. Tickets to their functions were
sold at one dollar each.

Five hotels ministered to the creature comforts of large
numbers of migrants while nine saloons took care of some
other needs. Over the years a total of six mills was kept busy
crushing and refining the ores that were brought down the
hill from the mines. For the building trade, a shingle mill and
a brick kiln went into production. Near the edge of town,
a stone quarry was opened up. Before closing, it supplied
some of the material used to erect the new state capitol edifice in Denver.

After a fire department had been established, hose cart
races became a common attraction, with keen competition
between the local runners and those from Georgetown, Central City, and Denver. Rock drilling contests were also a
source of much local interest. An active baseball team was
formed to play against teams from nearby camps. Their
athletic field was the vacant lot across the street from the

now-abandoned second school. From the Payrock Mine came a fine community band. In 1904, a circular bandstand was erected near the center of town. Although it is no longer used, it still stands.

Transportation at the Plume began with somewhat less effort for the residents since the town was built in a meadow adjacent to the Bakerville Road. Later, in 1879, this same grade became the Ten Mile Toll Road, described by its contemporaries as "dry and dusty." Daily mails and stagecoaches came up from and went down to Georgetown. One of the earliest operators was W. P. Ferris who ran an omnibus line to Georgetown and Brownsville. In 1874, his first year, Ferris cleared $9,135.

Railroad connections arrived in town by way of the incredible Georgetown Loop. Although Georgetown is only two miles or so away, as the crow flies, it is a full thousand feet lower than Silver Plume. To gain the necessary altitude and connect the two villages, a tremendous loop of track was built, filling the valley and circling back across its own lower grade. It took five years to construct the necessary trestles that held the four miles of track. By 1884 it was completed and six locomotives each day came whistling and puffing into Silver Plume. Geography texts of the nineteenth century commonly showed the Georgetown Loop alongside the Grand Canyon and Niagara Falls as examples of the wonders of America. Before the tracks were torn out in 1939, a thoroughly amusing but extremely jumpy motion picture was made, showing a ride over the loop. In nearly every scene, ridiculously attired tourists fill every window of the cars, waving white handkerchiefs at the photographer as the tiny engine hauled its load up to the 9,175-foot elevation of the Plume.

In 1905, Silver Plume acquired its second railroad. Edward Wilcox, a former Methodist clergyman, discovered that there was more money in Colorado mining than in the salvation of souls. On August 1, he started construction of the Argentine Central line to Waldorf and eventually on to the crest of Mount McClelland. In deference to his former calling, this became the only railroad in the United States that never operated on Sundays.

Population statistics seem to have run the usual gamut with 175 to 200 reported here in 1875. Four years later a figure of 600 was given, with a winter population drop to 120 people. When George Crofutt came to town in 1881, he reported that about 600 lived there. By far the most exaggerated statistic encountered was a figure of 2,000 as early as 1875, a completely irresponsible estimate.

Catastrophes of the usual sort also figure in the story of life at Silver Plume. Fire swept the town for the first time in November of 1884. Shortly after midnight, an overheated stove in the back room of Pat Barrett's saloon got out of control. Pat was burned to death and some fifty buildings in the business district went up in smoke before control was effected. No waterworks had yet been installed. A brigade, wielding one hundred leather water buckets, formed a line from the stream and put up a good fight. Fortunately, a pumper and crew came up the hill from Georgetown. They were able to stop the fire just short of the church. Silver Plume purchased its first pumper from St. Louis in 1885. It is still stored in town. Until recent years it was often sent to participate in parades around the state.

By far the most serious catastrophe in Silver Plume's history was the avalanche that struck on February 12, 1899, a Sunday morning. Both the slopes and crests of the surrounding mountains were blanketed by drifts that averaged three feet in depth. Unexpectedly, a thaw materialized and caused huge masses of snow and ice to detach themselves. Down it came; picking up trees, rocks, and loose materials. Pushing a massive wall of debris before it, the slide gained momentum, stopping with a resounding crash when the base of the canyon was reached.

Large numbers of miners of Italian extraction had built

their homes high on the steep mountainsides above the valley. Zigzag paths led up the rocky slopes from the town. A straight line path to any of these houses would have been impossible to negotiate. It was in this declivity that the slide ran. Obviously, the victims had no warning. As it was, nearly all were caught in their cabins. Most were buried, after first being carried two or three hundred feet down the mountain.

One version tells us that there were actually two slides which ran simultaneously, moving several hundred feet before combining above where the shanties were struck. In extent, both masses were about four hundred to five hundred yards long and about half as wide. The near-impossibility of extracting people from the slide, either dead or alive, becomes apparent when we realize that the solidly packed mass was upward of ten feet deep at the point where it stopped. Rescue parties did succeed in taking out a few badly mangled people. Miraculously, most of them recovered.

The exact number of dead was unknown until summer when the snow had melted. At first, it was thought that about a dozen persons had perished. When the mass melted, revealing its victims, the final tally was around twenty.

Great damage to mining property also resulted. Huge shaft houses from several mines were swept away and the mouths of most tunnels were filled with snow, rocks, and uprooted trees. Ten days later, a second slide came down. A partial precaution for the people was to keep out of the probable path of an avalanche. Regrettably, it was often difficult to tell where those tracks would be.

In the March 23 issue of *Leslie's Weekly* for that year there was a report detailing how the Rockies had been covered with one of the heaviest snows ever known. Those railroads which ran into the mountains lost thousands of dollars. Both tracks and marooned trains were shoveled or plowed out

Silver Plume as it looked prior to the turn of the century

Silver Plume in June of 1965

time and again, only to be snowed in the next time there was a storm, and the whole process had to be repeated.

Silver Plume is a quiet, peaceful village, just off to the side of Interstate Highway 70, west of Georgetown where the grades begin to incline upwards toward Loveland Pass. In winter it is often possible to watch herds of mountain sheep who come down close to the town in search of forage. When hungry, one may sometimes approach them close enough for photographs. In the town, a small local museum and many original buildings establish a pleasant tie with the past for those who enjoy firsthand exploration of nine-teenth-century history.*

---

* In this same general area, see also Fall River, North Empire, Gilson Gulch, Freeland, and Brownsville.

51.

SILVERTON

CAPTAIN CHARLES BAKER was a restless sort of frontiersman who had spent a considerable amount of time just knocking about from one mining camp to another. In the course of his wanderings Baker frequently heard Ute Indian rumors to the effect that gold had been found in the San Juan Mountains. Consequently, Baker assembled a party of six men and set out for southwestern Colorado in July of 1860. His employer, S. B. Kellogg of Oro City, had become infected by Baker's enthusiasm and had agreed to underwrite the expedition financially. The party traveled south down the Arkansas Valley, took on provisions at Fort Garland, and then turned straight west toward the high San Juan Range. Inevitably, word got out and they were followed. After crossing the towering eastern peaks, Baker's party dropped down to a beautiful, 9,200-foot-high alpine park, situated on an elevated level plain, a two-mile-wide tract of land above the Animas River that was completely encircled by high, snow-capped mountains.

To shelter themselves, a series of rude log and brush huts was hastily thrown up and the whole thing was called Baker City. Here they wintered, living in almost constant dread of the Utes since, at best, they were little better than trespassers on the Indian lands. With this settlement as a sort of headquarters, they worked their way up the Animas Canyon, panning for gold as they went. Some gold was actually found at a point roughly corresponding to the later location of the city of Eureka. Although the actual returns were rather meager, gross exaggerations found their way to the outside world and a small migration devolved upon Baker City. When the true facts became apparent, Baker was blamed and put on trial by the miners. The *New York Times* carried an account of the trial in which Baker pulled a "Perry Mason" and won acquittal from the threat of hanging by panning some gold on the spot.

When word of the Civil War filtered in, Baker made his exit via Fort Garland and returned to fight for his native Virginia. By 1868 he was back, only to lose his life at the hands of Indians near the mouth of the Little Colorado River. Inevitably, others also returned, following in Baker's footsteps. Baker City expanded. The Brunot Treaty of 1874 ended the Indian problem and opened the land for settlement. Somewhere along the line the name was changed to Silverton. When F. V. Hayden was there during his monumental survey of 1874, he recorded the presence of twelve houses. Although it occupied the older site of Baker City, the beginning of Silverton is ordinarily dated from 1874.

A tremendous number of rich silver properties was found in the area. This resulted in a influx of population that one source estimated as 4,000 people by the end of 1874. A more reliable source records only 3,000 people at Silverton during the peak of its boom several years later. When George Crofutt was there in the 1870's, he reported only 850 residents. At that time springwater was hawked through the streets at fifty cents per bucket. The mail was brought in from Antelope Springs. Dogsleds brought in the freight in winter. After each trip the dogs were rewarded with a shot of whiskey. In winter, Silverton was often isolated by snowslides.

As the town grew, all of the usual improvements arrived. There were stores, saloons, stables, restaurants, three sawmills, schools, a Masonic Lodge, Order of the Eastern Star, Eagles, and an Odd Fellows Lodge. The First National Bank of Silverton and one other did huge businesses. Isaac Grant operated the first hotel in town, the Grand, opened in 1882. It later became the Grand Imperial and was taken over by W. S. Thompson, an Englishman. Later, the Walker and Silverton Hotels were opened. The *La Plata Miner,* Silverton's first newspaper, appeared in July of 1875. At a later date it became the *Silverton Miner.* A second paper, the *Silverton Standard,* came along a few years later.

Greene Street became the principal business artery while Blair Street, just a block south, became the "Honky Tonk" district. Many dance halls and gambling houses were scattered in among the thirty-seven saloons that lined the street. At one period the underworld gained control of Silverton and ran the town from their dens on Blair Street. When vigilante groups were formed and failed in their attempts to restore order, Bat Masterson was hired to come in from Dodge City and was placed in charge of the Police Department. Although Masterson failed to close Blair Street because he enjoyed partaking of the creature comforts available there, he did tame things down a bit. The taming process was furthered by the arrival of families and the establishment of churches. By the 1880's there were four: a Congregational, an Episcopal, a Methodist, and a Catholic church. Some other diversions were provided by boxing matches and a racetrack.

The list of mines that contributed to the prosperity of Silverton is nearly endless. Among the better known were the Pelican, Victor, Terrible, Silver Crown, North Star, Aspen, Titusville, Idaho, Susquehanna, Gray Eagle, King Solomon, Mammoth, Parker City, Lackawanna, Prospector, Seymour, Dakota, Pompeii, Isle of Beauty, Cleveland, Creedmore, Belcher, Potomac, and the great Shenandoah-Dives. Several refineries of one sort or another kept up a busy schedule. The Walsh Smelter was situated at the entrance to Cement Creek and the Green and Company Smelter was at the edge of the city. Nearby were the Silver Lake-Aspen, North Star Mill, Martha Rose Smelter, Shenandoah-Dives Mill, Kendrick and Gelder Smelter, and the Silver Lake Mill which started up in 1907.

Silverton's economy really gained in prosperity when the Denver and Rio Grande Railway built north up the canyon of the Animas River from Durango, arriving at Silverton in July of 1882. An impatient crowd went wild and Silverton was caught up in the throes of a giddy celebration. Otto Mears also started three narrow-gauge lines from Silverton. His famed Rainbow Route, the Silverton Railroad, went up over Red Mountain Pass to Ironton. The Silverton, Gladstone and Northerly went up Cement Creek to Gladstone, and his Silverton Northern climbed up the Animas River Canyon to Eureka and Animas Forks. In all, four railroads served Silverton. One of these, the Denver and Rio Grande, still makes daily trips up from Durango during the summer months, traversing one of the most spectacularly beautiful canyons in North America. If you choose to make this run, get your tickets well in advance. This, incidentally, is the only regularly scheduled narrow-gauge railroad in the United States and it has been widely used by Hollywood film makers in recent years. Access for other kinds of traffic was provided by way of Stony, Cinnamon, Red Mountain, and Poughkeepsie passes.

After the silver crash of 1893, gold was found and Silverton was spared the final indignity of becoming a ghost town. Over the years, something in excess of a quarter of a billion dollars in precious metals has been taken out of the Silverton area. In addition to being designated as a National Historical Site, Silverton also has the distinction of possessing the first city-owned public utility system in the United States. Although Silverton has been generally lucky, there have been a few sad times, too. For example, a flu epidemic in 1918 took the lives of nearly a third of the townspeople.

To see Silverton today, simply follow U.S. Highway 550 south from Montrose or north from Durango. There, just twenty-six miles south of Ouray, you will find one of the prettiest and most historic mountain-ringed communities in all of North America.*

---

* In this same general area, see also Camp Bird, Dallas City, and Ouray.

Rio Grande Archives
*With Sultan Mountain as a backdrop, Silverton looked prosperous
in 1909 with its new City Hall, then just a year old.*

Collection of Robert L. Brown
Greene Street in August of 1965 showed many changes and many points of comparison

52.

STUNNER

WHEN THE FIRST PROSPECTORS sought to extract precious metals from the mountain ranges south of Del Norte in 1879, no town had yet been established at the location which is to be the subject of this chapter. Initial prospects were found in the valley of Cat Creek or Cat Gulch. Because the current maps published by the U.S. Forest Service show no Cat Creek in the vicinity, this may have been "Gato Creek," since this is a Spanish translation of the word cat.

Most of the rather meager sources of information about Stunner tell us that the first construction at the site occurred in 1882. Here, as in so many early camps, more than one name was tried before they found one that lasted. Probably because it was barely across the line between Conejos and Rio Grande counties, Stunner first kited the name of Conejos Camp. Conejos is another Spanish word, meaning rabbit. Later, this name was dropped and for several years the town was known as Loynton. Thus far I have been unable to find any reason for this change. Finally, in 1887, it became Stunner, an equally obscure name. It seems possible that Stunner might have been the optimistic reaction of some miner to his claim of the moment although this is sheer speculation of the most reckless sort.

Geographically speaking, the townsite was located about forty-five miles southwest of Alamosa, just below the headwaters of the Conejos River. Both gold and silver properties were found and worked in the neighborhood but the sheer remoteness of the camp prevented optimum develop-

ment. Notable among the better properties were the Merrimac, Log Cabin, Eurydice, Pass-Me-By and Snow Storm
lodes. Population statistics for the town fluctuated considerably. The earliest figure encountered tells us of 150 people
who settled there by 1889. Between 1892 and 1894 this total
seems to have dropped to 100 souls. In between these two
estimates was one that showed only 20 people there in 1891.

An item in the library files of the Colorado State Historical Society indicates that 1886 was the best year the town
ever had. One other account tells us that the Denver and
Rio Grande Railway built a line into Stunner but the report is simply not true. It was, however, reached by a fine
toll road constructed by the Le Duc and Sanchez Toll Road
Company. Papers for this undertaking were filed at Conejos on July 2, 1884. With few exceptions, the road followed
the Conejos River from Antonito, passing through Platoro
which was on the north side of the water. Since mountains
separate these two towns, a series of switchbacks was cut
out to enable the road to cross over to Stunner. The total
distance was about forty-five miles. Where the road topped
the range between the Conejos and Alamosa Rivers, it was
named Stunner Pass and still carries a Forest Service marker
to that effect on its crest. Despite this, maps published by
the Colorado State Highway Department have labeled the
crossing as Celeste Pass for the past several years. Its elevation is 10,500 feet.

When the Colorado General Assembly met in 1891, an
appropriation for $12,000 was passed for the purpose of
cutting a wagon road across the range by way of Platoro
and Stunner. Beyond this, very little information is available. Whether it used the already existing grades of Stunner
Pass, or whether this became 11,775-foot Elwood Pass, is not
clear.

During 1890, a United States post office was established at
Stunner but the town lasted only a few more years. A shortage of any really rich ores, good enough to absorb the high

transportation costs, doomed the town. By the turn of the century there was nothing stunning about Stunner. The nearness of Summitville on the other side of the range made better ores available at a lower cost. Both transportation and communication facilities for Summitville were also much better developed.

Before you decide on a trip to Stunner, it might be well to look carefully at the accompanying contemporary photograph. With the exception of four early log structures on the hillside across the creek from the road, the town has almost completely vanished. Stunner is about as ghostly a ghost town as anyone could want.

Follow the same directions given in the chapter on Jasper as far as access roads are concerned. I prefer the twelve miles of paved road, State Highway 15, south of Monte Vista. Where the blacktop stops, turn right and follow the signs toward the Platoro Reservoir. This good dirt road passed through Jasper and reaches Stunner just before the roads fork to Elwood and Stunner passes. Platoro and Summitville are over the hills. Stunner was in the wide, open valley where the routes divide.

Currently, the Forest Service has a ranger station here and maintains a very beautifully located new campground facility just below the road to Elwood Pass. Called the Stunner Campground, it barely misses being on the exact site of the old town. It is also the home of some of the most vicious and numerous mosquitos that ever plagued a lover of the great outdoors.*

---

* In this same general area, see also Jasper and Platoro.

Rio Grande Archives
Stunner, photographed by George Beam when it was trying to be a prosperous mining camp

Collection of Robert L. Brown
Stunner today. The road at the right leads over Stunner Pass to Platoro

53.

TARRYALL AND HAMILTON

FROM THE STANDPOINT of community images, Tarryall probably suffered the worst set of public relations ever to devolve upon a mining camp. Without a single exception, all stock Colorado history texts to date have dwelled at some length upon the covetousness and downright greed of the town's original inhabitants. Also noted was the manner in which any newcomers were discouraged from settling there and how all promising claims had already been preempted. With such dismal prospects for the future and in view of their inhospitable treatment, the late arrivals moved on a few more miles across Red Hill and established a town of their own, called Fairplay, in mockery of their feelings about Tarryall. More often, they bitterly referred to it as "Grab-All."

Historically, many people have speculated that Tarryall was the site of that first nebulous gold discovery in South Park by James Purcell. While he was being detained by the Spanish at Sante Fe in 1807, Lieutenant Zebulon Pike heard the story firsthand from Purcell, an early fur trapper. In any case, during July of 1859, a party of eight disenchanted argonauts from Gregory Gulch decided to journey deeper into the mountains to try their luck a second time. Actually they had another purpose in mind, too. Just a month earlier five other prospectors from Gregory Gulch had been killed by Indians near Kenosha Pass. William Holman and Earl Hamilton were now leading a party into South Park to punish the Indians. At present Kenosha Pass they were joined by six men from Wisconsin who promptly named the crossing for their home city. Venturing down the other side into South Park, they succeeded in raising color on Tarryall Creek at Deadwood Gulch. Little time was lost in establishing a pick and shovel camp two miles downstream which they named Tarryall. William Holman, one of the founders, first called the place Pound's Diggings, in honor of Daniel Pound, who, it was rumored, had found scales of gold as big as watermelon seeds there. The name was misinterpreted and many thought it simply meant that one could take out "a pound a day."

Inevitably the word spread and hordes of men from the Denver area, Gregory Gulch, and other locations started for South Park. Soon both banks of the creek were lined with tents. It was a reaction to this unexpected influx that the original settlers became jealous and began running off indignant newcomers. Winter finished the job and really deserted the camp. By the spring of 1860, most of the people were back and had already resumed work. About 150 men had worked there in 1859. During 1860, some three hundred log houses were built. Irving Howbert, later a capitalist at Cripple Creek, moved to Tarryall with his Methodist clergyman father in 1860.

Another winter depleted the town once more but the spring of 1861 saw another revival of interest in full swing. An attitude of permanence now pervaded the area and steps were taken that led to the formal laying out of a town in 1861. One hotel, the Dunbar House, seems to have opened its doors that summer. The Parsons Mint also went into production here in the summer of 1861. Both $2.50 and $5.00 rectangular gold slugs were minted. I have also seen twenty-dollar pieces from the Parsons Mint. At this point it might be advisable to explain that privately minted coins were entirely legal as media of exchange, provided that the gold content of each coin was equal to that of the federally minted variety. Not until June 8, 1864, was private coinage outlawed. After that date all such operations constituted a counterfeiting operation.

Almost concurrently with the beginnings of Tarryall, a second town called Hamilton was started on the south side of the creek by some of the other people who had been driven out of Grab-All. Earl Hamilton, one of the original founders of Tarryall, led the dissidents and was the source of the town's name. Although the two communities were easily within shouting distance of each other, separated only by a narrow creek, rivalry between them was understandably intense. Despite the fact that many contemporaries spoke of Tarryall-Hamilton in the same breath, the towns steadfastly refused to merge. When Governor William Gilpin visited Hamilton in 1861, a hastily contrived excuse to visit Tarryall was fabricated and trouble was narrowly averted. At one point when Tarryall received the designation as the seat of Park County, several Hamiltonites nearly succumbed with apoplexy.

One visitor described Hamilton as consisting of one long narrow street running parallel to the creek. There were no sidewalks. Constant traffic from oxteams made this thoroughfare a dust bowl in summer and a mudhole in the spring and fall. Something between 3,000 and 6,000 people are alleged to have lived at Hamilton. If the latter figure is accepted, surely Tarryall must have been included in the estimate. Among the commercial enterprises were several saloons and gambling houses, a post office, the St. Vrain and Esterday General Store, three boardinghouses, a drugstore, six grocery stores, a meat market, two physicians, a sawmill, one hotel, an attorney and a justice of the peace.

W. N. Byers, founder of the *Rocky Mountain News*, once started a newspaper at Hamilton which he called the *Miner's Record*. Byers assigned O. J. Goldrick as a roving reporter and the actual printing was done in Tarryall. Curiously, only eleven issues were published. Hamilton also had a theater that managed to attract a variety of the traveling shows that crossed Colorado's frontier. Gambling was always a popular pastime but the professional merchants of chance usually deserted the mountains each winter, even after the towns were established on a year-around basis. Since gold was plentiful, life was both hard and exciting at Hamilton and Tarryall.

During the summer rushes that swelled both of these embryonic communities in the beginning years, the old original Indian trail across Kenosha Pass proved to be inadequate for the immense volume of wagon traffic. Consequently, most traffic from Denver and the east traveled south on the old Santa Fe road, east of the Front Range. Just north of Pikes Peak, the primitive wagon road up Ute Pass provided access to South Park. Merchants at Colorado City spent $1,400 on bridges and road improvements to make the route more attractive. In the process, migrants kept Colorado City green by bringing money. Generally, this route paralleled the present U.S. Highway 24 to Lake George. There the trail turned north up Tarryall Creek into South Park. Twice each week, the Central Overland California and Pikes Peak Express Company ran four-mule coaches over this route from Denver to Tarryall and Ute Pass. The C.O.C. and P.P. was often maligned by its employees as standing for "Clean out of Cash and Poor Pay."

Although placer deposits are rarely satisfactory producers of long-term wealth, those at Tarryall-Hamilton were exceptional. The best locations were found along both sides of the old creek channel, extending westward all the way to the mountains. Beginning in the summer of 1859, gold flakes as large as watermelon seeds were recovered regularly. In value, these were worth anywhere from $.35 to $1.25 each. Most men took out gold that was worth between $2.50 and $25 per day per man. Thirteen hydraulic installations were already at work by July of 1861. One source also reports the presence of primitive ore-crushing arrastras. One particularly rich placer claim was worked by 150 men during a single winter and earned the name of Whiskey Hole. Here, allegedly, a thirsty man could always pan out the price of a drink, providing he spent it in the local saloons.

For many years after the coming of white men to South Park, both the Utes and Arapaho Indians fought for the privilege of hunting among the game herds at the south end of the park. Sometimes, when they grew tired of giving each other their lumps, both tribes would travel jointly up Tarryall Creek, pitching their lodges among the cabins of Hamilton and Tarryall. All animosity was forgotten as they watched in amazement while the white man alternately dug and panned the yellow metal from Tarryall Creek. One such encampment is shown in the accompanying photograph. For a time, aboriginal social and aesthetic aspirations were submerged while the warriors licked their wounds and attempted to figure out the intricacies of this gold business. Finally, in despair, they would journey southward again to resume the more practical aspects of their warfare around the buffalo and elk herds.

Although Tarryall Creek yielded two million dollars in gold between 1859 and 1872, trouble began as early as the water shortage that first became apparent in the fall of 1861. By 1872, Tarryall was dead. Ten families still resided in the valley but all made their homes in Hamilton. While the shortage of water was a factor in the abandonment, a more compelling reason was the end of profitable placering in 1875. When the Denver, South Park and Pacific Railway entered South Park in 1879, it bypassed the towns completely and the last residents moved a few miles south to Como. When George Crofutt was here again in the 1880's, he mentioned only Hamilton and referred to it as a station on the Denver, South Park, and Pacific with one hundred and fifty people in residence, indicating a possible short revival as a railroad town. Later, when much of South Park was subjected to extensive dredging, the sites of Tarryall and Hamilton were

This photograph shows some of the structures of Tarryall and Hamilton in 1880

*Here is the empty site, of the two towns in 1967. Boreas Pass crosses
the mountain at the right of the picture.*

buried under tons of rock. Such is the status of the towns at present.

To see the site today, take U.S. Highway 285 across South Park to Como. Drive through Como for two miles on the road toward Boreas Pass. At the point where the road drops sharply down to Tarryall Creek, huge piles of boulders will be seen on every side. Look north (left) toward Mount Silverheels. Hamilton and Tarryall are under the tons of rock that now fill the valley. This is also the point from which the accompanying photographs were made. A brief moment to compare these pictures with the actual site will quickly reveal the approximate locations of two of Colorado's earliest mining settlements, Hamilton and Tarryall.*

---

* In this same general area, see also Boreas, Como, Dyersville, and King City.

54.

TELLURIDE

IT SHOULD BE MADE CLEAR right at the start that Telluride is not a ghost town in any sense of the word. It is, however, one of the most beautifully located small cities in Colorado, and one with a history that reaches far back into the silver- and gold-mining history of Colorado. In addition, it is my own opinion that Telluride is one of the most friendly communities in the state.

Familiarly known as the "City of Gold," life began here in 1878, although one source places the founding two years earlier. Certainly there was mining here in 1875 and people had to have a place to live. Many people came over the range from Silverton to work in the San Miguel River placers. Some of them appear to have arrived as early as 1874. In those days it was known as Columbia and at that time it was a part of Ouray County. The altitude here is 8,300 feet and Columbia was built just a mile up the road from the earlier community of San Miguel City. The initial head count showed one hundred people there although one source kites it to three hundred. During those early years, commercial and mining supplies were all brought in by oxteams, mule packtrains, or by horses and freight wagons. Under such conditions, costs were almost prohibitively high.

Columbia became Telluride in either 1881 or 1883; two dates have been found. In February of the latter year, San Miguel County was carved out of Ouray County and Telluride became the county seat. The new name for the town was derived from the prevalence of tellurous ores found

Photo by Dr. Gerald G. Coon
The author and his son Marshall are shown here on the sheer ledge over the vertical cliffs above Telluride. They are heading down the Black Bear Road toward the town, visible at the extreme left in the valley far below.

*Taken from across the valley, the zigzag switchbacks of the Black Bear Road are clearly
visible. The mill and town of Pandora can be seen in the lower right corner.*

nearby. Quite a number of excellent mineral-producing properties were found among the mountains above Telluride. Among them were such famous names as the Liberty Bell, found by W. L. Cornett in 1876, and the great Tomboy, which was located in 1888, high up on the Savage Fork of the Marshall Basin. Other good producers were the Alta and Gold King, over the crest of Boomerang Hill; the Cimarron, Columbia, Japan, Black Bear, Argentine, Snow Drift, Cleveland, Red Cloud, Bullion, Hidden Treasure, Champion, Ajax, Emerald, Andrews, and the incredible Smuggler-Union. John Fallon made the initial discovery on the Sheridan claim, a fabulously rich property that included the Smuggler-Union and the Mendota, all on the same tract. In August of 1875, he took out ores that were worth $1,200 to the ton. Beneath the mines, something in the neighborhood of 275 miles of underground tunnels were dug. Although they are still there, most are now unsafe and should be avoided. By 1909 the combined production of gold, silver, lead, zinc, and copper had reached $60,000,000. In the intervening years this total has been pushed upward beyond the $300,-000,000 mark.

When L. L. Nunn built a power plant near Ames to supply electricity to the Gold King Mine, an extension was strung over the hill to Telluride and it is still in service. This became the first long-distance high-voltage alternating current line in the world. With a ready supply of electrical power, Telluride began to achieve its potential. The population soon reached five thousand. A courthouse, school, and opera house were built. In the early days, religious services for the Congregational, Catholic, and Methodist faiths were held in the courthouse. After 1890, these three put up church buildings of their own. In addition to the usual businesses, a water-powered sawmill was erected on the San Miguel River.

Telluride became so prosperous that twenty-six saloons were located there. In addition there were eight bawdy houses and a dozen dance halls. Business was so good that license fees and "fines" from these establishments produced enough money to run the municipal government for many years without a general tax levy. Some of these now-empty establishments are still standing on Pacific Avenue but twenty-one of the saloons were destroyed in a big fire and Telluride's city government is now supported by a more conventional tax structure.

Telluride really boomed when Otto Mears, pioneer road builder of the San Juans, built his narrow-gauge Rio Grande Southern Railroad from Durango, around the southern tip of the range and up to Rico, and all deliveries became much faster. Prosperity had arrived at last.

Over the years, three factors operated to the detriment of Telluride. First, because of its beautiful location at the bottom of sheer canyon walls, the city has been unusually prone to damage from snowslides. One of these even carried off the Liberty Bell Mine Buildings, leaving only an ugly scar in its wake. On several occasions the community itself sustained extensive damage. Second, there were bloody labor troubles in 1901. Peace was not restored until Governor James Peabody sent in the state militia under Major Z. T. Hill in January of 1904. This event is detailed in the chapter on Tomboy. The prolonged strikes opened many wounds that were slow to heal. Third, Telluride was badly hurt by the effects of the panic of 1893 and the slump in silver mining. However, unlike many places, gold was found here and a gradual recovery was made.

Telluride today is a prosperous and pleasant little community. The huge new mill of the Idarado Mining Company processes 1,800 tons of crude ore daily. This is the largest installation of its kind in Colorado. On at least two occasions, Hollywood motion picture companies have gone on location here and have taken advantage of the unparalleled scenery. To visit Telluride, take State Highway 145 in southwestern Colorado. It leads directly into the town. A fine campground, good fishing, hair-raising Jeep trips, and many other activities may be combined to make you wish that you could stay longer.*

---

* In this same general area, see also Pandora, Tomboy, and Vanadium.

Pack mules, loaded with timbers, crossing Main Street in Telluride

Today, Telluride still has most of the original structures seen in the picture above

55.

TOMBOY

WHEN THE ICE CHUNKS stopped floating down the San Miguel River and warming breezes blew across the deep valley, a golden treasure was tapped on the peaks above Telluride. In this mountain stronghold, more than three thousand feet above the town, the rich Tomboy vein was first located in 1880. But in the decade or so that followed, the San Juan country was caught up in the throes of a monumental silver boom and this above-timberline strike on the Savage Fork of the windswept Marshall Basin was somewhat neglected for the moment. Many chapters in this book have ended with the demonetization of silver in 1893; this story begins with that unhappy event.

The cry of "gold" at Cripple Creek and in the San Juans electrified the depressed state with news that the much-sought yellow metal had once again been found in paying quantities. When the news seeped out, it sent a fresh new stream of humanity into San Miguel County, stirred by the desire for adventure and by their own acquisitiveness. Off they swarmed, across Colorado's eastern prairies, into the canyons and mountain passes, risking their resources and even their lives on a search for subterranean riches. Before the end of the 1893-94 winter, hundreds of gold seekers were already on the trail to southwestern Colorado.

To shelter those who came in search of a livelihood, a small settlement was started near the mine in this unlikely location. Although it was never formally incorporated as a city or town in its own right, all the necessary elements were there.

As a first designation, it was called Savage Basin Camp. Several stores were established, many sturdy cabins were built, and there was even a school. Two livery stables supplied mules and horses for the hair-raising ride on the cliff-hanging trail to or from Telluride.

The Tomboy name seems to have come into more general use during the 1894 gold boom when production was heaviest. During that year the property was sold for $100,000. It was later resold to the Rothschilds of London in 1897. The price was a cool $2,000,000. Regardless of ownership, the name was usually the same: The Tomboy Gold Mines Company. Less than a half mile away, the Columbia and Japan lodes were found. Many of the men who worked in these shafts also lived in the Tomboy area.

L. L. Nunn built a transmission line across lofty, 13,114-foot-high Imogene Pass, which crosses the range in a saddle between Telluride Peak and Imogene Peak. Through the Savage Basin to the top, then down into the Imogene Basin on the east side, early scouts had blazed the way for the hundreds who would follow. By air, the distance is a scant four miles from Sneffels to Telluride. By the old trail, the distance is much longer. Early packtrains, loaded with ore, coal, and supplies, wound their way across from the Camp Bird Mine, then down to Ouray and Silverton. As prosperity continued, a daily stagecoach brought both passengers and mail from Telluride by way of the narrow road that still zigzags its way up and then runs along the face of a vertical cliff. Frequent but narrow turnouts and a tunnel help somewhat to quell anxieties among the uninitiated. Among the miners, ever alert for new thrills, a unique practice was tried on this road for just one winter. Wings were installed on toboggans for a faster "schuss" down to Telluride. Needless to say, frequent wrecks discouraged the practice.

Beginning in 1890, the Rio Grande Southern Railroad had established service in and out of Telluride. Their station still stands beside the San Miguel River. From here supplies and ores from the Tomboy and other nearby locations could be shipped in or out of the district.

Another unusual means of transportation became a reality when a tram was built down the steep mountainside to the Smuggler-Union Mill at Pandora. Visitors who rode this conveyance were required to waive all claims to liability. In 1919 the Tomboy Gold Mines Company of Telluride bought up a total of sixty claims from the Revenue Tunnel Mining Company, at Sneffels, on the mountainside above Canyon Creek. About twenty-one of these claims were on the Ouray side of the range. To connect these extensive holdings, a vast amount of traffic was carried over the wild road across Imogene Pass.

In the years immediately following the turn of the century, labor troubles characterized the manner of life at Tomboy. The Western Federation of Miners had officially espoused a belief in Socialism during this period. In 1901 they called their first strike in the Telluride district on the issue of the contract work system. Here, as at Cripple Creek, the union won its opening battle. In a hard-fought, hand-to-hand battle, the nonunion men lost and were herded out of the district across Imogene Pass. The hated contract system was abolished.

Later, when the Tomboy Mill began using nonunion laborers, a second strike was called on October 31, 1903. About one hundred workers from the Tomboy walked out. On November 5, members of the Mine Owners' Association asked Governor James H. Peabody, a conservative Republican ex-banker, to send in the state militia. This, they figured, would enable them to reopen the mines with nonunion help. When nothing happened, they issued a second request on November 17. On the eighteenth, Peabody asked President Theodore Roosevelt to send Federal troops to restore order. But in the days that followed, no help from Washington was forthcoming. It became increasingly certain that

This picture shows both sides of the medal that was awarded to members of the
Colorado National Guard following the turn of the century labor wars.

Above Tomboy, visible at the left of the cliff, is the 13,114-foot crest of Imogene Pass.
Chicago Peak is in the foreground and Mount Sneffels is visible in the right background.

the burden for any action was back on the shoulders of Governor Peabody.

Under the command of Major Z. T. Hill, state troopers arrived in the troubled San Miguel Valley. During January, the troops arrested twenty-two union troublemakers and lodged them in jail. Even more ruthlessly, Hill loaded the agitators onto the train and deported them to Ridgway with a "don't ever come back" warning. Meantime, Major Hill took another step and imposed a military censorship on the press. Next he took over control of the telephone and telegraph lines. With most means of communication with the outside world under his thumb, Hill ordered beatings for the more obnoxious union leaders and for some of the miners as well. In one case, a union leader was publicly chained to a telephone pole on the streets of Telluride.

On March 14, 1904, about one hundred men from a group that called itself the Citizens' Alliance, conducted an armed search of the town. Their investigation flushed sixty unionists and some sympathizers who were kept incognito in a vacant store until it was dark. After midnight they were marched at gunpoint to the railroad depot beside the river. All were packed into two coaches, given the admonition about what would happen if they returned, and shipped off to Ridgway.

Meanwhile, up at Denver, Union President "Big Bill" Haywood boarded the train for Ouray with Harry Orchard, as foul an assassin as ever skulked across the pages of Western history. For a price, Orchard did the union's "dirty work" for them. Among others, he murdered Governor Frank Steunenberg, of Idaho, who had been unfortunate enough to incur the wrath of the Western Federation of Miners during labor troubles in the Coeur d'Alene district. As a start, Orchard doctored up some dynamite to make it resemble lumps of coal. Little time was lost in adding these fiendish contrivances to the fuel piles at the Tomboy and other mills. He next debated the pros and cons of poisoning Telluride's

Evelyn Brown and a friend at Fort Peabody, above Imogene Pass

Ghost town souvenirs. From the collection of Evelyn Brown

water supply with potassium cyanide but his one experience with poisons had been such a disappointment to his personal pride that he remained a career dynamite man ever after. Rubbing his hands with anticipation, Orchard gleefully considered rolling dynamite down the steep mountainsides into Telluride while it was under military rule. Before he could do anything about it, Haywood sent Harry back to Denver to assassinate Governor Peabody. Orchard had few failures and served his masters well. Peabody was one of the failures. An unfortunate newsboy tripped over the wire and was blown sky-high. Peabody lived to a ripe old age. Meanwhile, Harry was getting hot, so the union shipped him off to Cripple Creek where he performed magnificently, in his own way, during that strike.

By April 5, the Telluride Mine Owners' Association was tasting the fruits of victory. They issued a remarkable document which declared that there was no strike in the district and nothing to settle. Unanimously, they refused to negotiate with the Western Federation of Miners and agreed to recognize no union in Telluride. Unlike the results of the 1901 strike, this one broke the power of the union. High on the peaks above, work was resumed at the Tomboy, and at other properties, with nonunion labor.

In one of the accompanying photographs you may see both sides of a medal that now reposes in my collection. Originally these were given to all members of the state militia who had served in any of the four cities listed on the top plate, above the ribbon. In each location there were strikes which required the use of troops. The pendant carried a likeness of Governor Peabody on one side and the State Seal on its reverse. Among union men, these medals became the most hated pieces of hardware in Colorado. Years later, there were instances of wearers being put off trains, assaulted, or publicly insulted. As the years passed, fewer and fewer of the veterans of the Colorado labor wars chose to wear their citations publicly.

Beyond the Smuggler-Union Mine (in the foreground), there was the Tomboy, in
Savage Basin above Telluride, at an elevation of 11,500 feet.

Empty ruins mark the Tomboy site, at the end of a thrilling, cliff-hanging road

To see the Tomboy, why not start off where many of the pioneers did? From Telluride, get on the zigzag county road at the north side of town. Aside from a "Jeeps only" turn to the left that goes to the Marshall Basin, you can't get off this road. Along the way you will be treated to some of the most throat-clutching vistas in Colorado. The road is still a narrow cliff-hanger and the valley below you seems to grow progressively deeper. Ahead of you, the tunnel is still there, as are several of the old turnouts in case you meet another car. For the record, I have seen conventional cars at the Tomboy many times. As your climb continues, the Smuggler Mill at Pandora can be seen far below. Among the other sights is a view of Bridal Veil Falls and the treacherous Black Bear road across the canyon to the southeast.

Extensive ruins cover the Tomboy site today, along with a number of original buildings. Beyond it, a four-wheel-drive road goes on up and stops at the top of Imogene Pass, from which you may enjoy a magnificent panorama of the surrounding ranges. For the experienced hiker, this will be a worthwhile jaunt. For the rest of us, it is a challenging walk. Long after the return home, you will remember the trip to Tomboy as a real road to high adventure.*

---

* In this same general area, see also Vanadium, Telluride, and Pandora.

56.

TUNGSTEN

LIKE SO MANY of the towns written about in this book, Tungsten started out as a gold- and silver-mining camp dating from the period of the Nederland boom. Although good strikes were being made all around it, no really outstanding finds were discovered to justify the existence of this new town. In the beginning the settlement was known as Stevens Camp, named for Eugene Stevens, an early-day resident and prominent mining personality of the district. This name, rather than the later designation of Tungsten, will be noted on the accompanying photograph. Following a decline of the surrounding mining territories, Stevens Camp underwent a slump for several years. When it reemerged under a new identity, a completely new substance was being mined there. In the meantime, Barker Dam was built in 1910 just to the west of the old and temporarily abandoned townsite.

When magnetic iron oxide was first discovered, it was called magnatite. Later, the hard, white, heavy, metallic element was found to be useful in the manufacture of filaments for electric lamp bulbs. With the addition of 18 percent quantities of tungstic oxide, a yellow powder, it was found that tool grade steel could be hardened much more effectively. When these uses were discovered and tungsten was found in the nearby hills of Boulder County, little time was lost in reactivating the old town. Although the presence of tungsten had been a well-known fact during the earlier mining boom, nothing had been done about it since there had been no market for the stuff. Actually, the first tungsten discovery in this area dates from 1900. Now, all that was changed. In the meantime, World War I had started, providing a tremendous demand for tungsten and a real shot in the arm for Boulder County's sagging mining industry. By 1917, tungsten claims covered an area of twelve square miles, extending from Boulder Canyon to Magnolia.

In the midst of all this profitable excitement, the Boulder Tungsten Production Company invested $30,000 in opening up the old town and for installing milling facilities. Their investment paid for itself in just thirty days. During the peak of the war years, population for the town reached 5,000, with 20,000 given for the total number who worked there. Laborers commuted to Tungsten from Eldora, Hessie, and Nederland. An influenza epidemic in 1917 brought the town to a standstill, but not for long.

When the wheels started turning again, there were seventeen mills running in the town. Many of them were in operation on an around the clock basis. Among them were the Colorado Tungsten Corporation, the Tungsten Mining and Milling Company, the Primos Company, the Boulder County Mining Company, and the Wolfe Tongue. While the town was booming, new people came in to seek jobs. From Boulder, fleets of Stanley Steamers were used to transport the incoming migrants up to the tungsten mines. The Stanley Steamer was used because it was one of the few automobiles capable of making the long pull up Boulder Canyon.

After the war ended, the demand for tungsten declined and took the fortunes of the town along with it. For a variety of reasons, the price of tungsten increased on the domestic market. In the face of boosted prices, American steel companies began to import the cheaper tungstens from abroad, particularly from China. Almost overnight the Boulder County mines closed, the mills suspended their operations, and the people moved away.

To see Tungsten today, drive up Colorado State Highway

Collection of Florence and Bob Staadt

A panoramic view of the settlement of Tungsten

Collection of Robert L. Brown

From just below the highway, barely east of Barker Dam, one may match the view with that in the picture above. Note the enlarged dump and the rock outcroppings on the background hill.

119 from Boulder toward Nederland. Just a mile east of Nederland, and at the foot of Barker Dam, was Tungsten. An equally pleasant ride will take you up State Highway 119 from U.S. Highway 6 west of Golden, through Black Hawk and Rollinsville to Nederland, and finally to Tungsten.*

---

*In this same general area, see also Camp Frances, Eldora, and Salina.

57.

TURRET

FOR MANY YEARS prior to the discovery of precious metals in the valley of Cat Creek, a sawmill stood on the future site of Turret. There are records of extensive timbering operations here as early as 1885, a full dozen years before the discoveries in the summer of 1897 that ultimately brought settlers to this high and remote valley. When fall came, tents, cabins, houses, and about a hundred anxious people were already there. In point of time, the settlement was platted in September of 1897 as Camp Austin. After a very brief period of use, the name was discontinued in favor of Turret. Although the town was actually built on the south side of Nipple Mountain, a spur of Turret Mountain, the more picturesque name was chosen. One source went a step farther and referred to the infant camp as "Turret City."

By 1898 there was a huge demand for building lots in the growing town. New homes and business structures were going up as fast as freshly sawed green lumber became available. Rather large amounts of Cripple Creek money were invested in both real estate and in the mines around Turret. Daily mail service became a reality in 1898 when a post office was established in the town. Across the main street from it stood the Hotel Gregory, a rather pretentious two-story building with a front balcony on the second floor. Just a few doors away, the inevitable saloon had been established. Scattered about in the business district were several stores, a couple of assay offices, and the usual number of restaurants.

One butcher shop supplied the hungry populace with fresh meat and poultry.

By May of 1898, the peak year, there were three hundred people there according to the *Rocky Mountain News*. Later, of course, a one-room school was built. During that same year, Turret got its own newspaper, the *Gold Belt*. From another source we hear that 1899 was also the peak year. That same article tells us that there were only five hundred people there at the time. The disparity between the 1898 and 1899 population statistics is difficult to reconcile. As noted elsewhere in this book, such figures were rather irresponsibly handled, a factor that was completely beyond the control of the newspapers which published these accounts. In the early years of the town, a stagecoach came up twice each week from Salida. By 1899 the service had been expanded to a daily run.

For the pioneers who came to Turret, there were employment possibilities in any of the several mines that contributed to the well-being of the settlement. The Gold Bug was owned by a group of Salida businessmen. It had a 200-foot tunnel and a 50-foot side shaft. Gold, silver, and copper ores from this property assayed at $60 to the ton. Its main vein pinched out rather early in the game. Two men named Crosby and Miller discovered the Vivandiere Mine in 1896 and later operated it on an $18,000 lease. Jasper quartz worth $43 to the ton, was taken out of the Last Chance property.

Both the Golden Wonder and the Monongahela Mine were owned by the same syndicate. The Mollie Gibson property was close to the upper end of the town. Ore from the Altman shaft was regularly sent to the cyanide works at Florence for refinement. Three men named Martin, Welch, and Hart, from Goldfield, operated the M. W. Lode. A three-ton shipment from their holdings netted them only fifty dollars to the ton. At first the Deerhorn seemed to show promise and it was worked through the winter of 1897-98 but the high hopes were soon shattered. The Copper King and the Inde-

C. E. Skinner, of Salida, made this early picture of Turret

Empty ruins now mark the site of Turret, west of Salida

pendence shipped their output to one of the smelters at Pueblo. From the Turret Copper Mining and Reduction Company, came shipments of copper and gold which continued as late as 1916. Other properties in the vicinity of the town were the Hattie, Cashier, Monterey, Little Jack, Anaconda, and the Lady Du Bois, which was being worked on a $25,000 lease.

The decline of Turret seems to have started about 1900. From time to time there were resurgences of interest but nothing that became permanent. Enough people stayed on so that postal authorities did not discontinue the post office until 1941. No particularly sophisticated reasons are attributable to the decline of Turret. It was just another mining slump.

A good dirt road that once bore the designation of State Highway 180 runs northeast from the gasoline storage tanks on the northern fringe of Salida. Cross the railroad tracks and follow the main road for twelve miles to Turret. Keep to your left at any main intersections. From time to time there have been Forest Service signs along the road with posted distances to Turret. Those other roads that turn off to the right go to the empty site of Calumet and to the handful of cabins that was once the town of Whitehorn.

Quite a few buildings still stand at Turret, nestled among a quantity of weirdly shaped rock formations. There's more of the town around the corner to the right and one of the mines can be seen at the end of this road. On my last several visits, the town had been completely deserted. If you happen to have camping facilities with you, this is a fine spot for a rest and the chance to get the dust and smoke out of your lungs. If you go in summer, keep a wary eye out for rattlesnakes. After the sun goes down, the wind whistles cool all night, smelling of pine trees and rain and sometimes of snow from the high Collegiate Peaks.*

---

* In this same general area, see also Bonanza and Crestone.

58.

VANADIUM

MOST TOWNS ARE NAMED for their founders, for prominent people who once lived there, for nearby mountains and streams, or for geographical features. This one was named for the rare substance that was mined there. Quite apart from the fact that Vanadium is a completely abandoned ghost town today, its period of life came about later than that of most of the other somewhat obscure communities written about in this book. Vanadium occupied a rather brief spot-in-the-sun during the era surrounding our participation in two World Wars.

When mining first began here, the name of Newmire was initially attached to the small cluster of cabins that sprang up in the vicinity. Essentially this deposit was an extension of the Hermosa-Barlow Creek Lode that apexed west of Telluride. Because the area was quite remote at that time, all of the early output was packed in by horses or on pack mule teams. There are stories in circulation which infer that the ores used by Marie Curie when she isolated the element of radium came from here, but details are nebulous. In view of the chronological disparity, this seems an unlikely possibility. It is entirely possible, however, that materials for their later research could have come from the Uncompahgre Plateau.

Shortly after the start of World War II, the name was changed from Newmire to Vanadium. Over the years, population figures have fluctuated between seventy-five and four hundred people who lived and worked there. The town's location is in San Miguel County, at an altitude of 7,700 feet upon the plateau, roughly eight miles northwest of Telluride. When the Vanadium Corporation of America took over a total of seventy-two claims in southwestern Colorado and Utah, a reduction plant was erected at Vanadium.

To supply the miners' needs, there was at least one general store here. Within it, the inevitable post office was established. For those families with small children, a single-room log schoolhouse was built and used for thirty years. During the New Deal era of the 1930's it was replaced by another one-room structure, but this was built of native stone and was financed from PWA funds. Incidentally, the Vanadium school district was composed of 13,000 acres, presumably the extent of the mineral holdings of the company. For many years, Otto Mears' narrow-gauge Rio Grande Southern Railroad served Vanadium. In fact, a small station house, with facilities for a passenger and freight agent, was built here. Much of the ore was shipped to the refinery at Durango until an unexpected cloudburst sent a wall of water coursing down the San Miguel River and washed out the tracks.

Vanadium, the mineral element, is the source of bombastic uranium as well as the source of radium. Fissionable materials used in America's first atomic bomb are definitely known to have come from here. Additionally, vanadium was classified as a critical and essential material during both of our World Wars. Found near the tops of high mesas, below the slick rims, vanadium is one of the finest steel alloys the science of metallurgy has developed. During both wars, it was widely used to harden the steel used in rapid-fire gun barrels and in making armor plating. Demands for accelerated output of all strategic materials were increased, particularly during World War II.

After the first atomic bomb had been detonated, Major General Leslie Groves made a personal congratulatory telephone call to Blair Burwell, vice-president of the Vanadium

Vanadium, on the Rio Grande Southern Railroad north of Telluride

Vanadium is now an empty shell beside the highway

Corporation of America. The date was August of 1945. This call ripped the veil of secrecy from the furtive activities around Vanadium. Prior to this, the presence of armed soldiers, elaborate secrecy precautions, and very little positive information had effectively kept people in the dark about what it had all been about. Quite unwittingly, the residents of the remote San Miguel Valley had played a small role in the faraway events that suddenly catapulted America into the Atomic Age.

Quite ironically, the site of Vanadium today looks somewhat like a miniature Hiroshima. Nearly all of the surface buildings are gone. Those that remain have been severely gutted. The railroad grade has been all but obliterated. Only a gigantic ugly scar on the plateau side remains, almost as if a bomb had removed Vanadium from the face of the earth. To see the site, drive northwest out of Telluride on State Highway 145 for about eight miles. Vanadium was above the road on the right side and will be recognizable from the accompanying photographs which were made from a point facing northwest. If you reach Saw Pit, you have missed your destination. Turn around and retrace your route for three miles to see Vanadium, an honest-to-goodness twentieth-century ghost town.*

---

* In this same general area, see also Telluride, Pandora, and Tomboy.

59.

VIRGINIA DALE

FOR WELL OVER A YEAR after the discovery of gold in Colorado the incidents connected with settling a frontier had been passing quietly into history. Then, in 1861, the country was severely divided as men took up arms against one another in a major Civil War that lasted four years. Generally speaking, this drew few complaints from the Plains Indians who relaxed and watched with profound pleasure as the whites counted coup on each other. Under the circumstances neither the North nor the South could spare troops for large campaigns against the aborigines.

Hardly a clean page exists in the entire record of our dealings with the American Indian. Taken as a whole, the trail of broken promises and systematic mistreatment was far too long. Probably the growing tribal restiveness had nothing to do with any grand Indian plot hatched to take advantage of the nation's preoccupation with its fraternal war. Nearly everything they attempted in the way of intertribal cooperation met with failure. Burying the hatchet was a fine practice, just so long as it was buried in some other Indian's skull. Preoccupation with religious trivia and cultural differences that shouldn't have made a difference served to keep the tribes divided.

Nevertheless, sporadic raiding and pillaging began to reach serious proportions in the summer of 1862. Such groups as the "Dog Soldiers" of the Cheyennes struck at isolated ranches, poorly guarded wagon trains, and at the vulnerable stagecoach relay stations. One particularly troublesome spot was in southern Wyoming. Here the stagecoaches on the Overland Route to California were using the old original Oregon Trail. Ben Holladay, erstwhile "stagecoach king," was forced to reroute his stages because of the Indians. From the Oregon Trail his new route headed south through Wyoming, across the Colorado line, and then along the South Platte River to Denver. On the return, it went north through La Porte and on to rejoin the Oregon Trail through Fort Bridger and Salt Lake City.

Virginia Dale was established on this cutoff in the summer of 1862. Actually, the route was not particularly new. General William Ashley had used this low pass on his fur trading expedition of 1824-25. Again in 1843 it saw use when John C. Frémont and his expedition are known to have traversed it. By 1849 it had a name; the Cherokee Trail. When faced by the need to change the stagecoach route, Joseph A. (Jack) Slade was chosen to supervise the building of several stagecoach stations along the way to Denver. He named this one for his wife, Virginia Dale Slade.

To assure protection from the Indians, Slade also constructed a stone tower on top of the ridge east of the station. From this point, a lookout could keep a sharp eye on any approaching hostiles. Through 1867, the station was also used by about fifty to one hundred emigrant wagons every day. It became a favorite campground and the Overland Stage people never discouraged the practice since there was safety in numbers.

In the annals of the American West, Jack Slade is best known as a notorious gunfighter. In this, as in so many confused records, he is credited with having killed somewhere between two and forty-five men. Mark Twain credited him with twenty-six. Under Slade's administration, Virginia Dale inevitably became a notorious rendezvous for desperados. Their lookout point on the mountain to the northeast is still known as Robbers' Roost. Slade, of course, knew when loads of rich bullion were due in or out of Denver on the coaches. Working closely with the desperados, Slade tipped them off and shared in the loot from their robberies.

At one time Schuyler Colfax, later Vice-President of the United States, 1869-73, was detained at Virginia Dale with his party. This particular event transpired during the severe Indian raids of 1865. Apart from visits by a few notables, Indian depredations, and the drunken behavior of Slade, life was quiet here. His affinity for the grape eventually caused Ben Holladay to fire Slade. His replacement at Virginia Dale was Robert J. Spotswood who later achieved a well-deserved measure of fame when he ran stagecoaches across South Park between Denver and Leadville.

Fortunately for all concerned, the firing of Jack Slade by Holladay did not result in the violence that accompanied another firing with which Slade was connected. During the spring of 1860 Jules Beni (or Reni), founder of Julesburg, ran the Leavenworth and Pikes Peak Express Company station at that location. The record seems to indicate that he operated pretty much to suit himself. Among other things, mail deliveries often went to the wrong destinations. After a prolonged feud, Slade fired Beni.

Old Jules brooded and bided his time until his tormentor came through Julesburg on a routine inspection tour. Amazingly, Slade was unarmed. Jules met him at the door and promptly emptied the contents of a Colt cap and ball pistol into him. Without the assistance of liquor, Slade staggered around the building. By this time Beni had a double-barrel shotgun loaded with pistol balls which he also discharged at his wounded adversary. Either treatment would have killed most men.

When the physician arrived from Fort Laramie he recovered a handful of pistol balls from Slade's body. Miraculously Jack recovered and at once vowed to rid society of old Jules. When the spring of 1861 rolled around Beni was at Cold Springs, east of Fort Laramie. One version would now have us believe that his friends tied Beni to a post until Slade arrived, drunk, and shot away various parts of his victim's anatomy. Afterwards Slade cut off Beni's ears and wore them for watch charms. The other story says Slade killed him with two shots in an honorable fight, and then cut off the ears.

Later, after his connections with Virginia Dale, Slade left Colorado and continued his alcoholic career in Montana where he made a general nuisance of himself in Virginia City. Finally, the Vigilantes hanged him for a crime he did not commit, thus ending his "eary" career.

For many years stagecoaches continued to run beside Dale Creek in the Cache la Poudre Valley. When Indian raids threatened the well-being of Virginia Dale or the other stations, the operators sometimes tried running two coaches at a time for protection. The full name of the company that operated stages along this route was the Central Overland California and Pikes Peak Express Company.

So, gradually, as Indian raids diminished after 1867, Virginia Dale was abandoned and activities other than transportation came to the forefront. Today the Poudre Valley is a prime agricultural district.

Taken as a whole, the ride to what remains of Virginia Dale is an easy and a pleasant one. Drive northwest out of Fort Collins on U.S. 287 toward Laramie. Just five miles south of the Colorado-Wyoming border is the Virginia Dale sign by a filling station. This is not the early Virginia Dale. Just north of the sign is the Colorado State Historical Society marker. A few feet north of its stone foundation, a good dirt road takes off to the northeast. Follow this road, staying on the most-used section and disregarding the tributary roads. The rocky base is rough in spots but not dangerous. Any car can make it on this good, short farm road. Winding around and up and down over the uneven terrain, the grade drops into and across Dale Creek on an old bridge. Shortly the destination is in sight. Since this is private property, ask

William H. Jackson made this early plate of Virginia Dale

Virginia Dale, a bit off the beaten path, is still there

permission before you start looking around. The stable is gone now but the old station house with its huge fireplace is still here. Few historic spots can boast of a more unusual background than Virginia Dale with its Indians, stage-coaches, and characters.

60.

ROADS TO HIGH ADVENTURE

AT THIS POINT a few notes on the early roads and trails of
the state would seem to be appropriate. An occasional di-
gression away from the neon and asphalt along any of our
Colorado pioneer trails can be a pleasing and unforgettable
journey into the past as you retrace the routes of the gold
seekers. Our motives today are quite different from the grim
purposes that impelled brave men and women to strike out
into the uncharted wilderness. Currently, the United States
Forest Service estimates that there are some 12,500 miles of
back-country trails in Colorado alone. Many of these came
into being during the mining period.

Since the birth of our nation, Indian trails have served as
our earliest roads. More than a century ago, argonauts re-
blazed many of these trails by notching the trees that bor-
dered them. For miles on end, summit roads and passes
slithered around over most of the ranges of our Colorado
Rockies. In fact, three fourths of America's real estate above
ten thousand feet lies within the borders of Colorado. In
general, Colorado's mining boom occupied the second half
of the nineteenth century, leaving a heritage of old roads
and trails among the timber. Through the foothills and into
the high interior ranges, early settlers and scouts blazed the
way for the thousands of pioneers who would follow.

From well-worn Indian trails, more than one of these
routes have developed into our most important pioneer roads.
Bullwhackers and mule skinners rammed their wagons and
packtrains across hundreds of scorching miles. With the

passage of time, many of the original trails were widened and improved. As new areas opened up, new roads met the need for getting people to Tin Cup or Leadville or Cripple Creek.

Since there was no State Highway Department in those days, private citizens secured a charter for five dollars and built their own grades. In such instances, many, like the intrepid Otto Mears, adopted the toll road motif to defray expenses and turn a tidy profit as well. Within a few years, many prime roads were sold and subsequently became railroad beds. The heyday of railroad sight-seeing came during the mining boom. Most of the larger mining towns were served by one or two day loop railroad excursions. Other early trails became stagecoach routes, lumbering, or freight roads to the early mining camps.

With each chapter in this book, specific instructions have been given for reaching your individual destinations. Most of these roads, except where noted, are accessible by private car. For the others, a four-wheel-drive unit of some sort is desirable, but there are other ways. To see those more remote spots, horses can often be rented. With sturdy footwear and adequate clothing, short hikes to some of the old towns can be pleasurable. We often leave our Jeep and walk the last few miles, just for the enjoyment of it.

In winter, except for those valleys where snowslides constitute a peril, snowshoeing is an invigorating diversion. Our family of four often spends the winter weekends in this way. For example, the short one and a half miles up to Saints John from Montezuma is an excellent first trip and the scenery above the deep snow is majestic. Snowshoes can be rented at a nominal fee from a variety of places. Although slower, this is a safer way to see the backcountry under its mantle of white.

If you are the sort of person who perpetually wonders what is at the end of this or that unmarked road, a few suggestions may be of some help. Highly detailed quadrangle

Photo by Ron Ruhoff
*A snowshoe **trip** makes for an interesting method of visiting ghost towns in winter*

Collection of Robert L. Brown
On a hiking trail to a ghost town

maps are available for a most reasonable sum from the United States Geological Survey offices. In my own opinion these are unsurpassed for information about the more remote regions. A fine book, *Guide to the Colorado Mountains,* by Robert M. Ormes, is published by Sage Books for the Colorado Mountain Club. In size and weight, the book is easily carried and contains a remarkable amount of information. Marshall Sprague's fine book, *The Great Gates,* is a monumental contribution, the most comprehensive book on the early mountain passes at this time. He covers not only Colorado but the other Western States as well.

Furthermore, any of the following trails offers a chance to get away from it all, look at handsome mountains and at a road that is rich in history. In only a few instances will you find these passes on oil company maps. Most are much too old and far too remote for that. From the reservoir west of Georgetown, a road branches off the main road and goes up to the old town of Waldorf. In the early days Argentine Pass crossed the peaks above Waldorf at an elevation well above thirteen thousand feet to the Argentine-Chihuahua mining district in the valley of Peru Creek. From Waldorf, the approach twists up across the above-timberline tundra. Although Jeeps can still make it, many people walk the remaining miles from Waldorf. The west approach, from Peru Creek, is now gone. Also from Waldorf, a second road follows the old grade of the Argentine Central Railroad to the top of Mount McClellan and a picture-postcard view of Grays and Torreys peaks.

Not far away, as the crow flies, is Webster Pass. From Montezuma, drive on through town and up the Snake River Valley to the United States Forest Service sign. Turn left here. Regular cars have made this one at times. At the top, you must turn around since the road on the other side washed away years ago. From the top, much of Summit County is visible.

Between Fairplay and Alma, a dirt road turns west to Mosquito Pass, highest crossing in the United States. For the past few years, passenger cars have been getting across the steep cuts and exposed talus slopes to Leadville but the experience is a far cry from driving over Loveland or Berthoud passes. In the early days, Father Dyer crossed the Mosquito Range on snowshoes. During the Leadville boom, it became one of the busiest roads in Colorado with regularly scheduled stage-coaches, ore wagons, and pack outfits moving in both directions.

Southwest of Buena Vista, from Nathrop, the Chalk Creek road leads to St. Elmo. From there, a good dirt road for passenger cars goes to the top of Tin Cup Pass, 12,154 feet above sea level. The west side, however, is a wild Jeep road down Willow Creek past Mirror Lake to the early town of Tin Cup in Taylor Park. Tin Cup Pass dates from the early 1880's. Only the east side is now maintained. Back at St. Elmo again, a second road goes up to Hancock and then traverses Hancock Pass. On its westward descent to Pitkin, it passes the trail to the Alpine Tunnel. The actual top of the pass itself remains a Jeep road, crossing a handsome panorama of tumbled peaks above Brittle Silver Basin.

Scofield Pass is only 10,700 feet high. From time to time a conventional car gets over it from the west side although this is certainly not a recommended procedure. From Crested Butte, go up the valley of the East River to the old ghost town of Gothic. At the opposite end of town from the way you came in, the road climbs up and passes Emerald Lake. In the open meadow at the top is the site of Scofield. Here the Crystal River begins its descent to the northwest, cutting deeply into the beautiful Crystal Valley. At one point there is a twenty-seven-degree grade, hardly to be recommended for the family sedan. Crystal City and Marble are on this road. Soon afterwards you will come to pavement and access to Carbondale and Glenwood Springs.

Southwestern Colorado contains the finest assortment of old passes in the state, located among one of the most magnificent settings to be found anywhere. Four of the better ones will be noted here.

On U.S. Highway 550, at a point five miles south of Red Mountain Pass, a dirt road branches left to Ophir Pass and Telluride. Originally opened as a toll road in 1880, Ophir never kept up with progress and remains as a four-wheel-drive road today, with extensive and potentially treacherous talus slopes on its western approach. Although Ophir only reaches a height of 11,700 feet, the scenery that unfolds before you at the top is magnificent. Among others, Lizard Head Peak, Wilson Peak, and Mount Wilson tower above the valley spread out below you. From Ophir's base, good roads lead to Telluride, Rico, or Dolores.

Stony Pass was once the main route to the San Juans. To-day it is a rather long and time-consuming trail from Cunningham Gulch, above Silverton, to the extreme upper headwaters of the Rio Grande River on the Del Norte side of the range. At the Rio Grande Reservoir, a fine campground will be found. Stony Pass was completely inaccessible for many years. Roughly a decade ago, it was cleared to permit four-wheel-drive vehicles to cross its 12,594-foot-high summit.

Anyone who has crossed Cinnamon Pass will remember it as one of the most stimulating journeys in Colorado. At its crest, Cinnamon crosses the range at 13,009 feet.

From a well-worn Indian trail, this pass developed into one of our most important pioneer roads. Later on, it was used by the Hayden Survey party. Still later, it was widened for use with wagons. In its existence as a true road, it was both built and allowed to decay during the final quarter of the nineteenth century. From Lake City, a high, twisting shelf road climbs sharply above Lake San Cristobal and the Lake Fork of the Gunnison River. Along the way you may see remains from the towns of Sherman, Whitecross, and Burrows Park. On the western side, a sharp descent puts you down into the upper reaches of the canyon of the Animas River. Here at the foot of the pass is old Animas Forks, and below it are Eureka, Howardsville, and Silverton.

*Cinnamon Pass was first used by Charles Baker in 1860. Enos Hotchkiss
widened the crossing into a wagon road in 1877.*

*In August of 1965 the east side of Cinnamon Pass showed little
change from what was recorded in the photograph above.*

Beginning back at Lake City once more, Otto Mears blazed another trail over the range and called it Engineer Pass. On August 10, 1877, the first stagecoach crossed its 12,800-foot-high crest and connected Lake City with Animas Forks, twenty-five miles away. Below the crest on the western side, the trail forks, allowing passengers for Animas Forks or Silverton to go by that route. A turn to the right and you drop sharply down to Ouray by way of the upper Uncompahgre River and Mineral Creek. When followed by Jeep today, this route offers some of the most breathtaking travel in Colorado.

More than a century ago, pioneers spent many weeks or even months traveling these trails into the unknown recesses of the Colorado Rockies. Today, in a four-wheel-drive vehicle you can telescope those journeys into a one- or two-day trip that will long be remembered. For the hiker with a well-planned pack and sturdy boots, the possibilities are limitless.

In some instances, major highways parallel or cut across several of the historic trails that have played important roles in the development of Colorado. For the lover of the great out-of-doors, these early roads offer access to scenic beauty so remote that the American national flower, "Kleenexus Americanus," does not even bloom here. In most instances the beer can and other contemporary highway markers are also conspicuous by their absence. Why not start off like many of the pioneers did? In this way you may still see some of the best of Colorado, reliving history as you go, seeing the old and all-but-forgotten ghost towns. Gone now are the lawns, the beds of flowers, and the tidy streets that once fringed the cabins that stood among sun-dappled groves of aspen trees. In their place one now finds long rows of dilapidated little cabins falling into ruin. Beside the quiet stream beds that once held miles of ditches, are the remains of rotting sluice boxes among the tons of rock and gravel. Hundreds of these deserted hamlets may yet be seen along the thousands of miles of backcountry roads to high adventure.

*Engineer Pass was constructed by Otto Mears and first opened
to traffic in August, 1877.*

This vastly improved Jeep road now traverses Engineer Pass

INDEX

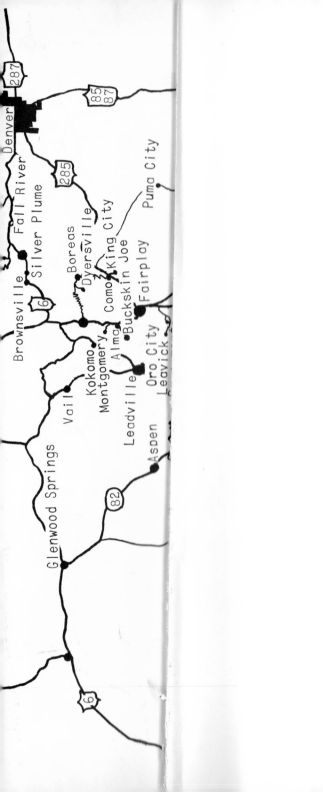

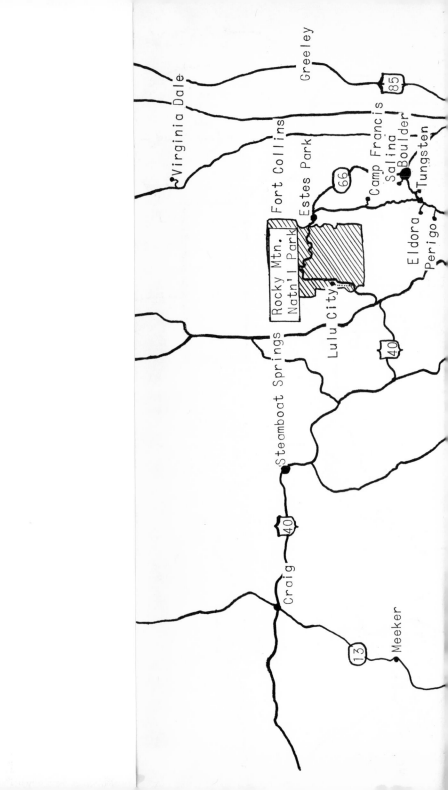

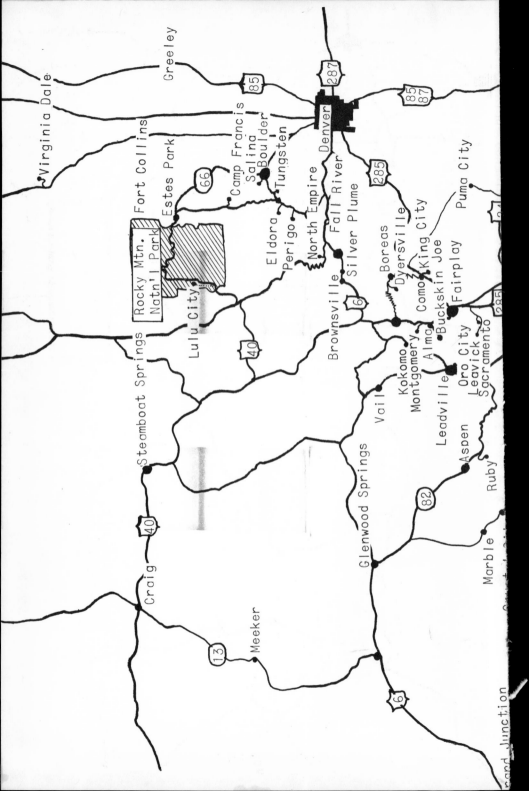